TOY
SOLDIERS

Also by the author:
CODE CONQUISTADOR
THE MASAKADO LESSON

TOY
SOLDIERS

William P. Kennedy

ST. MARTIN'S PRESS
NEW YORK

Library of Congress Cataloging-in-Publication Data

Kennedy, William P.
    Toy soldiers / by William P. Kennedy.
            p.   cm.
    ISBN 0-312-01478-3 : $19.95 (est.)
    I. Title.
PS3561.E429T6   1988
813'.54—dc19   87-27327
                                                     CIP

First Edition

10 9 8 7 6 5 4 3 2 1

For
Eileen
Karyn
Bob
Patti
Bill

and all the
children
who are trapped
in Saint Anselm's

TOY
SOLDIERS

April 14

early morning

He hadn't figured on the moonlight.

In Billy Tepper's imagination, each of the rooms had been black and formless, making him invisible as he entered. He had studied the rooms in detail during his casual visits so that he would be able to find each lamp, each radio, each tape deck in the dark. It would take more time, but he had the whole night to work with. The inky stillness would be his ally in case one of the students happened to be awake.

Instead, there was light streaming through the small panes of the leaded windows, which reached from just above the floor almost to the ceiling. The sparse dormitory furnishings were plainly visible, along with the photographs of happy parents and scrubbed brothers and sisters that stood on each desktop, the plastic models that separated the books in the bookshelves, and the randomly scattered sports gear. The pale glow would make it much easier to find the lamps and appliances and switch them on. But he would also be perfectly visible entering and leaving each room. The odds that a restless schoolmate would catch him grew with each door he pushed open.

He stopped with his hand resting on the doorknob to Charlie Noble's room. Maybe this was one he should pass by. Charlie was dangerous. The little snitch lived in the headmaster's office, and the Old Mouse hung on his every word. If Charlie saw him, there was no chance of making him a partner in the prank. No, Charlie would just put on his silk bathrobe, step into his slippers, and pad over to the new building and pound on the Mouse's door. Ten minutes later, Billy would be standing on the headmaster's Oriental rug, listening to threats about being sent packing back to his father in Cincinnati.

He started to back away from the door, then asked himself what good was a prank unless it got Charlie pissed off. Half the fun was watching Charlie run to the headmaster, then get on the phone and call the boardrooms of a dozen Eastern banks until he found his father so that he could complain. Billy pushed the door open and stepped quickly inside.

To one side, he saw Charlie's desk stacked with the labeled folders that held his homework assignments. The framed picture showed Charlie's father in a severe Bachrach pose, the light falling on a stern face and hands that held a silver letter opener. Jesus, Billy thought, what kind of father sends his kid the portrait from his company's annual report? Charlie was sleeping angelically in the bed on the other side of the room. A folded bathrobe rested across his feet and shoe trees protruded from the cordovans that waited on the floor.

Billy flipped the wall switch, but the overhead light did not respond. Silently, he crossed to the desk and snapped on the switch to the lamp, again with no reaction. He clicked on the radio and turned the volume knob all the way up. The radio remained silent. Then he moved to the tape deck, hit the button marked PLAY, and pushed the volume lever all the way to its stops. He glanced at Charlie, who was still lost in sleep, his hands folded under his face. Then he stepped silently from the room and closed the door behind him.

Jimmy Bradberry's room was next, easily identified by the whistling sound of his breathing. There was nothing to worry about in getting caught by old Snuffy. His asthma kept him out of sports, which made it hard for him to make friends, so he joined in anything just to be one of the guys. If Jimmy was awake, Billy would just explain what he was up to. Then Jimmy would double over with laughter until his excitement got ahead of his lungs and he would collapse into one of his coughing fits. Billy opened the door. In response, Snuffy tossed violently in his bed. But his eyes never opened. Instead, he settled comfortably into his bundle of blankets, and in an instant the shrill whistling sound picked up where it had left off.

There was no portrait on Snuffy's desk. Instead, there was a huge bulletin board hanging on the wall that was cluttered with clippings from *The Washington Post* and *The Philadelphia Enquirer*. Each clipping showed a dynamic pose of Senator Thomas Bradberry pounding a podium or jabbing a finger into the air. The caption underneath each picture described a hard-line conservative who advocated saturation bombing as the solution to nearly any social ill. Poor Snuffy, Billy thought. He hated being away from home. But he couldn't cut it in any of the prep schools in Philadelphia or Washington, and the good senator had sent him to study abroad just to get him out from under foot.

Billy hit all the light switches, including the reading lamp that hung over Jimmy Bradberry's bed, then cranked up the stereo to full volume. None of the lights came on, and the stereo system remained mute. As he was leaving, he noticed the electric shaver resting on the night table. Quietly, he plugged it into the wall socket and flipped the switch to on.

The silent operation was repeated in every room on the top floor, which housed the upperclassmen, boys fifteen or sixteen years old, who would be in the ninth and tenth grades of schools in the United States. There was no problem with the empty rooms whose usual occupants were away for the weekend. Tad Bliss had gone to Paris to be with his father who was head of European operations for an American computer company and wouldn't be back until tomorrow afternoon. John Richmond was spending the night at a hospital in Rome visiting his Hollywood mother who had been taken ill on the set of a movie she was making. John hadn't been overly concerned because his mother always took to a hospital whenever a director cut one of her scenes. But some of the rooms were scary. Billy didn't want to mess with Henry Giles, who was already six-foot-four and who had been sent abroad by his family of oil barons as the most palatable alternative to the prison sentence he would have received for beating up two Houston police officers. Said policemen had overtaken his convertible one night, which was cruising at close to a hundred miles an hour, and had mentioned that they were fed up with spoiled, rich punks. Henry had over-reacted. And Billy wasn't comfortable around Joey Trotta, either, a swarthy, brooding kid with a thin mustache who didn't let anyone get close to him. Trotta was said to be the son of a New Jersey gangster. There was no point in aggravating someone who had probably helped pour fresh cement around the feet of some of his father's business associates.

But Billy had steeled himself and entered every room. In each room, he had turned on every light, every radio, every stereo, every appliance. Still, the corridor remained dark and silent. Now he was making his way down to the second floor where the younger boys slept, the thirteen- and fourteen-year-olds who filled the school's seventh and eighth grades. He knew all of them by name, and had teamed with most of them in athletic contests and mandatory social events. But they weren't his friends. The passage between the eighth and ninth grades was a one-way street. There was no turning back.

Again, he went from room to room hitting all the switches and turning up all the volume controls. Only once did a resident wake, sitting up in bed and staring at Billy with glassy eyes. "You're dreaming. Go back to sleep," Billy had explained, and the boy had nodded obediently and slipped back under his covers.

Finally, he reached the ground floor, which lodged the primary school children in the fourth, fifth, and sixth grades—the "brats," as they were called in everything but the school's most official correspondence. The problem here was that the brats lived in pairs, so that if he woke one of the ten-year-olds, he would certainly wake two of them. And once they were awake, there would be no calming them down. Brats got hysterical over anything—one kid wet his bed every time it rained—and took their howling complaints directly to Miss Manetti, who had been hired as much to mind them as to teach them. It was also likely that some of them would be awake despite the late hour. You could always count on at least one brat having a stomachache whenever a teacher scheduled an examination for the next day.

But on the ground floor, Billy Tepper got a break. The high hedges that surrounded the building had blocked out most of the moonlight. The rooms were darker, giving him a greater sense of security. Cautiously, he made his way from door to door, again entering each room and turning on all the radios, televisions, and lamps. He missed just one room, where he could hear giggling and muffled laughter. He noticed that one of the names on the door was the same as the brand of tire that his family had on all four of its automobiles. But he wasn't particularly impressed. Half the kids in the school had names that were familiar to any consumer who had spent the first fifteen years of his life in the United States. If you met a boy named Ford, you just assumed he was one of the twigs on the family tree of the automobile family. A kid named Kennedy was probably one of *the* Kennedys. And the ones without familiar names were probably the sons of corporate czars who headed up firms with three-letter names that you saw on half the things you were ever likely to buy. The brat named after the tires probably had one of the smaller allowances in the school.

In fact, Billy chuckled as he worked his way up the curved stairs to the top floor; he had just completed a tour of the United States power structure. In addition to Charlie Nobles, he had visited the rooms of the sons of three major international banks, one automotive company, the second- and third-largest computer companies, an oil company, a brewery, a national mass merchandiser and the head of a regional discount chain (those two guys hated each other), a household brand of blended whiskey, and, counting himself, the country's largest soap manufacturer. Besides Snuffy

Bradberry, there were four other sons of nationally known political figures—another senator, a Southern congressman who headed up the Armed Services Committee, the Secretary of the Interior, and the governor of Indiana. And then there was the real money. The kids with insignificant names like Joey Trotta who weren't exactly sure what their fathers did to pay the school's outrageous tuition, and the sons of actresses who had no idea what ten percent of the gross of a new movie could possibly be worth.

It would take Billy about three minutes to blow them all out of their beds and send them screaming into the halls. And it would take the Old Mouse about two weeks to calm down all the outraged parents who would threaten to pull their kids out of school and send their financial support to a headmaster who could enforce discipline and give the children a satisfactory start in a world of law and order. Face it, Billy told himself. This isn't one of your best ideas. But it's still early in the term!

He slipped back into his room and closed the door behind him. Then he stepped into his closet, snapped on his flashlight, and pushed the hangers of designer jeans and Brooks Brothers blazers to one side. In the glow of the flashlight he found his lap-held battery-powered computer and knelt down on the floor in front of the keyboard. Then he snapped the old telephone handset into the slot on the edge of the computer and began typing a command. When he was done, he checked his entry.

"Good morning, everyone," he whispered. "It's time to get up." Then he hit the Return key, sending his signal down the telephone lines.

It traveled down the hall to the equipment board that was mounted on the wall of a broom closet. There, it entered a cable and dropped through the building to the ground floor. From there, it moved across to the "new" building, which had been added as a wing to the old mansion. Then it dropped down into the basement to a point where the telephone lines came together with the electric power lines before they were all carried out of the building to a utility pole. At that point, the telephone signal tripped a relay that Billy had installed across the power lines. And the electric power he had disconnected with a computer command before he had begun visiting each of the rooms was automatically reconnected.

He had hardly lifted his finger from the Return key when every light in the building came on with a flash that seemed like a lightning strike. In every room, students sat bolt upright in their beds. A second later, radios exploded in a cacophony of shouting voices and howling music. And then added to the deafening shriek he heard a rumble as three dozen stereos sent full-volume signals to oversized woofers.

Students of all ages nearly tore the handles off their doors as they made their panicky escapes into the hallways. Snuffy Bradberry fired out of his doorway only to be trampled by Henry Giles, whose huge frame had gathered enormous momentum in its flight from the horror that had invaded his room. Charlie Noble forgot his slippers, and as the door he had thrown open bounced shut, it caught the tail of his bathrobe. He felt the robe tearing in half but was too frightened to stop running. Billy Tepper poked his head out his door into the bedlam of the corridor and asked innocently if anyone knew what was going on.

In their flight down the stairs, upperclassmen were interrupted by the hoard of underclassmen fleeing the madness that had exploded on the second floor. The ensuing collisions sent bodies sprawling down the steps. And when they reached the ground floor, they were greeted by the horrible wailing of the brats, most of whom were frozen in their beds in terror.

"Holy shit," Billy mumbled as he looked at the curved steps leading down from the top-floor landing. His schoolmates looked like passengers going over the side of the *Titanic*. It was every man for himself, with the bigger boys pushing past the younger ones in their panic to reach the safety of the front door. From the sound of angrily cursing voices and the sight of bouncing bodies, he knew someone was going to get hurt. His little prank had turned into a disaster-in-the-making.

Teachers with dormitory duty began appearing from their rooms and shouting explanations to the boys. Harold Hutchings, who taught European history, had pulled on a pair of trousers over his pajama bottoms. "It's a bomb," he said reassuringly. "Nobody panic. Move quickly, but nobody panic."

"It's a bomb," students shouted to Elias Metz when he tried to control the flow of traffic exiting the second floor. "Walk slowly," the math teacher ordered as he pushed his way toward the stairs.

Within two minutes, all the upper- and lowerclassmen had made good their escape and were gathered on the front lawn looking up at the blazing building. Although the roar of the radios was nearly deafening, they could still make out the hysterical crying coming from the rooms on the ground floor. "We've got to get the brats out," Joey Trotta yelled at a group of the older boys. He started to charge back into the building but stopped short when he realized that no one had joined him.

"What are we waiting for?" Billy Tepper yelled, taking up Trotta's battle cry. "Let's get the brats out." With Billy's urging, the upperclassmen joined in, and raced up the steps to the front door.

Maria Manetti stopped them in their tracks. She was wearing a heavy bathrobe over what appeared to be men's pajamas, a horrible contrast to the snug-fitting blouses and sweaters that made her an obvious target for the upperclass boys endless sexual jokes, and her long dark hair was a tangled mess that stood up from the top of her head. But her blazing dark eyes fixed on them as soon as they entered the building, and when she shouted for them to stop, the rescuing army screeched to a halt.

"Joey, Billy," she snapped. "Please go into each room and turn off all the radios. Turn off all the lights except the ceiling lamps. Do you understand?"

"Yes, Miss Manetti," Billy said obediently.

"Now the rest of you," Marie ordered, "get out of here right now. Nobody needs to be rescued."

"It's a bomb," Charlie Noble shouted as a desperate warning.

"There's no bomb," Miss Manetti explained, barely able to control her anger. "Someone turned on all the lights and all the radios, and now Joey and Billy are going to turn them off. Do you understand?" Her question was directed at the two boys, and they broke ranks and started down the hall and into the rooms. Soon the roar began to quiet and the blaring lights began to dim.

"I guess we should turn off our lights and radios," Henry Giles explained to the other upperclassmen in the rescue party.

As they started up the stairs, they met Edward Ferrand on his way down. "It's just the lights and the radios," Giles said to the English teacher who was also his soccer coach.

"I know that," Ferrand answered through clenched teeth. "Go back to your rooms, turn everything off, and get back to sleep. You've got a practice in the morning, and I plan to work your tails off."

Ferrand poked his head into the ground-floor corridor and saw that Miss Manetti had things under control. The brats were standing anxiously in their doorways, and she was explaining what had happened. Two of the brats were leaning against her, holding onto her bathrobe as if it were a lifeline.

"Why did everything go on at once?" one of the wet-eyed children asked, interrupting her explanation.

"Someone was playing a joke," she said. "It wasn't a very funny joke."

Ferrand went through the front door and was immediately surrounded by frightened lowerclassmen and an equally frightened Elias Metz.

"What's going on?" the math teacher asked, appointing himself spokesman for the lowerclassmen.

"Somebody's idea of a joke," Ferrand said. "They must

have turned off the power, then turned all the lights and radios on, and then turned the power back on. Get everyone back inside, Elias, and have them turn everything off. Then let's get back to sleep."

Metz nodded, then started to lead his charges back into the old mansion. He stopped when Dr. Enrico Palma fluttered through the doorway and out onto the steps. Palma was fully dressed in his inevitable gray trousers and dark cutaway coat. His pince-nez, which he regarded as the traditional identification badge of European scholars, were set firmly on the end of his beaky nose, and the white tufts of hair, which stuck out from behind his ears, were smoothly combed. Apparently no bomb was as threatening to him as the prospect of making an undignified appearance.

"Is everyone out? Is the building safe? Why are you going back in, Metz, when you should be going out?" He walked with rapid, tiny steps, talking as he walked and heaping one question on top of another with no pause that would permit an answer. His head seemed to bob up and down with each syllable he pronounced, a mannerism that, together with his rodent-like features, had earned him the title of "Old Mouse."

"No problem, Dr. Headmaster," Metz tried to explain over the blur of questions. "It was just . . ." Metz forgot what the exact explanation had been, and he turned to Ferrand for help.

"It was a student prank. A joke," Ferrand said, his face showing no appreciation of the attempt at humor.

"A joke?" the headmaster asked, his lips trembling through one of his rare loss of words. "A joke? You think it is funny to frighten little children? You call this a prank?"

"I don't think it's funny," Ferrand explained. "But one of our students does. If I find out which one, I'll change his mind in one hell of a hurry."

The Old Mouse hadn't heard Ferrand's explanation. "Who could possibly think that such a thing is funny?" he demanded. He sniffled to show his distaste, and his mustache wiggled like a mouse's whiskers.

Billy Tepper walked out the front door and started down the steps.

"Well, the panic is over," he said casually. "All the brats are back in bed." Then he looked up at Elias Metz. "Anyone know what happened?"

Metz shrugged his shoulders the way he did when a student was bewildered by one of his explanations of mathematical logic. "Mr. Ferrand thinks it was a joke," he answered.

"Some sick joke," Billy Tepper added. "Half the brats wet their beds." He looked around at the circle of stern faces and noticed that Edward Ferrand was staring directly at him.

"Well, guess I better get back to sleep. Good night, Dr. Headmaster." The Old Mouse nodded without looking at him. "Good night, Dr. Metz." Metz had already started back into the building and made no response. "Good night, Mr. Ferrand." He started to turn.

"Mr. Tepper!" It was Ferrand's voice, and it wasn't friendly. "Can I see you for just a few minutes? In my room."

Billy forced a yawn that he was able to stifle with the back of his hand. "Now?" he asked. "It's kind of late. I think I have an exam in second period."

"Now," Ferrand said with no trace of sympathy.

"Who could think that such a thing was funny?" Dr. Palma asked again, as if the answer might possibly come from the moon.

"Now," Ferrand said, closing off any possibility that he might change his mind.

"Yes, sir," Billy Tepper answered. He started across the lawn toward the door of the new wing. Edward Ferrand's room was on the second floor.

Billy was seated in the chair next to Ferrand's desk when the teacher entered the room. He jumped to his feet, watched Ferrand circle the desk and settle menacingly into his chair. He was mad; as mad as Billy had ever seen him. And Mr. Ferrand wasn't someone you wanted to mess with when he was on edge. He was big, well over six feet tall, with most of his weight in his arms and shoulders. Hell, he was an athlete. He could run faster and kick a ball farther than any of the boys. He even looked like an athlete, with his dark hair cut short and his long face clean shaven. Most of the teachers tried to outsmart you. But Ferrand could run right over you. Billy tipped his head in respect, then he started to sit.

"Stay on your feet, Mr. Tepper," Ferrand commanded. "You don't sit until I invite you to sit."

"What did I do?" Billy asked, outraged innocence filling his blue eyes.

"We both know what you did," Ferrand said. "What I want you to tell me is how you did it? And I want you to tell me now."

Outraged innocence hadn't worked. Billy switched to indignant anger. "I don't know what you're talking about, Mr. Ferrand. What is it that you think I did?"

"Mr. Tepper," Ferrand answered, "I'm tired. Your stupid stunt has cost me a night's sleep, not to mention the four or five days of hell we're all going to go through while the headmaster tightens the screws. Now I'll give you just one minute to explain to me how you did it. One minute, starting right now."

Billy thought quickly. Ferrand wasn't a bad guy. He had caught Billy in pranks twice before and had never turned him in. Maybe if he came clean, Ferrand would give him another chance. But he remembered the teacher's warning when he had found Billy bringing two whores into the wine cellar. "No more chances, Billy," Ferrand had threatened. "Next time you pull one of your stunts, you're going back to soap city."

It wasn't that Billy hated Cincinnati. It was just that he knew his father wouldn't keep him there. If he was bounced out of Saint Anselm's American School, his father would only become more disappointed than he already was, and would pack him off to another private school in still another foreign country. Italy was a hell of a lot nicer than Switzerland. And God knew, it had to be better than Germany. That's what his father had told him when he had sent him to Saint Anselm's. "It's a fine school, Billy, located right in the middle of Renaissance culture. I think you'll enjoy it and profit from it. If not, then I have a school in mind that you won't enjoy at all. It's in Germany, and it is famous for its roots in the Prussian tradition. So I would advise you to make good at Saint Anselm's." It was a bald-faced threat, just like his father's promise to visit him whenever his business brought him to Italy.

Billy made his decision. Given the problems he had just caused, he couldn't trust anyone, even a nice guy like Ferrand, with his secret.

"I'm sorry, Mr. Ferrand," he said as his minute was about to run out. "I can't think of anything I could have done to cost you a night's sleep." Then his face lit up with disbelief. "Hey, Mr. Ferrand, you don't think I'm the one who turned on all the lights and radios?"

Ferrand rose from his chair, indicating that the interview was over. "You're restricted to your room," he told Tepper, "until I find out how you did it. As soon as I finish with soccer practice tomorrow, I'm going to turn into an electrician. I'm going to trace every power line in this building, from the utility pole right to the wall outlets. I'll find your switch or your relay or whatever you used. It will probably take me most of the day. But I'll bet you a week of your allowance that I'll have you on tomorrow night's flight to Cincinnati, with your father waiting at the airport to welcome you home."

Billy decided it was time to try for pity. His eyes misted over and his apple cheeks sagged. In a cracked voice, he began to plead. "Hey, please, Mr. Ferrand. You don't know what that means. If you bounce me out of here, my father will send me to a concentration camp. He already has one picked out, I swear. It's in Germany. Run by Nazis!"

Ferrand surpressed his laughter, unsure whether he was more amused by Tepper's pathetic demeanor or by the concept of a prep school run by Nazis. "What school?" he demanded.

"Schiller," Billy said. "One of the kids at my last school spent a year there. He said they called it Shriller because the kids spent the nights screaming. It has wire fences and lights up on towers. The whole works."

Ferrand couldn't hold back a smile. "Mr. Tepper, you're pure horseshit. I've heard of Schiller. It's a fine school. Maybe a little heavy-handed on the discipline, but that's exactly what you need. It will be good for you. Now get to your room and stay there. And in your spare time, you might start packing your bags."

"Please, Mr. Ferrand. What makes you think it was me? I mean, it could have been any of the kids. Maybe even one of the underclassmen. Some of those kids are crazy."

Ferrand walked around his desk and opened his door, indicating to Billy that his time had run out. "I don't think it was you, Tepper. I know it was you. Just like it was you who called the travel bureau and changed Dr. Palma's tickets, so that instead of getting a flight to Paris, he found himself in Moscow."

"That was last term," Billy protested. "You said we would forget that one."

"I said I wouldn't turn you in, and I didn't," Ferrand corrected. "But I could hardly forget about a student who tried to ship his headmaster behind the Iron Curtain."

"But I learned my lesson—"

"You learned nothing," Ferrand interrupted, "because a few weeks later you rigged a video camera into Miss Manetti's washroom and patched it into the television in the upperclass recreation room."

"That didn't even work," Billy answered, as if the failure of the scheme put the accusation to rest.

"Only because Miss Manetti heard the noise of the panning motor a few seconds before she undressed. Didn't it ever occur to you how difficult it would have been for her to hold the respect of students who had watched her undress and take a bath in their rec room?"

Billy still hadn't started toward the open door. "I apologized to her," he pointed out. "She said she forgave me."

"True. But she also gave you a lecture on the respect that you owed to women. And what did you learn from that lecture?"

Young Tepper understood the implication of the question. "You're talking about the hookers," he suggested.

"Yes, the hookers. Two months after she forgave you and saved you from the headmaster, you found the entrance to the old wine cellar behind the kitchen shelves and decided it would be fun to turn the wine cellar into a brothel. If I hadn't wondered why there were two new cooks in the kitchen at eight o'clock in the evening, you probably would have gone into business."

"I wasn't serious," Billy said lightly.

"The upperclass students who had prepaid you for the cooks' special services thought you were serious," Ferrand reminded him.

"So, a couple of little mistakes make me guilty of anything that happens around here," Billy protested.

Ferrand repeated his gesture toward the door. "When someone pulls off a cosmic prank, I look for someone who has a habit of cosmic pranks," he explained. "And that leads me to you. I'll find your latest invention somewhere along the power lines. And when I do, you'll be the owner of a one-way ticket back to the States. So, get packing."

Tepper was desperate. He pointed toward the door. "Close that thing, will you please, Mr. Ferrand. I need to talk to someone."

Ferrand's eyes narrowed. "About what subject?"

"Switching the power off and on," Billy confessed, and he collapsed into the chair next to Ferrand's desk.

It took him ten minutes to diagram the circuits he had used to cut the power with a command from his personal computer and then turn it back on again. "I thought it would be funny," he pleaded. "I never thought about people getting hurt. I'm sorry, Mr. Ferrand. Honest."

Ferrand tried to hide his admiration for Billy's innovative electronic design. "And because you're sorry, I'm supposed to forget that this ever happened?"

"Heck, no," Billy offered. "Just tell Henry Giles! He'll beat the shit out of me, and I won't tell anyone what happened. So, I'll be punished, but at least my father won't find out and I won't have to go to that Nazi prison camp."

"Can I watch?" Ferrand asked in mock eagerness. He saw Billy's eyes narrow in confusion. "Can I watch Henry Giles beat the shit out of you? I mean, shouldn't I get some satisfaction for all the times you've lied to me? All the times that you promised it would never happen again? I'd really enjoy watching Henry Giles bounce you off a couple of walls. Maybe break all your fingers so you couldn't play games with your computer. Maybe Miss Manetti should watch, too. She'd probably like to see you humiliated the way you were going to humiliate her. And I know the headmaster would want a ringside seat once he learned you were the one who sent him to Moscow. Hell, all the kids would want to watch."

Billy's chin had sunk onto his chest. "If you want," he mumbled. "Just don't send me to Shriller."

"It's Schiller," the teacher corrected. "No, I don't want. I would take no pleasure in watching you get bloodied. But I'll tell you what I do want. I want a complete explanation—a confession—in writing. And I want it in an envelope addressed to the headmaster."

"The Old Mouse?" Billy blurted.

"Yes, the Old Mouse. But use his more formal name, 'Dr. Headmaster.' And I swear to God, Mr. Tepper, that the next time a light bulb burns out in this building, the next time a car doesn't start, the next time anything goes wrong, I am personally going to slide your confession under the Old Mouse's door along with the cheese you've been sliding under his door every Friday night. Do you understand?"

"How did you find out about the cheese?" Billy asked admiringly.

"I didn't," Ferrand said, "until you just admitted it. Now get back to your room and start working on the confession. I want it in my hands before practice tomorrow. And I am going to break your butt at practice. Do we have an understanding?"

Billy was all smiles. "Thanks, Mr. Ferrand. And don't worry, because I've pulled my last prank. I've learned my lesson this time."

Ferrand walked to the door and held it open while Billy skittered through. "I'm not worried," he reminded the boy. "But you better worry. Because if there's another problem, the headmaster gets the confession with no questions asked."

Billy was nodding vigorously at the fairness and generosity of the settlement.

"And, Billy," Ferrand called after the chastened youth. "No more cheese."

Billy crossed himself as he walked backward toward the stairs. "Honest," he said, his final lie of the evening.

Ferrand was laughing before he had the door closed. He walked back to his desk and picked up the crude circuit drawings that Billy had explained to him. The kid was a genius, and his spirit was exciting. He had more potential than any kid Ferrand had ever had in a class. How could you stay mad at a boy with enough gumption to ship the headmaster to Russia? Jesus, but what he wouldn't have given to see Dr. Palma trying to figure out what Russian soldiers were doing at the Paris airport? And the whores. How many kids would have had the imagination to try to turn the abandoned cellar of a prestigious American boys' school into a bordello? Besides, he owed Billy a favor. The incident with the television camera had led to his first conversation with Maria Manetti. Since then he had used the wine cellar for an occasional rendezvous with her whenever one of them had weekend duty and they couldn't get together in Rome. How could you turn in someone who had introduced you to the woman you loved, and turned up a place for you to be together with her?

He walked to his window and noticed that there was only one light burning in the old mansion. It was Billy's room on the top floor, where he hoped the boy was busy working on his confession. But if he knew young Tepper, it wasn't a confession. More than likely he was working on a circuit diagram for a system that would kill all the electric power in Rome.

afternoon

Paul Frattiani was only a messenger. But he had the respect of Sharif because of whose messages and money he carried. He represented Albert Trotta, the largest single buyer of the hashish that Sharif gathered from all over the Middle East and delivered to market in Marseilles. It was Albert Trotta's cash, all of it untraceable, that paid for the guns and the grenades that Sharif's agents bought in East Germany, in Cuba, here in Libya, and even in Israel.

Frattiani climbed the steps along the outside wall of a private residence in Tripoli and started across the roof garden. Before he had taken five steps, he was aware that two men had fallen in behind him, and before he could turn, two others had stepped from behind a corner of the apartment and were waiting in front of him. He smiled at the faces he recognized, boys in their late teens and early twenties, noticed the machine pistols they were carrying, and stopped abruptly. He set his leather attaché case on the ground next to his feet and raised his hands straight into the air.

"Good morning," he said, as hands reached from behind him and began patting the sides of his body. "It's taped to my leg," he volunteered.

The hands continued down the outside of his trousers until they reached the pistol. Then his trouser leg was lifted and the gun removed from its flat holster. Another man picked up the briefcase and carried it forward to the two men who had appeared from behind the corner of the building.

"It's not locked. Open it," Frattiani offered.

One of the young men didn't wait for the invitation. He had already lifted the lid of the case that was held before him, noted the number of stacks of bills, and snapped the case closed. Then he returned Frattiani's smile, showing the space vacated by two missing teeth under his dark mustache.

"Sharif is waiting for you," he said pleasantly, almost like a headwaiter telling a regular patron that his table was ready. He handed the case back to Frattiani and opened the door to the rooftop apartment.

"Ah, Paul. How good to see you." Sharif rose from his chair at the head of a plain wooden table and walked toward the door to express his greeting. He was tall, with a lean body that marked him as a man in his early thirties, but with a dark, tired face that suggested he was much older. He was wearing blue work pants with an open-collared denim shirt, the cuffs turned back from his wrists. His hair was bushy and ungroomed, and the stubble of a beard covered his cheeks and chin.

This was the Sharif that Paul Frattiani met two or three times each month. But he was well aware that there were other Sharifs who appeared in poorly focused newspaper photos and streaked electronic transmissions that were often cut into sections of the evening news on television. Those Sharifs were sometimes immaculately dressed in European business suits, hair precisely parted and thin mustaches trimmed close to the upper lips. Or, they might be bearded figures in military jackets, adorned with campaign ribbons and decorations, their heads hidden in the hooded folds of tribal burnooses.

The costumes fitted his many personalities. To Arab extremists, he was a quasi-divine figure, a flaming sword from the desert who would drive the infidels from sacred land and bring a strict reading of the Koran to strengthen the spirits of his people. He nurtured the image, even though he had never seen the desert and despised the pretensions of religious leaders of all faiths. To the exiled governments of landless people he was a rebel. Impatient with years of impotence at bargaining tables, he had broken away from the traditional leadership, setting up his own government in exile. Now he claimed to be the legal spokesman for Palestinians living in Syria and throughout Lebanon and threatened assassination of anyone else who tried to speak on their behalf. To the legitimate governments of Middle Eastern countries he was a constant danger, rallying their minorities to revolution and demanding a seat at their conferences. To Western governments, he was a terrorist, a shadowy figure who seemed to have a hundred sponsors among exiled governments whenever his plots succeeded, and who was disowned by all who claimed legitimacy whenever his plots failed.

To Paul Frattiani, he was a dope pusher who supplied the opiates that his don sold on the streets of New Jersey, and who laundered the money from the don's other enterprises.

Sharif wrapped his arms around Frattiani and brushed the stubble of his beard against Paul's cheeks. "The last shipment was satisfactory?" he said as he pulled away to arm's length.

"To the gram," Paul answered. "Your merchandise is always perfect." He held up the briefcase. "Which is why we keep coming back for more."

They spoke easily, as if they were the closest of friends. But the contrast between the two men was remarkable. Frattiani was well tailored in a dark but lightweight business suit. His white shirt was buttoned to the throat and decorated with a conservatively patterned tie. His hair, like Sharif's, was dark, but it was worn short and perfectly groomed. Where Sharif was tall and lanky, Frattiani was short and stocky. And while Sharif flaunted the street-wise education of the refugee camps where he'd been born and raised, Paul was obviously the product of a liberal education on an East Coast campus.

Sharif took the case and dropped it casually on a covered sofa as he returned to his chair. He gestured to the other chair that was across the table from his own.

"Please," he said, as an offer of hospitality, and Paul joined him at the table. "We'll drink some coffee."

Frattiani accepted with a nod. The coffee was brought by one of the guards, who carried the ceramic coffeepot under one arm, his fingers hooked through the handles of the small cups that he set in the center of the table. The other arm was occupied by a machine pistol. It reminded Paul of Don Trotta. There were few people that Trotta could turn his back on. His bodyguards doubled as his personal servants and were always armed against the possibility of an unwanted intruder.

"I'm afraid I won't be delivering any more," Sharif said as he poured the syrupy coffee for his guest. "This next shipment will be my last."

Paul looked startled. Trotta and Sharif had a perfect business arrangement, profitable for both. He knew that the don would not be pleased.

"Mr. Trotta has other sources?" Sharif asked. "This will not be too difficult for him?"

"I don't know about Mr. Trotta's other business dealings," Frattiani lied, "but I would like to give him your reasons for ending the arrangement. Is there another buyer . . . a matter of price. . . ?"

Sharif dismissed the suggestion with a wave of his hand. "No, of course not. The price has been perfectly fair. It is just that the time has come for a change. Hashish has served its purpose. At least, for me. It's time for me to move on to more important things."

Frattiani nodded his congratulations at the change in status that Sharif was obviously implying. But he probed for more information. "What about the many people who benefit from your business? Will someone else be handling their output?"

Hashish was more than just a cash crop for Sharif. In many ways, it was the basis of his power. The tiny hemp plants were grown all over the Middle East, on every small farm, alongside herdsmen's homes, on the roofs of the stacked buildings in the refugee camps, in the window boxes in the Moslem sectors of Beirut and Tyre. They had been grown for thousands of years, to be ingested in small quantities as a mild narcotic in much the same way that an Englishman would take port after dinner. It was Sharif who, as a cadre leader in one of the Lebanese camps, had decided the people could do without their port. He began gathering their output, paying for their plants with favors—the kind of favors that only a military commander could deliver. Sometimes it was money. Sometimes it was physical protection from real or imagined enemies. Often it was rank within the governing committees or within the structure of his paramilitary command. But generally, he paid nothing more than a sense of belonging. Turning over the plants gave a refugee, who belonged nowhere, a sense of participation in the revolutionary cause. Withholding plants, on the other hand, became evidence of treason against one's neighbors.

By collecting the tiny hemp plants, Sharif also collected followers. And when he distributed the money and the guns that he bargained the plants for, his followers became an elite group. At first, his efforts had been praised by the leaders of the liberation armies. Sharif was empowering the people that they ruled. Later, as the people's loyalties shifted to Sharif, the more traditional political chieftains became uneasy. They fawned over Sharif in an attempt to win his allegiance to their constantly splintering factions. Before they realized that his loyalties were vested only in himself, Sharif had outstripped them in power. He controlled the source of the money, and with the money he controlled the source of the guns.

When the refugee army went to war against the Israeli tanks and planes, Sharif withdrew his troops to neutral ground. He had no intention of wasting his frail forces in a war that he knew couldn't be won. And he had stood on the sidelines while various Moslem sects and Palestinian factions tore themselves to pieces in a struggle that no one could win. Instead, he had conserved his energies for the kind of war that he could fight quite well, a barrage of terrorism against the imperialists who had ravaged his lands. When the bloody fratricide was finally finished, it was Sharif who emerged as the new leader of the Arab extremists. Well armed. Well financed. Well known throughout the world as a dangerous man.

It was inconceivable to Paul Frattiani that Sharif would walk away from his base of power, the millions of people who grew hashish and poured it into tributaries that grew into a mighty river as it flowed through the Middle East. The hashish was more than their source of income and protection. It was their pledge of loyalty to their leader.

"Production will continue," Sharif said in response to Paul's question. "The people will be paid. But it will be done by others. Trusted associates. No longer by me."

"Will Mr. Trotta continue as a customer?" Paul asked.

Sharif nodded over the edge of his coffee cup. "If Mr. Trotta needs the output, his interests will be protected. I give my word."

"And your own interests?" Paul asked politely. "I assume you will still be in a position of respect?"

Sharif's black eyes sparkled. "Respect?" he repeated, and then his teeth flashed in a smile. "Yes, certainly. In a few days my people will learn to worship me. I will be the only star in the Eastern sky."

Frattiani nodded slowly, indicating that he understood. Sharif was about to strike again. But this time the mission would be more daring than ever before. So daring that it would give him a new base of power, freeing him from the need to traffic in hashish.

In the past, he had met with Sharif immediately after his terrorists had blown up American government offices in Germany, killing scores of people, or after hijackers had thrown a series of freshly killed bodies out the door of a surrounded Israeli airliner. He had made it obvious that he took no joy in whatever successes Sharif had achieved. "I feel sorry for the innocent lives," he had told the terrorist. And Sharif had nodded in sympathy, but had defended his actions. "War always takes innocent lives," he had reminded Paul. "Were the hostages any more innocent than the children in our camps who were killed by Israeli tanks, or the shells fired from your battleship?" Consequently, they had learned to avoid the subject as a condition of their business arrangement. But now Frattiani took it up again.

"Sharif, you know that they can never give in to you. So the hostages are as good as dead when they fall into your hands, unless you back down, and then you lose respect with your people. You have to kill innocent people just to save face. That's not the same as people being killed in a war."

"This will be different," Sharif corrected quickly. "They will have to meet my terms. This time I will hold them by their hearts. There will be no question of allowing the hostages to suffer. They will beg me for terms. This time . . ." He stopped with his thoughts formed on his lips. He wanted to justify himself, but he realized he had said too much already. Suddenly, he dismissed the subject with a wave of his hand. "You will understand," Sharif concluded. "You will not be offended."

They finished the coffee in silence, and then Sharif rose to signal the end of the meeting. He pointed toward the briefcase that he had discarded so casually. "Convey my thanks to Mr. Trotta, and tell him his business interests will be respected."

"You should count the money," Paul said with a smile. "We always count the cargoes you send to Marseilles."

Sharif laughed. "Tell Mr. Trotta that I am a world figure. World figures don't count money."

The guards were waiting when Paul stepped out onto the roof garden. They walked beside him until he reached the top of the steps. He waited while one of the men bent down and replaced his pistol in the holster that was strapped to his leg. Then he walked down the steps and climbed into the back seat of a car that was driven by one of Sharif's men.

At the airport, the Libyan authorities accepted a nod from the driver and waved Frattiani through the passport checks. He boarded an airliner and flew to Naples, where he was met by relatives of Don Trotta who watched over the family interests in Italy.

"I'm changing my travel plans," he told one of the Italians. "Please get word to Signor Trotta that I will be visiting his cousin in Virginia. I will be a day late in returning home." The relative looked puzzled. Paul smiled reassuringly. "It's all right. Signor Trotta will understand." At the counter, he changed his tickets, cancelling his return flight to New York and booking a first-class seat on a plane to Washington.

The don's cousin wasn't a cousin; he wasn't even a member of the closely knit family of feudal chieftains that managed Albert Trotta's convoluted chain of cash businesses. Rather, he was an employee of the federal government on the staff of the Central Intelligence Agency.

Three years ago, the Agency had come to appreciate the extent of Don Trotta's business dealings throughout the Mediterranean and Middle East. During an investigation by the Justice Department into organized crime, the director had been awed by the professionalism of the don's organization, particularly the intelligence channels that protected his businesses. "The son of a bitch has better sources than we do," the director had explained to the attorney general. "The goddamn gangster even makes the KGB look like a bunch of amateurs."

The Justice Department was determined to put Albert Trotta out of business. The CIA was determined to bring him into the business. The heated dispute went all the way to the White House, where the president came down on the side of national security. So, while the attorney general fumed, the CIA had enlisted Trotta's help. The don had agreed. As an immigrant who had made his fortune in America, he felt he owed his adopted country a debt. And the don always paid his debts.

Paul Frattiani implemented the arrangement. He listened carefully during his visits to Syria and Libya, recording the names of people in power that were mentioned and the meetings that they had attended. The names and places enabled him to trace the changing alliances that shaped the emerging revolutionary leaderships. His eyes photographed everything he saw. He noted the kinds of guns his contacts carried and the shipping instructions on the sides of the ammunition cases. This told him which groups had found favor with Communist-block countries. He even noted the clothes people wore, sure evidence of the countries in which they were operating. It was trivial information, to his mind not important enough to justify his frequent visits to Washington. Frattiani never understood why the don's cousin was always so impressed and extravagant in his gratitude.

But this time the trivia was important. As he sat in the window seat of the Alitalia 747, Frattiani knew he was carrying critical information. The problem was that he wasn't sure exactly what the information was. Sharif was planning something big; so big that it would carry him to the pinnacle of prestige in the Arab world. Paul listened carefully to their conversation as he played it back in his mind. "In a few days my people will learn to worship me." The terrorist was moving up the ladder, so far, in fact, that he would no longer need his power base in hashish.

There were only two targets that could have such a drastic impact on the status quo in the region. One was Israel, hated by even those moderate Arab governments that had come to an understanding with the "Zionist state." Even the Egyptians and Jordanians, who talked of negotiated settlements, would side with anyone who could humble the Israelis. The other possible target was the United States, distrusted by its friends for its support of Israel, and hated by all others for the shells it had hurled into Lebanon and the bombs it had dropped on Libya. Wringing concessions out of the arrogant

Americans would make even a terrorist a giant among his people.

Those were the most probable targets, but also the most futile. Both countries had established policies against negotiating with terrorists. There was little chance of winning even minor concessions from either of them. And yet, as he swirled his drink over the ice cubes in his glass and glanced down at the lights of Paris blazing to the north, Frattiani recalled Sharif's most frightening comment. "This time I will hold them by their hearts. There will be no question of allowing the hostages to suffer."

What could be so different, he wondered. Who were the hostages who could hold Israel or the United States by the heart? Even when terrorists had held Israel's Olympic team at gunpoint in Munich, the Jews had refused to negotiate. The spectacular plot had ended in brutal carnage, hardly earning respect for the terrorists, even from Israel's bitterest enemies. American journalists and teachers seemed to be permanent prisoners in Lebanon. The United States had tried to deal for them under the table, but it refused to offer the public concessions that the terrorists demanded—the kind of concessions that Sharif would need to become the only star in the East. What did Sharif think was so vital to the Israelis or Americans that would force them to meet his terms?

He tried to think of people so important to those governments that they would not dare risk them no matter how great a price was demanded. Clearly, they couldn't be government officials. Neither country could afford protection to its politicians that it had denied its private citizens. Was there a religious leader so revered in Israel that the people would demand his freedom at any price? Was there an American poet or scholar whose life would be more valuable than the prestige of the government? It probably wasn't just one person. Probably a group. Some group of important people who could be taken all at once. Like the Olympic team, but much more important? Who or what in God's name could be so important?

Or maybe it was nothing. Perhaps Sharif was boasting, hinting at a bigger victory than he could possibly achieve.

Frattiani tossed down the rest of his drink just as the dinner tray was set before him. What was the point of torturing himself? He didn't know the answers. He wasn't expected to analyze the information he carried. He would just lay it all out for the don's cousin. What he did know was that Sharif seemed confident he had found the perfect target. Something so dramatic it would vault him to leadership in the Middle East. Something so important the target country would have to give in to his demands. And also that the Flaming Sword would strike soon; certainly before Paul's next scheduled visit, which would be in just two weeks.

Was he sure of his information? Probably not. It was possible that Sharif had gotten into his own hashish and was hallucinating his future hour of glory. But as he raised the first mouthful of pasta, his fork stopped in mid-air. He remembered the sparkle in Sharif's dark eyes and heard him say, "You will understand. You will not be offended."

The man was sure his intended victims wouldn't die. That they would be ransomed at any price. Frattiani set down the fork and pushed the tray away. Once again, the litany of people began to run through his mind. He knew there would be no rest until he had unburdened himself to the don's cousin.

"Ferrand, you ball-buster," Billy Tepper muttered to himself as he tore off the grass-stained sneaker and fired it against the back wall of his locker. He began tugging at the laces of the other sneaker. "I hope you're having fun kicking my ass"—the second sneaker set the metal walls of the locker resonating like a bass drum—"because I sure as hell am going to have fun getting even."

Ferrand had been all over Billy during the soccer practice, which extended a full hour beyond the normal gym period. He was working on field position, which was a useless exercise at best. The American boys had no grasp of the game's strategy and wandered like gypsies, giving the ball all the direction of a pinball ricocheting off lighted posts. Ferrand yelled at them all. But he sent Billy on endless laps around the field every time he had caught him out of position.

"Does the idiot really expect to beat the Italians?" Tepper demanded of no one as he pulled the sweat-soaked shirt over his straw-colored hair. Ferrand had booked a game with an Italian school that had just won its regional championship. "Goddamn Italians are born kicking a soccer ball," he muttered as he walked toward the showers. He had seen Italian kids holding animated conversations while they kicked the ball back and forth over their heads with their heels. "An Italian can get laid while he's dribbling a soccer ball," Billy said to the towel rack.

While he showered, he fumed at the details of Ferrand's retribution. The coach had ordered him to run wind sprints and laps until he staggered off into the bushes and threw up his breakfast. Then Ferrand berated his play. True, he missed an open net, but Christ, the ball hit the post. The other kids couldn't even come close, and the coach didn't single them out for abuse. Ferrand didn't even try to hide his pleasure. The bastard damn near laughed every time he ordered Billy to take another lap. "Enjoy yourself, Ferrand," Billy now mumbled. "We'll see who gets the last laugh."

The first thing he had to do was get rid of the relay he had used to turn off the power. Ferrand would probably make good on his threat to look for the evidence, and he didn't want the proof of his prank to fall into enemy hands. Billy didn't yet know how, but he was determined to get even with his tormenter. If he was going to get Ferrand aggravated, he'd better make sure that the teacher had no hard evidence to back up the confession he had extorted.

As soon as he was dressed, he walked across the tiled hallway to the toilets and closed the door behind him. A fast glance under the doors of the booths told him he was alone, and he quickly jumped into the last booth and climbed up onto the toilet tank. In a second, he had snapped the screen off the ventilation duct and pulled himself into the opening, drawing the screen back into position. The space was small, but he fit easily. Not that he was still a boy. His body was well along in its changes to manhood. But the boundless energy that fueled his imagination also incinerated the vast quantities of food he consumed during each of his waking hours. As a result, he was wire thin with a frailty that disguised his stamina.

Once inside, he lifted the bottom plate of the ventilator shaft and slid it aside, then dropped silently through the opening. It put him in a narrow space between the stone foundation of the old building and the cement blocks that formed the wall of the new building. The space didn't show on any of the school's plans. When the facilities had been expanded, the builders had decided it was too dangerous to tamper with the wall of the old mansion. Instead, they left it intact, building the new building adjacent to the old, and then sealing the space with a common roof and exterior walls. Billy had found it by accident; just "fell into it," as he liked to remind himself. He had climbed into the ventilation duct, sure that he could follow the sheet-metal tunnel through the building to the screen over the file cabinets in the administration office. That would get him into the office at night, when the door was locked and the place was empty. And that, he hoped, would get him copies of any exam the night before it was scheduled to be given. In his mind he had worked out an elaborate tariff under which his classmates could participate in his good fortune. He realized he couldn't sell all the questions, because then everyone who took the test would get a perfect grade. Even someone as dumb as the Old Mouse would smell a rat. But he could sell lots of people half the questions. As long as each student had different questions, there would be no obvious pattern of right and wrong answers. And he could charge just as much for half the questions as for all of them. After all, it wasn't as if he had any competition, and the one thing his classmates at Saint Anselm's had in limitless supply was spending money.

"Hell," he had persuaded himself, "it would be good for them to put some of their money into their education instead of wasting it all on candy bars and soft drinks."

So he had climbed into the ventilation duct and was crawling through the metal tunnel when the floor had fallen out from under him, dropping him into the space between the two buildings. After cursing his luck, he snapped on his flashlight and found that he had landed in a Pharaoh's tomb of possibilities. Every electrical line, phone line, water pipe, and gas pipe that ran between the buildings passed through the open space he had just discovered. If Saint Anselm's had a nervous system, he had just found its spinal cord.

On his first few visits, he had done nothing more enterprising than tap a few telephone lines and listen in on the conversations. It was exciting at the start, but then boredom set in. Adult conversations were dull, and the Old Mouse's line was impossible. The jerk spoke Italian, French, German, and a couple of languages that Billy didn't even recognize. He hardly ever used English. So, instead of listening, he had started ringing telephones randomly, figuring he could probably drive the administration crazy by having the telephones ring all the time, with every line dead when it was answered. That kept him out of mischief for a few more days.

Then he had gotten one of his cosmic ideas. Suppose every phone in the building rang at the same time—say three o'clock in the morning. That would be good for a few laughs. But as he drew up the circuit diagram and began assembling the parts he would need, he realized that he was tiring of the telephone. There were still the water pipes and gas pipes and power lines that he hadn't even touched.

He had decided on the power lines. It would be child's play to kill all the power, but he needed to figure out the appropriate time. Maybe in the middle of the commencement exercises, or during final examinations. Or how about a general assembly when the Old Mouse was showing slides of some boring museum he had visited?

Christ! It had struck him as a vision. Any fool could turn the power off. The real fun would be turning it on. Wait until the middle of the night. Kill the power. Turn on every light and appliance in the building. Then turn the power back on. God, it was brilliant!

Now, he traced the power line to the cement block he had loosened in the wall of the new building. He slid the block out of position and aimed his flashlight at the back of the circuit breaker panel that was mounted on the other side of the wall, in the basement of the new building. Carefully, he lifted the induction coil from the main breaker. Then he detached the wires that connected the coil to the power line and the signal wire he had installed from the coil to the nearby telephone line. He pulled his homemade device back through the opening and started to replace the cement block. Let Ferrand tear the building down. He wouldn't find the answer to last night's episode.

He reached for the flashlight he had wedged behind the power line while he was replacing the block, and it flipped over, sending a beam of light to the top corner of the space, where the outside wall joined the roof. High above his head, Billy noticed a cable he had never seen before. He pulled the flashlight from behind the power line and aimed it at the new cable, tracing its run with the beam. It came out of the wall of the old building, crossed the open space, then disappeared into the wall of the new building. Billy was puzzled. He had worked on the telephone lines and on the power lines. What other kinds of cables were there? He tried to remember what part of the old building was behind the wall where the cable originated. What kind of equipment was located there? The cable had to connect to something.

Of course! It wasn't an electrical line. It was a coaxial cable for the television security system. It was for the goddamn spy cameras that looked down all the corridors so the security people could spot intruders in the building. At least that was what they said the cameras were for. All night long, television cameras panned the tops of the walls and the entrances to all the buildings as well as the student hallways. The teachers said they were for the students' protection, to keep people out. Bullshit! They were there to keep the kids in. To keep them in their rooms and to catch them if they tried to go over the wall. They had never spotted anyone breaking in. But lots of kids had been caught trying to break out.

Billy stared at the cable. It's just a dumb wire, he thought. It doesn't know what it's carrying. Hell, it doesn't even know it's a cable! All you'd have to do is connect a video recorder to it and you could change the picture on the screens of the monitors.

His fertile mind nourished the possibilities. The monitors were located in the guard shack at the front gate and in the security office across the hall from the administration office. There was no point in sending a different picture to the guard shack. The watchmen stationed there never looked at the monitors anyway. They put their feet up on the desk and slept all night instead. But there was always someone in the security office. Teachers and secretaries were assigned there around the clock. They didn't really stare at the small screens that displayed different sections of the wall and the various entrances and corridors. Most of the time they brought work with them and only glanced up occasionally to see if any of the kids were trying to escape. But they would be bound to notice something different.

Like, say, a porno movie.

He could get a real grunt-and-grinder. Not the Swedish stuff. That would put a voyeur to sleep. Italian! A real flesh-pot Italian porno. He could connect a video recorder to the coaxial cable and show a hard-core movie on one of the screens in the security office. All he would have to do is check the duty schedule and find out when one of the old-bat secretaries would be assigned to security. He could even use the timed-start on the recorder. That way, he could arrange to be coming out of the administration office, looking right through the door into the security office, when his feature film cut onto one of the screens. God, he could even catch the old bat when she screamed and fainted.

Billy smiled at the idea. But he would have to file it away for the time being. His priority was Mr. Ferrand, and before he spread himself too thin he needed to find a way to pay the coach back for kicking his ass all over the practice field. He snapped off the flashlight and started toward the square of light that fell from the open panel in the ventilation duct. But before he had taken his second step, he stopped abruptly. He turned slowly, looked at the walls on both sides of the space, and then methodically began to pace off distances.

The hidden entrance to the old wine cellar was in the back of the kitchen in the new building. That meant the steps went right underneath the point where he was now standing, reaching down beneath the stone wall of the old building. If he could mount a camera somewhere in the wine cellar, he could lead his cable to the steps. Then he could bring the cable through the top of the stairwell and up through the ground into his secret room, where he could tap into the security system.

He felt a chill of excitement. "Porno flick, my ass," he said through a thin smile that was beginning to spread across his face. "I'll give them real live porno." He slapped his hand over his mouth to stifle the delicious laughter. Ferrand and Manetti in carnal knowledge, he thought to himself, and the joy broke through his fingers so that he had to bite down on his hand to keep from roaring in delight. They sometimes met in the wine cellar when the duty roster kept them at school. He could record their liaison. Images of torrid, panting sexual gymnastics flashed through his mind, and the suppressed laughter began to explode in his chest until his sides were aching.

He wouldn't use the panning camera that he had rigged in Miss Manetti's bathroom. The noise would give it away. It would have to be one camera, pre-focused, which meant he would have to do without the graphic close-ups. And there would be no sound because the security system had no sound capability. But the stars of his production would more than make up for the technical shortcomings.

The hell with shocking some old bat of a secretary. For this epic he would want a prestigious gathering. The Old Mouse, for sure. And as many of the teachers as he could assemble. He would have to record the encounter and then connect his video playback unit to the coaxial cable. Then he would have to figure out a way to start the playback remotely, maybe using the radio control system from Snuffy Bradberry's model airplane. He could hang around the administration desk until he found the perfect audience gathered in the security office. Then . . . showtime! He'd hit the remote control button and watch a picture of the top of the wall turn into Ferrand on top of Miss Manetti. Jesus, maybe he would wait until Ferrand was near the security office so he could be called in to watch his own performance. Brilliant! Why, he could even arrange to be talking to Ferrand outside the security office and then simply put his hand into his pocket and press the remote control button. That way, Ferrand would never be able to blame him. He would have the perfect alibi.

There was no holding it back. Laughter broke through his smile and he had to run back into the far corner of the room so he wouldn't be heard through the opening by someone in the bathroom. Finally, he was able to calm himself down, but as soon as he started back toward the opening he was once again convulsed with laughter. This was a classic, by far his best effort ever. And it was so simple! Hadn't he heard it a hundred times—the best ideas were the simple ideas. It would only take him a day or two to gather the pieces and assemble the equipment. Then maybe a few hours to drive a piece of pipe down through the ground and the top of the stairs. Then all he had to do was wait for Ferrand and Miss Manetti to have overnight duty. Their television debut probably would be within the week.

"You want to play hardball," he said to an imaginary Edward Ferrand as he began lifting himself back up into the air duct. "Then we'll play hardball. The Old Mouse will make you run a wind sprint all the way to America." He had reached the vent screen when he felt more laughter coming on, and he sat in the duct behind the screen for a full ten minutes biting down on his fingers before he trusted himself to move on.

When Billy came out of the bathroom, Ferrand was sitting on the bench in the locker room taking off his sneakers. Their eyes made contact, and for a second Billy was afraid that a look of guilt would give his whole scheme away.

"How are you feeling, Mr. Tepper?" the teacher asked with feigned solicitude.

"Just great," Billy answered with a huge smile. He sauntered past Ferrand. "Great practice," he said with bubbling enthusiasm. "We're really starting to get those passes down. I think those Italian kids are in for a big surprise. We're really going to kick ass out there."

Ferrand turned to watch Billy disappear through the door. The boy's optimism could mean only one thing. He was already launched on his next prank. Ferrand knew he should be worried. And yet he couldn't wait to see what Billy Tepper would come up with next.

April 15

late afternoon

Otis Brown didn't look like a spy. His thin white hair, combed in strands across the bald crown of his head, and the thick frameless glasses, which were always slipping down to the end of his nose, were the stage makeup of a clerk. His frail physique, with most of its weight fallen to the belt line, made him an unlikely model for a trench coat. But there were hidden qualities that accounted for his rank as the CIA's top man in anti-terrorist activities. And even though he had never captured a single terrorist, he had come close enough on several occasions to earn daily private meetings with the director and dozens of appearances before the National Security Council.

His title was "senior analyst," which was an accurate description of the tasks he performed. He gathered information from thousands of sources, wrote computer programs that organized the data according to hundreds of variables, and studied the results for interesting patterns that seemed to defy the general laws of probability. It was Brown who had studied the geographic locations of terrorist acts and correlated them with the airline schedules of international flights originating in Damascus, Tripoli, and other terrorist havens. His analysis enabled him to assign probability factors to certain flights as potential candidates for hijacking. Based on his warnings, Italian police had found guns and grenades secreted in the toilet of a Boeing 727 that was about to load passengers for a flight from Rome to Athens. Four Palestinians who had been standing in the waiting room with their boarding passes disappeared abruptly when the level of police activity around the airplane became obvious. His warning that there were too many Americans sailing the Mediterranean in cruise ships was being coded for transmission to friendly governments when Arab extremists boarded an Italian liner in Alexandria. And, based on his analysis of suitable targets for IRA soldiers, the British prime minister had cancelled reservations in a hotel that was later rocked by an explosion in the very suite she would have occupied.

Brown's subordinates stood as he entered the secure conference room in Langley and remained standing until he had deposited twenty-five pounds of computer printout on the conference table and taken his seat. Then they crushed out their cigarettes and fanned at the fumes in deference to a mild allergy that caused his eyes to water in the presence of tobacco smoke.

"This one will require quite a bit of overtime," he said, tapping the mountain of printed data before him. "We need some prime targets. Targets that will be fully ripe within the next two weeks. And we need them immediately."

He explained the background. A trusted source with the highest possible confidence factor had been in direct contact with Sharif less than twenty-four hours earlier. Eyes widened in recognition of the name that had become the inevitable subject in their recent analyses. Sharif, Brown explained, had indicated he was about to strike at a target of extraordinary importance. Something so important that it would wrest immediate concessions from the government it was aimed at.

"Where?" one of the assistants blurted. Then he withered under the glance Brown threw him over the top of his glasses. The question was naive coming from someone who had spent even a short time working on Brown's team. There were only two critical target countries.

"We have alerted the Israelis," the senior analyst continued. "They're running their own evaluation. We'll concentrate on our own interests. Personally, I think we're the ones who will come up with the right answer. We've had other information to indicate that Sharif is going for a knockout. I think this is the one we've been waiting for."

"A target within the United States?" another of the assistants asked, expecting an affirmative answer. The threats of Arab extremists to bring their holy war to the streets of America were too numerous not to be taken seriously. There was an assumption in the intelligence community that it was just a matter of time.

"Quite possibly," Brown answered, "but not certainly. The United States lives all over the world. As always, a strike against the United States can take place anywhere.

"All the obvious targets have already been alerted. Warnings went out to embassies, military bases, trade missions, and so forth early this morning. There's not much more they can do. These days, our people overseas live on full-alert status anyway. But the evaluation of the information indicated that they should receive a special warning. This is much more than a routine threat."

He could see from their expressions that his urgency wasn't registering. Terrorist threats were a daily occurrence, relayed with monotonous regularity from every listening post in the world. The simplest fool in any aggrieved population knew he could take on instant importance by pretending to be on the inside of a plot aimed against real or imagined oppressors. Hopeless Puerto Ricans, Irishmen, Lebanese, Palestinians, Indians, Egyptians, Moluccans, and Bantus posed as terrorists to impress women they were attempting to seduce, push their job applications to the top of the pile, or gain the admiration of their children. Inevitably, their threats were as empty as their pockets. But still, Brown and his team of analysts had to treat them as genuine. A real gunman had stepped out of the dismal litany of Indian plots to gun down Nehru's daughter. A real bomb thrower had emerged from the rumors of Puerto Rican rebellion to kill the lunch-hour customers of a Wall Street restaurant. Some of the rumors turned out to be true.

"Gentlemen," Brown said, jumping up from the table to break the atmosphere of complacency, "I'm convinced that this information is absolutely accurate. I'm positive that we're going to be hit and hit hard. If we let this one get by us, there could be a procession of body bags to remind us that we didn't do our job. We've got to give it our maximum effort."

He had their attention.

"Now, what exactly are we looking for?" He began to pace around the table, circling behind their chairs, sharing his thoughts rather than delivering a lecture.

"Something within two weeks. Our informant is positive on this point. Sharif indicated clearly that the strike would be history by the time he and the informant met again, and they would normally meet again two weeks from yesterday. It could be within hours, but it won't be any later than twelve days from now."

"Something very dramatic," one of the assistants offered. "If Sharif is behind it, it has to be big."

Brown nodded in agreement. Sharif believed in bold gestures big enough to make banner headlines across the front pages of the world's newspapers and to cause television networks to abandon their regularly scheduled programming. He also believed in huge demands that required hours and even days of negotiating. It wouldn't be a kneecapping or a kidnapping. And it wouldn't be a hit-and-run raid. Sharif wasn't interested in a quick kill or a demand that could be easily resolved or ignored. He needed to keep a mighty leader or a great power locked in agony, giving the whole world time to relish the giant's helplessness and to appreciate his own genius. He had captured airliners and traded the passengers for Arab prisoners. He had locked the French national soccer team in a hotel wired with explosives and bargained their lives for the cancellation of a French arms contract with the Israeli air force. He had hijacked a Spanish passenger train and held it in a mined tunnel, threatening to bring the mountain down on top of it if Spanish troops were not withdrawn from an international peacekeeping force. Some of his attacks had been bloody fiascos in which innocent hostages had been murdered, terrorists killed, and his demands ignored. Others had won him concessions, although never a victory on the grand scale he had envisioned. But all had caught the attention of the world and held its population pinned to their seats while he acted out his role as the Flaming Sword from the Desert.

"Yes," Brown mumbled. "Something big. With Sharif involved, we have to expect a raid that will give him a large number of hostages to bargain with. Or some very important hostages. Our informant was quite sure there would be a hostage or hostages so important that the target nation wouldn't even think of risking lives."

But there was more. In his head, Brown replayed the taped conversation between the assistant director and the unknown but highly reliable informant. He had been impressed by the sincerity in the informant's voice. The man had answered all of the assistant director's questions, but kept interjecting personal observations—references to Sharif's eyes, his smile, his gestures. The man knew Sharif. He was positive Sharif had not been boasting or posturing, that the terrorist was absolutely convinced he had found a way to bring a powerful government to its knees.

Brown was groping for the notion that had impressed him as he listened to the voices. The man knew Sharif. He had met with him after some of his previous terrorist attacks. But he seemed convinced that this attack would be very different.

"Something unusual," Brown said suddenly, breaking free from his thoughts and turning on his assistants. "Look for something different than we've ever seen before." Their expressions told him they didn't understand.

"What usually happens when these bastards take hostages?" Brown demanded. Then he answered his own question. "Both sides dig in their heels. The country that is attacked can't give in because it can't compromise its national honor. And the terrorists can't give in because they have publicly committed themselves to dying for their cause. So they kill a few hostages, and then we attack to free the hostages. If we're lucky, the hostages live, and if we're sloppy, the hostages die along with the terrorists."

Heads nodded in acknowledgment of the accuracy of the grim scenario Brown had just painted.

"For the terrorist to be sure of success, he has to take a hostage so valuable that the country he is attacking wouldn't even think of jeopardizing the hostage's life. They won't stall because they can't risk having the hostage killed. And they certainly won't attack. All they can do is give in immediately and meet all the demands. I think that's what we're looking for here. I think Sharif is going after the 'superhostage,' and he's pretty sure he can get his hands on him within the next two weeks. Our informant told us Sharif has found a hostage who will 'grab us by our hearts.' Someone we love so much that national policy won't even be a consideration. That's what we're looking for."

The faces around the table were puzzled. Suddenly, a voice from the end challenged his premise. "Otis, we have a national commitment not to give in to terrorist demands. Christ, even if they took the president, the vice president couldn't simply cave in. He would have to treat the president as if he were any other citizen."

"What if they took Prince Charles?" Otis Brown demanded.

Mouths dropped open around the table.

"Do you think the British government would refuse to negotiate? Or do you think the prime minister would order the commandos to give it their best shot and hope that the next king of England didn't get his brains blown out in the cross fire?"

His meaning was getting through.

"Or suppose they grabbed the pope? Can you imagine the Italian government standing on principle and waiting to see the Holy Father come flying out the door of an airplane? Or let's say they took over the Louvre and poured gasoline down the halls underneath half of the world's art treasures? Do you think the French would start throwing hand grenades in through the windows? When they kidnap a bunch of anonymous tourists, we can stand on principle. But if they capture the right people . . . or the right place? If they can make the price high enough or the pain intense enough, then maybe we have to compromise our principles."

"What do you think they're going after, Otis?" a chastened voice asked.

He shook his head in despair. "I don't know. I feel sure the United States is the target and that they're going to take something different. Something we love. Not just a few soldiers. Not just a few tourists or businessmen. It's going to be something that grabs us by the heart. Something we can't risk. Something that will have the whole country begging the president to cave in to their demands."

"Then we should ignore the obvious things," an assistant suggested.

"We won't ignore anything," Otis Brown corrected. "We'll warn all the airlines and put the airport and rail terminals on alert. But we won't stop there. We'll analyze every bit of this information from every possible angle." He waved his hand at the huge pile of data he had left at the head of the table. "We'll examine every possible target. And we'll test them to see if there is anything about them that makes them different. Makes us more vulnerable. As I said at the beginning, this one is going to require quite a bit of overtime."

He returned to his place at the head of the table and began distributing the thick packets of computer printout.

"Here are bookings for tours that will be overseas during the next two weeks." One of the assistants accepted the material and winced as he measured its thickness with his fingers. "Look for unusual combinations of people. Church leaders traveling together, children's choirs, families of government officials—anything that puts a large number of valuable targets together in one place at the same time." The assistant nodded.

"These are business conventions," Brown said, pushing a folder toward another assistant. "We're after a large gathering of special people in any city or resort that might be particularly vulnerable. But it has to be people who would cause a public outcry if they were kidnapped. Something more than those bankers who were living it up at that ski chalet on top of a mountain in Italy." They all remembered. It had been such a perfect target for a terrorist act that Brown had spent several frantic days trying to get the meeting cancelled. Finally, he had persuaded the Italian government to surround the mountain with troops. Nothing happened, and Brown endured a hundred jokes about Italian soldiers hiding behind the trees on the ski slopes. But, in Brown's mind at least, there was always the possibility that perhaps the reason nothing happened was the fact that armed troops had out-numbered skiers.

"Family information on U.S. government officials," he said as he handed over another statistical listing. "See if members of government families will be together anywhere." He had always worried about family members, a fear that had proven fully justified when the daughter of the president of El Salvador had been kidnapped by leftist revolutionaries. The government had caved in to all the kidnappers' demands.

"Art exhibits," he announced, pointing to another printout. At any time, there were priceless collections of art objects being shipped between the museums of the world, as well as being exhibited in vulnerable cities. Would we stand on principle if the work of Van Gogh was about to be tossed into a fire?

Brown worked his way through the other folders, delivering days of work to each of his assistants with the understanding that he needed results within hours. "Have we missed anything?" he asked when he had cleared all the data from in front of him. The response was an outburst of laughter. Otis Brown, they all knew, didn't miss anything.

"Boy Scout meetings," an assistant joked for the mutual amusement of his colleagues. Brown joined the laughter but then shook his head. "No. If they're traveling more than a hundred miles, you'll find them under the tour information."

The meeting ended and the waiting began.

Alone in his office, Brown paced the carpet that had begun to show the signs of wear from all the previous analyses he had directed. These were his worst moments, when he had assigned the work and then had to wait uselessly for the results to be returned. "What have we missed?" he asked himself over and over as he paced like a caged animal. "Something obvious," he answered in response. Something that Sharif has discovered entirely by accident, without the help of the powerful mainframe computers that were now sorting his information. Something so obvious that, when it happened, it would leave him sick at the thought of his own ignorance.

He realized that the light through the windows of his office had faded. He reached for the light switch but changed his mind. He didn't need to see; he needed to think, and he thought better in the dark. It had been four hours since he had turned his staff to the work. It was already eight o'clock in Washington, two o'clock in the morning in Europe, nearly dawn in the Middle East. Another day was beginning, perhaps the day that Sharif had circled on his calendar for his victorious attack against the hated Americans. Somewhere in the data Brown had gathered was the target that was perhaps being surrounded or boarded at this very instant. What had they missed?

An assistant charged into the room, then stopped abruptly when he became aware of the darkness. "Get the light," Brown's voice said from one of the invisible corners. Otis blinked at the sudden flash of brightness.

"I've got a couple of things," the assistant said as he pulled the side chair up against Brown's desk. Brown stood beside him, peering over his shoulder. The man began consulting his computer reports.

"This is from the tour information. Here, next Tuesday." He had found a line of information and was pointing at it with a freshly sharpened pencil. "The new fashion showings in Paris. A group of government wives are flying to Paris to do some shopping. Three senators. The head of the SEC and the head of the Federal Reserve. There are also three women from one of the big consulting firms." Brown understood the code in which wives were identified simply by the positions and titles of their husbands. "They're all on the same flight direct to Paris. All at the same hotel. And they're all booked on the same evening cruise up the Seine."

Brown nodded. "Jesus, wouldn't that be a coup. Can't you see the television pictures of Sharif's guerrillas holding the big-spending wives of American government leaders for ransom on the decks of a river boat."

"Here's another," the assistant said, thumbing to another page. "The Harlem Globetrotters. They're playing a game in Athens next Wednesday, passing through Athens airport twice . . . on the way in and on the way out."

Half the hijackings in the world seemed to begin at the Athens airport, Brown knew. And there probably wasn't an American who didn't know and love the team of basketball wizards. They fitted nicely with Sharif's plan to go after something that a target government wouldn't risk at any price.

"One more," the assistant said, turning furiously through the pages. "Here. A group of clergymen on a visit to the Christian shrines in Israel. Three of these guys are Catholic bishops and one is head of one of the Methodist churches."

Brown nodded. "Possible," he allowed. But he wasn't very excited. Clergymen were questionable targets simply because they were spiritual brothers to the terrorists' own holy men. He wasn't enthused about the congressional wives in Paris, either. Or even the Harlem Globetrotters. Harm to any one of the groups would be tragic. But he kept hearing the informant's voice repeating that Sharif's target would grab America by its heart. Women and clergymen and athletes had all been taken before. This had to be different.

"Anything else?" Brown asked.

"We're about halfway through," the assistant said, gathering his papers. "We'll keep you posted."

On the way out, he collided in the doorway with one of his colleagues who was rushing in with more reports.

"What have you got?" Brown demanded of the new arrival.

"Not much," the man apologized. "We've run all the conventions. About all I've learned is why it's damn near impossible to get a doctor. They're always away on conventions."

Brown laughed for the first time in days.

"Plastic surgeons are meeting at Nice. Dermatologists are knocking heads in Venice. All the world's proctologists are gathering in Bermuda. Do you suppose Sharif would demand a cut of all their Medicare dollars?"

"Terrible targets," Brown joked. "If all the American doctors were wired with explosives, we'd all be rooting for Sharif to push the plunger. Every American buried under medical bills would become an Arab sympathizer."

"There is one," the assistant said, returning to a serious mood. He found an entry in his data. "It's a film festival in Milan. Lots of beloved figures from the movies. They'll be together each evening in a theater, which would make it easy to get them all just by locking a few doors."

"Do you think Americans would grovel to save a few movie actors?" Brown wondered.

"My daughter would," the assistant answered, "if it happened to be a rock star."

An hour later, another assistant dropped a mountain of reports on Brown's desk. "Washington families," he said. "The possibilities are endless. This Saturday, for example, the congressional wives are playing in a golf tournament. Someone who took over the locker room could withhold marital sex from half the men in Washington. On Sunday, most of the same ladies are gathering for a flower show."

The families of government and commercial leaders were an impossible target to protect. In the Washington suburbs, in the posh communities north of New York, west of Boston, and surrounding Chicago, Detroit, Dallas, and San Francisco, they congregated like bees. Generally, there was nothing more to protect them than a suburban police force of cigar-store Indians.

"I know you hate shortcuts," the assistant said, "but I've tried to concentrate on things overseas. For example: Did you know that a whole group of government wives are going to be in Paris for the new fashions?"

"I've heard," Brown said.

"And this. There are over sixty college students—all sons and daughters of government officials—who are spending their junior years at European schools. Any one of them would be a kidnapping target."

"That's frightening," Brown admitted. He had felt the same chill of fear countless times before. We were vulnerable everywhere. "But one American in a university doesn't make it a very dramatic target."

"There are three congressional families with children traveling together, taking a college semester at sea."

Brown looked puzzled.

"I knew you'd ask," said the assistant. "It's a ship fitted out with classrooms. The kids take college courses and get to drop in on different cities as part of their education."

"Jesus Christ," Brown said. "Where's the ship now? What ports will it be hitting in the next two weeks?"

"Barcelona, and then north to Cannes," the assistant said, consulting his notes.

Not the most dangerous cities, Otis Brown consoled himself. But in these times, what wasn't dangerous. "I'm worried about that one," he said. "It would be easy to hijack a ship. I'm going to push the director to put a Navy destroyer alongside until this thing blows over."

"If you're worried about schools, take a look at this one." The man thumbed through his pages until he found the entry he was looking for. "Saint Anselm's American School, just outside of Rome. Look at all the government people who have their kids parked there. Even 'Warhawk' Bradberry. Do you think he'd be demanding we 'bomb the bastards' if his own son was inside?"

Brown scrutinized the list. "My God . . ." was all he could manage.

"That's just the government people," the assistant continued, happy to have captured his boss's interest. "Here's a list of students, and these are the companies that their families are connected with. It reads like the Fortune Five Hundred. Some of these families were at the president's inaugural ball. Nobody would wait around to see one of these kids get thrown out of a window, and I can't see the president ordering the Marines over the walls tossing grenades ahead of them."

"Christ," Otis Brown mumbled. "What's the most important thing in your life? The thing you love most. The one thing you would sacrifice anything to protect?"

The assistant shrugged. "My children, I guess."

Brown nodded. It was perfect. Half the power structure of the country had its sons in one school. To save their sons they would demand immediate concessions. It was exactly what Sharif had described. He would hold the United States by its heart. He could demand any price in return for the boys' safety.

Brown picked up the phone and told the operator he wanted a call to the American ambassador in Rome to be placed immediately. Then he sat silently, staring through his assistant while he waited for his telephone to ring.

"This one has gotten to you," the assistant commented. He had never seen Otis Brown's eyes as frightened as they were at this moment. "Why this one?"

"Maybe because it's so perfect," Brown said quietly. "Maybe a flash of brilliance. Probably just a hunch. But I'd bet my life that Sharif's commandos are about to take over the Saint Anselm's American School in Rome."

April 16

early morning

Maria Manetti turned her back to Ferrand as she pushed back the covers and slipped her arms into the nightgown that had been carelessly discarded a few hours earlier.

Ferrand found himself smiling. It was impossible to explain her rigorous sense of modesty. They had been lovers for six months, and yet she still wouldn't dress or undress in front of him. He had even caught her closing her eyes as he was taking off his trousers.

Each time they had come to the small hotel, she had known exactly what was planned for the evening. She had stood right at his side and watched him sign *Mr. and Mrs. Smith* into the register, then had stared down the old woman who looked up suspiciously at them when she read the name. Once inside the small room, she would throw herself eagerly into a congratulatory kiss, but always brushed away his hand when it wandered to her breasts or down the back of her leg.

"Pig," she sometimes teased. "Can't you wait until we are in bed?"

She would pull away from him, pick up her overnight bag, and disappear into the bathroom, reappearing in a few moments in a buttoned-to-the-neck nightgown. She would cross the room fully covered, draw back the blanket, and join him beneath the sheets. Immediately, she would undo the buttons and awkwardly wrestle the nightgown up her body, making certain she was always covered by the blanket. Miraculously, the bunched-up nightgown would appear above the edge of the covers, where she would slip it over her head and arms and drop it aimlessly beside the bed. Then, as if transformed by some magical power, she would turn to him in frightening, open-mouthed passion.

Modesty never inhibited her lovemaking. Within seconds, she would be kicking at the covers, pushing them down to the bottom of the bed and out of their way. She would begin to explore his mouth with a darting tongue and bite at the edge of his lips, simultaneously guiding his hands to the underside of her breasts or down across her belly to the cavern between her legs. Sometimes she would rise up, letting her nipples dangle against his lips. Or, she might begin to move downward, tugging at the hair on his chest with her teeth and kissing across his stomach toward his reddening erection. He often found himself embarrassed at her thoroughness.

When they were making love, Maria seemed to rejoice at exposing the details of her body. And she carefully inspected all the secrets of his own. She enjoyed describing the effect his touch had on her, using his fingertips to trace the sensations that flowed outward from her breasts and miraculously reappeared down the insides of her thighs. She challenged Ferrand for information. "What does it feel like?" she would ask while stroking some speck of his body she thought she might not have touched before. "Wonderful," he would answer, but the word wouldn't satisfy her. "Not wonderful," Maria would demand. "Tell me exactly what it feels like."

There were no limits on the positions for entry. Nor did she hesitate to say exactly what felt good and what might feel better. "Go slowly," she would beg on occasion, or "Please, harder," on another. Her frankness in explaining her desires was completely disarming.

But the moment they were finished and lying together basking in the afterglow, her mysterious modesty would return. She would reach down and draw the covers up over them, making sure to pull them high enough to conceal even the very top of her cleavage. And when it was time to get up, she would be careful to keep her back turned toward him until she was completely covered by her nightgown.

Tonight had been their most exciting night together yet. But her moments of puzzling modesty were no different. They had been able to get away from the school earlier than usual, although that had required them to violate one of their rules. Generally, they left the grounds separately. This time they had left together, signing out at the gate house on two consecutive lines of the log that the guard kept and, presumably, the headmaster was entitled to inspect. They both wanted to keep their affair a secret, because Dr. Palma had reasonable rules about the propriety his faculty displayed before his students, and because they knew how easy it was to become the boys' favorite topic of locker-room conversation. They weren't so naive as to think their attentions to one another would go unnoticed forever. In fact, both had caught the conspiratorial winks the boys exchanged whenever a group of the students found them walking together or sharing a tray in the dining hall. And they had watched the Old Mouse's twitching nose dart from one of them to the other if they happened to sit together at a faculty meeting. Billy Tepper certainly knew they were lovers. He had even come upon them in the pantry that led to the hidden entrance to the wine cellar. "Great stuff down there," he had commented casually in passing. But still, they were determined to be discrete. It was one thing to be suspected. It was quite another to leave a trail of glaring evidence.

So, they had arrived at the hotel nearly two hours earlier than usual and bought a bottle of inexpensive wine and borrowed two glasses to take to their room. Because they were in no hurry, there was no rush to the bed. Instead, they spent half an hour on the small sofa, talking and sipping the wine. Ferrand attempted to ease his hand up the side of Maria's leg while they were chatting, and later tried a bold foray through the buttons of her blouse. Both times she had pushed him away without interrupting the flow of conversation, clearly determined to keep her chastity from being compromised. When they had finished the wine, she retrieved her overnight bag and disappeared into the bathroom. When the door opened, she was completely covered by the nightgown.

"Am I ever going to see you in your underwear?" he had asked.

"You like underwear? Go down to the stores and gape through the windows with all the other dirty old men!"

Ferrand had roared with laughter, and it was in the laughing rather than the lovemaking that he realized he was hopelessly in love with Maria. At that instant, it became unimportant to him to finish the school term and then return to a business career in the United States. More than likely, he would try another year of teaching at Saint Anselm's—assuming that Maria stayed true to her plan of spending another year with her beloved brats.

They had made love, and then, while lying together in near silence, Ferrand gathered his courage and asked her to marry him. It was a subject they had danced around the past few weeks in their conversations about his plans to give up teaching and build a money-making career in America and about her devotion to school children and her love for her native Italy. Maria answered that she would marry him, without questioning which of their career paths they would follow together. In celebration of their commitment, they made love again and then fell into silence, simply holding hands beneath the sheets.

Now she was gone, vanished back into the privacy of her dressing room, leaving him lying in bed, happier than he could ever remember being.

They left their key and the wine glasses at the desk, where the old woman glowered her suspicions. "We have to come back here after we're married," Ferrand told Maria as they turned into the street and walked toward the tiny Fiat he had borrowed. "I want to see her expression when we sign in under a different name."

"She'll be delighted," Maria answered. "That's why she looks at the register so carefully. She has been waiting for us to get married, and she is disappointed every time we sign 'Smith.' It means we're not yet sure that we're in love. Italians feel badly for people who haven't fallen in love."

Ferrand held the door of the Fiat while Maria contorted herself into the small passenger space. Then he walked around the car and climbed in, taking a position that brought his knees up on both sides of the steering wheel. He winced. "I think I pulled a muscle in my leg," he said, and then they laughed together, wondering which of their positions had proved too acrobatic for him.

"Perhaps you should limit yourself to looking at the underwear in store windows," she teased. "That can't be too demanding . . ."

They drove to the end of the street and got on the highway that headed north. It was a short drive, only five minutes on the divided highway and then fifteen minutes on the winding road that climbed through the hills to Saint Anselm's. The school sat on a hilltop, surrounded by dense stands of trees and cut off from the countryside like a medieval city by a high stone wall. There was only one access road, and it led directly to the single gate in the walls.

It was a longer trip for Ferrand, because he always returned the car to a garage that was halfway down the winding road. Maria would suggest they leave the car and walk the last mile to the school together. But Ferrand would insist on driving her to the gate, then retracing his route back to the garage. From there, he would return to St. Anselm's on foot. It was a proper courtesy, with the added advantage that they signed back into the school at different times. If the Old Mouse happened to check the log, it wouldn't be so obvious that they were spending their evenings together.

Ferrand steered through the tortuous turns of the switchbacks that took the road up the final mile of the hill. It was in this stretch that he usually found himself cursing the Fiat's inadequate engine. He was shifted into low gear, which made the small four-cylinder block screech like a banshee. It seemed as if the noise would wake every teacher and child in the school and that the flash of the headlights would be an obvious announcement of their simultaneous arrival. It was impossible to sneak up the hill in a Fiat, he decided.

He swung the car in a circle a few feet from the wall, pointing it back down the hill. Maria leaned over and kissed him quickly and reached for the door handle. But Ferrand drew her back, took her into his arms, and kissed her gently, expressing a new feeling of belonging. She understood clearly what his kiss was saying. From now on, they were more than lovers, and she responded to the message. They held each other closely for several minutes.

"I'm getting excited again," Ferrand confessed impishly.

"I'd better leave," Maria answered, slipping out of his grasp. "If you try anything in this little car, you'll do more than pull a muscle. You'll probably break your neck!"

The door opened, and in an instant she was gone through the gate in the wall. Ferrand dropped the car into gear and turned his attention to the road. The engine screamed as he started back down the hill.

Maria walked through the stone arch and approached the wooden guard shack, which was illuminated by a single desk lamp and the white glow of the security monitors. She was surprised to see it was empty. There were two old men who split the night duty, one working to midnight and the other until morning. She had never seen the shed without one of the men waiting at the window, anxious to talk with her while she signed the log.

The book was resting on the desktop. When she leaned over it, she was startled to see dark matted stains sprinkled across the page. She touched one of them and it smeared under her finger like jelly. Then she noticed other stains on the desktop surrounding the book—long, thin streaks that seemed to have been fired onto the desk from behind the guard's chair. She looked back over the chair and saw that one of the windowpanes was shattered in a spider-web pattern. At the center of the web was a perfectly round hole no bigger than the thickness of a pencil. She looked back at the desk and noticed that the stains fanned out as they crossed the blotter and log book. The sticky material had originated at a point, somewhere over the back of the chair, in perfect alignment with the hole in the window. She touched another one of the dark blotches and lifted her finger into the light that was streaming from the desk lamp. In the glow of the light bulb, the dark stain turned to deep crimson.

Her shocked reaction was illogical. She should have rushed back through the gate and followed Ferrand down the hill. She knew what had happened. Whoever had killed the guard was inside the school. There was nothing she could do by herself. She should have gone after Ferrand, and together they could have gotten help. But the crimson stain had shattered her reason. Instead, she began running up the road toward the school buildings, thinking only of protecting her

children. There was a murderer on the grounds, and somehow she had to save them.

She saw lights ahead of her when the buildings should
have been dark, another warning that something was terribly
wrong. But instead of stopping to think, she ran harder, con-
tinuing in stocking feet after she had stumbled out of her
shoes.

She never saw the figure that lunged out of the bushes by
the roadside. She tried to scream when a hand clutched at
her arm, but her breath was coming in short gasps and she
couldn't make a sound. She spun around, struck blindly at
the slender form, and for a moment broke free. Suddenly
there was another form in front of her, silhouetted against
the lights of school. She recognized the shape of a gun,
which was being lifted toward her, but even that didn't snap
her to her senses. Instead, she charged blindly, grasping at
the weapon and raking her fingernails across the shadowy
face. The man cried out in pain but stood his ground, swinging his free arm around her neck and tearing the gun from
her hand. She kicked violently, but the wiry arm tightened
like a cable around her neck. And then she saw the first man,
a dark face with black eyes that were cold with rage. A fist
flashed out and exploded against her cheek. For an instant
she was lost, but then she felt herself fall and hit heavily on
the pavement. She started to push herself up from the
ground, saw a heavy boot firing toward her, and felt a sickening pain as it crashed into her side. The two faces above
her drifted out of focus.

She heard words hissed in a language she didn't understand. Her hands were torn away from her blazing side and
pulled back over her head. And then she was dragged, the
pavement tearing at her back like coarse sandpaper. The men
reached under her arms to lift her up the steps and used her
as a battering ram to push open the door of the new building.
Then they tossed her on the tile floor under the glaring fluo-
rescent lights of the dining hall.

Maria looked up as she climbed to her knees. Several of

the teachers were already in the room, their hands extended against the far wall. Two of the men were still in pajamas, a third with his trousers pulled loosely under a pajama top. The three women were in bathrobes. She saw a soldier striding toward her and braced herself for another kick. Instead, his hand twisted in her hair and dragged her to her feet. She was pushed staggering toward the wall and thrown into line with the other teachers. She didn't understand the order that was screamed in her ear, but she reached forward and braced herself against the wall.

Across the dining hall three more teachers were being marched in by one of the soldiers. The headmaster was last in line, clutching to hold up the trousers that weren't even belted, his jacket open over a white nightshirt. He was squinting in an unfamiliar attempt to focus without his glasses.

She was kept standing for more than an hour after all the teachers were assembled, her knees trembling as the pain from her side spread throughout her body. Glancing down the line, she studied the faces of her colleagues that hung beneath the row of extended arms. They looked like corpses, she thought, eyes either closed or staring blindly at the wall, skin pale, with lips stitched tightly. The learned minds had been shut down by fear—not so much a fear for personal well-being as a fear of the unknown.

The invaders were unknown. They were dark-faced youths who seemed to enjoy violence, exchanging brief commands in a language that seemed from another planet. Even their weapons seemed strange. None of the teachers had ever handled a gun, which made the flash-shielded muzzles, the oil-slick bolts, and the long curved cartridge clips seem that much more deadly. And their purpose was still unexplained. Since the teachers had been rousted out of their beds, there had not been one word of explanation. Even the silence was threatening in a room that was generally filled with shouting and laughter. Most numbing was the separation from the children. Without the boys, the teachers were deprived of purpose. They might act to protect their students, but how could they protect children who were locked in another building? Each of them had imagined the possible outcome of their imprisonment, then closed his mind to the images of carnage. It was easier to lapse into unconsciousness than to visualize the reality.

"Good morning!" A voice in Oxford English brought their senses back to life. "You may take your hands down from the wall and then turn very slowly and face me." The headmaster staggered as he tried to gain his balance and fell into the arms of Harold Hutchings, the history teacher. Maria saw that Hutchings' lips were split and his mouth bloodied.

"Good," the pleasant voice continued. "Now, please give me your attention. There are a few procedures that I want you to understand."

He was tall and thin, dressed in khaki shirt and trousers, a black fatigue cap pulled low over his forehead. The eyes beneath the brim were black, yet illuminated with a joyous vitality. Perfect white teeth glistened beneath an evenly trimmed mustache, and there was a small diabolical goatee at the point of his chin. Unlike the other soldiers, he had no weapon slung over his shoulder. Instead, he wore a small holster attached to a leather belt. The white handle of a revolver showed above the top of the holster.

"My name is Gamel. I am commander of the Holy Liberation Army, loyal to Sharif, the true hope of the Palestinian people." Hutchings' eyes widened. He already understood the words that would follow.

"It is in the name of General Sharif that I have captured this school and taken you all as prisoners in our war of liberation. You will remain our prisoners until satisfactory arrangements are made to return you to the imperialist forces."

Maria broke the shocked silence. "What about the children?" she demanded.

"They are our prize prisoners," Gamel answered logically. "The Americans put a much greater value on their children than they do on their teachers."

He turned and paced slowly before the ranks of his hostages. "First, let us evaluate your situation." He bent down and lifted a thin wire that was stretched across the floor near the wall. "You will notice wires like this one stretched throughout the room. Each is connected to an explosive charge placed somewhere in the school buildings." Gamel reached into his pocket and removed a small box that looked like a cheap transistor radio. "This is the detonator, which means that I can destroy the buildings and everyone in them by simply touching a switch." He held the small electronic device out at arm's length and turned slowly so that everyone could see it. "Is there a science teacher here?" he asked politely. Paul Prinz, the small, dark man wearing trousers under his pajama tops, cleared his throat and raised his hand tentatively. "Good." Gamel smiled. "Perhaps you can explain to them how a radio-frequency detonator works. Perhaps you can make them all understand that there is no hope for rescue by any outside force. If soldiers or police come through the gates or over the walls, no one here would live to greet them." He slipped the device carelessly back into his pocket.

"Now, about escape. Obviously, we cannot be watching all of you at every moment. It might seem as if you could slip out of the building and onto the grounds. It might even appear as if you have a fair chance of making it over the wall. I have two words of caution.

"First, these soldiers are used to killing. Many of them have seen their parents slaughtered by Israeli tanks or American shells. Some have watched their sisters being raped by the lackey militia that do the work of the imperialists in our countries. They have even seen children blown to pieces; sometimes their own brothers and sisters. You have taught them well. So I wouldn't advise you to expect a great deal of compassion from them. If they find you, or any of the children outside the buildings, they will simply fire. Your lives mean very little to them."

He walked slowly toward Maria, smiling as their eyes met.

With his fingertip he lifted her chin and turned her face toward the light. "You have already learned what it means to disobey their orders," he told her confidentially. "Perhaps you will share your wisdom with the others." Then he walked down the line until he reached Harold Hutchings and placed a brotherly hand on Hutchings' shoulder. "This man didn't open his door when he was told to. Instead, he made a telephone call to alert the local police. It was a stupid bit of heroism, because we had already called the police to tell them that we were in control. I think he has learned that it is more sensible to do exactly as he is told."

Gamel turned his back on his audience and walked back to the center of the room, where he slouched easily on the corner of a table.

"My second caution is that even if you should escape, you might want to think about those you are leaving behind. Your fellow teachers. And, of course, your students. For every one of you that escapes over the walls, we will kill five and throw the bodies over the wall after you. It might be heavy baggage for you to carry with you for the rest of your life.

"So. There can be no rescue. There can be no escape. And, finally, there can be no confusion. Your job is to keep the students under control. They must be in their rooms at night and here in the dining hall during the day. If they begin milling about, we won't be sure of what they are up to. If we become confused, we become even more dangerous. Do you understand?"

One or two heads nodded. The others remained motionless.

Gamel jumped to his feet and rubbed his palms together. "Now, are there any questions?"

"How long?" Maria asked immediately in a strong voice. "How long will we remain your hostages?"

His eyes narrowed. "Prisoners," he corrected quietly, "not hostages. You are prisoners in a war of revolution. How long you will remain prisoners is up to the government of the

United States. General Sharif will present terms for your
release. It is up to the United States to accept those terms.
Perhaps the authorities will do so immediately. Or perhaps
they will impose endless conditions and delays. The time
isn't important to us. We have been prisoners for two generations, so we are used to waiting."

His shining eyes ran down the line of dead faces. "No
more questions? Good! Then it is time to wake the students.
Have them dress and bring them here to the dining hall. All
of them. Breakfast will be served as usual. But please remember. There is a guard at the end of every hallway. Make
sure you maintain order. No confusion. Confusion could be
very dangerous."

No one moved.

"Now!" Gamel ordered, his voice harsh with authority for
the first time. The change in his manner was more startling
than the command. The teachers moved quickly across the
dining room toward the hallway that led to the old mansion.

As Maria filed in front of him, Gamel held up his arm to
block her path. She stopped and turned to face him, looking
defiantly into his eyes. For a moment he held her gaze with a
cold stare. Then his lips parted in a smile.

"You are not afraid," he said curiously.

"I'm afraid for the children," she answered immediately.

"Good," he said almost as a compliment. "But be afraid for
yourself as well. I have been in this situation several times
before. Courage can be a problem. In every case, the prisoners who were most courageous were always the first to
die."

morning

Colonel William Smiles pushed the peak of his baseball cap
back from his tanned face and raised the field glasses to his
eyes. The airplane seemed to be floating on a lake. The midday heat rising from the desert floor distorted the light so

that the landing gear was invisible and the hard-packed sand rippled like water. He could make out the shapes of the cockpit windows, but he couldn't see the figure inside whose voice was crackling over the radio receiver that was mounted behind him in the back seat of the jeep.

"We want the fuel truck to drive directly in front of the plane, no closer than fifty yards," the voice ordered. "Then have it turn and drive past in the other direction so that we can see the other side. Then it should park directly in front of the nose. Do you understand?"

"Understood," replied another voice immediately. "Two passes in front of the nose and then park in front of the plane. No closer than fifty yards."

"Begin now," the first voice said.

Smiles lowered the glasses and turned to the captain seated next to him behind the steering wheel. "Smart son of a bitch. You trained him well."

The captain nodded. "You said you didn't want us to make it easy."

Both men turned their attention to the squat tanker truck that suddenly appeared from behind the corrugated metal hangar. The brutal sun reflected off its windshield as it began rolling across the scorched ground toward the Boeing 727. The truck turned to its left before it reached the plane and rolled slowly in front of its nose. Then it turned sharply to its right and came back past the 727, showing its other side. Again, it made a right turn and drew directly in front of the plane, coming to a stop facing the windows of the cockpit.

"Is that satisfactory?" a voice asked over the radio. There was no response from within the plane.

"What's wrong?" Smiles asked the captain.

The captain shrugged. "They're thinking," he ventured.

"Now listen carefully," the terrorist commander said suddenly from inside the cockpit. "We want the man who will connect the fuel hoses to get out of the truck and stand in front of it. Just one man, do you understand?"

"Understood," the second voice responded.

"We want that man to walk in front of the truck until it is under the wing. No one else is to get out of the truck for any reason. If we see a door opening, we start shooting."

"Understood," the voice answered. "Only one man outside the truck."

Smiles raised the field glasses again and watched the passenger door of the fuel truck swing open. A single figure in work coveralls climbed out of the cab and walked into the space between the truck and the plane. As he continued walking, the truck lurched forward and then followed slowly. The colonel felt the knot in his stomach pull so tight that it was difficult for him to swallow. The rescue operation he had code-named Trojan Horse was about to unfold.

He had orchestrated it perfectly from the moment the terrorist force took over the plane with its one hundred and forty-three passengers and forced it down for refueling. "Rabat," he had been told, and within two hours he was on his way from Texas aboard an Air Force jet, with a mid-air refueling scheduled over the Atlantic. Behind him, a force of thirty men was boarding a C-5 cargo plane, accompanied by a truck that had been freshly painted in the colors and Arabic legends that were common at the Moroccan airport.

The situation he had found was hopeless. The terrorists had taxied the captured airliner out into the hard-packed desert, nearly half a mile from the airport's hangars and administration buildings. There was no cover anywhere near the aircraft, no way to move troops toward the captured Boeing without their being spotted immediately. The first words from the terrorist commander was that the plane was wired and would be blown up if anyone approached. They demanded to be refueled, but under conditions he would dictate.

Smiles had begun negotiating, striking a delicate balance between total compliance with the terrorists' demands and enough delaying tactics to enable him to assemble his assault force. He needed time. The C-5 couldn't be seen landing at

Rabat. He had to bring it in at Kenitra, then drive his truck and attack force into the Rabat area. And even that had to be done under cover of darkness. He had to assume the terrorists had a collaborator somewhere in the vicinity of the airport who could warn them if any military force or special equipment was being assembled.

He also needed time to let the sun do its work on the terrorists and the hostages. With its engines shut down, the Boeing had no ventilation and no air-conditioning. In a few hours, the sun's beating down on the metal shell would turn the cabin into an oven. The heat would wear down the hijackers' stamina and take the edge from their reflexes. It promised to be a minor advantage, but in the first moments after the landing, the terrorists held all the advantages. Just as important, the heat would exhaust the passengers and render them docile. Smiles wanted them collapsed in their seats, totally passive to the events happening around them. The last thing he needed was a heroic passenger who might enrage his captors.

His radio talker had begun the negotiations, first with assurances that the terrorists were in complete command and that all their demands would be met. But the terrorists had no demands. Those would be announced after the plane and its hostages had reached an unnamed destination. All they needed was fuel.

Smart, Smiles had thought. Demands for release of captive terrorists or for political and economic concessions took hours, even days, to communicate and resolve. Terrorists often surrendered the advantage of urgency while they negotiated the details of their demands. These guys weren't going to be trapped. They were going to refuel and get to a friendly country—perhaps even take the passengers from the plane to a secret prison—before they got involved in time-consuming negotiations over demands.

Smiles had begun bargaining for substitute hostages. Instead of innocent tourists, he would provide officials of the United States government. They could be brought to the airport in a matter of hours and substituted for the men and women aboard the plane. The terrorist commander dismissed the suggestion immediately. There would be no exchange of prisoners, no excuse for opening the plane's cabin door, no opportunity to create confusion with cars and buses moving back and forth between the plane and the administration building.

Smiles next ploy had been a plea for release of some of the hostages. "I have the passenger list," the radio talker explained in a slow, calming voice. "There are fifty-two women and twelve children aboard. Let's get them off the plane. You don't need them. Certainly, you're not going to hide behind women and children. All they are is a problem for you."

Smiles hadn't been that concerned with the special needs of women and children. His sole concern was to delay the refueling and create a reason for opening the door of the Boeing and allowing trucks or buses to approach the hijacked aircraft. The terrorist leader understood what the colonel was trying to do. "Perhaps the women and children will be released when we reach our destination," he countered. "But not now."

The colonel had then tried for the release of the passengers who were not American citizens. "Some of these people may be friendly to your cause. We can give you the names of passengers from non-aligned or friendly countries. You can check their passports and release them." But the commander aboard the aircraft clung to his single purpose. All these issues could be resolved later. He demanded fuel immediately.

Smiles had struggled to keep the conversation going. Could they change flight crews? If the journey were protracted, they would need rested pilots. Where were they headed? Flight routes would have to be cleared and landing arrangements made. Finally, he exhausted the patience of the terrorist commander. He was given thirty minutes to have a fuel truck appear in front of a designated hangar. If the truck were not there, a passenger would be executed and dropped from the airplane. A new body would follow every thirty minutes thereafter. Smiles was able to extend the deadline to one hour, arguing that the fuel truck had to be filled and a volunteer to drive the truck to the plane found. At the moment the terrorist was agreeing to one hour, Smiles' C-5 was discharging its crew and the newly painted fuel truck at a Navy airfield some thirty miles away.

Now the truck rolled toward the wing of the aircraft, following the workman, who had raised his hands to shield his eyes from the sun. It pulled up alongside the fuselage, stopping with the cab hidden under the wing and the back end of the fuel tank beneath the cabin door. It was a parking position that Smiles' hand-picked troops had rehearsed often. From inside the aircraft, the terrorists could only see the top of the truck. The side of the truck closest to the plane was well hidden from the sightlines offered by the cabin windows, and the far side was hidden by the shape of the truck itself.

"Stop," the voice ordered from inside the plane's cockpit.

"Jesus," Smiles muttered. Were the bastards on to him? Or were they falling into his trap? He squinted into the field glasses, hoping to read the mind of a terrorist commander whose form he still couldn't see through the cockpit windows.

"Order the man to stand behind the truck where we can see him." There was a delay as the message was relayed, and then the workman walked around the outside of the truck and appeared next to the nose of the Boeing. He stood there waiting for what seemed like an eternity.

"What the hell are they up to?" Smiles demanded of the captain without taking his eyes from the glasses.

"I don't know. This is something new."

"We're opening the cabin door," the terrorist's voice suddenly announced. "We want to inspect the truck."

"You bet your ass you do," Smiles said, a hint of a smile straightening his lips. "You bet your ass you do."

The hard voice sounded again on the radio. "When we open the door, one of the passengers will be in front of us. If anyone fires into the cabin, she will be the one hit. Do you understand? When we open the cabin door, we will be using a passenger as a shield."

"Shit," Colonel Smiles hissed. He made an instant decision. "It's one passenger or all of them," he told the captain. "Keep it moving."

"Don't be concerned," Smiles heard his radio talker say lightly to the terrorist commander. "Nobody is going to do any firing. All we're trying to do is get your plane gassed up."

Smiles saw the shape of the cabin door appear in the side of the airliner as the pressure locks were released. The door backed into the cabin briefly, then swung out as the hatchway was opened. Through the glasses he could make out the form of a woman moving from the darkness inside into the bright glare of sunlight. There was a darker form behind the woman. The two seemed to pause for an instant, and then a man pushed up next to the woman and into the sunlight. He was dressed in fatigues and carrying a small automatic weapon under his right arm.

"Now," Smiles ordered.

There seemed to be no response. The man leaned out of the open doorway and looked down at the truck.

"Now, goddamn it!" Smiles yelled.

In response to his command, two hatchways swung open from the side of the fuel truck facing away from the Boeing. Smiles' assault troops, dressed in flak jackets and riot helmets, rolled out quickly, crouched low, and moved to the ladders that were fitted to the side of the tank. In the aircraft's doorway, the terrorist continued to scan the scene slowly, holding the woman hostage close to his chest. The truck hid the troops from his line of vision.

The radio crackled and then a voice came from inside the airplane. "Have the workman climb up on the truck and connect the hoses."

"Understood," the radio talker said mechanically. "Our man will climb up on the truck and connect the fuel hoses."

Nothing happened. The workman continued to stand like a statue near the nose of the airplane. The troops waited motionlessly behind the truck. The terrorist commander hovered in the open cabin doorway with his human shield.

"For Christ's sake, get moving," Smiles ordered the workman through clenched teeth.

"It takes a few seconds to relay the messages," the captain explained, aware he was giving the colonel information he already knew.

At that moment the workman moved crisply toward the fuel truck and climbed the ladder that was attached to the back of the tank. He started down a catwalk along the top of the truck, then stooped down and picked up one of the large rubber hoses. With the hose under his arm, he began moving toward the wing.

Smiles' breathing stopped.

Suddenly, the workman wheeled toward the open doorway. His hand snapped up from the open end of the hose and aimed a pistol toward the terrorist and his hostage. A trace of smoke appeared between the pistol and the open hatch, and, in the same instant, a flash of light filled the inside of the cabin. Then the doorway disappeared in heavy smoke.

No sooner had Smiles seen the smoke then he was aware of his assault troops climbing to the top of the truck. In two columns, they charged toward the doorway, firing into the smoke-filled opening.

The next three seconds seemed like an eternity. As the assault team rushed forward, the airliner door began to swing closed. The flash of the grenade had been intended to stun the terrorists, and the acrid smoke to drive them from the doorway. But someone inside had kept his senses and was pushing the heavy pressurized door back into the opening. The first member of the assault team dropped his weapon and threw himself at the door. A second and then a third assault trooper slammed up against him. For an instant, the door seemed to balance, balanced between the forces on either side. Incoherent voices screamed over the radio as the door began to fold back into the airplane, then stopped.

Suddenly there was a new sound coming over the radio—a mechanical chatter like a motor's starting. It was muffled somewhat by the static and screaming voices, but Smiles recognized it immediately. It was the sound of automatic weapons being fired inside the plane. The field glasses slowly dropped from his eyes and he turned his face away from the battle.

"They've got the door," the captain yelled. "We've got a man inside. They're fighting in the doorway."

Smiles nodded, but all he could hear was the chattering of the machine guns that vibrated the speaker of the radio. In his mind, he could see the terrorists moving down the aisle, firing indiscriminately at the cowering passengers. Two men, emptying their ammunition clips at point-blank range, could each kill three or four people a second. They would pause only for the instant it took to snap in a new clip. While his troops were battling for control of the hatchway passage, the hostages were being shot to pieces. The rescue had turned into a bloodbath.

"That's enough," Smiles said.

"Do you want to end the exercise?" the captain asked.

"I said that's enough," the colonel snapped. "I want this fucking fiasco stopped right now." He was already out of the jeep and walking out onto the desert toward the smoke-shrouded airliner.

He had done everything right. The troops had been hand-picked and meticulously trained. Their equipment—flak jackets, riot helmets, lightweight automatic weapons—had been carefully chosen and then modified to fit the demands of the rescue mission. He had worked with top university psychologists to train his radio talkers in techniques for keeping terrorists calm, assured, and involved. He had invented the Trojan Horse, a lightweight replica of an airport fuel truck that served as a troop carrier and access ladder. He had tried hundreds of grenades to get exactly the right combination of flash and paralyzing smoke. He had even organized a terrorist force, thoroughly trained by his staff, and given them an airplane filled with volunteer hostages. "Don't tell me how or where," he had ordered his adjutant. "Just put the plane down someplace and issue your demands. I want the rescue mission to be as realistic as possible. Everything except live ammunition."

The captain had made it very realistic. He presented the situation exactly as Colonel Smiles' rescue force would face it. And the rescue had failed.

It had to fail, Smiles admitted to himself as he walked across the blazing sand. There were too many imponderables. How could you be sure, for example, that a shocked and stunned enemy would fall backward, away from the door? The only thing that had gone wrong with the exercise was that a "terrorist" had been smart enough to reach out through the dense smoke and push the door back over the opening. He hadn't even succeeded in getting it locked. But that simple action had delayed the rescue team by perhaps ten seconds. And that ten seconds had caused half the "hostages" their lives.

It was an insane kind of war, where the most important weapon was madness. The side most deprived of reason, the force with the least concern for human life, was inevitably the winner. There would be no problem stopping the plane from taking off. It would be simple to overcome the terrorist force; they wouldn't stand a chance against his trained troops with their sophisticated weapons. But there was a catch. He had to do it without harming any of the hostages. And as long as the terrorists were perfectly willing to turn their guns on the hostages, they held the most decisive weapon.

Smiles' rescue team had practiced in other situations. They dropped onto the roof of a simulated embassy and crashed in through the top-floor windows. It had taken only twenty-four seconds to secure the building, but only twenty seconds for the soldiers playing the role of terrorists to machine-gun all thirty hostages inside the building. The "mission" had been a failure. They had hurled grenades of paralyzing gas through the windows of an airline terminal. The gas had put everyone—terrorists and hostages—to sleep in just five seconds. But within three seconds, one of the terrorists had pushed the handle of a detonator that, in a real attack, would have blown the terminal to pieces. Another failure.

The willingness to slaughter was the only weapon that counted. And there was no strategy that could deprive terrorists of that weapon.

The Israelis had faced that fact years ago. Official policy counted hostages in the hands of terrorists as already dead. Since they were already "dead," the terrorists' willingness to slaughter was an empty threat. The response was simple. But the Israelis only learned the lesson after years of confronting people willing to slaughter, and by counting the hundreds of bodies that piled up in their attempts at rescue. Americans hadn't often confronted an enemy who had no regard for innocent life, and so they still believed that the threat to kill hostages was more bluff than real.

Smiles reached the Boeing and walked into the center of the circle of troops that had gathered next to the Trojan Horse. A corpsman was tending to the injuries that were an inevitable price paid for a realistic training exercise. Two members of the terrorist force had been burned by the smoke grenade. One member of the rescue team had caught his hand in the closing door and broken it badly. Another had fallen from the top of the truck and seemed to have a broken ankle.

"Who closed the door?" Smiles asked. A sergeant dressed in fatigues raised a burned hand. "Nice work," he told the man. "That stopped the rescue." Then he heard the murmur of despair from the commander of his rescue team. "Don't any of you men get down on yourselves," he snapped at the assault troops. "You got inside damn fast. You probably would have saved over half the hostages."

"We would have lost the other half," one of the men responded.

Smiles nodded and turned back to the terrorist leader.

"Why didn't you just blow the plane? You had the damn thing wired, didn't you?"

A lieutenant shook his head. "That was just a bluff, sir," he answered. "We thought we had a good position where no one could approach us, so we didn't want to take a chance with explosives."

"The truck took you by surprise?" the colonel asked, his expression showing only the modest amount of satisfaction he could allow himself.

The lieutenant laughed. "That was beautiful. We were real worried about the truck and the people who would be involved in the refueling. But it seemed clean. You scared all hell out of us when there was suddenly a squad of armed troops outside the windows. If the sergeant hadn't gotten on the door right away, you probably would have had us. The truck is a great idea."

"So, maybe we've learned something," Smiles said. "Let's get back home so you guys can catch up on your leave."

As he walked back toward the jeep, he decided exactly what he had learned. As long as he valued human life, he could never lead a successful rescue mission of hostages. There was no way to guarantee that everyone would live. His military bearing seemed to wilt under the sudden realization of failure. The muscular frame seemed to soften and the square shoulders to slump. The firm stride slowed to a shuffle, and the proud head leaned forward. He seemed smaller than his nearly six feet, and older than his thirty-eight years. When he lifted his cap to wipe the sweat from his brow, the sandy brush-cut hair was streaked with white.

The captain climbed out of the jeep and walked out to meet him.

"We've got a problem," he announced. Smiles looked up wearily. "We just got orders to get our unit to Rome. They want us there immediately."

"Rome?" Smiles asked.

His adjutant nodded. "They've taken over a boys' boarding school just outside the city. They have sixty kids locked inside."

"We're helping the Italians?"

The captain shook his head. "No, this is our show. It's an American school. All the kids are Americans."

The colonel glanced back at the plane still clouded in the smoke from the grenade. He thought of all the lives that would have been draining out onto the carpets and seat cushions inside the cabin by now.

"Jesus Christ," he said.

Maria knew she should be talking to the brats. Their frightened eyes were asking questions that needed to be answered. But she kept her head turned to one side so they wouldn't see the purple welt on her cheek, or the blood that had matted her hair. Her battered face would only add to their terror.

The boys were all seated in the dining hall, their hands flat on the tables just as they had been ordered. At one end of each table were two teachers, standing as monitors to keep their charges completely still. At the other end, a soldier stood guard, an oily machine gun dangling from his shoulder, the muzzle swaying back and forth across the faces of the children.

The older boys understood. They were prisoners, and their lives depended on making themselves invisible. All they had to do was blend in with their classmates, make themselves transparent just like they did in the classroom to avoid being called on. No sudden movements. No sounds. Nothing that would attract attention. If they tried hard, they might even be able to shut the entire ordeal out of their minds. Then the bell would ring and the class would be over. They knew how to survive danger.

The brats were the problem. They were babies being force-fed the manners of young men. Officially, they were students and addressed as "mister" by their teachers. Actually, they were infants, secure only in the arms of a caring adult. When hurt, they needed to be consoled. When frightened, they made themselves highly visible, wailing until someone came to their rescue. Now they were terrified, caught up in events as unreal as a fairy tale. It was only a matter of time before one of them would scream and rush to the safety of a teacher's arms.

And what would the soldiers do? Would they understand that a frightened little boy was no threat to them? Would they have the sense to turn their guns away? Most of the terrorists were only boys themselves. Maria guessed that two or three of them were probably only fifteen or sixteen years old. The oldest of them couldn't have been more than twenty or twenty-one. Did they know how easily children were blinded by fear? Did they remember their own terror of noises in the dark? They were frightened themselves. Maria could see it in their faces and in the fingers that flexed nervously around the triggers of their weapons. The guns were their only protection, the only thing that separated them from the boys they held captive. Would they fire defensively at anything that moved? Would they steel their own courage by punishing the first uncontrolled violation of their orders?

She had to keep the brats calm. She had to talk with them, even laugh to break the tension they weren't equipped to handle. But if they saw her face? She had seen the younger boys become hysterical at the sight of blood from their own skinned knees. What would they do when they saw blood oozing from their teacher's cheek?

They had roused the children, carefully explaining to the older boys that the school had been captured and that they were being temporarily detained. "Probably for just a few hours," Harold Hutchings had assured the boys, and then waited for the first screams of panic.

"Does that mean that classes are cancelled?" Billy Tepper had asked casually. "Because I was looking forward to your history test. I really studied the stuff, and I was going to ace it!" The boys looked uncomprehendingly at Tepper, and then

Snuffy Bradberry began to laugh until his lungs fell behind and he began to cough furiously. That started all the boys laughing and brought a smile to Hutchings' cracked lips.

Elias Metz had explained the situation to the under-classmen, beginning with the boys who seemed most mature. There was no hint of bravado in their reactions, however. They were plainly frightened, some struggling to fight back tears. He heard the word *hostages* pass between two of the boys and hastened to correct it. "They don't want to keep us," he had lied. "Plans are already being made for our release." But he knew they didn't believe him. They were old enough to have read the papers and understand their situation. Yet they were too young to cope with the obvious danger. He could feel their terror. "Discipline!" he reminded himself. It would require strict discipline to keep them from bolting in exactly the kind of confusion that Gamel had warned against. "Gentlemen," he ordered firmly, "there will be no more talking. Dress immediately and be back out in the hall in three minutes. We will walk in silence and take our places in the dining hall."

No one had questioned his authority. Instead of thinking for themselves, they had done exactly as they had been told.

Maria had assembled the brats and guided them into the lavatory, explaining the essentials of the situation as she directed them through the normal morning rituals. "The soldiers will be using our buildings," she had said confidently, "so we will not have our normal classes. But bring your textbooks with you. We will hold our classes in the dining hall."

A dozen voices had called her name and asked why and when and other questions that she waved away. She was determined to keep her explanations as simple as possible and to get the boys involved in some sort of school work immediately—anything that would keep them from fixing their attention on the dangers that were all around them.

She had noticed some of the children staring at her face, but it wasn't until she saw herself in a washroom mirror that she realized her physical condition gave the lie to her calm manner. Her cheek was swollen, with a purple welt running beneath her eye. The skin was split beneath the welt and there was blood smeared down to her chin. Maria soaked a paper towel in one of the washbasins and tried to wipe the blood away, but the warm water opened the wound and the blood just flowed more freely. She dabbed at the stains in her matted hair but they stayed there, turning from black to their original crimson. She was making the situation worse. From then on, she was careful to keep the battered side of her head turned away from her charges.

They all assembled in the dining room, the upperclass boys sneaking glances at the expressionless soldiers while the brats stared in open-mouthed amazement. Thankfully, there was more curiosity than fear, at least at first. The silent breakfast went off without incident.

Gamel then ordered the teachers to their positions at the ends of the tables and posted his guards at the opposite ends. He and his officers would search the buildings room by room, he explained. Telephones and radios would be removed. When he was satisfied that there were no weapons available nor any means of communication with the outside, the children would be returned to their rooms.

And now they were waiting in endless silence. Hours had dragged past. The older boys were becoming bored and the brats increasingly restless. Maria knew she had to gather the children and talk with them. She had to begin some sort of make-work lesson just to capture their attention. The longer they sat in silence, the more certain it became that one of them would demand attention. And that demand, if ignored, could lead to an outburst. Then the situation would be in the hands of the soldiers. It would depend on instant evaluations and quick decisions by the teenagers who were nervously fingering the automatic weapons they held at the ready. Maria wasn't afraid of their cruelty. Despite Gamel's warning, she couldn't believe that any young man would enjoy slaughtering children. No, what she feared was their fear. The terrorists themselves were terrified by the strangeness of their situation, by the danger to themselves that was everpresent while they were holed up in the midst of an alien country. The probability that their captors would panic was the most obvious danger her children faced. Somehow she had to prevent any outburst from her babies that could trigger even an instant of panic.

afternoon

Ferrand was exhausted. He had been under interrogation since the Italian police car had pulled up next to him as he was walking back up the hill toward the school. First it had been the local civil police in blue uniforms with ridiculous three-cornered hats. They had asked dozens of questions about the identity of the terrorists and seemed unwilling to accept the fact that he had no idea what they were talking about. Next he had sat through a jurisdictional dispute while the *carbinieri*, in their brown uniforms, took control from the locals. A weatherbeaten lieutenant kept offering him cigarettes while asking the same questions as the locals. Who were these "freedom fighters" who had captured the school? Why did they let him leave when they were holding everyone else hostage? He finally smashed his fist on the package of cigarettes that was left on the table. He didn't know that the school had been taken over by anyone. All he knew was that he had dropped a young woman—a teacher—off at the front gate and she had walked innocently onto the school grounds. Was she safe? Had anyone heard from her?

The lieutenant had left him alone for a moment and argued on the telephone with two different callers. Then he ordered Ferrand driven in a jeep from the police station to the farm house where he had left the Fiat. The transformation was miraculous. A dull-brown antenna dish stood next to the front walk, with cables leading through one of the two small windows in the irregular stone facade. The stuffed furniture in the small living room had been replaced with banks of radios and a telephone switchboard. A map table and three desks had been squeezed into the kitchen, looking ridiculous next to the stained porcelain sink and the rusted iron stove.

Otis Brown was waiting in the kitchen office. After introductions were made, Brown listened to Ferrand, readily accepted that he was unaware of the takeover, and then explained what had happened. The Italian police had received a call from a man who claimed to be a colonel in a Palestinian liberation army. The caller said he had captured the school in the name of Sharif and threatened to kill all the inhabitants if anyone tried to enter the school grounds. Minutes later, there was a second phone call from a teacher at the school, who screamed that the buildings were being invaded by a foreign army. The teacher asked for help.

"Because it's an American school, our embassy was notified," Brown explained. The small scholarly-looking man glanced at his watch. "That was about nine hours ago . . . actually two A.M. Washington time. I just landed, so I don't have very much to add. Except that the calls are genuine. Jerusalem picked up a radio broadcast in which Sharif claimed to have seized the children of America's ruling class. He called it the 'turning point' in his 'holy war of liberation.'"

Ferrand had tried to ask about Maria again and the safety of the children, but Brown dismissed his questions. It was he who needed information. "How many children in the school?" he had demanded politely but firmly. Ferrand counted: twenty-two upperclassmen, nineteen in the middle grades, and twenty-three brats.

"How many teachers?"

There were twelve faculty members—two of the women were really secretaries—plus the headmaster and the assistant headmaster. Then he corrected Brown's total, pointing out that he himself couldn't be counted in the total of imprisoned faculty members.

"Any staff?" Brown demanded, writing Ferrand's figures in his memo pad.

"There are three housemaids," Ferrand remembered, "and three people who take care of the dining hall—a man and his two sisters. Then there are two groundskeepers. But none of them would be there at night. They come up each day from Rome. And there are two men who guard the front gate. One is on from six to midnight, the other from midnight to six. I guess it's the guy on the late shift who would have been caught inside."

Next Brown had probed for Ferrand's impressions of the atmosphere at the school. First, the teachers. What kind of people were they? Could they be counted on to keep order in a crisis? Could they control the boys?

"They're teachers," Ferrand answered logically. "Scholars. Not people used to dealing with life-threatening crises. They're devoted to the children. I guess they're courageous enough. But I wouldn't say that there are any natural leaders. Nobody who stands out as a potential hero."

"That's fine," Brown commented. "We don't want any heroes. Just people with enough common sense to size up the situation and know that they should do exactly as they are told."

Then he had asked about the children. Were they well disciplined? Could they be counted on to obey their teachers? Were there any with serious physical problems that might require a doctor's attention?

Ferrand raised his hands helplessly. "They're children— like your own, or like the children you went to school with. Some are mature. Some are babies. Some will straighten their shoulders when they sense a problem. Some will wet their pants. I guess the upperclassmen will take some responsibility for the grade-school kids. But I really can't be sure. I don't think there are any medical problems. We don't accept kids who need special medical attention."

As Brown kept probing, Ferrand had become more and

more aggravated. He had some questions of his own. Like, who were these people who were holding his colleagues and students captive? Were they dangerous? What the hell did they want with a bunch of schoolkids? And what was being done to set the teachers and children free? A whole day had gone by, and all the police and Otis Brown had seemingly done was ask a lot of questions. Wasn't anyone going to do something?

He also had questions about Maria. Had she turned around at the gate and escaped? Or was she one of the prisoners inside? An attractive woman in a camp of invading soldiers had very special problems. Was anyone thinking about her safety?

But Brown had no answers. Only questions. And he had the infuriating habit of simply nodding at the answers Ferrand gave without revealing their significance. He wrote everything down carefully, as if time were of no importance.

Ferrand had just jumped to his feet to demand action when a military officer stormed through the door, exchanging salutes with everyone in sight. Brown greeted the officer with a report that consisted of all the data he had copied into his pad. Then he introduced Ferrand and explained his unique position as an insider at the school who happened to be outside when the attack occurred.

"Colonel Smiles will have some further questions for you," Brown had finally told Ferrand, and he had given his place at the table to the Army officer.

Smiles had lots of questions. He began with the physical layout of the school. How high were the buildings? Were the roofs flat? Were there stairs and connecting doorways leading to the roofs? Were the grounds level or hilly? Were there open fields, or was the entire area planted in trees? How high were the walls? Were there other gates into the grounds? Were there any breaks in the walls? How did the security surveillance systems work? How many cameras covered the walls? How many were aimed at the outside of the buildings?

Ferrand could only guess at most of the answers, and he could tell that his vague responses were irritating to the officer. "For chrissake," he finally exploded, "why don't you just fly a goddamn helicopter over the place and find out for yourself?"

The colonel had stared at Ferrand for an instant, then smiled an apology. "I'm sorry," he said. "I guess this questioning has been pretty relentless. We're taking pictures. Not from a helicopter, because a helicopter would upset the terrorists. They might think it was an attack. But there are two U-2 spy planes over the place right now, probably at eighty or ninety thousand feet. We should have the pictures by morning. It's just that the photos will mean a great deal more to us if we know what we're looking at."

Before Ferrand could apologize for his outburst, a young lieutenant had entered the house with the rolled-up blueprints of Saint Anselm's school. Smiles gave Ferrand the plans and asked him to review them. He was trying to draw in all the changes that had occurred since the days of Italian unification, when construction on the old mansion had begun.

Construction had started in 1870, when the whole of central Italy was the possession of the pope, protected by France in order to keep a rival country divided. With the fall of Napoleon III, the Papacy lost its patron, and with him any hope of defending the Papal Estates. The original builder had abandoned the project shortly thereafter, leaving just the walls and the stone foundation of the manor house.

Work had resumed at the turn of the century after the property was claimed by a landowner from the north. He had kept the outside walls but redesigned the interior to his personal taste. The land within the walls became the estate gardens, with the surrounding hillsides planted in citrus trees and share-cropped by imported peasants. By the time the house had opened, the original drawings were already obsolete.

The house was again abandoned when the citrus trees failed, and remained empty until it was given to one of Mussolini's henchmen at the beginning of the Fascist era. Decorators were brought in to give the home a more contemporary decor, and once again the floor plans were changed. All that was left untouched were the sweeping marble steps that rose two floors through the core of the building.

The manor became a fortress when the Italian peasants turned on the Fascists during the Second World War. The walls were rebuilt to a new height and topped with sharp stones and imbèdded spikes. The national leaders kept their families inside and their soldiers stationed at the gates.

When Rome fell, the house became a field headquarters of the German army, which made the Allies pay a heavy price for every mile they advanced to the north. Kesselring himself had used it as a command post, drawing Air Corps and RAF bombing raids as a result. Once again, the interior was gutted, leaving only the outside walls as a reminder of its past glory.

American troops had billeted on the grounds for a time, and then the property had been taken over by the Red Cross and used as a depot for foodstuffs and medical supplies. It was the international relief agency that had rebuilt the manor, giving its interior over to small, practical rooms at the expense of the graciousness of the original design. The marble was used to rebuild the grand staircase, but on a much more modest scale.

In 1950, the hotel-like structure was purchased at a modest price by the Anglican Church, which established it as a school for the young male offspring of the English aristocracy and named it after Saint Anselm, the Benedictine monk from Canterbury who had been England's greatest religious scholar. It was the Anglicans who had added the new building in the early sixties, devoting most of the space to an assembly hall faced by a modern stone pulpit.

Postwar economic realities had, however, taken most of the discretionary wealth of the English and put it in the hands of American bankers and industrialists. In 1965, the buildings and grounds had been sold to a group of Americans, who established a school for the sons of the New World's newly wealthy. The churchlike interior of the new building had been converted to more worldly pursuits. The dining hall was enlarged and the spacious lecture halls were divided into small classrooms.

Ferrand studied the plans, tracing the thin lines that represented walls and rooms with his finger. He called out the names of each room he could identify, then cursed the lines that wandered into a bewildering maze. "This is crazy," he muttered when he found himself hopelessly lost, and finally, he pushed the scrolled sheets away and buried his face in his hands in frustration.

"These things are all wrong," he told Colonel Smiles without bothering to look up. "They're goddamn useless. I'd get lost in my own bathroom if I tried to follow them."

"They're old," he heard Smiles' voice say. "But they're all we've got. What you have to do is update them."

Ferrand nodded and reached out for the blueprints. Once again he tried to reconcile them with the familiar image of the buildings that was stored in his memory. "Jesus, Colonel, I'm not an architect. I don't know where to begin. The proportions seem to be way out of whack."

"Proportions aren't important," Smiles said. "What we need is the arrangement of the rooms and the position of the doors. We need to know which way the doors open—into a room or out. We need the locations of windows and their size."

"The size of windows," Ferrand repeated sarcastically.

"In general terms," the colonel interrupted. "Could a man break through, or would he have to crawl through? Could two or three men fit through a door at the same time?"

Ferrand nodded, then stretched the curved corners of the drawings and flattened them with his palms. "I'll do what I can," he promised for the second time in the past fifteen minutes.

"Do better than you can," Smiles told him. "A lot of lives could depend on just how well you do."

Ferrand looked at drawings of the old building that showed ballrooms and libraries where he knew there were bedrooms and drawings of the new building that detailed church pews where he knew there was a kitchen. After a few moments, he discarded the drawings and simply traced the outlines of the structures onto blank tissue paper, filling in the details from memory.

Before he was half finished, he could see the problems that Colonel Smiles was facing. The frequent renovations had turned the floor plans into a maze, with endless, convoluted corridors leading to scores of small, irregularly shaped rooms. Each passageway would force a squad of assault troops into a single line from which only the first soldier would be able to deliver effective rifle fire. Each doorway led to a new battlefield from which a single defender could pin down a whole company simply by firing at each face as it appeared. It was impossible to sweep in suddenly and take command of the entire school. Each room would have to be taken individually, one at a time.

The topography promised a dreadful loss of life. But more significantly, it guaranteed an appalling loss of time. From the moment Smiles' assault troops burst through the front door, they would be stretched out in a single line and under constant fire from the defenders. Minutes would be lost securing each corridor, each room. There would be ample time for the terrorists to dynamite the buildings. There would be more than enough time for each of the students and each of the teachers to be executed ceremoniously. Clearly, with sufficient resources and unflagging determination, Smiles could eventually overcome the terrorists and take over the ruins of the buildings. But just as clearly, none of the hostages would survive his attack.

Smiles was coming to the same conclusion as he watched Ferrand draw in the interconnecting lines. The buildings were a potential minefield, territory he would have to avoid if he were to assault the area. He had just finished an exercise where there was only one doorway. Ten seconds lost in penetrating that doorway had cost dozens of lives. Now there were a hundred doorways, and the terrorists had already had a full day to prepare their defenses.

He left Ferrand to complete the plans and wandered to a window where he could look up the road that led to the school. He could get glimpses of the high stone walls through the trees and see clearly the narrow gates that opened into the grounds. He realized he could lose a whole company of crack troops just breaching the walls. Above the tree line, he could see the gabled roof of the mansion with its irregular lines and sloping tiles. There was no way to land on the top of the old house.

It occured to him then that more than a hundred years ago, a builder had fancied himself a feudal prince and built his home like a medieval fortress to protect his civilized lifestyle from the barbarians. Now the barbarians were inside the fortress, armed with the most effective weapon ever conceived—their willingness to commit mass murder. There was no way Smiles could get to them.

The colonel crossed back to the table just as Ferrand was laying down his pencil. "Finished?" he asked, looking down at the neat lines that cut the area into countless rooms.

"I think so," Ferrand said. "But let me work on it a little longer. I'm trying to imagine myself walking through these lines to see if I can remember anything. There have to be lots of things I haven't thought of yet."

Smiles noticed a dotted line that sealed off a large area to one side of the main house. "What's that?" he demanded, tracing the line with his finger.

"The wine cellar," Ferrand answered without looking up.

"Wine cellar?"

"Not really," Ferrand said, aware of the officer's sudden interest. "I guess that's what it was originally. It's about six feet under the foundation of the building. During the war, the Germans built concrete walls and used it as a bomb shelter. I think the Red Cross used it as a supply depot."

"What's it like?" Smiles pressed.

Ferrand remembered vividly. "Just a big square room with whitewashed walls. There are a couple of industrial lights—bulbs encased in wire mesh—a few old chairs, and a couch. One of the boys discovered it. He was going to use it for . . . a clubhouse."

"Discovered it? You mean it's not in use?"

Ferrand shook his head. "I don't think most of the kids even know it's there. Maybe the headmaster knows, but the teachers don't. When they put the kitchen in the new building"—he pointed to the area he had ruled off—"they built storage closets right across the door to the wine cellar steps. It was probably a dustbin until one of the boys found it and decided he had a use for it."

"Would the terrorists be likely to find it?"

Ferrand raised his eyes. "Probably not. You'd have to be looking for the door before you'd recognize it."

Smiles nodded. "That's a break. If they herded the kids into that cellar, with only one narrow entrance, we'd never get them out. You could level the damn buildings and the bastards would still be in control, holding onto their hostages." He walked away from the table shaking his head. "A wine cellar . . . that's all we need."

Otis Brown returned to the room, the pouches under his eyes darkened by lack of sleep. "How are you doing?" he asked Ferrand, glancing down at the nearly finished plans. Ferrand gestured toward Smiles with a nod of his head. Smiles responded by throwing up his hands in despair.

"It's a goddamn fortress with a concrete bunker in the basement. That fucking school has better security than the White House."

"How long would it take to secure the buildings?" Brown asked. He opened his note pad and was prepared to write down the answer.

"Too long," Smiles said without an instant's thought. "If

they were willing to kill the hostages, then they would all be dead before we made it through the first room—"

"Would they?" Ferrand interrupted.

Both men looked puzzled by his question.

"Would they be willing to kill the hostages? These are just children. Schoolkids. I know they can threaten to. But if it comes right down to it, could they just turn machine guns on a bunch of little boys?"

Otis Brown removed his wire-frame glasses and pinched the bridge of his nose between his thumb and fingers. "That's usually a very good question," he said as he refitted the glasses. "When terrorists slaughter their hostages, they cease being patriots and become criminals, even in the eyes of their own people. They win by gaining concessions, not by wanton killing. Usually, if you don't force their hand, the hostages are reasonably safe. So you would figure that the children would be safe unless we did something very stupid, like botch an attack on the school."

Ferrand seemed relieved.

"But in this case," Brown continued, "the person holding the hostages is a man named Gamel."

"Gamel!" It was Smiles' stunned voice coming from the other side of the room. Brown nodded slowly in the colonel's direction.

"Gamel seems to enjoy killing," Brown said to Ferrand. "Even when we've been prepared to strike some sort of a bargain, Gamel finds a reason to kill."

Ferrand's eyes narrowed in confusion. If they were about to win concessions, why would they risk their victory by killing unimportant hostages?

"Fortunately," Brown went on, "our discussions will be with Sharif. Sharif has risen in stature to the point where he sees himself as a world political figure. He wants concessions that he can flaunt before the world. The last thing he wants is bloodstained hands. So we can probably count on Sharif to keep Gamel under control. But Gamel doesn't want world stature. Gamel wants revenge. For him, the concessions mean very little. The killing is the victory."

"Revenge?" Ferrand pressed. "He'd kill children over a land dispute?"

Brown shook his head. "It's more personal than that," he said. He would have stopped his explanation there, but Colonel Smiles drew a chair up to the table and Ferrand was plainly unsatisfied with half an answer. Brown decided to tell his associates what he knew about the man they were up against.

Contrary to popular belief, not all Palestinians were impoverished refugees. Gamel's father had amassed a fortune, first by selling land to Jewish settlements, and then by providing a market for the foodstuffs they produced. He had reached a position of power before the Israeli militants had defeated the combined Arab armies, and was waiting with open arms for his fellow Palestinians when they fled north into Lebanon. They needed everything—clothes, shelter, food. They needed connections to gain jobs, as well as to gain entry into the closed and suspicious communities that became the refugee camps. Gamel's father provided it all, but at a very dear price. He relieved thousands of refugees of the cash, jewels, and heirlooms they had carried with them as they fled, making himself one of the wealthiest men in the Moslem community of his new country.

Gamel was educated privately in schools run by the Europeans. He knew of the poverty of his people who lived in the camps, just as a young American growing up in the suburbs knows of the poverty of other young Americans in the inner cities. But it didn't touch him directly, so, like his American counterparts, he didn't let it concern him. Instead, he finished his middle school education and was packed off to England for Oxford. His father had been certain that a few years of gentlemanly leisure abroad would polish the rough edges and raise his son well above the petty squabbles of the Palestinian people. But Gamel refused to follow the script. Instead, he took his studies very seriously, particularly his reading of the history of his own people. It became obvious to him that much of the suffering of the Palestinians had been inflicted on them by their own leaders and that his father had benefitted handsomely by the diaspora of the Arabs out of the Holy Land. His own wealth, therefore, was blood money. In time, he determined to return to Lebanon, not to a position of privilege, but rather to serve his own people.

Despite his father's threats and rantings, Gamel moved into one of the ghettos in Beirut. He wasn't able to do much. He had no trade or commercial skills. But he did what he could. He set up a small school and began teaching the children to read and write. In a community dominated by armed militants who trained daily for a war of liberation that would probably never come, he was a harmless enough figure. He had no interest in or involvement with the politics of the camp and simply refused to join its militia. He survived without joining any of the factions simply because he wasn't a threat to any of them. And he was careful to limit his instructions to numbers and letters, never commenting on the convoluted politics that raged outside the door.

Eventually, Gamel married a young girl in the camp, and they had a daughter. He and his family lived in a single room above the room that served as his schoolhouse. Often, he brought the baby girl into his classroom, where she slept in a basket while he worked with the children.

After the Israeli invasion, the situation in Lebanon became chaotic. Christian and Moslem militias battled to sieze power of what, for a brief instant, promised to be a unified national government. United Nations troops tried to keep a fragile peace and, when they faltered, the United States landed Marines in the hope that an American presence could solve feudal disputes that went back generations. The Moslem militias saw the Americans as supporters of the Christians and began firing on the Marine's positions near the Beirut airport. The Americans retaliated by bombing Moslem positions, and then by shelling their ghetto strongholds from a battleship cruising off the coast.

Gamel was taken by the Moslem leaders to act as an interpreter in the futile negotiations that were going on among representatives of the United Nations, Syria, Israel, and the Lebanese warring factions. His young wife, with their baby daughter in tow, took over the school. They were all in the classroom when a shell from the battleship crashed into the building.

"The sixteen-inch guns on the *New Jersey*," Brown said, concluding his story, "fire a projectile about the size of an automobile. When Gamel returned home, there was no sign of the building. It was just a ditch filled with debris and stagnant water. The neighbors hadn't even tried to dig for survivors. There was no point. The shell had crashed through the wall of the building and the structure had collapsed under its impact. Then it had exploded, creating a geyser of pulverized concrete and a cloud of smoke and dust that took half an hour to clear. There were no sounds, no voices crying for help. The dozen or so children in the school, Gamel's wife, and his daughter had simply been vaporized. Gamel stood looking at the wreckage and asked that it simply be plowed over. Everything he loved was buried in a mass grave."

Ferrand and Smiles were silent. "A stray shell," Smiles finally said. Then he explained to Ferrand. "It can happen. Somebody reads the wrong coordinates. Or maybe one of the power charges is a dud, so the shell falls short."

Brown nodded. "Miscalculations are terrible killers. That's why we can't have any miscalculations here. Sharif isn't dangerous, because Sharif is a man who wants to be king. He has a great deal to lose. But Gamel has nothing to lose. Gamel is a man who simply wants to die."

Ferrand wasn't able to sleep. Even though he had been awake for over thirty-six hours, he tossed fitfully on one of the folding beds that had been set up on the second floor of the farmhouse. It was difficult enough for Otis Brown and Colonel Smiles to deal with the danger posed to innocent hostages. But it was agonizing for him. To him, the hostages were faces and voices. They were real people, capable of fear and vulnerable to pain. They were scholars who loved their narrow little specialties enough to want to share them with others. He could see their eyes brighten as they traced mathematical equations to their elegant conclusions or tapped their fingers to the meter of a sonnet. He could hear the laughter in their voices when they read the first hints of comprehension in the amateurish essay of one of their students. They were boys cautiously examining the footings of the bridge to manhood. Some were too proud to admit they were frightened and covered their doubts with daring and boasting. Others thought they were the only ones who were apprehensive and tried to hide their shame by blending anonymously into the crowd. And others simply fled, waiting to be consoled and coaxed back to the crossing. Each of them, at some moment of the day—perhaps an instant of stress in the classroom or on the athletic field—reminded him of what his own rites of passage had been like. They were as real to him as his own memories.

And there was Maria. Otis Brown had her listed in his pad as "teacher, Italian national," a footnote to remind him of a possible diplomatic problem should she become a victim of an American rescue attempt. To Smiles, she was merely a number, another factor in the calculations by which he determined the statistical probabilities of lives lost should he be ordered to attack. But Ferrand knew the excitement of her skin and the scent of her hair. He could read the changes in the color of her eyes and understand the meaning of the subtle tones that sounded in her voice. He had held her close. They had shared the same breath. Her life was his life.

When he closed his eyes, he saw faces. He heard words that pulled together the sense of whole conversations. He was part of every one of them. Of the teachers. The boys. Of Maria. They were all part of him. He shared their uncertainty and felt their fear. Most of all, he felt guilt that he had somehow escaped sharing their fate.

There could be no sleep. It was easier to force his eyes open and look up into the blackness of the room. To look for a sliver of daylight that might call him to act. He had to do something. He couldn't simply wait for events to overwhelm them all.

Ferrand was out of the bed before he heard the knock on the door. He pulled it open and recognized the form in the dark hallway. Smiles' adjutant started to apologize but interrupted himself when he saw that Ferrand was fully dressed. "Colonel Smiles would like to see you," he ordered. "Something has come up."

Smiles and Otis Brown were huddled at the dining room table with a blue-uniformed police officer. Smiles was having difficulty maintaining his composure. "Everyone," he was saying to the officer, speaking slowly in an effort to make his English clear to the Italian. "The boy. Your officer who took the phone call. The men at the police station. Your driver. Everyone who might have heard about this message. They must all be arrested. Held in quarantine. Do you understand?"

"But that is not possible," the Italian officer was trying to explain. "They have done nothing . . ."

"They could get a lot of people killed," Smiles said. "One careless word could kill all those children."

"They haven't spoken to anyone," the officer shouted back. "I have given strict orders—"

"Orders my ass," Smiles snapped. "There are newspaper reporters all over your police station. One of your people is going to want to see himself interviewed on television. And the sons of bitches who hold the school are going to watch that interview. Or maybe the boy is going to boast to his friends. You have to understand, there are lives at stake. We can't take any chances."

The policeman wasn't going to allow himself to be bullied by the American. It was his country and his district. The boy was an Italian. The police were under his command. He jabbed a gloved finger toward Smiles' face. "There will be no arrests. I have given orders to my men and my orders will be obeyed."

"We understand," Otis Brown interrupted, trying to calm the Italian and protect him from Smiles' barely contained rage. "And we appreciate your help. Perhaps if you would just explain to your officers how sensitive the situation is." The Italian tipped his head curiously. "Dangerous," Brown said, trying for a more common word. "It would be very dangerous if anyone learned about this message. If the terrorists knew that someone in the school was talking to us, they would tear the place apart to find him. And they might kill him. They might kill several people."

The officer nodded. "I understand. No one will know."

"And it would be very helpful if the boy were brought here. We would like him to help us. We want to establish a direct link into the school."

The officer smiled. "Of course. That is possible. I'll have him brought here immediately."

Brown rose and pumped the hand of the Italian police officer. The man snapped the uniform cap from under his arm, fixed it squarely on his head, and saluted Brown and Smiles. The colonel managed to return the salute.

"The ass," Smiles growled as soon as the Italian was through the front door.

"I'll get the embassy," Brown said reassuringly. "We'll get Italian troops up here to take over the police station."

"What's going on?" Ferrand asked, looking at the two troubled faces.

Brown removed his glasses wearily. "A kid in Rome—fifteen years old—called the local police station. It seems he's a computer buff. He exchanges computer messages with other kids through some sort of electronic mail drop. A couple of hours ago he dialed in and got a message that he was supposed to deliver to our local Keystone Kops. It was addressed to you."

Ferrand looked startled. Brown handed him a scrap of perforated printout.

"'Mr. Ferrand. These guys are complete jerks. They took out all the telephones but they never even looked for a computer. So we can send messages back and forth. Even if they're listening in it will just sound like static. Let me know when the Americans are going to take this place. I'll get everything ready here. Boy, are these goons in for a surprise. We're really going to kick some ass.'"

It was signed, "Billy Tepper."

Senator Thomas Bradberry bounded out of the limousine even before the Marine guard had the door fully opened and disappeared through the side door of the White House. He charged ahead with long strides and took the service stairs two steps at a time. A secretary rose to greet him as he reached the entrance to the Oval Office, but he was by her in a flash, nearly colliding with half the double door that the president's assistant, John Powers, had hastened to open for him.

He found the conference already assembled on a sofa and in two soft chairs with four straight-backed chairs pulled over to complete the circle. The president, in shirt-sleeves, was in one of the chairs, looking down a row that included William Clemmons, director of the Central Intelligence Agency, Martin Potter, the secretary of state, and the uniformed admiral who was the current chairman of the Joint Chiefs of Staff. The vice president occupied the soft chair at the other end of the sofa. Seated in the straight-backed chairs were Senator Richard Moore, a Republican from Ohio, North Carolina Congressman Briggs Stratton, the long-reigning chairman of the Armed Services Committee, and Matthew Topping, a former professor of geology who had been named secretary of the interior as a sop to the nation's environmentalists.

"I think we're all here," the president announced after nodding a greeting to Bradberry and gesturing him to an empty chair. "Let's get started. I know some of you have been traveling all day and have a difficult night ahead of you."

He began with a mumbled word of sympathy. Bradberry, Stratton, Moore, and the secretary of the interior had sons at Saint Anselm's. As soon as President Reynolds had heard of the takeover, he had sent word to them. Stratton was at home in Washington. But the secretary of the interior had been on an acid-rain inspection in New England, and Senator Moore had been addressing a manufacturers' convention in Ohio, where most of the acid rain originated. Bradberry, who had poorly disguised presidential ambitions, had been meeting with fundamentalist religious leaders in Tennessee. All three had been rushed home by special Air Force flights. None of the men belonged to the inner circle of advisers that had been locked up with the president since the terrorist takeover of the school had been confirmed. But Reynolds had arranged the briefing because of their special interest in this particular assault on their country.

"This is going to be a particularly rough ordeal for you," the president continued, "so I wanted you to have the information we have gathered firsthand. And, of course, I'll value your counsel and personal insights on this mess for as long as it lasts." Heads bobbed in expressions of appreciation. President Reynolds was a fixture in Washington, with a twenty-year career in the House and Senate. His capabilities had numerous critics, but his personal loyalty and concern for his colleagues had never been questioned. "I'm told that the late network news will have the story on the takeover of the school. They may have the names of the kids and make the connection with all of you. But even if they don't, you can expect that the press will be after you for comments sometime during the night. I thought you should be informed." It was a typical Reynolds' kindness. He was genuinely concerned with the personal tragedy that each of the men was facing. But he was also aware that they were public figures with reputations to protect. If they were going to be questioned about a national crisis, they would want to sound deeply involved and fully in control.

Reynolds pointed with the eyeglasses he was holding toward the secretary of state. "Martin, I think perhaps you should start."

The secretary opened a file folder that had been on his lap. "First, it seems certain that we are dealing with Sharif. Two or three other groups have been on the radio claiming to be involved, but they're the typical fringe lunatics who try to take credit for every disaster. Sharif notified our embassy in Cairo that he had occupied the school and then issued a statement to Cairo radio. He had all the details necessary to support his claim."

The information wasn't at all startling to the men gathered in the room. When they had been summoned, they had been informed it was Sharif's faction that was responsible.

"The demands," the secretary continued, "were delivered late this afternoon to the Syrian embassy and passed on to me by the ambassador—"

"The Syrians?" Bradberry interrupted.

"Just as good-faith messengers," the secretary answered without hesitation. "The ambassador doesn't know the source of the documents, and he went out of his way to express his sympathy. That doesn't mean that Damascus won't applaud the action; but it probably means that they were as surprised by it as we were."

Bradberry launched into a denunciation of Syrian duplicity, but was silenced by a gesture from Congressman Stratton. "What are the demands?" the congressman asked the secretary.

"They're tough," the president answered impulsively. "Goddamn near impossible."

The secretary of state nodded in agreement, then consulted his notes. "Immediate release of specified Palestinian prisoners now being held in Israel, Italy, and Cyprus. There are a hundred and five names on the list. Ninety-three of them are in Israel. We're checking with those governments to confirm that the people named are actually being held and what their status is."

"Will we consider a trade?" the congressman asked.

"Of course not," Bradberry answered.

"Our policy is not to trade," the secretary agreed, "but we should know what we have to deal with just in case we have to reach some accommodation." Those assembled agreed that it would certainly be prudent to gather all the available information concerning the people on Sharif's list.

"Next, he wants us to pay an indemnity for war damage caused by our forces and by the military support we have given the Israelis. We're to provide one billion in a mix of currencies—dollars, deutsche marks, and yen. Sharif will use it for economic investments in countries that have refugee populations. It's a nice public-relations touch. He specifies that the money will not be used for military supplies."

"Unbelievable," Congressman Stratton said, his voice already tinged by despair.

"It gets worse," President Reynolds interjected.

"Much worse," the secretary of state agreed. "Sharif wants us to respect a twenty-one-mile limit on the eastern and southern coasts of the Mediterranean. In effect, he's demanding that the Arab nations be considered out-of-bounds to the Sixth Fleet."

"That's asinine," Senator Bradberry snapped. "He's giving us demands he knows damn well we can never consider."

"He's smart," President Reynolds snapped back. "Look at the package. If we free the prisoners, he becomes an instant folk hero. The son of a bitch would have more charisma than Ronald Reagan. If he pushes the Sixth Fleet away from the coast, he becomes a military hero. And with a billion in investment capital he could run his own Marshall Plan. He'd be the biggest thing to hit the Middle East since Mohammed. What Sharif is demanding is that we anoint him king of the Moslems."

"They're impossible demands," Congressman Stratton said, summing up the mood of those present. He looked at the faces of his colleagues and found one blank expression after another. Then he turned back to the secretary. "Can we get any diplomatic help?"

The secretary shrugged. "Nothing worth a damn. Every Middle Eastern government is sitting on a powder keg. They're all frightened out of their wits by the Moslem fundamentalists within their countries. They can tell us privately that they're sympathetic. They can promise to use their influence to protect hostages. But in public they have to be very understanding of the rights of terrorists to fight with every weapon available to them—even hostages. Half their populations think terrorists are heroes. Basically, the governments are going to sit on the fence with their fingers in the air testing the wind. If Sharif falls on his face, then they'll condemn him and point out that only legitimate governments can represent the needs of a displaced people. But if Sharif wins, then they'll make a grandstand play of the support they gave him."

"Don't we have any friends at all in the Middle East?" Senator Moore asked rhetorically.

"Israel," the secretary of state answered, "but the less they have to say, the better."

In the gloomy silence that followed, the president turned to Admiral Kimball. "Admiral, I think you have some additional bad news for us to consider."

Admiral Kimball had been confirmed as chairman of the Joint Chiefs only six weeks earlier. It was his first audience with the president; his first meeting ever with Senator Moore. He looked apprehensively into the faces of Senator Bradberry and Congressman Briggs. Both men were dedicated advocates of a strong military who had steered hundreds of billions in military appropriations through the House and Senate. He knew perfectly well what he was about to tell them: that all the sophisticated weaponry they had wrung out of the public coffers at the expense of every program of social concern couldn't buy their sons back. It wasn't a message he was anxious to deliver during his first visit to the Oval Office.

"I have received a military assessment from Colonel William Smiles, commanding officer of the Delta Force unit on the scene," Kimball said, his voice barely audible. "His recommendation is that no military action to relieve the school be considered."

Bradberry came out of his chair. "Jesus Christ," he said in exasperation and moved around the gathering until he was standing next to the admiral. "Isn't that why we have a Delta Force? All they're trained to do is attack terrorists. And when we need them, they tell us not to attack."

"My understanding," the admiral continued, "is that the school is a virtual fortress. We would lose much of the attack force, and in the time it would take to secure the buildings, the hostages—the children—could all be . . . executed. Colonel Smiles is making a recommendation based on—"

"To hell with Colonel Smiles," Bradberry shouted. "I'm fed up with military men who keep telling us why we can't use our military forces. Don't we have one damn soldier in the entire Army who can get the job done?"

"Thomas," the president said calmly to Bradberry, "why don't we get all the information on the table. Maybe we do have to consider a strong military response. But let's work with the facts we have in hand."

Bradberry finally nodded and walked back to his chair.

The director of the CIA took this as his cue, opened his briefcase, and launched into a tutorial on the intelligence gathered from the Middle East. His summaries of the political situations in each of the major countries were remarkably similar. Everywhere there seemed to be weak governments trying desperately to hold together populations assembled from different nomadic tribes that were separated by centuries of tradition and militantly defended religious differences. "About all that keeps them from each other's throats," the director said, "is a shared hatred for Israel. If

Israel didn't exist, the Arab leaders would have to invent it just to lend some semblance of unity to their own countries.

"That drummed-up hatred spills over to us. A victory over the United States is seen as weakening Israel. So you can understand why they can't turn against Sharif. But at the same time, they don't want to see him succeed. A triumphant Sharif would be one hell of a threat to their already fragile governments."

"Come to the point, Bill," the president finally said.

"The point," the director responded, "is that we can't let Sharif win this one. If he does, there is an enormous risk that he could topple some of the existing governments, most of which are privately cooperative, even if they are publicly hostile. Any concessions we make will have to be relatively inconsequential. But Sharif can't accept a token victory. He needs a big win. The bottom line is that we don't have a great deal of room for neogiating."

Stratton jumped in with a summation of the information that had been presented. "We can't free the kids with military action, and we can't free them by negotiations. What's left?"

No one wanted to handle the question.

"There's one more intelligence item that tends to support the decision of the Delta Force commander," the director offered. "The commander of the terrorists at the school is the same man who took that synagogue in Vienna. He has absolutely no regard for innocent lives. I wouldn't even hint at a military assault unless we had an ironclad plan that was completely assured of success."

They all remembered the synagogue incident some nine months earlier. Gamel had promised to kill a hostage every three hours until his demands were met. The bodies were thrown out the door like clockwork until the Austrian government released the five terrorists they were holding from a previous airline hijacking. Gamel took three of the hostages with him on the helicopter and then on the airplane that had been provided for his escape. They were to be released when he landed safely in Libya. But they weren't aboard the plane when it landed. Once inside Libyan airspace, he ordered the plane down to a low altitude, opened the rear door, and threw them into the Mediterranean.

"We'll be working toward some middle ground," the president told the meeting. "Remember, Sharif gains nothing if he comes away with nothing but the blood of children to show for his efforts. Publicly, we have to sound very tough—uncompromising on our principles. But actually, we'll be bargaining. We'll be looking for concessions that are better than nothing but short of what Sharif needs to make himself into the hero of the refugees and fundamentalists."

"What will they be?" the secretary of the interior asked respectfully.

"Damned if I know," the president admitted.

After his guests had left, he sat alone in his office with a temperate dash of scotch poured over ice and a clandestine cigarette that his advisors had told him could hurt his image. He thought sympathetically of Thomas Bradberry, a potential rival in the next presidential election and a decent man who truly believed in America's right to mediate justice to the rest of the world as well as its ability to solve the planet's most convoluted problems. He could count on Bradberry to demand that the country take a hard line regardless of the safety of the hostages. "Negotiate," Bradberry had insisted repeatedly, "and you just encourage the next act of terrorism." Except this time the hard line would cut squarely through his own son. Abraham, the president mused, had been such a fervent believer that he had raised his knife over his own flesh and blood. And God, according to the Bible, had sentenced His own son to die for a cause. But Bradberry probably wasn't Abraham and certainly wasn't God. His beliefs probably wouldn't stand up to the test.

He thought of the meeting he had scheduled for early the next morning. There were a dozen industrialists and financiers descending on the city with their grief-stricken wives, all demanding that he act immediately to free their children. The nation's diplomatic clout and military might had made the world safe for their offshore factories and international cartels. But it had also put their own children in jeopardy. What would they decide? To uphold the righteous principles that protected their economic empires? Or to save their sons?

Where had we gone wrong? Reynolds asked himself. We saw ourselves as a haven for the world's defenseless and disenfranchised masses. Yet it was some of those very same people who hated us so much that they would rally around a fanatic who threatened to kill our children. The best and brightest of three generations of American leaders had grappled with the problems of the Middle East, Africa, Latin America, and Asia and had succeeded only in making us the enemy of every peasant and laborer on half the earth's continents. Now, in this moment of crisis, there wasn't a single mind among the world's great leaders that had any idea of how to save us.

Maybe that's the answer, Reynolds told himself. Maybe great men couldn't save us. Maybe our hope is in children. Could it be that the thought of children in danger might finally cut through all the complex politics and self-serving rationalizations? Could the simple fact of a child's life turn out to be the only important issue?

April 17

morning

Billy was still in bed when he heard the computer in his closet turn itself on. He bolted up and pushed past the hanging clothes just in time to watch a message write itself across the display screen.

Billy. Don't send messages. It would be very dangerous if the men heard the signal and knew you were
using a computer. Just wait. We will contact you if
we need to deliver information. Ferrand.

"Fantastic," he whispered. His message had gotten
through. The Italian kid had finally done something right.
Billy hadn't been too hopeful when he had addressed his
message to Giorgio with instructions that he should deliver it
to the police. Giorgio wasn't the quickest kid he had ever
spoken with over a computer link. Sometimes it took him
half a day to log on, and then another half day to answer the
simplest question. Like when Billy tried to line up a couple
of bimbos for his wine-cellar massage parlor.

I need two hookers, under twenty, at the break in
the wall about eight o'clock tonight. Real stunners.
One-third of the take for you. Can do? he had typed
into his terminal.

It was a simple, businesslike message. But it was after ten
by the time Giorgio had gotten around to reading his mail,
which meant that Billy had to cancel the evening's scheduled
events. That didn't improve Henry Giles' disposition! And
then Giorgio had replied with a question.

What's a hooker?

For God's sake, where was this kid raised? In the Vatican?
Billy responded immediately with his most tactful descrip-
tion of the services he had in mind. So what did Giorgio do?
He fired back another question.

Under twenty what?

No wonder the Italian economy was in shambles!
Billy understood Ferrand's message perfectly. The Americans didn't want to compromise the computer link with idle

chitchat. That made sense. They probably wouldn't talk to him until their attack plans were all set. And he should talk to them only with the essential information that they absolutely needed. But he had to get busy. Even if they didn't have their troops in place yet, it wouldn't take the Screaming Eagles long to get ready. They'd probably be coming over the wall in a day or so.

Billy knew all about the Screaming Eagles. They jumped out of planes with these special parachutes that they could steer like gliders. They'd probably come crashing through the windows, guns firing before their feet even hit the floor. Then we'd see how tough these greasers really were!

There were a lot of things he had to do. First, there were the stupid television cameras that kept panning the walls and buildings. One man, sitting in front of the monitors, was as good as an army of sentries patrolling the grounds with a kennel of bloodhounds. The Americans would lose the element of surprise. Stick your face over the wall and the bastards would be able to tell the color of your eyes. They'd put a hole through your head before you could say "Gung ho!"

Billy had tested the cameras, so he knew the damn things worked. Once, he had set up a rendezvous with Giorgio, but the teachers had already found the break in the wall by then and wired it over, so his only way out was over the top. He was halfway up a tree that had a branch reaching out over the wall when all of a sudden the old man from the guard shack was under the tree, poking around with a six-cell flashlight. He had to drop behind the old guy and run like hell to keep from getting sent back to Cincinnati.

Now he had to figure out a way to turn the cameras off. Only he couldn't just cut the coaxial cable. These guys were real nervous. If the monitors went dead, there was no telling what they would do. Somehow, he had to get them watching something else. They had to think they were looking at the walls when really they weren't looking at the walls. Some kind of distraction. And the Americans had to come in at exactly the moment when the Arabs were distracted.

The second problem was the explosives. He had watched his captors stuff the white putty into every nook and cranny in both buildings. Talk about overkill! They had installed enough plastic to level Manhattan. And then they strung more wires than Western Union. With all the wires running through it, the dining hall looked like a giant harp.

But you had to hand it to them. They were pretty smart. There was a separate wire to each explosive charge, and all the wires were in different places. Even if you cut half the lines, there would still be enough wires connected to charges to bring down the building. So what good would it do for the Screaming Eagles to take over the buildings if the bastards could set off the detonator?

They even had their own power source. All the wires connected to a radio receiver that was powered by its own batteries. Even if you killed the power to the building, they could still send current up the lines to the plastic charges.

What he had to do was disable the complete system. The head sleeze carried the detonator transmitter around in his pocket. He got his kicks out of showing it to the teachers and rubbing his finger across the button. Billy had to find a way to put the transmitter out of commission. Only he had to do it while the transmitter was still in the creep's pocket. Well, what the hell! Nobody said it was going to be easy.

And then there were the guns. Each of these guys carried a machine gun with a clip that had to be a foot and a half long. The Americans might get most of them within a few seconds. But even if two or three of them had the time to start firing, they could put a lot of holes in a lot of kids. The problem was that the guns were never in one place. The jerks were scattered all over the two buildings. There was one at the staircase landing on each floor and another in the lobby at the bottom of the stairs. Then there was one in the hallway that connected the two buildings. There was a guard in each corner of the dining room, one at the door to the administration office, and still another standing just outside the front door. And there were probably a couple more of them out near the front gate. They each had a gun, and none of them ever took his finger off the trigger. There was no way he could put all of the guns out of operation at one time. Some of them would always be pointed at some of the kids. What he had to do instead was figure out a way to get all the guards out of the buildings at the same time. Or, maybe a way to get all of the teachers and kids out from under the barrels of the guns, even if only for a few seconds. That's about all the time the Screaming Eagles would need.

But before he could tackle the big problems, there were a few little ones. One was language. It was important for him to find out which of the guards could understand English. He needed to gather information, and he needed to spread that information among the teachers and students. With the guards everywhere, any conversation was certain to be overheard. So he had to know which of his captors wouldn't understand what he was saying.

He also had to do something about the total discipline the terrorists had imposed simply by their presence. In the dining hall, all the boys sat at the tables in neat rows. And between the dining hall and their rooms, they marched in straight lines, one behind the other. Anyone who stepped out of line would be immediately noticed. If he was to accomplish anything, he needed the freedom to move about the buildings without attracting attention. That meant he had to loosen up the atmosphere. He had to get all the kids moving randomly and, more important, had to get the guards used to seeing the kids wandering about. Only then could he come and go without being watched.

Billy carried the answer under his arm as he left his room and joined the silent line filing down the corridor toward the stairs. Who the hell would get suspicious over a kid carrying a soccer ball? Isn't that what kids were supposed to do? When he was halfway down the hall, he let the black-and-white ball slip out of his grasp. He kicked it accidentally, without breaking stride, sending it rolling toward the stone-faced guard who was probably only a few years older than the boys he was watching.

"It's a ball, you jerk," Billy said under his breath. "You know what you're supposed to do with a ball. Kick it back!"

The boys in the line flinched as they saw something roll past them toward the armed guard. The simple break in the careful decorum seemed like the battle cry of a revolution. They fully expected the guard to lower his weapon and shoot the soccer ball to pieces. The guard was as startled as they were. Since the moment his raiding party had broken through the front gate, he had expected to be attacked. Consequently, he watched each of his prisoners carefully, alert to any sudden move that might be the first step of a rush toward his throat. Now the attack was coming in the form of a rolling ball.

"Kick it," Billy prayed. The guard seemed to take a step back as the ball reached his feet. "Kick it. It's a ball, not a bomb," his prayer continued.

Suddenly, the guard danced to his left, his hand releasing the machine gun as he raised his arms for balance. His left foot shot out like the tongue of a snake and snapped the ball behind him. The right foot swung in a tight arc so that he caught the ball with his heel, tapping a perfect pass right into Billy's outstretched arms.

"Great kick," Billy yelled. Then he thrust his fist into the air in an athlete's victory salute. "Let's hear it for the guy." He let out a cheer. The boys' heads turned in bewilderment to the smiling terrorist and then back to Billy, who was gesturing like a cheerleader. They took the cue and began exchanging high-fives as they yelled their approval. The guard joined in the laughter.

Billy stepped out of the line and walked straight toward his captor. He shook the ball triumphantly in front the guard's face, laughing in appreciation of the great shot. "Hell of a pass," he said. The terrorist smiled modestly. "Why don't you take this ball and stick it up your ass," Billy suggested, his face still bright with admiration. The guard nodded in agreement, then pointed to his own feet and, repeating his dance step, gave the boys an instant replay of his footwork.

Great, Billy thought as he fell back into line. You could plan a nuclear strike in front of this guy and he wouldn't understand a word.

"You crazy?" Henry Giles hissed into Billy's ear as soon as they had started down the stairs. "You trying to get us all killed? I oughta rearrange your face!"

Billy started to explain but then thought better of it. Why be hard on Henry? All the poor sap could do was play the cards he had been dealt. It wasn't his fault he had only half a brain.

He reran his little skit as soon as they reached the dining hall. He let the ball slip, then awkwardly kicked it as he pretended to pick it up. As it rolled across the tile floor, he watched the guards' eyes leave their prisoners for the first time and follow the ball all the way to the wall. "Sorry," he apologized to the nearest guard as he walked across the room to retrieve it. He circled around the ball when he reached it, took two quick, short steps, and kicked a shot toward Davey Moore, the goalie on the soccer team.

"Score," he shouted. Davey lunged toward the shot just as he would have on the soccer field. His hand flicked out and knocked the ball away. "Great save!" Billy Tepper yelled.

The teachers' eyes widened in horror.

"Did you see that block?" Billy demanded of the guard closest to him.

The guard started to nod, but then his smile stiffened. "No ball playing," he ordered.

"Yeah, right," Billy agreed, "but that's one heck of a goal-tender."

"Good save," the guard agreed.

Billy studied his face. That's one guy I'll have to remember, he thought. No conversations when he's around.

The soccer ball had broken the spell of fear. Immediately, the boys began whispering to one another. Maria rearranged the straight lines of the tables and began gathering her brats into a circle. Elias Metz climbed up on a chair and announced the order in which the boys would file into the kitchen to get their breakfast. The kids at the first table he selected cheered his decision and bolted toward the kitchen door. Suddenly, things seemed normal. For an instant, it was possible to forget the straight-faced guards in their drab coveralls. It was even possible to forget the machine guns.

But Billy kept his attention fixed on the guards. He watched their darting eyes and tried to measure their reactions. One screamed command, even in their incomprehensible language, would freeze the room. One gesture of authority would instantly turn all the boys back into zombies.

It never came. With their prisoners now involved in the casual routines of the day, the guards' square shoulders slackened. For the first time, their hands seemed to relax and slip away from the trigger housings of their weapons. Their eyes, until now riveted on the teachers and students, lost their focus. They began to glance easily at one another.

Before he had kicked the soccer ball at Davey Moore, the two groups had been in terror of one another. Certainly the students had. The sight of the guns was reason enough for fear. And the bloodied faces of two of the teachers had made the danger completely real. But the terrorists were also frightened. They were little more than boys themselves, in a strange place surrounded by hostile faces. Danger was everywhere, in the people they held prisoner and in the country that lay only a few hundred feet away, just outside the walls of the school. Their survival depended on keeping their prisoners healthy and alive. Yet it also depended on their willingness to slaughter their captives. If the students and the teachers turned on them, they would certainly begin shooting. But their own chances of survival fell with each body that dropped under their guns. Of course they were prepared to die. That was exactly what they had rehearsed over and over again since they were old enough to raise a weapon. But they had trained in the security of their own camps, surrounded by friends and admirers. Now they were surrounded by the reality of death.

Since Billy had broken the spell with his soccer ball, the teachers and students were able to look away from the awful weapons. And with the spectre of death gone from their faces, the terrorists were no longer looking at a mirrored reflection of their own fear. At least for the moment, horror had been banished from the school.

Paul Prinz had moved to the kitchen door to supervise the first group of boys filling their breakfast trays. Billy Tepper left his table to join the second group and pushed to the head of the line so he would be standing next to Prinz. It was time to get to work on his more important problems. Prinz was a scientist, and Billy needed information about the radio transmitter that the terrorist leader had flaunted so proudly. If he was going to disable it, he had to understand exactly how it worked.

afternoon

Edward Ferrand tried to look confident when he pulled open the door of the black Fiat sedan and slid into the seat next to Otis Brown.

"You're sure you can handle this?" Brown asked.

"I'm okay," Ferrand said. "Let's get going."

Brown started to speak, then thought better of it. He put the car into gear and pulled slowly away from the farmhouse. "Is there anything you want to go over? Anything that's not clear?" he asked as they turned onto the road that led up to Saint Anselm's.

Ferrand shook his head. He was afraid that if he said even a word, his voice would crack.

They had rehearsed him for nearly three hours, ever since Gamel had demanded an emissary. Gamel simply dialed the local police station, by then secured by a company of Italian troops, and suggested that the ranking American at the scene call him at the school number. Otis Brown marveled that he could simply place a telephone call to an enemy whose ruthless tactics might well have come from another age, or even another planet.

Gamel had wanted one man—a civilian with no connection to either the American or Italian governments. He suggested a reporter, perhaps from the international press corps. Brown agreed to a civilian but balked at the idea of a reporter. If negotiations reached a sensitive stage, he didn't want American options debated in the newspapers or on television. While they were talking, the American intelligence officer noticed Ferrand standing alone by the window, looking quietly up the hill toward the school. It was then he had suggested a teacher, one familiar with Saint Anselm's and deeply concerned with the well being of its inhabitants. The idea appealed to Gamel, and they agreed that Edward Ferrand would carry messages between them.

Colonel Smiles had led off the briefing. He had aerial pictures of the outside of the buildings and Ferrand's rough drawings of the inside. He even had photographs taken through the school windows by powerful cameras that were positioned in observation posts that he had set up in the surrounding hills. But there was much more that he needed to know.

"The detonator is the most important factor," Smiles had told Ferrand. "Look for wires—thin bell wires. They may be taped to the walls or just hung loosely. They'll be stretched throughout the buildings, but they'll all terminate at one point. I need to know exactly where that point is. If we have to go in there, we have to neutralize the detonator immediately."

Ferrand understood. "Won't I be blindfolded?"

Smiles nodded. "You may be. But we're hoping you can convince Gamel to let you have a look around. We want you to ask to see the children so that you can be sure they haven't been harmed. It's a reasonable demand. He shouldn't see any danger in it."

"So while I'm being shown the kids, I'm really looking for wires," Ferrand concluded.

"And for the locations of the boys," Smiles added. "Does he have them scattered throughout the buildings or are they all herded into one place? Where are they kept during the night? During the day? Once we get to the detonator, our first priority will be securing the students. We have to know where the boys and their teachers will be."

Ferrand's quick nod indicated he understood.

"Now, the next thing is the locations of the guards. We can see some of them through the windows, but we don't know how many we can't see. How many are there? Where are they positioned? What kinds of weapons are they carrying? When you get back, we'll want you to redraw the building plan with every detail you can remember."

Ferrand had glanced hopelessly at Otis Brown.

Brown had read his uncertainty. "You won't remember it all. And you certainly won't have the opportunity to see everything that we'd like to know. But every bit of information helps. Something may even be critical."

Smiles had continued with his shopping list then. Weapons. He briefed Ferrand on the various types of guns and grenades so that Ferrand would be able to identify what he was seeing. Security. Were there trip wires around the buildings? Were there lookouts posted, or were they relying entirely on the television security system? Communications. Was each of the terrorists carrying a pocket radio? How would one guard alert another guard? Discipline. Were these trained troops with a military bearing? Or were Smiles' specialists confronting a gang of thugs?

When the colonel had finished with his questions and suggestions, Otis Brown had leaned in over the table. It was essential that Ferrand stick to his role as messenger. He should make no comments on the demands that Gamel would make, nor should he answer any questions about the identity of the Americans at the scene, their numbers, or their attitudes. "You should appear to be totally neutral,"

Brown advised. "If he wants to go into a diatribe about American aggression, just listen without comment. If he demands to know your views, just tell him you're not interested in politics. Your only role is to verify that the boys haven't been harmed, and to carry his instructions to us."

"Couldn't he have given you his demands over the telephone?" Ferrand had asked.

"He could have, but he obviously wants someone from out here to go in there. Maybe he wants to make sure we understand that the hostages are in a hopeless position. Or maybe he wants to know what's going on out here. Remember, he's locked in with his prisoners. He has no way of knowing whether he's winning or losing. That's why I don't want you to make any comments. I'd like to keep him guessing."

Now, the black Fiat was cresting the hill and Ferrand could see the gate that Maria had disappeared through only a day earlier. In the entire briefing, Maria had never been mentioned. Still, she was the one question that tormented him. When she had kissed him and stepped out of the car, the terrorists were already on the school grounds. They were probably in the very process of taking over the buildings and rounding up the teachers and students. All day long he had been envisioning the moment. The terrorists moving through darkened buildings, guns poised, ready to fire at anyone who made a threatening move. Maria coming upon them unexpectedly, perhaps bursting through a door and startling a trigger-happy guard. Or maybe she'd come upon a soldier who was terrorizing one of the boys or abusing one of her precious brats. She would have attacked without even hesitating to notice a raised weapon. . . .

He needed to see Maria. He needed to know that she was alive and unharmed. He would trace wires. He would try to identify weapons. But more than anything else, he would look for her. And if he found her, he would . . . he would . . . what? There was nothing he could do for her. Certainly, there would be no opportunity for them to speak. And he couldn't risk a gesture of encouragement. Any sign of recognition would arouse the suspicion of the guards. If they thought he knew her, if they guessed she had some special standing with those on the outside, then she might immediately be marked as their most promising victim. If she had any protection at all, it was in the obscurity she shared with all the other teachers. She was just one of many anonymous hostages.

He felt the car stop. The gate was only a few feet ahead. "Good luck," Brown said. "I'll be waiting right here. You'll probably be back before the engine gets cold."

Ferrand forced a smile. Then he lifted the door handle and stepped out.

"Wait a minute," Brown said. "You should have something to identify you. Take out your handkerchief and keep waving it over your head."

The teacher looked bewildered.

"A white flag," Brown called from inside the car. "You should be carrying a truce flag."

It seemed ridiculous, Ferrand thought. Did people still carry white flags to signify that they were off limits? Had Gamel's snipers been schooled in the niceties of European gentlemen's wars? "Are you serious?" he asked through the open door.

Brown nodded. "I'm not sure. But I think you should be clearly marked as the emissary. I think it's a good idea."

Ferrand reached into a pocket, then began searching all of them. "I don't have a handkerchief," he finally told Brown.

In response, Brown dug his hands into his own pockets. Ferrand watched incredulously, and then the anger he had been stoking during the day began to flare up. With children's lives hanging in the balance, America's expert on terrorists couldn't decide whether he needed a white flag. And if he needed one, there wasn't one to be found. He turned abruptly and started through the gate.

"I found it," Brown called after him.

Ferrand looked back and saw the intelligence officer waving his handkerchief out the window of the car. "Save it for the surrender," he shouted back in disgust. He kept walking and picked up his pace as he turned onto the path that led to the new building. The deal with the handkerchief had snapped him out of his stupor. He had spent the day as a ridiculous dummy, with the United States government pulling his strings. He had allowed himself to become a helpless victim. But there had to be some way to fight back. There had to be something he could do to help the people who were trapped in Saint Anselm's. He didn't know what it was. But he sure as hell was going to find out.

He had nearly reached the door to the new building when he heard the voice behind him.

"Halt."

It was just one word, probably rehearsed by someone who wasn't quite sure what he was saying. Then a hand grasped his shoulder and turned him around. He was greeted by the tiny circumference of a machine gun barrel pointing squarely at his forehead. Behind it was the shape of a young face with narrow dark eyes and teeth set like a vise. Smiles had told him a dozen things that would help him identify the weapon, but all he could see now was the lethal hole, smaller than a dime, threatening him with obliteration. For a moment he thought he was going to be sick.

He heard the door behind him and then footsteps rushing down the stone staircase. Suddenly there were hands on his back, patting down the sides of his arms, then under his arms and down the sides of his body. The search was thorough, but Ferrand paid no attention to it. His mind was riveted on the gun barrel that hung unwavering just a few inches from his face.

He was turned around again, this time by the man who had searched him, a mustached figure with a shock of hair falling over his forehead and a gold chain showing under an open-collared shirt. The man turned and started up the steps. The gun prodded his back, indicating he should follow.

They walked in a procession through the doors of the new building, passing the security office that was bathed in the gray light of the television monitors and then the door of the administration office. Smiles' first question was immediately answered. Wires in small bundles were squeezed through the tops of the two closed doors that led to the dining hall as well as the open window at the far side of the building. They converged at the doorway to the administration office, signaling the location of the detonator. Ferrand had been told to count the number of wires, but his mind was anxiously racing ahead to his meeting with Gamel. He couldn't think clearly enough even to guess at the number.

They turned to the right at the end the administration office, entering the short hallway where the headmaster had his office, and stopped at the wood-paneled door. The guard who had searched him knocked softly, and a pleasant voice told them to enter.

Gamel was seated at the headmaster's desk, a small leather-bound book opened before him. He slipped in a marker to save his page, closed the book, rose in greeting, and indicated the chair on the opposite side of the desk. Then he nodded to the two guards, who stepped out of the room, closing the door behind them.

"Caesar," he said, lifting the book. "I haven't read Latin since I was a boy. The teachers at the European schools had a very high regard for Latin. I suppose they thought it would have a civilizing influence on Arab barbarians."

Ferrand was too confused to respond. He had expected to find a glassy-eyed fanatic swathed in bandoliers and other bloody tools of his trade. Instead, he was sitting across from a man who seemed perfectly comfortable behind a headmaster's desk.

"You have received the terms for the prisoner exchange from General Sharif?" Gamel asked by way of beginning the meeting.

"I don't know," Ferrand managed to say. He was surprised by the calmness of his own voice. "I was told that I should do two things: make sure that the children were safe and bring your instructions back to the American you spoke with."

Gamel nodded. "The children are safe," he said. Then he jumped up and walked around the desk toward the door. "Come with me."

Ferrand followed him out of the office and past one of the guards who was waiting outside the door with his machine gun at the ready. Gamel opened one of the doors to the dining hall and stepped back so that Ferrand could see.

The boys were gathered in groups around the teachers, using the dining hall as a common classroom. Textbooks were strewn on the tables along with the debris of loose-leaf binders and open notebooks. Elias Metz was in his high-pitched whine, jabbing his finger into the pages of a book that was opened in front of one of the upperclass boys. Harold Hutchings was droning on about a fine point of Italian history, oblivious to the fact that half his audience had fallen asleep.

He focused quickly on Maria. She was sitting on one of the tables, her feet resting on a chair, reading a story to the brats who were gathered around the table. Some of the younger boys seemed interested, but most were fidgeting and playing games with their fingers. Her back was toward him, so he couldn't see her face. But she seemed calm, typically in charge and very involved with her students.

"We didn't want them to miss their lessons," he heard Gamel say. In his voice, Ferrand sensed the cynicism that he had expected. The bastard seemed to think that kidnapping a school full of boys was some sort of intellectual game.

He tore his eyes away from Maria and tried to position the guards for Colonel Smiles. There were six terrorists in the dining hall. Four were stationed around the tables, one at the door to the kitchen, and another at the door that led to the lockers and the washrooms. There seemed to be a steady flow of boys, moving one at a time, toward the washrooms, each glancing uneasily at the guard standing by the door.

"Do they sleep in here?" Ferrand asked, remembering that

Smiles wanted information about the boys' schedule.

"They sleep in their beds," Gamel snapped, "with a guard on each hallway. They're perfectly safe, as long as they do what they are told. So far, there have been no problems. The teachers are doing an excellent job keeping order."

"What about the teachers?" Ferrand pressed. "Do they stay with the children or in their own rooms."

"We keep them together," Gamel answered. Then he laughed softly. "We don't want them to get creative."

Ferrand switched his attention to the weapons the guards were holding. He mentally started through the list of details Smiles had told him to look for.

"So, you can report that the children are well," Gamel said, interrupting his concentration. "Good. Now there is something else I want you to see." He closed the door, blocking Ferrand's last glance toward Maria.

"These wires," Gamel began analytically, "lead to explosive charges set throughout the school. They are carefully placed. It would take about two seconds to turn this entire school into an inferno." He reached above his head, took one of the thin wires in his fingers, and pulled it down so that it was directly in front of Ferrand's eyes. "There is a separate wire to each charge. It would take much longer than two seconds to cut even a few of the wires."

His eyes looked directly into Ferrand's to make sure the teacher understood. "You should tell your military leaders this. I want them to understand that there is no way for them to come onto the school grounds without causing the death of everyone in these buildings—the teachers, the students, my own men as well. If they come over the wall they will rescue nothing but burning debris and dead bodies. The lives of my men are of no consequence. We have been ready to die for many years. But you probably value the lives of the students. I hope you will be able to persuade your leaders that not one student will survive their attack."

He let the wire slip through his fingers, then turned and started back to the headmaster's office. Ferrand followed silently, and watched Gamel circle the large wooden desk and settle comfortably into the headmaster's chair. Ferrand took his seat and waited.

"Point one," Gamel resumed. "Your people have received the terms for the release of the prisoners. You should tell them that those terms are not negotiable. They must all be met."

Ferrand dipped his chin, indicating that he understood.

"Good," Gamel continued. "Now, once they are met, I will need transportation for my men. We will require . . ." He paused and looked solicitously toward Ferrand. "Would you like to write any of this down? It's important that there be no confusion." He turned around a pad of paper that was resting on the desk so that it faced Ferrand and pushed a pencil toward him.

"We need two helicopters with pilots. Each should have a capacity of at least ten passengers. They will land behind the school, on the athletic field. We will board them along with five of our prisoners—four of the children and one of the teachers. This is a point at which your military people are apt to see an opportunity. They should know that the rest of the students will still be in the buildings, locked into one of the rooms. We can blow the buildings from anywhere—the grounds outside, even from the helicopters. So it would be very foolish for a few sharpshooters to try to prevent us from reaching the helicopters and taking off. You can understand that, can't you?"

"I understand," Ferrand answered. He continued writing.

"Good. Next, we will need an airplane. It should be a commercial jet, fully fueled, with a range of at least four thousand miles. There should be a flight crew aboard. No one else. Just the pilots and the flight engineer. The door must be opened, and there must be a boarding staircase in position. The plane will be parked at Leonardo, at the far end of a runway, with no trucks or other planes within a distance of one mile. There should be no traffic on any of the runways."

He paused to let Ferrand's pencil catch up.

"We will land one of the helicopters next to the plane, and some of my men will board it and conduct a search. If there is anything that is even slightly suspicious, the prisoners we are holding will be immediately executed. Do you understand?"

Ferrand nodded that he did.

"Good. If everything is in perfect order, we will land the second helicopter and board the aircraft. Then we will take off immediately—with our five prisoners."

Ferrand's head snapped up.

Gamel smiled in response. "We must continue to hold prisoners," he explained logically. "Otherwise our plane might prove to be an irresistible target for your military. I'm sure the price of an airliner wouldn't stop them from killing us. But I think the lives of four of the children—particularly the ones we will be taking with us—might keep them from foolish acts of reprisal."

"When will the five hostages be released?" Ferrand asked coldly.

"Prisoners," Gamel corrected. "Prisoners of a war that you have forced upon us. When will they be released? As soon as my task force is safely home and we see proof that you are living up to the terms of your agreement with Sharif. Perhaps a few days. Or maybe a week. It should not take very long."

Ferrand tore the page from the pad and set the pencil down on the desk.

"There's one more point," Gamel said. "Perhaps the most important message for you to convey. Your people should know that we have no intention of waiting endlessly for your answer. We want it immediately."

Ferrand reached to retrieve the pencil.

"It is now almost five o'clock. You have twenty-four hours to agree to all of Sharif's terms. He will telephone me here at this desk when he is completely satisfied." Gamel noticed Ferrand's eyes widen. "Yes, telephone," he repeated with a smile. "For a few coins we can use any telephone in the world." Then the smile vanished. "If he doesn't call me by five o'clock tomorrow, you will find one of your students at the front gate. He will be quite dead." Gamel enjoyed the expression of horror that paled Ferrand's face.

"Then we will start the clock again. At five o'clock the next day, you will find another body . . . and then another and another. One prisoner will be executed each day until Sharif informs me that you have agreed to all his demands. Do you understand?" There was no sympathy in his expression. Ferrand was looking into the empty black eyes of a shark.

"I understand," he answered. And then, after a moment of silence, "Is there anything more or can I go now?"

The menacing eyes held his gaze. And then suddenly they clouded in confusion. "I don't think you believe me. That would be most unfortunate. I hope you will not have to hold the first body in your arms before you understand that we are completely serious."

"I will tell them," Ferrand said. He started to rise, but Gamel waved him back into his chair.

"You don't seem concerned," he said challengingly.

"I'm just a messenger," Ferrand answered, remembering the instructions he had gotten from Otis Brown.

Gamel eyed him with obvious suspicion. "I understood you were a teacher," he said.

"I am." He kept his expression blank.

"Where did you study?" Gamel asked, suddenly becoming conversational, as if his grim instructions had never been given.

"Yale," Ferrand said.

Gamel's eyes widened in admiration. "Yale?" He smiled derisively. "I thought Yale produced bankers. I didn't know it was famous for teachers."

"I thought children were more important than money," Ferrand said. His voice was cold and factual. There was no hint he was ready to join Gamel in a friendly conversation.

"I thought so, too," the terrorist leader answered. He rose to signal the end of the meeting.

Ferrand reached the door to the office before he turned back to confront his adversary. "If children are important, how can you talk about murdering them one at a time?"

Gamel nodded that he understood the question. He gave his answer in a very soft voice. "You taught me that I was wrong. You murdered my children."

Brown was waiting in the Fiat just outside the front gate, but Ferrand didn't get in. Instead, he stood next to the car and looked around at the countryside that lay beneath the high point of the hill. He took in the shapes of the tall thin pines and the hues of olive and umber that made Italy different from any place else on earth. The world was a wonder, with room for hundreds of thousands of different kinds of natural treasures living side by side, at peace with one another, their variety blending in a glorious harmony. Differences turned into madness only among men.

He opened the door and saw the anticipation on Brown's face. The government agent was leaning forward, anxious for his report.

"The killing starts in twenty-four hours," Ferrand said calmly.

President Reynolds turned away from the television as soon as the secretary of state had stepped down from the podium in the press room at the State Department.

"He handled it well," he said to his assistant, who had joined him in his office to watch the press conference.

"Extremely well," the assistant agreed. John Powers watched the president search his pockets for a cigarette, then took the package that he always carried from his own pocket, handed the president a low-tar filter, and produced a lighter. Powers had been the president's political advisor for fourteen years, joining him when Reynolds had first left the House to try for the Senate. His new title of special assistant to the president was a transparent cover that gave a sense of national purpose to his work of keeping the party in line behind its leader.

"Think anyone believed him?" the president asked.

Powers shrugged. "Those who don't know any better should have been pleased. And those who do know better understand that he said exactly what he had to say."

It had been the standard theatrical production that three successive administrations had rolled out whenever terrorists had taken United States citizens. We were outraged at this barbaric assault on fundamental human decency. We were appalled at so flagrant a violation of the basic principles of international relations. No, we would not negotiate with terrorists. To do so would simply be to invite further acts of terrorism. We were marshaling the influence of decent governments all over the world and bringing the full weight of the international community to bear on these pirates.

The secretary had concluded with an implied threat. "If any harm comes to even one of these children, we will track the guilty parties to the ends of the earth and bring them to justice."

"Does that mean there will be military reprisals?" a reporter had asked.

"It would not be prudent," the secretary of state had answered, dodging the question, "to discuss at this time the exact measures we are prepared to take. But let me say that this administration will not yield to terrorists. Nor will we allow harm to any American citizen to go unpunished."

It was all farce, of course. Lines of communication to Sharif had already been opened via the Egyptian government. The entire administration was struggling to assess his demands and decide which concessions had to be made. Some of the Palestinian prisoners would certainly be freed. The Italians were already working on the excuse they would use to grant clemency to the prisoners in their jails. And the Israelis, though publicly assured that the United States would not ask them to free prisoners, understood it would not be wise to become a stumbling block in an American agreement to save the lives of its schoolchildren.

The "marshaled influence of decent governments" was an empty cannon at best. The French stepped lightly in Middle Eastern affairs because of their thirst for Arab oil. The Germans couldn't afford to upset a major market for their automobiles and chemicals. The Italians had reached an accommodation with the terrorists. Everyone would mumble a word of concern and sympathy. No one would lift a finger to pressure the Arab governments in the region.

Even the threat of retaliation was hollow. The terrorists, at the end of their mission, wouldn't be returning to a Beau Geste fort topped by a colorful flag. They would disappear into the refugee camps of Lebanon, Syria, and Gaza, or move into apartment buildings that they shared with a dozen families. The United States wouldn't be able to find them, even with its surveillance satellites and high-flying spy planes. And it wouldn't be able to bomb them, even with all the infrared and laser technologies. Not without risking international incidents with governments the United States was trying to influence. Not without killing more innocent people than the terrorists had killed themselves.

Still, Americans liked to hear their government talk tough. They enjoyed hearing their ethics called honorable while someone else's ethics were labeled barbaric. And they rallied around the promise that, in the end, their view of right would triumph.

The government officials who spoke these words, and the reporters who noted them, knew they were meaningless. But they also knew that, with its citizens held captive, a government was required to make a statement. And they appreciated the fact that governments couldn't make a habit of admitting their own helplessness.

President Reynolds drew on the cigarette. He despised the posturing and hypocrisy of politics. Why couldn't the truth be told? Was the image of invincibility that essential to the mental well-being of Americans? Did he really have to smoke his damn cigarettes in a closet in order to protect the purity of the presidency? Why couldn't he simply say, "They've got us by the short hairs. We're going to lose this one"? Wouldn't that make more sense than risking the lives of children? Why couldn't he just light up a cigarette in public and say, "Look, I'm addicted to the stinking things. If you need pure lungs, vote for someone else."

"Who's out there?" he asked, already certain he wouldn't like the answer.

"All the biggies," Powers answered. "If Sharif really wanted to bring us to our knees, he'd take over the Cabinet Room. There must be two dozen Fortune Five Hundred hotshots inside."

As soon as Reynolds had been told just who the fathers of the captured children were, he had sent each of them a note of sympathy together with an invitation to a personal briefing. They were important men—important to the careers of scores of congressmen and senators and only God knew how many local politicians who supported his party's fortunes. His expression of concern would be recognized and appreciated at every level of government. And besides, these weren't the kinds of people who would be satisfied by the vague pronouncements that the secretary of state had just made.

He crushed the cigarette into an ashtray bearing the presidential seal, stood and lifted his jacket from the back of his chair. "Let's face the music," he told Powers. The special assistant to the president was already opening the door.

Reynolds remembered most of the men who rose when he entered the Cabinet Room. Some had made top-level presentations before Senate committees on which he had served. Some had worked with government commissions. All had been approached for support during his presidential campaign.

Their names were associated with specific corporations. But because of their positions on the boards of numerous companies and civil commissions, their influence reached far beyond the business interests of just a few corporations.

They were the managers of the United States economy, the trustees of its educational institutions, the directors of its charities. They were the power brokers of a nation that liked to think it existed without benefit of power brokers. They paid the required respect to Reynolds as keeper of the presidency, but none was in awe of him. Each believed he possessed far more talent than the president of the United States. Each was confident he had a better grasp of the real workings of American government. Each was certain he had more wealth. All were true to the Constitution in that they saw the president as an employee of the people. And since they managed the people, the president was their employee.

Reynolds began with a quiet review of the obvious, avoiding the patriotic clichés that had liberally punctuated the secretary of state's presentation. Then he got down to the hard facts.

There was a Delta Force rescue team standing by at the school as a precautionary measure. If something went wrong inside Saint Anselm's that put the boys in immediate danger, the rescue squad would act. But they had no intention of storming the school. Any such show of force could easily result in harm to at least some of the boys, and the safety of the children was the primary concern.

He hoped to negotiate their release. This should have been shocking news to his audience, most of whom had somberly advised their shareholders, business groups, and old-boy networks that a "great nation cannot counsel with terrorists." But rather than shock, their faces registered relief.

"There are some concessions we can certainly make," the president said, "but there are others that we can't offer." When pressed, he told the business leaders assembled that the free movement of the Sixth Fleet in the Mediterranean couldn't be bargained away. "And, of course, we can't admit to Sharif's right to war reparations."

"So all we can discuss is the release of prisoners," the chairman of a major money center bank challenged.

"At this time, yes," Reynolds admitted.

"Will that be enough?" the president of a retail chain asked.

Reynolds started into an evasive answer but then remembered his audience. "We can't be sure," he said simply. Then his eyes dropped and focused on his folded hands. "Personally, I doubt if it will be enough." He looked up into narrowed, questioning eyes. "Every hoodlum who takes American or Israeli hostages wants to have prisoners released. In my opinion, Sharif wants to achieve a much larger success. He wants to do what no Arab leader has yet been able to do. And that's emerge as the unquestioned leader of the Arab people.

"But he doesn't want to kill children," Reynolds hastened to add. "That would stain him with blood that he'd never be able to wash off his hands. He holds us captive with the threat of an unspeakable crime. But that same unspeakable crime also holds him captive. So, I think he will accept something far short of his present demands. But at the same time, I think it will have to be something more than just the release of a few prisoners."

The room fell quiet. The president had already ruled out two of Sharif's terms. Yet he was implying that further concessions were necessary. With their sons' lives at stake, the business leaders needed something much more concrete.

"Perhaps," the bank chairman said softly over the stillness, "there are things we can do best as private citizens. Perhaps there are . . . investments we might make through Sharif that would . . . offset his economic demands."

Reynolds picked up on the implications immediately. "I don't think that would be prudent," he said, "at least not at this stage. We have national policies—vital interests to protect. We have to speak with one voice. It would be disastrous if our business leaders began negotiating behind the back of their government."

He was interrupted by the head of a large chemical concern. "We have more than national policies to protect, Mr. President. Our most vital interests are the lives of our sons." He looked around the table and found no one taking issue. "You said there was a rescue force standing by," the executive continued, "in case something went wrong inside the school. It seems to me that every minute we lose increases the chances of something going wrong. I think I'm speaking for everyone here when I say that I want my boy out of there right now. I think we've got to find a way to give Sharif what he wants and give it to him quickly. I don't want my son to pay the price if our delicate negotiations get *too* delicate."

Again there were no dissenters.

"I don't think," President Reynolds insisted, "that we can have two standards. We can't refuse to make concessions for some hostages and then rush to make concessions for others. We will do everything we can to get your sons out of there as quickly as possible. But appearances have value in international relations, and we have to maintain the appearance of a united government."

"You have to maintain appearances," the chemical executive said sharply. "I have to save my son."

Reynolds nodded. He understood the anguish of the men around him. But he also understood that he couldn't allow private citizens, no matter how powerful, to negotiate national policy. He stood at his place to signal the end of the meeting.

"Gentlemen, I will keep you completely briefed on every development as it occurs. We need additional time, but I hope to have positive news for you very shortly. As I said at the outset, my prime concern is the safety of your sons."

"How much time?" a voice challenged.

Reynolds paused on his way to the door. "Perhaps a few hours," he said. "I hope not much longer than that."

It was more than a hope. A few hours was all he had. He could see the United States government beginning to unravel. The war hawks, like Senator Bradberry, were thrashing about for some sort of decisive action—a precision strike that would give substance to their country's declarations of its own power. The only requirement was that it not endanger their children, which was also the only requirement that could not be met. And the power brokers were already rushing forward with concessions that had not yet even been demanded.

Could Sharif have known? Was he brilliant enough to understand the weaknesses of his enemy? Did he appreciate how easily the delicate balance of self-interests that was the United States government could be upset? Perhaps that was the reason why he was demanding impossible concessions. It was not the concessions he wanted but rather the total destruction of the American mystique.

Had he also taken an accurate measure of his adversary, the president of the United States? Reynolds had no illusions about himself. He wasn't a charismatic figure. He wasn't a great thinker. He *was* a skillful politician who had somehow managed to become the least offensive common denominator in dozens of political caucuses that had advanced his name in nomination. Did Sharif know he wasn't strong enough to command the powerful men in his own country? Had he realized that a least offensive common denominator couldn't hold the frail coalitions of American politics together if they were threatened with enough pain?

Reynolds had to move quickly. Time was on Sharif's side. The longer he applied the pressure, the more defections there would be from Reynolds' leadership. And each defection would accelerate the country's free-fall from its role as a world power.

When he reached his office, the hourglass that had fixed itself in his mind was abruptly turned over. The sand began to fall. His secretary handed him a message from Otis Brown, telling him of Gamel's promise. The first body would be at the gate tomorrow at five o'clock, Rome time.

He had only eighteen hours left.

night

He would never get it past his teachers. Billy Tepper carrying a leather-bound dictionary? They'd know immediately he was up to something. But these other creeps. They were so busy cocking their machine guns they wouldn't know a dictionary from a comic book. It would just look like another schoolbook that he was carrying down to the dining hall.

With a razor blade, he was carefully cutting the center out of each page, creating a space exactly the same size as his video recorder. It was monotonous work. The blade could only slice through about twenty pages at a time. And he was distracted by the definitions of words relating to sexual acts or parts of the female anatomy whenever he came across them. He'd read the definition of *breast* at least half a dozen times and had been amazed that *teat* wasn't spelled with an *i*.

Billy had already figured out the solution to one of his problems—the security monitors. The cameras were scanning the walls, sending images of the placid countryside to the monitors along the coaxial cable he had discovered in the vault between the two buildings. With nothing more complicated than the connector from his video games, he could tap the coaxial cable. Then he could record an hour's worth of exactly what the terrorist in the security office was watching. All he would have to do is pick his moment, then play the untroubled walls he had recorded earlier back into the monitors. The guard would be looking at yesterday's serenity while today's Marines were coming over the walls.

He placed the video recorder into the space he had made in the dictionary. It was still half an inch too high, so he would have to cut through the *R*s and into the *S*s. But at least the end was in sight. Once he was done, he would be able to carry his recorder right under the guards' noses without anyone getting suspicious.

His solution did have a few shortcomings. Like the possibility of a weather change. He had decided that the best time for the attack would be immediately after dinner, when all the boys were still assembled in the dining hall. But that was the time when clouds that had sucked up Mediterranean moisture during the day sometimes got together for a half hour of violent rain. Billy figured the guards weren't too swift, but even the slowest of them was apt to catch on if he were watching a rainstorm through the window and a glorious sunset on his security monitors. To make the scheme foolproof, he would have had to record a whole range of weather conditions so he could play back something appropriate. But there just wasn't enough time.

Another problem was the few moments it would take him to tap the cable. There would be an instant when the monitors in the security office would go blank. There would also be an interruption when he turned on his recorder to play back the tape he had made. The guard would be watching one section of the wall when suddenly the image would jump to a prerecorded section. What he needed was a distraction, something to take the guard's attention away from the monitors as he connected his tap, and later, in the final moments before the invasion, when he turned on the playback. It wouldn't have to be much. Maybe Snuffy Bradberry going into one of his fits in the hallway between the administration office and the security office. Or maybe he could get Miss Manetti to walk past the doorway. That would be guaranteed to get the guard out of his chair so he could watch her hips move as she walked away. Give him ten seconds of Manetti's body, and the guard wouldn't get suspicious even if he looked back at his monitors and saw a commercial!

Billy also knew what he had to do about the guns. There was no possible way of disabling them all at once. If there had been just two or three guards, he could have probably created some sort of commotion, moved in close to the guys, and dropped them with croquet mallets. But with half a dozen armed men in the dining hall, there was little chance of getting to them all. And even one guy with one of those Kalashnikov assault guns could hurt a lot of kids.

Since he couldn't remove the guns, what he had to do was remove the kids. And that meant getting them down into the wine cellar. The Screaming Eagles and the terrorists could shoot the whole school to pieces without hitting anyone in the wine cellar. And even if the explosives were detonated, bringing down the whole building, people in the wine cellar probably wouldn't even hear the blast.

From the tables in the dining hall, it was only a few steps to the kitchen. At the end of the evening meal, the boys would be milling in and out of the kitchen as they returned their trays and tried to steal second desserts. During that time, they would be under the supervision of just one of the guards, the one posted near the kitchen door. If they moved to the back of the kitchen, where the door to the wine cellar was hidden in a cupboard, every one of the boys could be made to vanish.

That was what he had to do. But he still hadn't figured out how to do it. The problem was, it had to be every one of the boys. And it had to be every one of the teachers. He wasn't going to leave a few stragglers in the hands of the guards to pay the penalty for the ones who got away. But if they all disappeared into the kitchen at the same time, even these jerks would get suspicious. So once again, he needed a distraction. Something had to happen that would get the guards out of the dining hall, even if only for a few seconds.

There was also an organizational problem to be solved. Everyone had to know exactly what was happening and exactly what he was supposed to do. But the brats were hopeless. There wasn't a chance in the world that all of them would follow instructions. Hell, it took a week just to teach them to play poker! What he had to do was divide the kids up into groups and appoint a leader for each group. Which meant he needed a messenger, someone who could move from room to room and tell the leaders which children they were responsible for and what they were supposed to do with them. He needed someone who could organize the brats. Which meant he needed Miss Manetti.

Maria glanced up from the homework she had been shuffling aimlessly—randomly arranged multiplication problems on sheets of blue-lined paper. She was supposed to be correcting the assignment, noting the mistakes in the margins with a red pencil and assigning grades. Instead, she was picturing each of the boys as she read his name at the top of his work.

They were holding up better than she had thought possible. In the first hours of the siege, she had been certain that at least some of the younger boys would collapse under the terrifying strain. She had been prepared, listening for the first sobs of uncontrolled crying, ready to scoop up the child before he could bolt toward an open door, before he could rush past a guard who might react instinctively by squeezing a trigger. But none of the boys had succumbed to panic. Instead, they drew more closely to her and became more involved in the make-work projects she laid out before them in the dining hall. The normal routine became their security blankets in the face of the monstrous interruption to their lives. The silly stories they read in their readers and the insignificant arithmetic problems she assigned were the perfect defense against the terrifying presence of the guns that hovered over them.

She glanced around at the other teachers, men and women all confined together under the searching eyes of a silent guard. They were herded into the faculty lounge, a carpeted room with a random arrangement of soft chairs and side tables. The clothes they had worn since the first hours of the takeover were rumpled from the few hours of fitful sleep they had been able to get curled up in the chairs or stretched out on the carpeted floor. Beards had appeared on the faces of the men who were generally clean-shaven, emphasizing the pallor of their skin. The women had aged in the absence of their cosmetics. They were all exhausted by the lack of sleep and primitive living arrangements enforced by the guards. But most of all, they were bending under the stress of imprisonment. Unlike the boys, who were able to lose themselves in the routine, the teachers were never unaware that even the most trivial incident could touch off a slaughter. The resulting fear was taking its toll.

She studied the headmaster, who was sitting perfectly straight in a leather chair, his palms resting on top of the curved stuffed arms. He was nearly catatonic, with his chin raised and his eyes staring vacantly into space. Of all of them, he had suffered the greatest shock. The sight of armed men, symbolic of a primitive world ruled by barbaric ignorance, was more than his mind could bear. Even a temporary triumph over his cherished world of civility and learning was beyond his comprehension. His brain had simply shut down to avoid the obscenity that was all around him.

Maria understood the terrorists' methods. They knew they had little to fear from the children, so they had no qualms about returning the boys to their separate rooms. Without the presence of an adult to organize them and lend approval to their plans, they were incapable of organizing an escape or mounting a counterattack. But the teachers, if left unsupervised, might begin to collaborate. They might weigh their options and develop some sort of plan. So they were kept under constant surveillance: in the dining room during the day while they kept the boys under control, and in the recreation room at night, where they were locked up.

It was a logical solution for a military mind to arrive at, but it made no sense to a teacher. To Maria, the greatest danger lay in the unpredictability of the boys. At any moment, any one of them could panic and try an impossible escape. She could picture any one of the older boys tying bedsheets together and trying to climb down the outside of the building. She could see one of her babies simply sitting up in the middle of the night and deciding it was time to run for the front gate. They needed the teachers with them at all times as symbols of stability, as counsellors who would discourage their impulsive reactions. Their separation, she thought, grew more dangerous by the hour. Somehow, she had to get to the terrorist leader and persuade him that the teachers belonged with the students at all times.

I have to see you. I'm talking with Mr. Ferrand.

Her head snapped up from the papers she was flipping through aimlessly. She read the message again, not quite sure what it was she was reading. Then she realized she was holding a bomb, and that her sudden interest might be noticed by the guard. She turned the paper into the stack of finished work and tried to look attentive to the next page of arithmetic problems. Slowly, she turned her head and glanced toward the guard. His eyes were focused on the other side of the room where Harold Hutchings was tossing in a chair as he tried to find a comfortable sleeping position. Carefully, Maria picked up the page she had just set down, a blue-lined sheet identical to the papers she was correcting. She read it once more. This time she noticed the name signed at the bottom of the page. *Billy T.*

She tried to think back. The younger children had been gathered around a dining hall table, working on the multiplication problems she had assigned. She had collected the papers and then placed the stack on top of her books at the next table. And, then, Billy Tepper squeezed between her and the papers on his way to the bathroom.

That's when it must have happened. He probably wrote the note while he was doing his own work, and kept it in his notebook waiting for a chance to slip it to her. When he saw the stack of schoolwork, he must have pushed his note into the pile knowing she would find it when she corrected the papers.

How could he be talking with Edward? They had ripped out all the telephones in the first hour after their invasion. She knew the phone lines were still working. The terrorist leader had received phone calls in the headmaster's office and had placed at least one outgoing call. But what good were phone lines without telephones? Could Billy be sending some sort of signals from his window? But how would he know where to send them? He couldn't possibly know where Edward was. She didn't even know.

"Dear God," she heard herself whisper. This was exactly what she was afraid of. If Tepper was signaling with a flashlight from his window, the guards would be sure to notice it. The takeover of the school was all a big game to Billy. He had no idea of the danger. He had even tried to get the guards into a soccer game. And now he was signaling to someone on the outside.

She folded the papers into her notebook and pushed them aside. She had to get to Billy Tepper right now, before he did something insane. Something that could get him killed, or that could bring reprisals down on other students. But she didn't want to call attention to him. She didn't want to ask for him by name. What she needed was a reason to go into the old building to visit two or three of the rooms so that Billy's room wouldn't be singled out.

Maria got up from her chair and walked carefully toward the guard. He was attracted by her movement and, when he realized she was coming toward him, pushed himself away from the wall he had been leaning on. The gun that had been sloping from his shoulder was suddenly erect and pointing toward her.

"Do you speak English?" she asked, trying to smile unthreateningly despite the gun pointed at her. The guard's jaw tightened but there was no comprehension in his eyes. Maria tried a few words in Italian. The man's expression remained unchanged. She began to pantomime, patting her hip to indicate the pistol that the terrorist leader carried. "Gamel . . . commander," she said, exaggerating the pronounciation. She pointed to herself. "I," she said, "need to talk"—she moved her hand in front of her mouth to show words—"with Gamel."

The guard's eyes didn't even flicker.

Maria started into her routine once more but was interrupted by a single shouted syllable. She didn't recognize the word but she understood its meaning and stopped abruptly. The guard pointed toward the chair she had just left. She knew he was ordering her to sit down. Once again, Maria pointed to the location of Gamel's pistol. "Commander . . . Gamel," she begged, emphasizing each syllable. The guard took a threatening step toward her, jabbing his finger toward the chair. Maria retreated, backing away for a few steps and turning back toward her place.

The guard remained poised, his weapon at the ready, until she was seated. Her mind began racing again. She had to find some way to get to Billy Tepper before he violated the uneasy peace that was keeping her children alive. She would see Gamel in the morning. He would be in the dining hall when the children were brought in from the old building. But Billy was probably at work right now, endangering them all.

She caught the guard's movement from the corner of her eye. He had backed up to the door, eased it open, and taken a half step out of the recreation room and into the hall. She heard him stage whispering in his unintelligible language, and then heard a response from somewhere outside. There were footsteps, and then the guard stepped back, clearing the doorway for Gamel.

The terrorist leader stood for a moment, staring directly at her, then beckoned her to follow with a toss of his chin. Maria could feel her knees weakening as she walked behind him.

Gamel turned abruptly as soon as she had passed through the door. "You have something to say?" he demanded. She wasn't sure whether it was a question or an accusation.

"I thought about the medication," she said, aware that her voice carried no conviction. "Several of the children take medication. Is anyone giving it to them?" For the first time since his initial monologue, he looked uncertain. "There is a nurse during the day," Maria forced herself to continue. "But she was outside when you . . . took over. We haven't been giving them their medication."

He weighed the question. "What medication? How many children?"

"Several," she said, trying to think of the names of those boys who were frequent visitors to the nurse's office. "Some of the smaller children, and two or three of the older boys."

"Prescribed medication?" He was pushing for specific answers, and Maria could feel her plan beginning to unravel.

"Yes," she finally managed. "For some of the boys. Others just get stomach medicines—the kind you buy in the store."

"Who gets prescribed medicine?" Gamel demanded. "Give me a name."

She searched her memory frantically. "Bradberry," she said. "The Bradberry boy. He has terrible asthma. He wakes up choking."

His hard face softened, but his smile remained cynical. "Then there should be a prescription bottle with his name on it. If you're telling the truth, we'll find the bottle. But if there is no bottle, then you must be lying, isn't that so?"

She tried to sound assured. "That's right. You should find his medication in the nurse's office. In the cabinet."

Without taking his eyes from her, he snapped off a command in his native language. The guard jumped to his side, and Gamel gave him brief instructions, incomprehensible to Maria except for the word *Bradberry*, which she heard him pronounce very carefully. Then the guard turned abruptly and rushed down the hallway, leaving Maria and Gamel standing together, their faces only inches apart.

"You're still not afraid," he said, puzzled by a woman wiling to risk his anger.

"I'm very much afraid," Maria admitted.

He nodded his approval. "You should be. Because if you are trying to trick me—if there is no medication with that name on it—I'm going to make an example out of you."

She suddenly felt cold. She had no idea what medication Jimmy Bradberry took. She had been bluffing, and he had called her bluff. She saw only a blur as his hand snapped up from his side, and stared in horror at the shiny surface of the pistol. The barrel circled in front of her face, then touched the skin of her forehead.

"Perhaps here," Gamel said thoughtfully. Then the pistol circled again like the head of a cobra about to strike. He touched it to the hollow of her throat. "Or perhaps here." He let the cold metal rest there for a moment. "Unless you're not certain," he offered. "Perhaps you were just imagining that they needed medication."

Maria tried to remember the prayers the nuns had taught her in school. Then she heard the footsteps of the guard returning with her verdict.

Ferrand wrapped his hands around the mug of hot coffee, hoping to stop them from shaking. He was physically exhausted after two days without sleep. And he was emotionally drained by his growing fear for the safety of the prisoners at Saint Anselm's. He knew the questions were important, but he was irritated by their constant repetition. Or was he irritated by the lack of precision in his own answers?

"Try again," Colonel Smiles was pressing him. "Just try to picture one of the guards you saw in the dining hall."

Ferrand squeezed his eyes shut.

"Look at his belt. What do you see? Is it a military belt? Is there anything hanging from it? Look for ammunition clips. Look for grenades. Is there anything you can remember?"

He was shaking his head even before Smiles was finished. "I'd be making it up, Colonel. I just never noticed the belts."

"And you never saw any radios," Smiles repeated. "No one ever used a hand-held radio."

"No one used a radio. I'm sure of that," Ferrand said. "I'm not sure whether anyone was carrying a radio."

Smiles began reviewing his notes. Ferrand knew he was disappointed by the number of unanswered questions.

"You've done one hell of a job," Otis Brown said.

Ferrand looked surprised. It seemed as if they had been asking him questions for the past three hours, and he had left most of them blank.

"Outstanding," Smiles said. "But I think you've had about all you can take. You better get some sleep."

"I haven't told you anything," Ferrand protested.

Smiles lifted the plans of the school grounds and buildings that Ferrand had redrawn. The overgrown areas of the grounds were shaded in, in contrast to the lawns and playing fields. The small break in the wall was marked. Within the buildings, the location of the detonator was clearly noted as well as the path of the wires as they emerged from the dining hall. The tables were precisely positioned along with the seating arrangements of the children and the stations of the guards who watched over them. Gamel's command center in the headmaster's office was circled.

"You gave us this," the colonel reminded Ferrand. "If we have to go in there, this is our field map. It's a hell of a lot more than we usually have."

He remembered then that he had given them a great deal of information. He had identified the communications link between Gamel and Sharif: the ordinary telephone that sat on the headmaster's desk. Sharif simply passed information to a collaborator in Italy. And the collaborator simply dialed the headmaster's office and relayed the message over the telephone. He had also been able to identify the types of weapons the terrorists were carrying. He remembered nothing of the gun that had been pointed at his eyes, but when Smiles had shown him photographs of dozens of weapons, he immediately recognized the Soviet Kalashnikov assault rifles the guards inside the dining hall were carrying. He had also given them the number of guards on the scene, verified that the security monitors were operating and that they were manned, and repositioned one of the doors he had originally drawn incorrectly.

Smiles and Brown had been particularly interested in his description of the calm that prevailed within the school. The children were relaxed and involved with their lessons. The teachers seemed to be maintaining normal order—more normal than during a typical school day. Ferrand seemed sure that the hostages would not give their captors any reason to panic.

And, of course, he had relayed Gamel's demands for his escape, detailing the written notes he had brought out of the building with him. Smiles had drawn the landing positions of the helicopters on the map and carefully studied the terrain between the buildings and landing point over which the terrorists and their hostages would have to travel. He had become emotional when he repeated Gamel's threat to begin killing hostages at five o'clock the next day.

"You believe him?" Otis Brown had pressed.

"Absolutely," he had replied.

"Why?" Brown had demanded. "Most threats are empty. The last thing terrorists want to do is harm their hostages. The hostages are their only security."

"I was sitting across a desk, looking right at him," Ferrand had reminded them. "It was like talking to a perfectly civilized, refined, polite human being. Like talking to one of the teachers, or the father of one of the students. Except when you looked into his eyes. It was frightening. You could see that the dignified person is only a shell. There's madness living inside. He wants us to miss his deadline. He wants to pick his first victim and leave the body at the gate. That's what he's here for. He didn't come to win a victory and fly away. He came to pay us back for his own children." He had repeated Gamel's final comment over and over. "You murdered my children." And he had finally challenged Smiles. "Did we really fire a shell right into his schoolhouse?"

Smiles hadn't answered.

Brown had finally nodded in agreement with Ferrand. "I think he means it. I agree with your assessment. He's here to pay us back."

Ferrand pulled himself up out of the chair and climbed the worn wooden steps that led to the bedrooms. He pulled off his shoes without untying the laces and fell back onto the pillow. His body tried to find rest, but his mind was locked onto the dining hall filled with boys. And there was Maria, sitting up on the table, teaching them to read and write.

Move them into a smaller room . . . take away the sunlight that streamed in through the windows . . . and it could have been Gamel's basement schoolhouse. Instead of Maria, it would be Gamel's wife sitting up on a table or another piece

of discarded furniture. Instead of the scrubbed, light-com-
plected faces, the boys would be dark and stained from the
streets. There would be no textbooks, just slates or sheets of
scrap paper. But everything else would be the same. The
children would be distracted, turning to one another in whispered conspiracies against their teacher. And the woman
would be working against all odds to bring about a miracle.
To teach them to read without their even suspecting that
they were being taught. To make them love learning before
they could begin to appreciate what it was to learn.

To Ferrand, teaching had been a pleasant distraction.
Something he could use to delay the more important decisions about a long-term career. Saint Anselm's combined his
love of sports with an interest in literature and threw an opportunity for foreign travel into the bargain. A pleasant way
to spend a year or two before he got serious. His arguments
with Maria had sprung from their different views about their
work and future. He wanted Maria to join him in something
important. She couldn't think of anything more important
than what they were doing now.

But he was beginning to understand what she had been
telling him all along. The schoolhouse was the most sacred of
all man's institutions. Any schoolhouse. Maria's. Gamel's.
What did it matter? They were all places where ignorance
was cured. And then crashing through the roof into that
sanctuary came the embodiment of all ignorance—a hot,
shaped projectile packed with explosives.

He could see the horror on the children's faces in the fraction of a second it took the projectile to detonate. The flash
was blinding, a pure white light so intense it bleached away
the color of skin and the shape of faces. Then all he saw were
ghostly silhouettes, the forms of bodies picked bare by the
heat. He couldn't tell whose bodies they were. Was it Jimmy
Bradberry and Henry Giles and Billy Tepper and the boys
who were kicking a soccer ball on the green fields of Saint
Anselm's? Or were they the boys that Gamel had gathered
from the crumbling buildings of a Lebanese refugee camp?

Was the woman Maria? Or was she a smaller, darker girl clutching at the ashes of her own baby? And the screams. What language were they in? Did agony have a language? Or was it the world's only universal language?

He felt his body trembling, not with pity but with rage. The schoolhouse, more sacred than any cathedral, had been violated. Learning, the only religion Maria believed in, had been defiled. Someone had to pay. But who? Who had been destroyed? He couldn't make out the faces. He couldn't understand the screams.

Ferrand sat upright in the bed. There was pounding on the bedroom door and a voice calling his name. But he was more aware of the pounding of his own heart and the sweat soaking through his shirt.

"Just a minute," he called as he swung his feet to the floor and tried to push them into his still-tied shoes. It took a minute for him to open the door and recognize Colonel Smiles' adjutant.

"There's a message from the school," the adjutant told him. "Colonel Smiles asks that you join him."

> Mr. Ferrand, I've figured out how to take care of the monitors. These jerks will never see you coming. If you attack at 7:30 right when were finished with diner I should be able to get all the kids and teachers into the wine cellar where no one will get hurt. I am still working on the bombs. I think I know what to do but I can't do it until tomorrow nite. So you should attack on Friday right after diner unless I have to change the plan. Billy.

"Sweet Jesus," he said as he handed the message back to Otis Brown.

"We told him to sit tight, to wait for instructions," Smiles said in frustration. "What the hell is he trying to do?"

"He's a kid," Ferrand snapped. "He's fifteen years old and he's absolutely sure we're coming in to rescue him. What he's doing is trying to help. For Christ's sake, he can't even spell. You expect him to figure out that all the brains in the United States government can't outsmart a dozen terrorists?"

"He ought to be able to figure out that he can get them all killed," Smiles shot back, squeezing the words through clenched teeth.

Brown raised his hands to put a stop to the exchange. "We're all tired. The boy can't understand what we're up against." He waited until Ferrand and Smiles had turned away from one another. "But we do have to stop him," he added. "I hate to use that telephone line again. Even if they don't know what a computer transmission sounds like, they may know that someone is calling in on one of the lines. It's dangerous. But I think it's even more dangerous to let this boy think that we're about to attack. I think we've got to send him an unmistakable warning."

"He's just a kid," Ferrand repeated. "He'll believe what he wants to believe."

Brown pushed his glasses up to his forehead and pressed the heels of his hands against his eyes. "Do your best," he told Ferrand. "You tell us what to say and we'll send it to his computer. I think it's essential that he stop whatever it is he's doing before he's discovered. We've got a very good chance of negotiating those boys out of there. A much better chance than we do of rescuing them. But if"—he looked down at the message—"Billy . . . gets himself killed, or gets a few other boys killed, then any negotiations could go straight to hell."

Ferrand nodded. He sat down at the table and took a pencil and a sheet of paper.

"What's this kid like?" Smiles suddenly asked from across the room.

Ferrand found himself laughing. "Like no kid you've ever met," he said. He started to write, then looked up at Smiles and told the colonel about Billy's phone taps. Before he'd finished the story he recognized that Smiles' interest was more than casual.

"You think he really can disable the televisions?"

Ferrand didn't hesitate. "Absolutely. I don't know how he'll do it, but if Billy Tepper says the televisions will go out at seven-thirty on Friday, I wouldn't book commercial time on a big TV special."

Brown interrupted. "I don't think we should be considering employing the skills of a child with so much at risk."

"Of course not," Smiles agreed. "But the kid is right. He saw something that we all missed."

Brown and Ferrand looked up at him.

"The wine cellar," Smiles said. "We saw it as a bunker where the terrorists could herd the boys so we couldn't get to them. We saw it as an insurmountable problem. But it's not. It's what Billy sees it as—a place where no one will get hurt."

"Much too dangerous," Brown said.

"I know," Smiles agreed. "But suppose we did have to go in there. Suppose the negotiations collapsed and Gamel started to do what we all agree he came to do. What would be our two biggest problems?"

Neither Brown nor Ferrand interrupted with an answer.

"The monitors," Smiles said. "With the monitors working they have half a minute, maybe even a full minute's warning that we're coming. The kids would be dead before we reached the buildings.

"And what about the kids themselves? With the kids in the dining hall or in their rooms, some of them would be bound to get killed even if we took Gamel by total surprise. But if they were in the wine cellar they'd be safe—at least for two or three minutes. And that's all the time we'd need to clean the place out."

He picked up the plans that Ferrand had redrawn. "Look," he said, pointing to the position of the kitchen door. "The kids are right outside the kitchen. At the end of the meal, they're probably going in and out of the kitchen. What are they—ten, maybe fifteen steps from the door to the wine cellar."

"I told you it was a heavy door," Ferrand added.

Smiles nodded. "You did. You said it was probably a blast-proof door left over from when the Germans used the place as a command center. If the kids were inside, it would probably take thirty seconds, maybe even a minute, for Gamel's people to get through the door. I can guarantee you that if the monitors are out, I can have troops in the kitchen within thirty seconds of the moment we fire the first shot."

"That would be twenty-nine seconds after Gamel had blown the entire school," Brown said coldly.

Smiles nodded. "I know. I'm not proposing we go into the place. But this kid has already figured out two of our biggest problems and found solutions for them." He looked at Ferrand. "You really believe he can fix those monitors?"

"I think you should write the message," Brown said to Ferrand before the teacher could respond. "We want to stop that boy. We don't want to encourage him."

Ferrand began drafting the words that would be sent to Billy's computer.

Maria heard the guard's footsteps but couldn't turn her head to find him. Her chin was tilted up by the top of Gamel's pistol with the barrel resting against her throat. All she could see was the thin white smile against the outlines of his face. She knew he was waiting for the evidence to be presented before he pulled the trigger.

She heard the musical words as the guard delivered his report. She saw Gamel raise a small medicine vial between his face and hers. She closed her eyes. Then she realized that the barrel of the pistol was no longer pressing against her skin.

"Good," she heard his voice whisper. Maria opened her eyes and watched him lower the pistol to his side. "You were telling the truth. James Bradberry needs his medication." He held out the brown glass container, and she took it from him. "There is also medicine for several other boys," he admitted, "just as you said." He took the keys to the medicine cabinet from the guard and dangled them in front of her. "Get whatever medication you need and take it to the children." Without turning from her he gave instructions to the guard. Not a single syllable made any sense to her.

"I have instructed him to accompany you. When you have administered the medications, he will bring you back to the faculty room. Signal to him when you need to return to the boys. He will understand." He dropped the keys into her hand.

"Thank you," Maria said. She turned to follow the guard.

"I'm making you responsible for the boys' behavior," Gamel said before she could leave. "You are very concerned for them, and they seem to respect you. Do whatever you have to in order to keep them comfortable and quiet."

Maria nodded. She was about to acknowledge what she thought to be a humanitarian gesture, but Gamel continued.

"I hope you will take the responsibility very seriously. Because if one of the boys gives us trouble, you will share in the punishment. We will kill the boy, whoever he is. And then I will kill you. Do you understand?"

"I understand," Maria answered.

"Good," Gamel said cheerfully. "We understand each other."

She followed the guard to the nurse's office and gathered the prescription medicines and other medications. Then she led the guard through the empty dining hall and into the old building.

She began on the ground floor where the brats slept, tapping gently on the doors that showed light spilling out into the hallways. Most of the boys simply needed to see her and hear her say "good night." A few complained of nausea and swallowed spoonfuls of the pink syrup used to calm nervous stomachs.

She tried to watch for the reactions of the guard. He followed her into the first room, but remained in the open door of all the other rooms she visited. When she reached the second floor, she knocked only on the doors where boys were supposed to be receiving prescribed medicine. Without exception, the boys were sleeping and seemed surprised to be awakened.

"I have your medicine," she told each one deliberately, looking directly into his eyes to stem any words of protest. The boys were surprised that medicine was being brought to them in the middle of the night. Generally, they stopped at the nurse's office during the day. But her pantomime told them they were to act as if everything were normal. "Yeah, thanks," was the typical reply, delivered under eyes that first searched her face and then looked suspiciously toward the guard.

She tried to make conversation, lengthening her stay in each room. Eventually, the guard no longer stood framed in the doorway. The whole procedure had become boring to him. He simply looked into each room she entered to make sure there was no one else inside. Then he would wander back into the hallway.

By the time she reached Billy Tepper's room, she had only one medicine bottle that she hadn't yet used—the one with Jimmy Bradberry's name on it. She knocked on the door and entered when she heard him say "Yeah, what do you want?" The guard glanced inside, saw one of the boys sitting at his desk, and turned away satisfied.

"Your medicine, Jimmy," Maria announced in an artificially loud voice.

Billy smiled. "You don't have to play games for that guy," he told her. "I don't think there's a language he *can* understand."

Her smile vanished. "What in God's name are you up to? How are you communicating with Mr. Ferrand?"

"I've got a computer in my closet. It's connected to one of the telephone lines. We send messages through a kid I know in Rome."

Maria's eyes widened. "Are you crazy? If they catch you talking to the outside they might kill you."

"Not a chance," he said brightly. "These guys couldn't catch herpes—" he realized he was talking to a teacher. "I mean . . . they're not used to computers . . . they can't read a computer message even if they're listening in on the phone. It's safe! Believe me."

"Billy . . ." she started to explain.

"Listen," he said, taking the medicine bottle from her hand and unscrewing the cap. "It's all set, but I need your help." He shook two of the pills into the palm of his hand. "Mr. Ferrand and a couple of regiments of Screaming Eagles are coming over the wall on Friday night. They're going to take these jerks apart."

Her mouth opened, and he knew he had to keep talking before she started to deliver a lecture.

"But we have to get all the kids and all the teachers into the wine cellar so that no one gets hurt. So we need to get them organized." He tossed the two pills into his mouth and swallowed. "I've listed all the kids and put them into ten groups. And I've picked one of the upperclassmen to be in charge of each group. I'll talk to the older kids who are in charge. But you've got to talk to the younger kids. Especially the brats. You've got to make them understand who they're supposed to follow. And you've got to get the word to the teachers." He shook two more pills into his hand.

"What in God's name are you talking about?" Maria demanded.

"Friday night, right after dinner, there's going to be a diversion that will distract the guards. I'll give a signal, and then everyone has to file through the kitchen and get into the wine cellar. We have to be sure there's no panic. The brats have to know exactly who they're supposed to follow. Here! The whole thing is written down."

He tore a piece of note paper from his desk pad, folded it quickly, and stuffed it into the medicine bottle. Then he screwed the top back on.

"Mr. Ferrand told you to do this?" Maria asked, her mouth open in confusion.

"He didn't tell me," Billy said immediately. "But he knows

exactly what we're doing. He's counting on us getting everyone into the wine cellar. Otherwise someone could get hurt."

He tossed the two pills into his mouth and swallowed. Maria suddenly realized what he was doing.

"How many of those are you supposed to take?"

He looked from her eyes to his own empty hand and then at the brown bottle. "I don't know," he admitted. "I don't take any pills."

Maria snatched the bottle from his hand and saw Bradberry's name. "Good God, these are Jimmy Bradberry's asthma pills. He's only supposed to take one a day!"

"I'll tell Snuffy I took them for him," Billy said, dismissing her alarm. "I'll tell him he's not allowed to sneeze until Saturday."

She started to leave. She had already spent more time with Billy than with any of the other boys. "Be careful," she told him. "Please don't do anything until Mr. Ferrand knows."

"Right," he agreed. "And listen. I need to talk to Mr. Prinz. Tell him there are about a dozen kinds of Nikka radio transmitters. Tell him I need to know which kind the guy is carrying."

She looked confused.

"He'll know," Billy said. "I already talked to him. Just ask him if it's the same kind you use to control model airplanes."

"Billy," she protested, "this isn't a game. These men are serious. They could hurt us all."

He was nodding in exasperation. "Please," he begged. "This is important. I have to know if it's the same Nikka transmitter that Snuffy has for his radio-controlled Spitfire. Tell Mr. Prinz I have to talk with him."

She turned and started for the door. The guard was still somewhere in the hallway, unaware of the conversation they were having. She looked back at Billy. "Okay. But don't do anything until you explain it to Mr. Ferrand. Do you understand?"

"Right," he agreed. "Mr. Ferrand knows exactly what we have to do."

* * *

Sharif had disappeared.

He had left Tripoli the moment that Gamel's force had taken over the school, traveling in the garb of a laborer and riding in the back of an open truck with two dozen drums of diesel oil. Three hours later, he switched trucks, climbing in with a cargo of grain seed and dressed in peasant attire. His itinerary aimed him first toward Benghazi, on the Gulf of Sidra. There, he met briefly with colleagues and arranged for his demands to be transmitted to the American embassy in Cairo. When he was sure that he had been seen proceeding to Cairo by truck, he changed places with a hired hand, sent the truck on its way, and boarded a small fishing boat. The boat put him ashore in Tobruk.

American intelligence services knew that he had departed Tripoli and that his messages were being delivered in Cairo. Arab leaders could confirm that he had passed through Benghazi. But he seemed to have vanished. With the exception of two of his intimates, no one knew where he was.

Emissaries delivered his messages and received the Americans' replies at the U.S. embassy. They used different telephones to call different locations within the city. Couriers with empty briefcases left Cairo on flights to Tripoli, Damascus, and Nicosia, closely shadowed by operatives of Israel, Syria, Egypt, the Soviet Union, and the United States. Meanwhile, the actual correspondence was on its way to Alexandria by automobile, where it was broadcast in a simple number-substitution code. Sharif's responses, also in code, came over a marine-radio band from a fishing boat off the coast of Tobruk. Sharif's agents knew they were in communication with their leader, although they had no idea where he was. All they could do was await his triumphant resurrection, which would come after he had humbled the American imperialists.

In the basement of a small house, one street from the waterfront, Sharif was enjoying the consternation of his enemies. He listened to the hedged statements of the Arab leaders, speaking on their national radios. They regretted the necessity of terrorism, yet spoke of it as a legitimate weapon of an oppressed people. They claimed to be mediating between Sharif and the Americans, hoping to avoid bloodshed while pressing the legitimate claims of the Arab nations. Privately, they were telling anyone who might have links to Sharif that they stood firmly in support of his glorious struggle. And, he imagined, through diplomatic channels they were telling the Americans that they were sickened by his barbaric tactics.

At the same time, he listened to the public utterances of the United States government, which refused to bargain with an unprincipled terrorist. Yet he knew that the prisoners he had demanded were being bathed and dressed by their guards in Israel and Italy, while he was hearing the first offers of American industrialists who were suddenly interested in consulting with him on investment opportunities within the Arab world.

The Middle East princes who claimed to be advising him were tearing the fingernails from informers in an effort to learn where he was. American satellites were capturing every telephone call in the Mediterranean and American computers were processing miles of magnetic tape in their search for a clue to his whereabouts. Reprisals? How could they attack him when they couldn't even find him? And how could they find him when he was nowhere and everywhere? And if they found him, how could they harm him? He wasn't a person locked in fragile flesh. He was the cleansing fire, blowing from the desert out over the crumbling structures of a fraudulent world.

They were all frauds, these so-called leaders who lived in fear of their own people, who paid lip service to discredited principles. They survived on lies, pretending to represent the common man while they helped shore up the fortifications of the privileged. But now they were exposed. Now the American leaders would have to admit their helplessness; the Arab princes would have to confess their duplicity. And the leaders of the Zionist entity, soon to be deprived of their American patron? They would eat the bitter fruit of their own arrogance.

The American reply to his demands was a lie, a transparent attempt to disguise their actions. They would not ransom their children by trading convicted terrorists. However, the Israelis and Italians had been considering amnesty for Palestinian prisoners as a humanitarian gesture for some time now. The United States would inquire whether the amnesty might be accelerated.

Nor would the Americans even consider war reparations. The victors didn't pay for the damages of war; the vanquished did. And the United States had certainly never been vanquished. But there were several Middle East development loans now pending with the World Bank that the United States had been blocking. Perhaps those programs could be reconsidered.

As for keeping the Sixth Fleet away from Arab coastlines, the United States could not even comment. The definition of the limits of coastal waters was a matter of international law.

It was laughable. Even with their children at risk the great powers couldn't allow themselves to be seen doing anything more than throwing crumbs to the Third World. The Americans didn't mind a defeat. They simply couldn't admit to a defeat. They would trade prisoners. They would pay indemnities. They just couldn't allow themselves to speak the words *trade* or *indemnity*.

After their farcical rescue mission had self-destructed on the Iranian desert, they bargained with Khomeini's henchmen. They avoided a public humiliation simply because the Iranians didn't force them to admit they were beaten. They bargained with El Fatah, trading prisoners held by Israel for American hostages on a captive airliner. Again, they avoided disgrace only because El Fatah allowed them to define a simultaneous release of prisoners as something other than a trade. But this time, Sharif was determined that they would not escape. This time they would be forced to treat an adversary as an equal. Only if the Americans treated him as an equal would he rise above the corrupt princes of the Arab world. He didn't want prisoners. He didn't want indemnities. He wanted power.

Sharif drafted his response carefully. The prisoners he demanded would be free in Damascus before the children of Saint Anselm's were free. The indemnity would be called an indemnity. The Americans would get only one concession: he would yield on the limitation of Sixth Fleet operations. But in return, they must honor Libya's claim to the Gulf of Sidra. His terms would represent a humiliation for the United States. And that humiliation would fan the cleansing fire from the desert.

Sharif handed the tightly worded response to his aide, who immediately began translating it into number-substitution code. In an hour, it would be aboard a boat ten miles offshore, being keyed to a receiver in Alexandria. In the morning it would be in the hands of the Americans.

He walked with his lieutenants down the narrow broken street that led to the abandoned piers of Tobruk, once the depot for the Italian and German armies that had rampaged through North Africa unchallenged for nearly a decade. The city and its harbor had been the linchpin of the battle for the southern Mediterranean, attracting great armadas of ships and a withering hail of bombs and shells. Now it was nearly deserted. The pipeline that sucked Libya's petroleum wealth out of the desert left the land where the cargo docks had once been and followed a catwalk out into the sea. Far offshore, tankers loaded to the incessant beat of giant pumps. No trucks, no hoists, no men were required. The oil seemed to run on its own toward the busy factories of Europe.

"A strange war," Sharif said in despair. His lieutenants understood. He was locked in a death struggle with the imperialists, yet the commerce between the two sides continued without interruption. There were Americans in the oil fields at one end of the pipeline who were getting rich pumping the oil out of the ground. And there were Frenchmen and Germans and Dutch at the other end getting rich processing the oil. And yet the Arabs remained poor. Only their leaders prospered. Freeing a few prisoners wouldn't change that obscenity. No, he needed to be swept into power by the Arab people. And for that to happen he needed to do what no other leader in the Middle East had ever been able to do. He needed to humble the greatest Western power.

They handed the messages to the hirelings on the boat, men who had no idea what the random numbers they were transmitting might mean, or whose message it might be. They assumed they were dealing with smugglers or drug dealers and were paid well enough to accept the risks without asking questions. In return, the boat crew handed over the latest messages they had copied, perhaps communications passed on from Washington, most likely the random observations of Sharif's agents in Cairo. Then they watched the boat head back out to sea until its lightless form disappeared into the darkness.

Sharif was sleeping easily when he heard his aide's voice next to his bed. He sat up and listened as the aide read one of the short messages he had just decoded.

"Contacted in Cairo by agent of your business associate, Trotta. He informs us that Trotta's son is in the school. He pays his respects."

Sharif rubbed his eyes, took the message, and read it himself by the shielded light of the oil lamp. "When is our next exchange with the boat?" he asked.

"In the morning. Nine o'clock," he was told.

He nodded. Then he climbed out of bed and walked into the dusty bare room that served as his command post. He drafted a short message to his people telling them to call the school and order Gamel to release the Trotta boy.

The aide looked startled.

"I'd rather have the United States as an enemy than Don Trotta," Sharif explained.

April 18

morning

Billy couldn't understand it. First the message from Ferrand that didn't make any sense at all. And now Snuffy asking a lot of stupid questions that he didn't have time to answer. It was a simple enough plan! Why was everyone trying to make it so complicated.

Ferrand didn't want him to do anything.

> We will have you released shortly. Don't do anything with the security monitors. Don't tell anyone about the wine cellar. If you do, it will be dangerous for the other boys and will make it difficult to free you.

What the hell was the matter with the guy? These dummies wouldn't be any problem for the Screaming Eagles. Jesus, they look like they'd gotten their uniforms at an Army-Navy store. And if they were going to be "released shortly," then the Americans must be coming over the wall soon—probably tomorrow night, like he'd told Ferrand in his last message. So it made sense that he should be ready to mask out the security cameras. The Eagles weren't going to stop on top of the wall and wait to have their pictures taken!

Of course he wasn't going to tell anyone about the wine cellar. What did Ferrand think he was? An idiot? Tell the kids about the wine cellar, and ten seconds later, they would all be trying to crowd through the door. They'd give the place away. He knew he couldn't tell them about it until the last second. And then he would only tell the group leaders he was organizing. Jesus, it was a good thing Ferrand could kick a soccer ball. Otherwise he'd have a tough time finding work.

And now Snuffy. All he was asking Jimmy Bradberry to do was throw one of his classic coughing fits. You'd think he was asking him to do something difficult. "Just do what you always do, Snuffy. Start hacking, double over, turn blue, and then fall on your head."

"But why does it have to be by the security office?" Snuffy kept asking. "Why can't I do it at the table?"

"Because I want the guy in the security office to come to your rescue," Billy explained.

"Why?"

"Jesus, Snuffy. You never ask any questions in class. Why do you save all your questions for me?"

"Because these guys have guns," Snuffy said. "Maybe they shoot kids who have coughing fits. And why does it have to be at exactly five minutes to twelve?"

"Because I won't be able to see you," Billy answered, his patience already drawn like a rubber band. "I told you. I'll be in the john. I need to know exactly when you're having the fit so I'll know exactly when to do what I have to do. What's the big problem?"

"You're sure this isn't dangerous? You don't think the guards are going to get mad?"

Billy reached for his trump card. "Aw, forget it, Snuffy. I'll ask Charlie Noble . . ." He started out of his chair as if he were going to move to the other side of the table.

"Charlie Noble?" Snuffy protested. "First thing he'll do is tell the headmaster. Besides, Charlie doesn't know how to throw a fit."

"Well, it's either you or Charlie," Billy said. "Are you in, or are you out?"

Jimmy Bradberry was nodding before Billy could finish the question. "Okay. Five minutes to twelve. Right in front of the security office."

Billy gave him the thumbs-up sign.

At exactly 11:45, Billy looked across the table and nodded

imperceptibly toward Joey Trotta. Joey picked his books up from the table and elbowed John Richmond. The two of them rose, walked past the bewildered stare of Harold Hutchings, who was only fifty years into the Hundred Years' War, and started to the washrooms. The guard braced slightly as the two boys came toward him, then relaxed when he realized they were involved in their own smiling conversation. He watched as they walked past his post and disappeared into the washroom.

As soon as they were through the door, Tad Bliss stood up with Henry Giles and repeated the procedure. On the way into the washroom, they moved aside for Joey Trotta, who was on his way out. Davey Moore rose from another table, his books under his arm, and went toward the washroom, passing John Richmond, who was heading back to his table. A few moments later, Tad Bliss came out of the washroom, passing two more of upperclassmen who were on their way in.

Billy watched the parade. But most of all he watched the reactions of the guards. They had all tensed when the first boys had gotten up from the table. But gradually they relaxed as they realized where all the activity was directed. The guard by the washroom door had seemed to scrutinize the activity at first. But now he was ignoring it. The return of the first boys seemed to lend credibility to the disappearance of the others through the washroom doors.

Billy had planned the pattern carefully. The boys who entered together left separately. The boys who entered separately, left together. It was impossible to keep a precise count. If one of the boys was a little slow in returning, the guard would never notice. It was time to strike.

He stood up, cradling his dictionary under his arm, and started to slide out from behind the table. His sole concern was remaining inconspicuous, and he tried to match the casual stride of the other boys.

"Just where do you think you're going, Mr. Tepper?" It was Harold Hutchings' gravelly stage whisper that hit him like a shot. He needed a quick, glib answer, but he was suddenly struck dumb.

"What's going on here?" Hutchings demanded through clenched teeth.

Not now, Billy prayed silently. Jesus, not now.

"Sit down," Hutchings ordered. Then he leaned close to Billy. "And don't ever leave my class without asking my permission."

Hutchings, you asshole, Billy thought. But his mind went blank as he continued to struggle for a response. He had already lost his anonymity. And now the timing of his whole plan was shot to hell. He had to get to the washroom during the heaviest traffic in order to be sure that no one would notice when he didn't return.

Hutchings was turning back to his notes. Billy couldn't just leave without creating an incident, and an obvious incident was the one thing he couldn't allow.

"Mr. Hutchings," he tried.

The teacher made a point of ignoring him.

His eyes darted to the guards. The one closest to him was looking directly at his table. He panned quickly to the clock. Eleven-fifty. He was running out of time.

"Mr. Tepper?" It was Hutchings again. Billy looked up into a stern face leaning close to his own. "May we have your answer?"

Jesus, he had asked a question. The world was about to explode, and here Harold Hutchings was asking questions about the Hundred Years' War.

"I didn't hear your question," Billy offered.

Hutchings' face began to redden. "You didn't hear my question," he said, dwelling on each word to hammer home his irritation. His voice was rising. One more sentence and he'd be wailing like a siren.

"It must be the breakfast," Billy blurted. "We're all sick. I think I'm going to throw up."

Hutchings pulled away quickly. "You're sick?" he asked.

Billy didn't answer. Instead, he tried to force a belch and covered his mouth with his hand.

"Well, leave the room," Hutchings said. He set down his notes. "I'll come with you."

Oh, Christ, Billy thought. He shook his head violently. "I'll be all right," he said bravely. Then he climbed out of his chair, scooped up the dictionary, and moved quickly before the teacher could offer any more help.

He tried to walk calmly toward the washroom. Hutchings had already turned him into a lighthouse, and he didn't want to attract any more attention. As he approached the guard, it seemed as if the terrorist was studying him, and he imagined the eyes of all the guards digging into his back. This isn't going to work, he told himself suddenly. For the first time, he considered giving it up. They were watching him go in, and they would be waiting for him to come out.

He passed the guard without looking up. He had planned to toss the jerk a casual smile but now he was afraid to see the guy's expression. He half expected to have the dictionary torn from his hands.

Billy turned into the white-tiled room and saw several of the boys waiting. As soon as he was inside, two of them nodded to one another and then left. Billy walked directly to the last booth and looked up at the ventilator screen. In a moment, the remaining boys would leave, and then in a few more seconds, two other boys would get up from their chairs and start toward the washroom. There was no way that any of the guards would remember who was still inside.

He looked up at the ventilator. If the guard came into the washroom while he was climbing through the opening his whole plan would be in ruins. But in about four minutes, Snuffy Bradberry would launch into his fit. So if he were to have any chance of disabling the security monitors, it had to be right now. He either had to start climbing, or hurry back into the dining room before Snuffy launched into his act.

*   *   *

Jimmy Bradberry watched the clock. The tall minute hand snapped to 11:53. What had he gotten himself into? In about one minute, he was going to get up, start coughing, stagger all the way across the dining hall to the double doors, push the door open, stumble toward the security office, and then fall on his face.

Some chance! The guards would converge on him before he cleared the dining hall. And they had guns. The guns would make such a racket that no one would even hear his coughing. He'd be dead before his act could convince anyone he was dying!

There was no way he was going to volunteer for target practice. He'd just have to think of an explanation for Billy. He could say that he'd started to get up, but that the guard had signaled him back into his chair. Billy would understand that!

Like heck he would. He'd be madder than hell. But all Billy could do was yell at him. The guards might blow his head off.

Billy had no choice. It was now or never. He jumped up on the toilet tank and pulled the wire grating free. Then he pushed his dictionary into the ventilation duct and climbed in behind it. Carefully, he pulled the grating back into position.

He was short of time. Less then two minutes to get down into the vault, pare the insulation from the television cables, and be ready to splice in his connector. It all had to happen at exactly 11:55. Snuffy couldn't keep coughing forever.

He slid back the bottom panel, dropped down into the space, and immediately realized he hadn't thought of everything. He needed to hang by both hands in order to shorten the drop to the dirt floor below. But he needed one hand free to carry the damn dictionary.

*   *   *

Snuffy was having second thoughts. Billy was counting on him. And he remembered what Billy had asked him: "What are they going to do, shoot you just because you have asthma?" Of course not. Heck, they could even ask the teachers. He really did have asthma.

All he had to do was get up and walk toward the last table. That way he would already be halfway across the dining hall. He could start coughing there and then run toward the water fountain near the doors. It wasn't so hard. The guards would certainly fall for that.

But suppose they didn't. Maybe nobody had asthma where they came from. Maybe nobody ever coughed. Even if they didn't shoot him, they might just slam the butt of a gun into his face.

He switched his attention back to the story he was going to tell Billy.

Billy braced his elbows against the sides of the opening while he clutched the dictionary against his chest. The drop was longer and the landing harder than he'd thought it would be, jarring the book from his hands and sending the recorder tumbling across the dirt floor. He didn't have time to look for damage. He scooped up the recorder and connector and scampered across the vault to the boxes he had piled up under the coaxial cable. Within seconds, he had the blade of his pocketknife against the cable's insulation and was carefully cutting through to bare the wires underneath.

Snuffy had counted to thirty after he had seen the second hand jump to 11:54. If he was going to collapse outside the security office at exactly 11:55, he had to move now. But he seemed to be frozen into his chair.

Billy checked the time on his wristwatch. He had reset it less than an hour ago, matching the time exactly with the minute hand of the dining room clock. In exactly thirty seconds he would splice onto the camera wires, momentarily killing the camera on the roof of the old building that was scanning the top of the north wall. One of the images in the security room would flicker, perhaps even black out for a few seconds, as he made the connection. But the guard wouldn't be looking at the monitor. He would be too involved with Snuffy.

Jimmy Bradberry made it to his feet and started innocently toward the farthest table. As he reached it, he sucked in a deep breath. Suddenly, he gasped, let out an explosive cough that turned every head in the room, and doubled over with his arms clutched across his chest. Before anyone could move, he straightened up and flung his arms out as if he were being crucified. Then he sucked in a great swallow of air, letting it whistle like a steamboat as it passed his teeth.

It was like a theater entrance. The paralyzing fear vanished the second he made contact with his audience. He knew he had the attention of every seat, and he began playing to the house.

"Water," he gasped, aiming a quivering finger toward the drinking fountain. Then he rushed toward it quickly, pulled up abruptly when he was halfway there, and gave them another steamboat whistle.

The guards were awestruck, half expecting that the deranged boy would explode. They looked toward the teachers for guidance, but they were just as stunned by the violence of the attack. All of them had seen Jimmy Bradberry break into fits of coughing and helped him from their classrooms to the nurse's office. But they had never witnessed anything of the magnitude of this convulsion.

Jimmy knew he had them eating out of his hand. So he began to pad his part. "Air," he hissed. "I need air." He changed his direction from the water fountain toward the double doors, staggered onward, allowed himself to drop to one knee, dragged himself for a few feet, then rose and fell against the door. He spun around, his arms flailing wildly until he was spread-eagled against the door, and looked out over the mesmerized crowd in the dining hall. Then he let out a gurgling sound, like the last measure of wine being poured from a giant wooden cask.

"My God, he's dying," Maria screamed. She broke ranks and began rushing toward him. The nearest guard released his grip on his weapon and also rushed toward Jimmy, the assault rifle swinging freely on its sling.

Jimmy nearly smiled in appreciation of his own talent. But he still had a distance to travel. He flopped over again, crashing his body against the door, which swung open under the impact, and let out a parting cough as he exited upstage. When he looked into the corridor, there was a guard waiting for him.

Billy's watch hit 11:55. He touched the copper tips of his connector to the wires he had bared. In his head, he could see the monitors break up with electronic noise and begin to roll vertically. Then, with trembling fingers, he began to wrap the splice.

Snuffy never hesitated. He toppled forward into the arms of the guard and wheezed, "Help me." Then he straightened up in the guard's grasp, threw back his head, and shot his face forward in a volcanic sneeze. The guard jumped back to escape the spray. Snuffy staggered directly toward the security office. The guard inside had heard the commotion and the echoing sneeze. He abandoned the panel of television screens and rushed to the doorway, where he nearly collided with Snuffy's pain-contorted body.

Snuffy looked straight into his eyes. He moved his mouth as if trying to form words; he rolled his own eyes, focusing just long enough to notice the horror in the guard's expression; then he launched into his final piece of business.

It was a full three-hundred-and-sixty-degree turn, made with his eyes staring vacantly, the back of one hand laid dramatically across his forehead. He finished with a gasp and then slowly began to sink, a death rattle sounding in his throat. He leaned backward, reaching out with his free hand and clutching at the terrorist's shirt. Then he fell, pulling the bewildered guard down with him. Jimmy landed with a thud, the guard firmly in his grasp. As an afterthought, he kicked his legs up into the air and let his heels fall crashing to the floor.

A dozen faces crushed in close. Hands tore at his shirt. He heard frantic sounds in the strange language mixed with words he understood: "artificial respiration," "mouth-to-mouth resuscitation."

He opened his eyes and saw Miss Manetti's face inches from his own. Her fingers were at his lips, pulling down on his chin to open his mouth. Had he been looking at the monitor, he would have seen one of them rolling, then abruptly refocus itself with a perfect picture of the outside wall. But he didn't care about the monitor. Just wait till he told Billy Tepper he had gotten mouth-to-mouth resuscitation from "Big Boobs" Manetti. Boy, would he be pissed!

All the boys were crowded up against the double doors when Billy sauntered out of the washroom. He passed the guard, who was so distracted by the commotion that he never even looked in Billy's direction, and pushed through the crowd until he could see over the heads of the shorter boys. Snuffy was being helped to his feet by Miss Manetti and one of the terrorists. He waited until Snuffy was looking in his direction. Then he held his thumb up and watched Jimmy Bradberry nod in recognition before he was dragged off in the direction of the nurse's office.

All around him were the signs of disorder. Books had fallen from the tables and several of the chairs were overturned. The guards had abandoned their stations and the kids were out of control.

"Jesus," Billy said to himself. "Snuffy must have given one heck of a performance. I'll probably have to listen to him bragging about it for the next hundred years."

*   *   *

The president was in a rare rage, tormented by the powerlessness of the nation's highest office. He was holding a response from Sharif that gave him little room to negotiate and a deadline from the terrorists in Saint Anselm's that gave him no time. He needed an immediate dialogue with the "camel jockey" who had become the headline of *The Washington Post* and the lead story on each hour's television news brief. But the keepers of his billion-dollar intelligence services had no idea where the man could be reached.

"Let me get this straight," he shouted at Director Clemmons. "I'm in life-and-death negotiations with a world figure, and you're telling me that with all our goddamn antennas and spy satellites and stealth airplanes, you don't have a clue as to where Sharif has his headquarters?"

Clemmons looked to the national security adviser for help, but found that his counterpart was more interested in the shine of his shoes. He looked back to the president. "His correspondence is telephoned to different people in the Egyptian government, each caller using a code word to identify himself as genuine. Our correspondence is picked up at the embassy and then phoned to different drop points within Cairo. We have no idea where it comes from or where it goes."

President Reynolds glowered at the CIA director, who continued with a description of the efforts of his agency. "We've been following possible couriers all over the Mediterranean. None of them seems to be in contact with anyone. Our people have concluded that they're decoys. Our best guess is that Sharif is in Cairo and that all this telephoning and courier activity is just to throw us off the track."

"Jesus," the president said. "I can't smoke a cigarette without a picture of me being on all the news wires within fifteen minutes. This guy hijacks a schoolhouse full of kids and the most sophisticated intelligence services the world has ever seen can't even figure out what continent he's on."

"No one can find him," the national security adviser reminded the president. "The Russians think he's on Cyprus. The Israelis are certain he's in Damascus. The Syrians claim to be talking with him in Beirut. The son of a bitch has vanished. All we know for sure is that he seems to be getting the correspondence we deliver in Cairo and that we're getting his answers in Cairo. But personally, I don't think he's in the city. It takes nearly eight hours for him to reply to our correspondence, which makes me think there has to be courier travel time involved."

Reynolds lit another cigarette and then shook his head in despair. "The CIA thinks he's in Cairo and the NSC thinks he can't be in Cairo. How in the name of Christ am I supposed to negotiate with the man? Maybe I should just wait until he sends a carrier pigeon to find me. He sure in hell knows where I am."

The national security adviser ignored the president's moment of pique and continued with his explanation. "I think the messages are being carried by courier to a broadcast point, maybe in Damascus, or maybe Alexandria. That way, Sharif can receive them without anyone, even the people who are sending them, knowing exactly where he is. But he would have to have a transmitter in order to respond, and he wouldn't want that transmitter located at his headquarters. It would be too simple to pinpoint his location if he were broadcasting from there. So he's probably using couriers between himself and his own transmitter. That would account for the consistent time loss."

"But you haven't been able to pick up any radio transmissions," Clemmons observed pointedly.

"We've probably picked them up," said the national security adviser, bristling at the criticism. "We pick up everything. We're analyzing all traffic in the Middle East and breaking everything that looks like a code. Sooner or later we'll identify his communications link. It's just a matter of time."

The president nodded without enthusiasm. "Time," he said quietly. "They're going to shoot their first hostage in less than six hours. And I'm probably not going to hear from Sharif for another eight hours."

Neither man could offer a word of encouragement.

The president had been awakened before dawn with Sharif's reply. There had to be an exchange of prisoners. A simultaneous release that disguised the exchange was not acceptable. And Sharif wasn't falling for promises of cooperation on grants and loans being considered by the World Bank. He wanted cash indemnities. The only concession was on the operations of the Sixth Fleet. And there, his substitute demand on conceding the Gulf of Sidra to Libya was equally impossible. The United States had made a great show of its right to hold fleet exercises in the gulf. A retreat from that position would be an unbearable humiliation.

The Arab leader's response had confirmed the president's worst fears. Sharif wasn't interested in the release of captured terrorists or a few dollars of investment capital. He was going for power, for a place at the table with the leaders of the Western world. By his threat he was attempting to vault over the heads of the tribal chiefs who claimed to speak for the Arab nations.

But power was the one thing that Reynolds could not allow the Flaming Sword from the Desert to seize. The countries of the Middle East were fictions, willed into existence by the British to reward all the chieftians who had helped them rule their colonial empire. Their leaders were frauds. But they were useful frauds. At least they served to keep one of the most backward regions of the Third World under control. And they lent legitimacy to the oil contracts and profit-sharing schemes by which the West got the petroleum reserves it needed. The sultans and sheikhs might rant against the unholy imperialists and promise their malnourished populations a day of reckoning. But in the meantime, they kept their people from the throats of the engineers and technicians who worked their oil fields. They kept the pipelines filled. And all they demanded in return were weekly deposits to the Swiss bank accounts they kept in their family names.

Sharif was not a fraud. He was a fanatic. If he should seize power, the frail structure of the relationships between the industrial nations and their energy suppliers would crumble. The wealth of the Middle East would be spent on its own people instead of being recirculated into the vaults of Western banks. The dream of Arab union and nationalism might well be realized. And then the fighter planes and cluster bombs that the Congress routinely provided to keep Israel free might not be enough. It would take all the might of the United States to help her withstand the onslaught.

Yet the price of defying Sharif was more than even the lives of the boys and teachers held hostage. Reynolds knew it was the very existence of his government. The fathers of the boys at Saint Anselm's could destroy his ability to rule simply by withdrawing from the consensus of interests that made democratic government possible. Should they begin to negotiate directly with Sharif, the country's elected officials would be left without authority. Nor would the government be able to appeal for the support of the people. The death of the children would cause an explosion of public outrage that would certainly lead to his defeat in the next election. If Jimmy Carter couldn't survive the capture of public servants, how could he hope to survive the massacre of defenseless children? Could a government that couldn't protect its own sons even ask to be returned to power?

Whether Sharif understood it or not, he was challenging America's role as a world power. He was leaving Reynolds with two choices. Either anoint Sharif a prince and suffer massive upheaval in the Middle East. Or watch as his own government was rejected by its outraged citizens.

"I was afraid of something like this," Reynolds finally admitted to the other two men. "I've had nightmares that at some moment of crisis, something would go wrong and I wouldn't be able to talk to the other side. I figured it would be the Russians, or maybe the Chinese. I'd learn that their missiles were being armed and their bombers were on the runways. I'd turn to the hotline and the damn thing would be dead."

The two men nodded.

"I want to get a message out to Sharif right now," Reynolds continued. "I want to tell him to appoint an emissary. Someone who can speak for him and deal for him. I want his people to meet with our people right now, and I don't care where. Cairo. Damascus. Right here in Washington even. I want to get this thing settled."

The two men looked at one another. "We don't know where to find him," the CIA director reminded the president.

"Put it out in the clear," Reynolds said. "Give it to the news services. All it has to say is that the United States is willing to negotiate the immediate release of the children and that we are sending representatives to . . . Cairo . . . wherever. Then let him find us."

"I'm not sure—" the national security adviser started to say.

"I *am* sure," Reynolds interrupted. "I know we say we don't negotiate. But if he's going to start shooting children, I want him to know that the whole world will know that the blood is on his hands—not mine."

"And we'll publicly discuss his demands?" Clemmons asked in amazement.

"I don't know what we'll discuss," the president said. "All I'm trying to do is buy some time. Dead kids aren't any good to Sharif. I want to make damn sure he understands that."

As the three men rose, Reynolds turned to the CIA director. "That rescue squadron at the school?"

"The Delta Force," the director corrected.

"Tell them to be ready to go into the place on my orders," the president said.

"It could be very risky."

Reynolds tipped his chin in agreement. "So is doing nothing."

afternoon

Smiles read the message in disgust, then tossed the paper on the table in front of Otis Brown.

"What in God's name is this supposed to mean?" he demanded.

"What it says," Brown answered without enthusiasm. "Be prepared in all respects to effect a rescue on the president's order."

"Does it mean we're going in?"

Brown shrugged his shoulders. "I'm as baffled as you are. They know we're ready. They also know our chances of getting those kids out alive are poor to nonexistent." He looked up at Smiles and shook his head. "I don't know what it means."

Colonel Smiles swore as he turned away from the table. His orders were coming from a committee of politicians halfway around the world, men with no conception of what their orders meant. "Be prepared in all respects . . ." he said softly to Brown. "Do you suppose those assholes have even a clue of what it takes to be 'ready in all respects'?"

Brown buried his face in his hands.

"They think they can turn a military operation on and off like a light switch," Smiles shouted, venting the rage that had been building up within him. "To be ready, I'd have to have my troops standing behind the north wall right now. Out there, where the chances of them being spotted are enormous and the danger to the kids is doubled. That's the last place I'd want them if we're not going in, but exactly where they have to be if we are. Someone in Washington has got to make up his damn mind!"

Brown knew that Smiles was right. He had been on both ends of terrorist operations. In Washington, the politicians were concerned with appearances. In the field, military commanders were concerned with lives. The lives generally turned out to be less important.

"What are we supposed to do with the kid in the school?" Smiles continued. "We tell him to do nothing because we're going to negotiate them out. Now we have to tell him to get ready because we need his help to shoot their way out. Jesus Christ, Otis, the kid is only fifteen years old."

Brown turned to face the colonel. "That's what I've been thinking about since we got the order," he said softly. "And I've come to the conclusion that we can't tell the boy anything. We have to let the previous message stand. We don't want him to do anything." He watched Smiles' eyes widen. "Look," he continued, lifting the wire-frame glasses from his nose. "Right now the biggest danger to the boys would be some sort of foolish escape attempt. Something that would get Gamel nervous. That's the last thing we want to encourage. We can't tell a fifteen-year-old boy that we 'might' be attacking. God only knows how he'd react—"

"But if we do have to attack," Smiles interrupted, "getting the kids into the wine cellar is the best chance they have. And if he really *can* kill those security cameras . . ."

Brown was nodding vigorously. "Right. *If* we are going in. And *if* the boy can actually do what he makes sound so easy. But let's take a moment and figure the odds. That's my specialty, Colonel. Figuring the odds."

He stood up, walked past Smiles, and stared out the window toward the school. The midday sun was high overhead, and the school stood like a stone fortress visible through the tall thin trees. "There's a better than even chance that the kid can't pull it off. I know that Ferrand thinks Billy Tepper is some sort of genius, but look at what we're expecting him to do. First, he has to fix a security system so that the cameras can't see what they're aimed at. He can't just break them. If the cameras simply went out, Gamel would know that something was up. So this kid has to trick an electronic system. Let's say he can do it. He obviously knows how to handle electronics, because Ferrand said he had the telephone system doing tricks. But that's only the beginning.

"The next thing he has to do is organize sixty-five children and a dozen teachers so that they all disappear on cue into a wine cellar. I don't know about you, but I can't get a staff of eight people into a conference room on schedule. And remember, some of these boys are only ten years old. They won't have much instruction, because Gamel isn't going to let Billy Tepper hold a class on escape techniques. They won't have any rehearsal. What do you think the chances of all them disappearing at one time are?"

Smiles nodded wearily. He didn't have to answer.

"Now we get to the tough part. The kid has to disable the explosive charges. He has no tools, no circuit diagrams, nothing. All he can do is pull on a few wires and hope he's pulling on the right ones. Personally, I don't want him to go near those explosives. One mistake, and there wouldn't be any hostages left to rescue.

"My guess is that Billy Tepper is a hyperactive kid with a vivid imagination. And I also think that when we order him to do nothing, we give him an excuse for not acting out his fantasies."

"You're right, of course."

"Wait," Brown said. "That's only half the equation. There's also Washington. I know most of the key players. The president. The secretary of state. There isn't one of them who would let himself be associated with an assault on that school. If one of those boys dies, their political careers would die with him. Forget about our cherished policy of not negotiating with terrorists. The leader of that line is Senator Bradberry, and his son is one of the hostages. We've given them our appraisal: if we attack, children are going to be killed. So the odds are they'll never order an attack. My guess is they'll give Sharif anything short of the keys to the White House to set those kids free. I don't want a fifteen-year-old schoolboy screwing up the odds."

The colonel watched Brown as the intelligence officer carefully wiped the lenses of his eyeglasses with a handkerchief and slipped the wire frames back onto his nose. "Then why are they telling me to make preparations for an attack?"

Brown looked sympathetically toward the Army officer. "So they can hang your ass if anything goes wrong," he said simply. "You're covering the downside risk."

He was right, the colonel knew. That was the new role of the American military—to fight wars without winning them, and to fight in such a way that they wouldn't anger the enemy. The civilians who commanded America's armies had no idea what they wanted them to accomplish. Smiles thought of the generals who stood guard at the line that divided Germany, the commanders whose only defenses were atomic cannons that only Washington could fire. The crisis, when it came, would come in Europe, and they'd have only minutes to decide whether to fire the nuclear projectiles or abandon Europe to the Russians. Washington would still be equivocating when the armies' positions were overrun.

The stakes at Saint Anselm's weren't nearly as high. The lives of sixty schoolboys were trivial compared to the fate of Western Europe. But that only made Smiles' situation that much more hopeless. If the leaders of the free world couldn't come to a decision on how to save Germany, how could he expect them to be decisive about saving an archaic schoolhouse. They would simply stand with a moistened finger raised in the air, testing the political winds until every hope of military advantage had been wasted. The boys at Saint Anselm's were held hostage to their vacillation.

Smiles had no illusions. A year of practice exercises like the debacle he had just rehearsed in the desert had convinced him that rescue operations were doomed before they began. He had no desire to lead his troops over the walls of the fortress. But if he was going to attack, he needed to be "ready in all respects." And it was dangerous to put an operation into motion if he wasn't going to be allowed to see it to its conclusion. All he could do was wait, placing his faith in Otis Brown's odds that no attack would be ordered.

But even as he was resigning himself to the futility of the situation, those odds were being recalculated by one of the prisoners of Saint Anselm's.

Joey Trotta had no idea why he had been singled out. He hadn't even noticed the headmaster standing with the terrorist leader at the open door to the dining hall, nor had he watched the Old Mouse shuffle across the room and whisper to Harold Hutchings. He was startled when he felt Hutchings' hand on his shoulder.

"The headmaster wants to speak with you," the history teacher whispered.

"What?"

"You're to go to the headmaster's office," Hutchings repeated.

"I didn't do anything," Joey protested.

Hutchings had to laugh. The boys didn't seem to be afraid of the machine guns all around them, but they were still terrified by a summons to the headmaster's office.

"It's nothing that you did," he told young Trotta. "I believe he has a message for you."

"What about?"

"Why don't you go and find out," Hutchings said, his voice carrying a hint of anger even though it came through a frozen smile.

Trotta pushed up from the table. "Be right back," he said to the others, assuring them that he could hold his own with the headmaster.

"I wouldn't count on it," Billy Tepper said mischievously. "He probably thinks you're the one who's been leaving him cheese."

"It's gonna be your ass," Henry Giles said by way of encouragement.

Trotta tried to look confident as he sauntered to the door.

When he turned into the corridor, the headmaster was waiting for him.

"It's good news, Mr. Trotta," the Old Mouse said. "There's nothing to be frightened of." He took Joey by the arm and guided him into the office, where the terrorist leader was waiting.

"Joseph Trotta," Gamel said from his seat behind the desk. Joey tried to answer but his mouth had gone stone-dry. He nodded his head.

"You're being released," Gamel continued. "If there is anything you need from your room, go and get it now."

Trotta stood frozen. He couldn't respond.

"Did you hear me?" Gamel demanded.

He nodded again, but still he didn't move.

"You're being released," Gamel repeated. "A guard will take you to the front gate. There will be a police car waiting."

Joey heard the headmaster's voice from behind him. "Come, Mr. Trotta. Get your things."

"No," he said suddenly, forcing the word through paralyzed lips.

Gamel had already looked down at the book he was reading. His head snapped back up. "You are released," he ordered. "Don't you understand?"

"Why?" Joey demanded, his voice suddenly becoming firm. "Why me?"

Gamel set the book down. A thin smile spread across his face. "Why? Because I said so. Or haven't you been taught to obey an order?"

"Why me and not the others?" Joey persisted.

"You, because of the respect we have for your father," Gamel answered. "Your father is a great man in our country."

"Please, Mr. Trotta . . ." It was the headmaster's voice.

"My father is a gangster," Joey said, his eyes fixed on Gamel. "I don't want him doing me any favors."

"You don't want to be free?" Gamel asked.

"Only if you let us all go," Joey said. "Otherwise, I'm staying with my friends."

"Mr. Trotta," the headmaster started to say, but Gamel raised his hand to silence him. Then the terrorist rose from his chair. "Please," the headmaster begged. "He's only a boy. He doesn't mean . . ." His voice faltered under Gamel's gaze.

The Arab leader came around the desk until he was standing directly in front of Trotta. His voice was scarcely a whisper. "You're right. Your father is a gangster. We don't respect him, but for the time being, we do need him. So we are giving him what he wants. And what he wants is your release. I am not releasing the others. I am releasing you. Do you understand?"

Joey's eyes were tearing in his rage. "I'm not leaving," he said, trying to match the determination in Gamel's voice.

Gamel stared at the boy, then raised his head and said a few words in his own language. A guard responded immediately, pushing past the headmaster and grabbing Joey by the arm.

"You *are* leaving," Gamel said softly. "You're leaving right now." He nodded to the guard, and immediately Joey felt himself being dragged backward and out through the door.

He was half pushed, half dragged down the hallway, past the entrance to the dining hall and toward the front door of the building. He struggled, twisting his body and digging in his heels as he tried to break the grip of the guard, who was forcing his arm up behind his back in a hammerlock. "Let go, you sleazy bastard," he yelped, doing an improvised dance step in an effort to twist his arm free. The commotion brought the guard from the security office out into the hallway, where he laughed at Joey's senseless struggle and shouted encouragement to his comrade. Trotta heard the guard who held him laugh in response, and, in his rage and frustration, he began to cry.

He had stopped fighting by the time they reached the front steps. The guard relaxed his hold and, with one hand on Joey's arm, began steering him down the path toward the front gate. His eyes, flooded with tears, were fixed on his feet as he shuffled each step of the way, and he felt himself drowning in the loneliness that had always run like a tide through his young life. People respected his father. Or they were terrified of his father. It didn't make any difference. Either way, they pushed Joey off to one side. Those who respected his father, revered the son. Those in fear, avoided the son. He was always an outsider. Always different.

In his hometown school, there had been whispers whenever he passed through the locker-lined corridors. The party invitations were always handed around him. There were rumors that if Joey Trotta came to your house, a black limousine would be parked across the street with guns trained on your windows. If you hurt him in a football game, two men wearing dark hats would ring your doorbell and break your legs. You could nod to him, maybe even risk a smile. But you couldn't talk to him because something you said just might make him mad.

In his home, everyone talked to him. Relatives pinched his cheeks and mussed his hair. Some made great shows of hugging him in their fat arms. Men he had never seen before brought him expensive presents that he didn't need and spent hours praising qualities he didn't have. None of it, he knew, was directed at him. He was just the telegraph wire over which they sent their obsequious tributes to his father.

Joey Trotta had done the only thing he could. He turned inside himself and away from everyone else. He rushed into school seconds before his first class, found the empty corner of the cafeteria near the garbage cans, and nibbled at the edges of his sandwich. He left the school grounds while the dismissal bell was still ringing. At home, he went straight to his room and locked the door behind him. He had tried to vanish from the face of the earth.

After a year of fruitless encouragement, and realizing that his son was being destroyed, Don Trotta had decided on Saint Anselm's. He would send his son away from his home and family to a school where no one would fear him or fawn over him. A school in Italy, where his native family could watch from a distance and make certain that no one would be tempted to use the boy to reach the don.

At first, it hadn't worked. Joey Trotta had sulked into Saint Anselm's, found his room, and left it only for the day's required ritual of classes, assemblies, and athletic events. In the classroom he found a back seat where he turned solemnly through the pages of his textbooks, never raising his eyes to the teacher or the other boys. In the dining hall, he ate silently, finished quickly, and sat staring at his half-empty dish until the end of the meal was announced. On the athletic field, he ran through the games, a competent but soulless player who never rejoiced in victory or showed the pain of defeat. He participated in everything but joined nothing.

His resurrection had occurred entirely by accident. Midway through the fall term he had been jogging after a soccer ball that was rolling toward the sideline. Suddenly Henry Giles, flashing like a guided missile, had exploded into him. The boys had bounced off each other, each skidding across the ground in an awkward tangle of legs and arms. Giles had recovered quickly and was on his feet while Joey was still struggling to his knees. He had rushed at Joey, twisted the front of his shirt in a strangling knot as he dragged him up, and shouted into his mud-stained face.

"Ya dumb dago. Who the hell do you think you're checking." Then he had pushed Joey back three full steps and charged toward him with a wildly swinging fist. Joey had ducked under the blow and felt Giles' momentum carry him across the top of his shoulder. He had straightened up quickly, sending the other boy tumbling through the air like a gymnast until he had crashed flat on his back.

He had jumped on Giles like a tiger. "You, you fucking farmhand," he had screamed as he whipped a fist across Henry's face. Giles had thrown him off with one hand, and in an instant the two boys had been locked in each other's arms, throwing short harmless punches as they rolled through a puddle of muddy water.

It had taken only a few seconds for Ferrand to break through the ring of boys that instantly formed around the fight. He'd pried them apart, held them at arm's length, and outshouted them until he had them under control. Giles face was a comical mask of mud, with blood seeping out of the opening that outlined his mouth. Joey Trotta's nose was bleeding and his left eye was already beginning to swell. But even as Ferrand had watched, the rage in Joey's eyes had begun to soften. Then a smile had turned up the corners of his mouth. Henry Giles had tried to beat the hell out of him, which meant that Henry Giles didn't give a damn about his father. And Ferrand was screaming at both of them as if they were both dirt. He'd begun to laugh. In an instant he was laughing hysterically.

"Jesus, Henry," he'd managed to say. "You should see yourself. You look like you're doing a minstrel show!" His laughter had been contagious. In a second, the whole circle of boys was howling at Henry. Miraculously, Giles had joined the laughter. "Yeah?" he'd shouted. "Well you ain't much to look at yourself. You look like you fell off the back of a garbage truck."

It had been easy for them to shake hands at Ferrand's order before they returned to the field. And as Joey had run toward his teammates, he'd heard someone shout, "Way to go, Joey," and then felt an open hand slammed across his back. It was the first time anyone had ever patted him on the back without thinking of his father.

After that, he had lifted himself out of his isolation and raised his eyes from the empty pages of his textbooks. He'd joined the jostling on the food line and become a partner in some of the plots that were directed toward the headmaster and the teachers. He'd found friends, the first he had ever known. And he'd begun to understand that he was not really alone. All the boys at Saint Anselm's were just like him. They were all the sons of gangsters.

Their fathers weren't in the same businesses as his father.

But they did the same things. They assembled giant commercial and government enterprises, and managed them for their own fame and fortune. They competed fiercely, rewarding those who served them well and destroying those who stood in their way. They amassed great power and used the power brutally to further their own purposes. They skirted the laws they could get around and ran roughshod over the others. They established themselves as supermen.

Some men respected them. Others feared them. Either way, they flattered or ignored their sons until the boys became completely invisible in the shadows of their fathers. As a result, none of the boys fit in. All of them had been shuttled from school to school with miserable experience piled on top of miserable experience. Finally, all of the fathers had come to the same conclusion: that their boys could survive only in the company of other boys who had also been made invisible. They had sent them to Saint Anselm's.

Now Joey was leaving. With the guard pressing against his arm, each reluctant step was carrying him closer to the gate. And the gate led to nowhere. He was more terrified of the emptiness outside than of the danger that hung over the boys and teachers inside. The danger wasn't frightening if he could share it with someone.

Trotta saw the guard from the corner of his eye—a boy perhaps a few years older than himself. The terrorist was an inch taller and slightly more filled out. And he was stronger. Joey remembered the viselike grip that had kept him under control in the hallway. But he wasn't as big as Henry Giles. And he probably wasn't as strong.

If he could just surprise the smug bastard and get his hands on the gun. Then he could turn the tables and do something to help his newfound friends. Bet the fucking guards wouldn't be so macho when he burst through the door of the dining room with a machine gun in his hands. Christ, Billy and Henry and the other guys would be all over them while the bastards were diving for cover. We could wrap these sons of bitches up in a minute and then we'd be kicking *their* asses down the path to the front gate.

Joey never thought of the danger. He had to act to save his friends or else he would lose his friends forever. He decided instantly. One moment he was a sniffling, beaten teenager being led like a dog on a leash. The next instant he was spinning like an enraged bull. He tore his arm free, turned on the guard, and raked his hands across the boy's face. The guard screamed in pain and backed away, his hand groping for the weapon that hung from his shoulder. But Joey's leg was already swinging in a powerful arc that scored directly to the guard's groin. The boy dropped as if his legs had been cut off at the knees and fell forward, his head striking the ground. Joey nearly tore his arm off as he ripped the gun away. In one step he was at full speed, rushing back up the path toward the school with both hands on the machine gun, his finger pressing against the trigger.

It had happened so quickly that the guard in the security office had not yet reacted. The first violent motion on one of the screens had caught his attention and he watched with detached fascination as the schoolboy disposed of his well-trained comrade. He stared for an instant as Joey rushed toward the building, growing larger on the television monitor with each step he took. Then he bolted from his chair, grabbed his gun from the top of a filing cabinet, and screamed a warning as he rushed across the hallway. He threw open the door to the dining hall and waved for the other guards to help him.

While he was screaming an explanation, the front door burst open behind him. His head snapped around and his eyes focused just in time to see Trotta framed in the doorway, pointing the captured gun at his head. He heard the gun explode at the same instant as he threw himself facedown on the floor of the dining hall. The door frame he had just vacated shattered into splinters.

The guards who had rushed from their stations toward the dining hall doorway now turned and rushed away, diving beneath the unused tables and the small administration desk. As they were scurrying for cover, Joey Trotta jumped into the open doorway. He fired first at blue trousers that were disappearing behind the desk, the bullets cutting up the tiles a few feet from his target, then moving in until they chewed holes through the back of the desk. Then he swung his sights toward the overturned tables and fired a burst that cut one of them in half.

The chattering of the machine gun turned the entire dining hall into a drum resonating with the ricochet of each bullet. All of the boys had seen gunfire in movies and on television, but nothing had prepared them for the terrifying sounds that pounded through the room, or for the grotesque destruction that exploded everywhere the gun was pointed. Most of them fled to the back of the hall, toppling tables and chairs in their panic to escape. But some of the brats remained frozen in fear, their hands clamped over their ears. Joey Trotta charged into the dining room, the gun at his hip swinging from side to side, and fired long bursts at each sign of movement, the shots straying upward with the recoil of the weapon. Pieces flew from another table, and then a row of folding chairs toppled over like dominos. "Let's get the bastards," he screamed at his schoolmates, but his words failed to carry over the explosive noise from his gun. "Come on," he yelled, still firing into one of the overturned tables some of the guards were using as a shield. As he looked for the help he was sure would come, the stream of bullets climbed up one of the walls. Suddenly, there was the shattering of glass, and one of the dining hall windows disappeared from its frame.

And then there was silence, colored by the echoes that sounded in the hills around the school. Joey was standing alone in the middle of the room, the spent gun hanging from his fingers. The terrorist troops began to crawl out from under the broken furniture they had used for cover. One of the younger boys began to cry.

Two of the guards realized the clip was empty and rushed

at Joey. One swung the butt of his gun, and Joey collapsed without making a sound. The guards were standing over his fallen body when Gamel walked into the dining hall.

It took the leader only a second to understand the situation. He had heard the gunfire and now he was looking at its effects. Joey was sprawled out on the floor, the assault gun resting under his hand.

"Shoot him," he said softly.

One of the guards looked questioningly toward his superior, then back down at Joey's helpless form. He turned to Gamel and mumbled a few words in their desert language. Gamel answered quickly in the strange tongue, and then the soldier looked back down at Joey and tipped the muzzle of his weapon toward the boy's head.

Maria screeched and started to rush forward, only to be caught in the arms of one of the soldiers who had stood up from behind a splintered table. "He doesn't know," she screamed at Gamel. Then she looked at the guard who was standing over Joey. "He's a child . . . he didn't know."

"Shoot him," Gamel snapped. The young guard's eyes darted from Maria to Gamel and then back down at the wild dark hair that hid Joey's face.

"Please," Harold Hutchings yelled. "We'll take care of him. It won't happen again." He began shuffling forward, reaching out toward Joey.

Gamel knew he was losing control. The teachers who had momentarily been stunned into paralysis were beginning to recover. The boys who had fled to the back of the room were edging their way forward. His trained troops had failed their first small test and now seemed on the verge of panic themselves.

He walked forward quickly, and pushed the two guards away from Joey. Without looking down at the motionless form, he reached to his side and drew the plated revolver from its holster, then held it over his head for all to see.

"Anyone who disobeys my orders will be punished," he said in the direction of Harold Hutchings. Then he looked down, pointed the pistol at the back of Joey's head, and pulled the trigger.

The noise was barely heard—a dull *pop* that had no echo. There was no flash and only the slightest trace of smoke. At first there was no reaction at all from Joey, almost as if Gamel had fired into a sack of grain. Then the body twitched and one of the legs stiffened for an instant before it relaxed.

"Oh my God," Maria gasped. She stood frozen for a second, then suddenly tore out of the grasp of the guard and rushed toward Joey. The other teachers started forward. Gamel took a quick step to position himself in Maria's path and, as she tried to push past him, grabbed her by the hair. He pulled her head back and spun her around so that she was facing the teachers and the boys, then pressed his pistol against the side of her face. The teachers stopped instantly, their concern switching from the lifeless body on the floor to their colleague who was struggling in the grasp of a murderer.

"We can kill you all," Gamel said, stating the fact without emotion. "One at a time . . . starting with this one." He yanked Maria's head back further and pressed the tip of the pistol further into her cheek.

Harold Hutchings began to back up.

"Good," Gamel said. "You understand."

The teachers were in full retreat, moving back toward their students.

"Now get all the children to their tables. Then we'll take a count, and when everyone is accounted for, the boys will be brought back to their rooms. Is that understood?"

The teachers backed toward their tables, their eyes still fixed on Maria.

"As for you," Gamel said into Maria's ear, "if I have to kill you, then there will be no one to control the little boys. So I will have to kill them, too, do you understand?"

She made no response. Gamel twisted the knot of her hair even tighter. "Do you understand?" he repeated.

"Yes," she was able to whisper.

"Good," he said. He slackened his grip. "I warned you to be afraid. Perhaps now you understand why you should be afraid." Then he took a quick step and flung her toward the teachers. She staggered a few steps, struggling for her balance, then fell forward on her face.

The terrorist commander waited for a few seconds to assure himself that order had been restored, then nodded with satisfaction. He turned to one of the guards and pointed with his pistol toward Trotta's motionless form.

"At exactly five o'clock, I want him thrown out through the front gate, do you understand?"

The guard nodded nervously.

"They've had their warning," Gamel explained. "Now they can have their body. Perhaps it will help them pay attention."

Each of the two guards took one of Joey's hands and began dragging him toward the door. A thin smear of blood traced his last journey across the dining hall.

night

Sharif broke camp.

He had heard the radio reports of Washington's willingness to meet with his representatives. Then his henchmen had confirmed the offer through their contacts at several non-aligned embassies. Not only were the Americans backing away from their determination not to negotiate for hostages, they weren't even bothering to disguise the negotiations. They were meeting with him as an equal.

He was on the verge of a triumph even greater than he could have imagined. Certainly greater than he had planned. And it was coming to him almost by accident. Sharif had realized that he was in mortal danger the moment he took over the school. Danger from the Americans, certainly.

They had already demonstrated a willingness to mobilize their clumsy military and blow up half a city in order to retaliate against a terrorist headquarters. Qaddafi's ears were still ringing from their laser-guided bombs. But he was also in danger from Arab leaders, who didn't want him to succeed where they had failed. He had already gotten wind of plots to drop his body at the Israeli doorstep. If they could kill him and place the blame on the Zionist entity, then they would achieve two goals. They would rid themselves of an upstart patriot with a growing following among the radicals, and they would fan the flames of hatred that they continually stoked beneath the Jews. But his victory over the Americans would be their defeat.

Still, it was the real dangers of his position that had driven Sharif into hiding. He had recognized the communications problems his disappearance would cause but felt them a reasonable tradeoff for his own security. But now the communications problems had become an asset. It was the Americans whose children were in danger and therefore the Americans who were desperate to make contact. They had failed to gain assurances for the hostages through normal channels, and now were forced to use extraordinary channels. It was his self-imposed exile that was forcing the Americans to go public with their desire for a meeting.

In the past, they had bargained in secret. They used intermediaries to plead their case so they could insist publicly that they weren't pleading at all. The terrorists were never given credit for their victory. But now there would be no subterfuge. The United States would be dealing publicly with Sharif, the Flaming Sword from the Desert. It was he who would receive their concessions and hold them up for all the world to see. He would become the only Arab equal to the American president; he would become the ordained leader of the Arab people.

He handed his coded instructions to the boat captain: the time and place of his appearance in Cairo in exactly twelve hours, and the arrangements for his triumphant procession to the Swiss embassy. There he would meet with the American representative, who, he'd ordered, must be the secretary of state or another public figure of Cabinet rank. They must come to written terms. He wanted a piece of paper he could wave to the crowds that would be assembled outside the embassy, and which he could pass among the reporters who would be gathered for his press conference. Then he wanted use of the facilities of Radio Cairo, so that he could read the agreement to the entire Arab world.

Sharif watched the boat turn out to sea, toward a position north of the Egyptian coastline. He would be gone by the time the instructions were broadcast, gone back into the desert from which he would shortly emerge in triumph.

He climbed into the back of a truck and squeezed past an electric pump that was the truck's only cargo. In the small space, swaying violently with each bump in the packed dirt road, he changed into an Egyptian laborer's clothes—a plain woolen tunic over cotton pants, with a small knitted cap covering his black hair. He struck a match to the papers that had described him as a Libyan mechanic for the pipeline company in Tubruk, watched them shrink into ashes, and then tossed them over the side. His new costume came with a new identity, which he would use when they crossed the Egyptian border. Then he curled up on the currogated cargo floor, determined to sleep for a few hours during the night, when the air would be cool.

The journey would take him south for three hours, to Jarabub, and from there across the unguarded border to the north of the Siwa Oasis. The crossing would be uneventful, through thin fields of grain and cotton, where the boundaries between farms were far more significant than the boundaries between countries. From the oasis, he would travel eastward on a four-hundred-mile route to the banks of the Nile. During the entire trip he would be out of contact with his loyalists in Alexandria and Cairo, neither receiving their messages nor daring to broadcast orders to them. The temporary isolation was necessary for his own safety, and it seemed insignificant. He already knew that American envoys were coming to meet with him and that by holding Saint Anselm's, he held all the chips that would be on the bargaining table.

Sharif pulled a packing cloth up over himself, folding a corner under his head to serve as a pillow, and threw his arm across his eyes. Great men, he mused, had always traveled a humble road to the heights of power. Abraham had traveled with a flock of sheep, sleeping under the animals' breath for warmth. Moses was floated to the pharaoh's palace in a straw basket. Lenin had journeyed across Germany from Switzerland in a sealed railroad car with blackened windows. And even the Americans remembered George Washington, sleeping on the snow with a greatcoat for a blanket, the night before his triumph at Trenton.

Someday, Arab children would be told the story of Sharif, journeying toward Cairo for his coronation as king. They would hear how he'd slept on the floor of a wheezing truck, wrapped in packing cloth and dressed in the disguise of a common laborer. He wondered about the American who was coming to meet him, riding a jet aircraft at the speed of sound. Could the American possibly suspect how his adversary was traveling? Did he see the parallels of history and realize that once again the common man was rising up to strike down his oppressors? Did he understand that his time had run out, just as it had for the pharaohs and the czars?

The motion of the truck rocked Sharif to sleep, and he rested peacefully, unaware of the murder at Saint Anselm's.

Joey Trotta's body hit the White House like a bomb, shattering the president's credibility and driving his followers into panicky flight.

Reynolds had assumed the boys were safe, that Sharif's ambitions demanded that the children survive. But Joey's life, drained out through a small wound in the back of his head, seemed to prove that Sharif had no fear of presenting himself to the world's leaders with blood on his hands. The timing of Joey's death was also terrifying. The body had been dragged down to the path and dumped at the world's doorstep at five o'clock—exactly as promised—even though word of the president's willingness to negotiate had certainly gotten through to the terrorists. Reynolds had been sure that his signaled concession would stop the grim clock that was ticking toward a daily murder. But the body left at the gate showed that the clock was still running. There would be a new body each day until the United States had caved in to all of Sharif's demands.

"We're delaying the prisoner release," the secretary of state was explaining to the small gathering in the president's office, "precisely because it's a concession we know we're going to have to make."

The president still didn't seem to understand the logic.

"If the prisoners are released before we meet with Sharif," the secretary repeated, "then we won't be able to use them as a bargaining chip. Sharif has to win something. So we're going to let him win something that we've already conceded."

"But everyone knows it," Reynolds insisted. "Aren't we past the point of playing games?"

The secretary glanced at Senator Bradberry, who had not yet contributed a single word to the discussion. "I think we're agreed that we should yield some points during negotiations, but that we shouldn't appear to have collapsed," he said, hoping that Bradberry would support his position.

Bradberry's head turned slowly. "I don't think I should comment," he finally managed. "I guess I have to disqualify myself on this one."

They all knew his views. In every previous hostage crisis, Bradberry had taken the hard line. "Great nations don't bargain with hoodlums" was both his public and private position. "Any concession would only encourage further acts of terrorism." But this time the hands of the terrorists' clock were pointing toward his son. The obligations of great nations didn't seem to be as important.

"What about the economic concessions?" the president asked. "Do we have any options left, or is that horse already out of the barn?"

"I think we still speak for the business community," the secretary said. "I think we can hold them in line for another twenty-four hours. As long as we seem to be making progress."

This was the area where the administration faced its greatest problems. The fathers of many of the boys at Saint Anselm's were already preparing package deals of their own. Certainly, it was illegal for ordinary citizens to negotiate policy with foreign governments. But Sharif wasn't a government. He was a kidnapper. And these weren't ordinary citizens. Each of the men had his own ideas about rescuing his son. Each was assembling a package of economic concessions—sound business investments, of course—that could be offered to Sharif. There was talk of jointly owned corporations that could build refineries in the Middle East, with a percentage of the profits going to Sharif's organization. An auto parts manufacturer was considering licensing African distribution to a company that Sharif would own. In one form or another, agents of the boys' fathers had rushed in panic toward the Middle East, bearing suitable ransoms. Reynolds knew that while government negotiations with Sharif would embarrass his administration, private deals that ignored the policy of the government would destroy it.

"So, we've got about twenty-four hours," the president concluded grimly. "Twenty-four hours to locate this desert rat and make a trade."

The secretary of state looked down at his watch. "Less," he said softly. "If they hold to their timetable, they will kill their next hostage in less than eighteen hours."

"Not much time," Reynolds agreed. "Especially when we have to spend half of it pretending that we're still running the show."

That had been the substance of the secretary's comments to a press conference that had been assembled moments after the death of one of the boys had been confirmed. "We regret to report," the secretary had read from a prepared statement, "that one of the children held hostage in the Saint Anselm's school in Italy has been brutally and needlessly executed. Brutally, because the deliberate murder of a child is certainly an act that defies every convention of human decency. Needlessly, because the United States, through diplomatic and private channels, had already expressed its willingness to address any legitimate grievances of the groups that hold these children captive." We were willing to consider legitimate claims, the secretary was implying. That was only fair. But we weren't making concessions. That would be beneath the dignity of a great nation.

Next he had offered the profound sympathies of the entire government to the parents and family of the boy whose name he refused to reveal. "Notification," he said, "is being made directly to the family as quickly as possible." That wasn't entirely true. There was a raging debate as to exactly how friendly the government should appear to be toward a leader of organized crime who was under indictment for drug trafficking. Reynolds had been advised not to talk to Trotta personally. But the CIA had wanted condolences from a high government official in view of Don Trotta's services to the Agency. For lack of a decision, the information had not yet been delivered.

Finally, the secretary had launched into a condemnation of terrorism, stressing that the murder of innocent civilians could never be justified by any government with pretenses to legitimacy. His comments avoided the fact that the United States wined and dined governments that murdered their own citizens with monotonous efficiency. "All governments," he said somberly, "including those that represent the very people Sharif is attempting to speak for, are revolted by this cowardly act."

It was in the question-and-answer session that the secretary had tried to preserve the facade of the administration's policy toward terrorists. "We will not bargain; we will not trade with outlaws who trample on the basic rights of American citizens," he answered forcefully. "We will, however, meet with these people and try in good faith to be responsive to their legitimate grievances."

"Are we going to trade prisoners for the students?" a syndicated columnist asked, obviously impatient with the double-talk.

"Certainly not," the secretary insisted. "We have asked friendly governments to review the status of certain prisoners, and the release of those who are no longer considered dangerous may well be accelerated. But this is entirely at the discretion of the governments who hold the prisoners."

"What about the demand for war indemnities?" a television reporter fired at the podium.

"There are no war indemnities," the secretary bristled. "But we do have to keep in mind the difference between indemnities and legitimate business investments."

Even in the mournful setting, the press could hardly control its laughter.

Bradberry remained behind when the others left, slumped in the chair with his eyes fixed vacantly on the carpet. The president waited a moment in silence, half expecting that the senator would rise and follow his colleagues. Finally, he walked around his desk and put his hand on Bradberry's shoulder.

"I wish I could make this easier for you, Tom," he said, making no effort to hide his sympathy.

Bradberry looked up. "You're doing everything you can . . . I'm grateful . . . very grateful."

"It's damn insensitive," Reynolds continued, "talking about our world image when your boy is in danger."

Thomas Bradberry waved the apology away. "You have to. You have to put the country first. That's your job." His head lowered until it was buried in his hands. "That's my job, too. I know exactly what we have to do. But with Jimmy involved, I just can't do it."

"Maybe you should sit this one out on the sidelines," the

president offered softly. "I think everyone would understand that this is one game you can't play."

The senator shook his head at the irony. "I'm already on the sidelines. Christ, I'm hiding under the bench. I'm letting you call the plays, hoping to God you'll go for the kids . . . for Jimmy . . . and the others."

"That's the way I'm calling it," Reynolds responded.

Bradberry bolted up from the chair and walked a few steps away from the president. He kept his back turned as he spoke. "But I should be battling you all the way. There's no way in hell we should be talking to these people. How can we sell out the country . . . sell out everything we stand for . . . just to save a few kids?" He wheeled to face Reynolds. "Don't we have to accept sacrifice, even our own children, to protect what we believe in?"

The president wandered back behind his desk. "I don't know," he admitted, glancing out the window to avoid facing his political rival. "Maybe we've lost sight of what we stand for. Of course we have to accept sacrifices to protect what we believe in. But what the hell else is there to believe in besides our children?"

It was so simple that Billy Tepper should have been laughing. The asshole terrorist leader kept flashing his radio detonator as if he were holding the cutting edge of high technology. And it was exactly the same kind of transmitter that Snuffy Bradberry had for his radio-controlled model Spitfire. Imagine the jerk! He thinks he's going to take on the United States with electronics that you can pick up for twenty bucks in any toy store. Was he in for a surprise!

But Billy wasn't laughing. What had happened to Joey Trotta was beginning to sink in. The numbness was giving way to rage, and as he moved the tweezers over the radio receiver that was fitted into the cockpit of the Spitfire, he was working in a cold fury.

Joey was dead. All the boys knew that. They had seen the pistol fired and noticed Joey twitch. They watched as his body was dragged across the tile floor and examined the sticky trace it left behind. They understood that he was dead. There was no doubt about that. It was death itself they didn't understand.

Death was for old people, like the grandmothers who always came for Christmas and birthdays, and then didn't come anymore. It was the end of living, something that happened after you lived long enough. It had nothing to do with kids. Kids were just beginning to live. So why should they have to worry about dying? There was enough to worry about. There were the tests the teachers were always dreaming up—five essay questions that made you write until your fingers hurt, and twenty true-or-false questions where you had to guess the answers. That was something that could keep you awake all night. And there were the trips to the headmaster's office, where the Old Mouse and one of the teachers would sit staring at you, shaking their heads sadly while you begged for one more chance. That was terrifying! There were the schoolyard bullies who would jab fingers into your chest and twist your arm up behind your back. That was humiliating. And then there were the groups of kids who would all decide that no one was allowed to talk to you. That could make you miserable. Jesus, it was hard enough without having to worry about dying.

They could understand that Joey had gone away. Kids were always going away. At the end of each term, some of the guys were always going back home, wherever that was, or being packed off to another school that sounded better than the one they were at. Sometimes they just disappeared. One day they were sitting next to you in history, and the next day you heard that their father had been transferred, or their mother had split, and that was why they were gone. You knew you would never see them again, but that didn't mean they were dead.

But Joey hadn't just gone away. Joey was different. The brats simply couldn't comprehend what had happened to him. They had closed their eyes, and when they opened them everything was just as it had always been. They could go back to coloring the pictures in their art books. Most of the older boys thought of Joey's pain. It had to hurt to have a bullet tear through your body, hurt worse than anything they had ever felt. They were sorry for Joey because he was hurting, and frightened that what happened to him could probably happen to them. They could share his agony, but they certainly couldn't share his death. They understood pain, but they had no idea what it was like to die.

Even Billy hadn't understood at first. They were playing a game, like cops and robbers. The terrorists were trying to hold them prisoners and they were trying to break away. It was fun, especially when you were winning, like when Snuffy threw his coughing fit while he cut into the security system. You expected to lose every now and then when something went wrong, like when the camera in Miss Manetti's shower made too much noise or when Mr. Ferrand figured out why all the lights had gone on. That was part of the game.

Sure, Joey had gone too far. So maybe the guy should have knocked him around a little or locked him in his room. But to take out his pistol. And then to fire it into the back of Joey's head. It was a game, wasn't it?

Billy had stood stunned in the dining hall while Joey was dragged away. He had watched the feet disappear around the corner of the door and stared after them into the empty hallway as if expecting them to return. He had seen it happen, but he couldn't believe what he had seen.

When they had been returned to their rooms, he had just dropped onto his bed with his hands folded behind his head and tried to think. Why did the son of a bitch have to shoot him? Joey wasn't doing anything. They had already taken the gun away from him and had him down on the floor. His little tantrum was all over. Nobody had been hurt. So why did they have to shoot him?

As his numbness had begun to ease, his confusion had turned to guilt. Maybe he should have understood the danger. Maybe instead of trying to outsmart the terrorists, he should have warned the other boys that their lives were at risk and told them to do exactly as they were ordered. Christ, he had scheduled all the boys in and out of the washroom just so he could get his recorder into the vault. Suppose they had been caught. Maybe some of the kids would have gotten themselves shot. If they had, it would have been his fault. Wasn't that what Ferrand's messages had been telling him? That it was dangerous for him to do anything except obey orders. Why hadn't he listened?

Then he'd felt guilty for not doing something to save Joey. The kid was his friend, yet he'd just stood there while the goons had beaten his head in and then while the fucking sleeze had drawn a pistol and shot him. Maybe he could have rushed forward and hit someone. Maybe he and Joey together could have taken the bastards apart. Or at least he could have explained that it wasn't Joey's fault. The kid was just different, always brooding until something got him mad, and then he just went out of his head for a little while. Hell, it was only during the last few months that he even talked to anyone. He should have told them that Joey didn't mean anything. That's just the way he was, so let's just shake hands and forget it. Okay?

But he hadn't done anything. Hell, even the teachers had tried. Horseface Hutchings had walked right out into the middle to try to save Joey, and Miss Manetti had nearly gotten her face blown off. Why hadn't he done anything for Joey? Even if it didn't work, at least he should have tried.

Billy wanted to convince himself that it was all his fault, but the chain of logic kept coming apart. How could it be his fault? He didn't even know who these guys were or where they came from. It was his school, not theirs. Nobody at the school had ever done anything to the bastards, so what right did they have to come in and start pushing people around? If they had a problem with the United States, then they ought to settle it with the United States. It was the governments that were crazy. What kind of problems could they have that were worth getting a kid killed? What was so goddamn important that it was worth Joey Trotta's life?

When he had bounded off his bed he was mad. Mad enough to slam his fist into the plaster wall and take the skin off two of his knuckles. Mad enough to kick over his chair and topple all the books from the bookshelf into a jumbled pile on the floor. But within a few seconds, he had begun to focus his anger. The wild fire had burned itself out as quickly as it had started and had been replaced by an icy rage.

"I'm gonna get that bastard," he'd told himself, seeing the confident grin on Gamel's face as he'd raised his pistol in the air for all to see. "Joey, I swear, I'm gonna get him."

He had reset his chair at the desk, opened the drawer, and removed the radio control unit he had borrowed from Snuffy. It looked complicated but was really ridiculously simple. So simple that Mr. Prinz had been able to explain everything he needed to know in just a few seconds while they were together on the food line.

Gamel had a transmitter—a tiny radio broadcast unit powered by a flashlight battery. If he pushed the button, the device sent out a low-powered radio signal with a range of just a few hundred yards. The detonator that was locked in the administration office was really nothing more than a radio receiver. All it did was recognize the signal from Gamel's transmitter and close a switch in response. The switch it closed did nothing more than connect a car battery to the wires that the terrorists had stretched throughout the school. The current from the car battery rushed down the wires until it reached the tiny explosive caps that were buried in the plastic charges. The caps flashed and set off the plastic.

"It's the frequency of the radio signal that's important," Prinz had whispered out of the corner of his mouth. "The transmitter and receiver are set for the same frequency, and it has to be a frequency well out of the commercial and specialty bands. Otherwise an ordinary radio signal could set off the explosives by accident."

"You mean you tune it to a frequency just like a regular radio?" Billy had asked.

"No . . . no," Prinz had answered with his usual impatience. "The frequency is preset. There's one chip in the circuit that determines the frequency. The manufacturers install identical chips in each transmitter and receiver set. But the chips in each set are all slightly different from the chips in any other set. That's why when Jimmy is flying his airplane, he can't control the airplane the boy next to him is flying. Jimmy's airplane recognizes just the frequency that Jimmy's control unit is sending. And the other boy's airplane recognizes only the frequency that his control unit is sending. You see?"

Billy had nodded, but he still wasn't positive of what the teacher was saying. "So the creep with the detonator can't control Jimmy's Spitfire."

"Of course not," Prinz had said. "If he could, then it would follow that Jimmy could set off the explosives. Now wouldn't that be a fine kettle of fish if every boy with a model airplane could blow up our school? We certainly wouldn't want that now, would we, Mr. Tepper?"

"We certainly wouldn't," Billy had agreed cheerfully. "And we wouldn't want the man to be able to fly Jimmy's airplane either, because he might fly it right through one of the windows."

"Exactly," Prinz had said as he raised his tray to accept a spoonful of baked beans. "So you see, Mr. Tepper, you've learned something today."

Billy had nodded. "You bet your baked beans, I have," he said under his breath.

Now he was studying the simple repair diagram that was pasted inside the battery cover of the flight controller aboard Snuffy Bradberry's Spitfire. The frequency chip was right where he'd expected it to be, on top, where it could be changed easily. It made sense that manufacturers would want to add the frequency chips to the transmitter and receiver immediately before the pair was shipped. That would save them the trouble of keeping the pair together during the whole manufacturing process. It also made sense that users might want to change their operating frequency. It had to be easy to take the old chips out and put new ones in.

All the components of the circuit were soldered together, then covered over with a layer of epoxy to protect them. The component that set the radio frequency was the exception. That was simply plugged into a pin socket. Billy pinched the square plastic package with the blades of the tweezers and began to rock it gently. It loosened immediately and began to pull free of the circuit board, its tiny metal legs slipping out of the holes. When it popped free, Billy lifted it out of the control unit and set it into the palm of his hand.

He was halfway home, but the half remaining was the hardest. Now he had to get into the administration office, where the wires from all the explosive charges came together and were attached to the detonator. The chip in his hand was useless. It had value only when it was connected to a radio receiver. But that was something he couldn't do alone. Not while they had him locked in his room with an armed guard at the end of the corridor. He needed help, and the only person who could help him was Miss Manetti.

Maria nodded toward the guard at the entrance to the old building and hurried past him on her way to the stairs. The steel tray covered with medicine bottles was her passport, and she carried it in front of her in plain sight so that the guards would understand her mission. While she was bringing medication to the boys, she had free run of the buildings.

She started up to the second floor and came across another guard waiting on the landing. His greeting was a smile that turned quickly into a leer. Even in the loose-fitting slacks and high-collared shirt that she had changed into, she was still a very attractive woman, made all the more desirable by the fact that she was the only young woman in the building. She had sensed the interest the guards were now showing toward her, and understood the gist, if not the actual words, of the comments they whispered to one another in their own language. It was her awareness of growing danger that had made her select the least attractive outfit she could assemble from her closet and led her to pull her hair back in a matronly bun.

Again she nodded as she passed the soldier, gesturing with the tray by way of explanation. When she had passed, she heard him call in a stage whisper to the guard on the ground floor, and then pretended not to hear as both of them laughed.

Once past the final guard on the third-floor landing, she moved directly down the hall to Billy's room, tapped lightly on the door, and stepped in as soon as Billy opened it. He was talking before she could even close the door behind her.

"Is everyone set? Everything organized?"

She shook her head. "It's too risky. I don't think the young boys understand."

"They have to understand," he said. "They're only going to get one shot at this, and it has to work."

Her eyes flashed with impatience. "They're babies, Mr. Tepper. You have to understand that. I've divided them into groups and made them hold hands so they'd know who was in their groups. And I had them each point at the upperclassman they're supposed to follow. But that's not enough! Even with a hundred rehearsals they wouldn't do it perfectly. It's too dangerous."

"Not as dangerous as leaving them in the dining hall when the shooting starts."

"There will be no shooting," she started to scream, and then checked her voice when she realized the guard might hear her. After a moment, she whispered forcefully into Billy's face, "I don't want another Joey Trotta, do you hear me?"

He nodded obediently.

Maria saw the model airplane on his desk with the radio

controller exposed. "What's that for?" she demanded suspiciously.

"I can disarm their explosives," Billy answered.

"Mother of God," she gasped. "Have you lost your mind?"

"It's easy," he snapped, annoyed by her lack of confidence in him. "It will take me about twenty seconds, and they'll never even know I did it. Ask Mr. Prinz. He'll tell you."

"Prinz? Prinz told you to disarm the explosives?"

Billy fidgeted in his chair. "He didn't tell me to do it," he finally admitted. "He told me *how* to do it. And it's a piece of cake. Anyone could do it."

She stared at the exposed circuits and thought they seemed hopelessly complicated. "No," she finally decided. "We're not touching their explosives, and we're not escaping into the wine cellar, do you understand? We're going to sit quietly and do exactly as we're told. Sooner or later we're going to be released, and when that time comes I want every one of you alive. Is that clear?"

He nodded meekly.

"Now put that thing away," she ordered, pointing to the electronics hanging out of the Spitfire. Billy pushed the circuits back into the body of the plane and closed the panel over them. Maria started for the door.

"They're attacking tomorrow night," he said as indifferently as if he were commenting on the weather. "Right after dinner."

Maria stopped dead, then turned slowly. "Who's attacking?" she demanded in a menacing voice. "How do you know?"

"Mr. Ferrand and the American army," he said excitedly. Then he jumped up from his chair, moved across the small room, and opened his closet door. He pushed the clothes aside so she could see his computer. "He sends messages over the phone line. I find them written here, on the screen. Then I write back." Maria stood dumbly, staring at the computer until Billy closed the closet door.

"Mr. Ferrand told you that they were attacking the school?" she finally managed.

He avoided the question. "It's all set. I've already fixed the security system so they'll never see our guys coming over the wall. I've told him that the kids would be safe in the wine cellar. And I've told him that I figured out how to disarm the explosives. Everything is going to be ready by tomorrow night, right after dinner."

"And he agreed . . . ?" Maria stammered.

"They're still working on it," Billy said confidently, "but they expect us to be ready by tomorrow night. That's why I need your help."

"My help to do what?" She wasn't even listening to herself. She had agreed to organize the younger boys only because she thought it might be useful if anything went wrong. Now she was beginning to understand that she'd been helping to plan an invasion.

"Keep the leader—the guy who shot Joey—busy tomorrow morning at exactly nine-thirty. Come up with something so that he has to be in the dining hall. Just make sure that he doesn't go into the administration office."

Maria looked bewildered.

"I'm going to be in the administration office at nine-thirty," Billy continued. "You have to make sure that he doesn't walk in on me, okay?"

She tried to assemble everything he had told her. They were planning to attack. No, that wasn't what Billy had said. He said they were considering it, perhaps as soon as the next evening. Considering it only because Billy had promised he could get the children to safety and disarm the explosives that were buried throughout the buildings. The Army—or maybe the Marines—was counting on a fifteen-year-old boy who was treating their invasion as if it were just another prank.

"Sweet suffering Jesus," she said aloud.

"Okay?" Billy repeated. "Tomorrow at nine-thirty?"

"No!" Maria nearly screamed. "No. Nobody is attacking the school. You get on that computer of yours and tell Ferrand that there will be no attack."

Billy was about to respond when the doorknob clicked and the door swung open. They both turned to see Gamel framed in the doorway.

Ferrand wasn't even aware of the darkness until the blare of a car horn penetrated his consciousness. He saw the headlights bearing down on him, broke stride, and veered off to the side of the road. The Alfa Romeo flashed by him, its driver too involved with navigating the curve to spare him a glance.

He stepped back onto the paved surface and tried to resume his pace, but he was suddenly aware of the pain in his legs and the dry fire that filled his chest. He staggered for a few steps, pulled up with his hands on his hips, and bent from the waist as he sucked in air.

He had been running for nearly an hour, along the edge of the highway, first southward toward the tall apartment buildings at the edge of the city, then, when the traffic had grown heavy, back toward the farmhouse. He had no idea how far he had traveled. But it had worked. Somewhere during the first few miles, the image of Joey Trotta's marble-white face faded into the recesses of his consciousness. The wretching sickness that had struck him at the police station went away.

Otis Brown had sent him to the station house as soon as they'd learned that a body had been dumped at the front gate. The news had thrown the command post into turmoil. "It's one of the boys," Brown had told him, holding his hand over the phone while he'd listened to the reaction from Washington. "Call me as soon as you identify him." He'd gestured toward the phone. "They need to know who it is."

"Get right back here," Colonel Smiles had added. "This may mean that we're going in."

Before he had been able to respond, two Italian soldiers

had been leading him toward a waiting car. They'd pushed him into the back seat, and then one of the soldiers had slid in beside him.

At first he had been confused. It must be some sort of a mistake. Washington assured them that negotiations were in progress. Brown and Smiles accepted the information and decided that the boys would be safe. They determined that the best course of action was to do nothing that could confuse or excite the terrorists. They told him to contact Billy Tepper and put a stop to his preparations. They seemed positive it was just a matter of time before the boys would be released. And he had accepted their assurances. After all, they were part of the United States government, experts in this kind of crisis. It had to be a mistake!

But as they'd driven on in silence, he had begun to realize that the report was true. He'd remembered the anxiety in Brown's eyes as he talked with someone on the other side of the Atlantic and the sudden change in Smiles, who had abandoned the role of tactician and was acting like a military commander. There had been a smell of fear in the air at the farmhouse. Crisis control had turned into crisis. And he remembered Gamel, calmly explaining the methodology by which one of the boys would pay with his life for each day of delay. Ferrand had begun to understand then that what had happened was exactly what Gamel had said would happen.

His confusion had given way to rage. There *had* been a mistake—a terrible error in judgment. The experts had miscalculated. They had made assumptions about the attitudes of the terrorists, and those assumptions had been wrong. They had tried to bargain when they had been warned that there was no room for bargaining. They had ignored the deadline, thinking it was only a threat and not a reality. The experts had been wrong. And one of the boys had paid the price.

Faces had begun to rush through his mind as if responding to a roll call. First those of the older boys on the soccer team who were his daily companions. Faces that were growing hard and square, colored by the first sparse traces of beard, with eyes narrowed in apprehension instead of wide open in anticipation. Faces trying to remain composed right up to the last instant when they understood where the lottery had pointed the gun. Ferrand had thought briefly of each of them, trying to come up with reasons why the body he was going to identify should be one and not another, and fighting the urge to value some more than others.

Then he'd thought of the younger faces, many with names he hadn't yet learned. Round, soft faces, with eyes that tended to wander in a thousand different directions. Faces that would fill with terror at the first hint of danger. It didn't seem right that it should be one of the babies. Their youth would give them an added measure of protection. Except that all the boys were young. And maybe Gamel would start with the child closest in age to his own slaughtered daughter.

Maria's face. Ferrand hadn't been able to think of the brats without seeing her. If Gamel's victim was one of her charges, then the bullet would certainly have destroyed her as well. He remembered his instinctive reaction when Otis Brown had said it was one of the boys. "Thank God it's not Maria." But then he understood that Maria would feel the pain of any child that was chosen for killing and that the pain would linger in her long after it had left the small lifeless body.

The car had come to a stop in front of an old building built out of massive brown stones and large ornate windows, with flags that he hadn't recognized flying over the entrance. He had been rushed up the steps, past wooden desks manned by soldiers who glanced up curiously as he disturbed their routine, and up a wide staircase to the second floor. An officer had greeted him in broken English, bobbed his head in a confused expression of sympathy, then opened a door and stood back so that Ferrand could enter.

The body had been on a bed, covered with a khaki blanket. Only the legs protruded, clad in faded jeans and white sneakers that were stained with grass along the sides.

"I'm sorry . . . very sorry," the officer had said as he reached in front of Ferrand and drew back the blanket.

"Joey Trotta," Ferrand had said instantly, forming the words before he could even react to the lifeless form. The officer's pen had hesitated above the clipboard he was carrying. "Trotta," Ferrand had repeated, as if he were filling out a questionnaire. "T—R—O—T—T—A. Joey . . . Joseph, I guess. He's an upperclassman. He graduates in June."

The Italian had written down the name, then reached for the edge of the blanket, but Ferrand had caught his hand. He'd stood for a moment, studying the face.

The swarthy skin had gone pale, nearly colorless, except for the blue that had filled his lips. There was a dark welt on the side of the head, just in front of the left ear, nothing more serious than the bruises all the boys carried home from the athletic field. The eyes were closed. He'd wanted to think that Joey was asleep, but it was obvious he wasn't. Death had its unique complexion, and Joey was certainly dead. He'd wondered whether Joey knew he was dead. He'd wondered whether Joey knew anything.

"It was painless," the Italian officer had whispered. "I'm sure he never felt anything. He never had time."

"That's what hurts," he'd answered. "He never had time."

Then he'd released the man's hand, and the officer had raised the blanket until Joey disappeared. They were outside the room in the dark hallway when Ferrand had felt the nausea. He'd leaned against the wall for an instant, then dropped to his knees and wretched. But he couldn't get sick. There was no food in his stomach, so there was no way to relieve the pain in his gut.

By the time he had returned to the farmhouse, the Italian police had already called with Joey's name. He had no message to deliver. Smiles was away from the command post, meeting with his Delta force. Otis Brown was busy with an endless series of telephone calls. He'd stood hopelessly in the kitchen, oblivious to the activity that was raging around him.

It was Smiles' adjutant who'd noticed him and asked if there was anything he needed.

"Can you get me a pair of running shoes?" Ferrand had answered. The adjutant had looked surprised, but then seemed to understand. He'd called one of the soldiers and ordered that someone be sent into the city to get Ferrand whatever he needed.

It was a ridiculous reaction. But it had provided the distraction he needed. He had run with self-destructive fury until the very act of running assumed total importance. He had passed through pain and into exhilaration, and the roll call of faces had disappeared. Even now, as he walked laboriously past the armed guard and up the path to the farmhouse, they still hadn't returned.

Inside the command post, the panic had passed. The sitting room with its faded furniture was empty. Otis Brown and Colonel Smiles were seated at the kitchen table, studying photographs of the school that had been taken with powerful lenses from the woods surrounding the fortress.

"Feel any better?" Brown asked as soon as Ferrand appeared in the doorway.

He nodded, still breathing too heavily to respond.

"The negotiations have been accelerated," Brown said. "We've got people on their way to Egypt for a face-to-face meeting with Sharif."

Ferrand nodded again.

"The first thing they're going to do is stop the clock. It may take a day or so to work out the details of the release—the exchange—but there will be no more killing."

Ferrand looked up from his shoes. "That's what you thought this morning," he managed to say.

Otis Brown accepted the reprimand. "We've got one problem," he continued. "It needs your advice." He lifted one of the papers from the table and held it out to Ferrand. It was a message from Billy, sent by his computer over the telephone line.

Everything is ready for tomorrow night at 7:30.
Don't be late. Don't worry about the bombs because
they won't explode. Lets make them pay for what
they did to Joey.

Gamel walked into Billy Tepper's room without saying a
word; his face was expressionless except for a knowing smile
that played at the corners of his mouth. He crossed to the
window, ignoring Maria, who was standing just inside the
door and holding the medicine tray, and Billy, who was
seated next to the desk. For a moment he stared out over the
grounds, able to see the tops of the trees against the lights
that flooded the walls. Then he pulled the shade down
slowly.

"I watched you come in here on the television monitor,"
he finally said, his back still turned to Maria and Billy. "You
have been in here for a long time. I wondered what kind of
medication took so long."

"They have to talk," Maria answered immediately.
"They're all frightened. Talking is more important than medicine."

He turned slowly and looked from Maria to Billy. "What
were you talking about?" he asked the boy.

"About getting out of here," Billy said.

Gamel nodded his approval. He noticed the Spitfire and
picked up the model to examine it closely, turning the plane
in his hands so he could see it from every angle.

"This is beautiful," he decided. "Did you make it?"

"No," Billy said. "I was just fixing it for one of the little
kids." He watched in horror as Gamel looked through the
plane's plastic canopy. The flight-control electronics could be
seen through the canopy when the Spitfire was held at a certain angle.

"Does it fly?" Gamel continued. He seemed to be looking
right at the circuits that were identical to those in the transmitter he carried in his pocket.

"Sometimes," Billy said. He jumped up from his chair and turned the plane over in Gamel's hands so that the terrorist couldn't see through the canopy. "But the wheels keep breaking," he lied, pointing to the tiny landing gear on the bottom of the wings. "I'm trying to figure out how to make them stronger."

Gamel released the model and watched as Billy set it upside down on the desk. Then he reached for the framed picture.

"Your mother and father?" he asked, looking at the two distinguished faces that were drawn close to one another.

"My father," Billy said. "She's his . . . new wife. I only saw her once."

Gamel set the picture down and looked around the room, taking in the books on the shelves and the posters of rock stars that were fixed to the walls. Then he crossed over to the closet and began to push open the sliding door. Billy couldn't remember whether he had pulled the hanging clothes back over the computer. His eyes shot to Maria, and the fear in her expression told him he hadn't. As the door opened a crack, he could see the machine's keyboard.

"Did you have to kill him?" Billy suddenly shouted. Gamel froze, his fingers resting on the edge of the closet door. He remained motionless for only a second, but it seemed like hours to Maria.

"He was just a kid," Billy added in a softer voice.

Gamel turned slowly away from the door, the cold black lenses swinging toward Billy Tepper.

"Don't pay any attention to him," Maria said nervously. "He's upset. They're all upset."

Gamel raised his hand to silence her, his eyes settling on Billy. Maria could hear the medicine bottles beginning to rattle on the tray, but she couldn't seem to steady them.

"He was your friend?" he asked.

Billy nodded. "Yeah, he was my friend."

"He didn't do what he was told," Gamel said. "Tell all your friends that they should do what they are told."

He never looked back toward the closet. Instead, he pointed through the doorway, indicating that Maria should leave the room. Then he followed her out into the hallway and closed the door behind him. He stood for a long moment staring at her, then looked down at the medicines that were shaking in her hands. Slowly, he reached out and touched the edge of the tray until the rattling stopped.

"You're learning to be afraid," he told her. "That's good. Make sure that all the boys stay frightened. It will help to keep them alive."

Her eyes lowered from his face toward the pistol that hung from his belt. She saw him turn and walk back toward the stairs.

"We have to stop him," Otis Brown said as Ferrand handed him back the computer printout. "We can't let him go on making plans for an invasion that isn't going to happen."

"I can send him another message," Ferrand agreed. "But he may not pay any more attention to this one than he did to the last one."

Brown wasn't satisfied with the answer. "Maybe he didn't understand the instructions we sent. I think this time we ought to ask for an acknowledgment. We'll tell him to do nothing and then ask for a return message that says he understands and promises he'll do nothing."

Ferrand nodded. "Okay, we can try." He left the kitchen and went upstairs to change into his clothes. Brown followed him into the bedroom.

"How do you think he'll react?" he asked as Ferrand stripped out of the running shorts and towled himself off.

Ferrand weighed the possibilities as he pulled on his slacks and shirt. "I think the acknowledgment is a good idea. If we get an answer from him, we can probably count on him to do what he says. My guess would be that if he doesn't want to follow your instructions, he won't send you an acknowledgment. You have nothing to lose by trying."

Brown followed Ferrand back down to the kitchen and watched while the teacher poured himself a cup of coffee.

"That's not true," he finally said. He saw that Ferrand didn't understand his comment. "We do have something to lose. I think each exchange of messages is dangerous. It raises the risk that a message might be intercepted. I wouldn't want to send another instruction unless you're very sure he'd obey it."

Ferrand answered with a hint of anger. "Christ, Otis, how can I give you assurance that he's going to follow your instructions? He's fifteen years old and trying to think this thing through without any help. Last time we told him that if he did nothing everything would be all right. We told him his friends would be safe. So he did nothing, or at least nothing that the terrorists were aware of. And then today he probably watched while they pulled Joey Trotta's name out of a hat, walked him outside, and put a bullet in his head. I don't know about you, but if I were Billy Tepper, I wouldn't have a lot of confidence in the brilliance of adults right about now. I'd probably figure the odds were just as good doing it my way."

Brown didn't seem at all affected by the stinging criticism. He simply absorbed what he heard and put it into his mental computer with all the other information he had gathered.

"I tend to agree with you," he concluded. "If we sent a new message, there's a possibility it would be intercepted. That would be dangerous for Billy and probably some of the other boys. And even if the message wasn't intercepted, there's the possibility that Billy would get caught trying to send back a response. There's also the possibility that Billy would ignore the message. In that case, we could lose eight, maybe ten, hours waiting for an answer that wasn't coming."

"There's another reason," Colonel Smiles said, suddenly lifting his attention from the photographs he had been studying. "If we do have to go in there, we're going to need the kid's help. We can't turn him off and on like a light switch."

Ferrand slammed down his coffee cup, spilling the freshly

poured coffee into the sink. "What do you mean, 'if we have to go in there'?" he demanded. His head snapped quickly from the colonel to Brown and then back to the Army officer. "Jesus, don't you guys know what you're doing yet? One minute you're telling me that the negotiations are being rushed and that there won't be any more killing, and the next you're talking about invading."

"There won't be any attack," Brown started to say, but Smiles cut him off before he could finish.

"That's right now, Otis," he said. "A few hours ago, when it looked like we were going to be able to negotiate, the politicians told me to prepare for an attack. Now, when it looks like we may have to take the school, they're telling us to stand down." He turned to Ferrand. "The fact is, you're absolutely right. We don't know what the hell we're doing."

"There will be no attack," Brown said with authority. "We already have representatives in Cairo waiting to meet with Sharif."

"If they can find the son of a bitch," Smiles fired back, holding his ground. "Look, Otis. If something goes wrong with the meeting, there's going to be another body waiting at the gate at five o'clock. Which means that by six o'clock the politicians will be in a panic and we could have orders to attack. So then what do we do? Send the kid another message and tell him that we didn't mean it? That we want him to go ahead and defuse the bombs we've just told him not to touch?"

"We have our instructions," Brown insisted.

"Which are good until they send another set of instructions," Smiles replied. "What I'm saying is that we ought to be ready in case they do another one of their flip-flops."

Ferrand stood at the edge of the table, his head turning as he followed the heated exchange. In spite of the argument, he felt himself tremble as if he were chilled. Simultaneously, Brown and Smiles became aware that they were performing before a critical audience. They both fell silent, Brown turning away from the table while the colonel looked back toward his photographs.

"You're guessing," Ferrand said softly. "You're guessing what Sharif will do, and Sharif is guessing what you'll do. And there's a hundred pounds of plastic waiting to explode if someone makes the wrong guess."

Brown slipped off his glasses and tried to wipe the lenses on the front of his shirt. "No one can be sure," he acknowledged honestly.

"I'm sorry, Otis," the colonel began to say, but Brown waved away the apology as unnecessary.

"We're all on edge," he said for everyone. And then there was a guilty silence, as if the three men had been caught conspiring in a hideous crime.

Colonel Smiles broke the spell. "It's just that if we had to go in there, that kid gives me a better chance than I've ever had before. Here, take a look at these."

He held up a series of photographs, which Brown took and then began passing to Ferrand.

"This is the dining hall," Ferrand said in amazement. "I can see the kids' faces. I can identify them." He looked at the Army officer. "When were these taken?"

"This afternoon," Smiles said. "They're taken from the next hilltop, a little over a mile away. Look at this one." He handed Ferrand a photo that showed the back of a man seated at a desk. "That's Gamel. This one was taken right through the headmaster's window. If we had a rifle that could fire that far with accuracy, we could have put a bullet right through the bastard's head."

"To what purpose?" Brown asked, taking the picture from Ferrand. "All that would accomplish is to put someone else in charge. Someone probably more likely to panic than Gamel."

"That's not the point," Smiles said. "What I'm trying to show you is that we can see into the dining hall. That solves one of the major problems we had. I was concerned that we might attack thinking the boys were safe in the wine cellar.

But suppose something went wrong at the last second and the kid wasn't able to get the other boys into the wine cellar. They'd all be caught in the cross fire. What I needed was some way to be certain the kids were safe the instant before we attacked. We have that now. We can look in and make sure that the dining hall is empty."

Brown looked up from the photo. "It would still be a terrible risk. The boys could get caught as soon as they started to escape. Some of them might get killed right before your eyes. And even if they did make it to the cellar, there're still the explosives. All Gamel has to do is touch that button and your attack is a failure."

Smiles turned to Ferrand. "What about the explosives?" he asked. "Can the kid disarm them?"

Ferrand thought a minute. "I don't know what's involved," he finally concluded.

The colonel shuffled through the papers on the table and found the computer printout. "'Don't worry about the bombs because they won't explode,'" he read. "Do you think he knows what he's talking about."

"He's only fifteen," Otis Brown interrupted, but the colonel's eyes never left Ferrand's face. He was waiting for a response.

Ferrand walked back to the sink and retrieved his coffee cup. He started to refill it, then stopped with the pot hanging from his hand. "Billy is pretty certain the bombs won't explode," he concluded. "He understands the mechanism, and he thinks he can fix it."

Brown's impatience flared. "This is ridiculous," he said, but once again the colonel kept his attention riveted on the school teacher.

"*Can* he fix it?" Smiles pressed.

Ferrand knew exactly what he was being asked. Tepper had said the bombs wouldn't explode. He knew Billy Tepper better than either Brown or Smiles. So Smiles was leaving the decision up to him. Should the colonel bet the lives of his men and the lives of the boys on Billy's promise that the bombs wouldn't explode?

"He can fix it," he answered.

Albert Trotta was sitting behind the massive wooden desk that had pride of place in the center of his library, a room walled with books that he had never read. He was surrounded by the symbols of his power—books and paintings, rich draperies framing tall arched windows that looked out over the Short Hills countryside, an expansive hand-loomed Oriental rug, a gun collection that dated back to the Revolution. Yet he looked frail and vulnerable. He was seated alone in his shirt-sleeves, the single desklamp glaring down on the top of his balding head.

When he looked up, his red eyes blinked into the light. Then his hand reached out and tipped the shade so that the glare was directed away from him. He sat motionless for several minutes. Then he touched the button under the edge of the desk and tried to square his shoulders to make a good appearance for Nino Lanza, his childhood friend and trusted business associate.

"I'm sorry, Don Trotta," Nino managed when he reached the desk, "truly sorry. He was a fine boy."

Albert Trotta nodded in appreciation. "Drink a glass of wine with me," he said. Nino went to the liquor cabinet and removed two wineglasses and a dark red decanter. He set the glasses on the desk blotter next to Trotta's hands and filled them both. Albert waved to the leather chair next to his desk, inviting Nino to sit.

"I won't wake his mother," he said, reminding himself of a decision he had made an instant after he had received the news. He took a sip of the wine as if to close the subject, but then looked at Nino and asked, "How am I going to tell her?"

"She's a strong woman," Nino said, as if that were an answer.

Albert leaned back, his eyes raised to the ceiling. "She

wanted to go over for his graduation. She thought we could start at the school and then travel through the old country and visit family. I told her we'd see, but I think I would have done it. I think I was looking forward to it."

"You should go anyway," Nino advised. "Take a boat. It will be good for you both."

Trotta nodded. He looked thoughtful, as if he were considering the trip. "He was ashamed of me," he finally said.

Nino objected. "He loved you, Albert." The don began to shake his head at the suggestion, but Nino persisted. "He was a boy. It was a phase. All our children are ashamed of us at some time. That's normal. But he loved you. I know he did."

Trotta tapped his fingers on the desktop as he considered his friend's words. Then he lifted his glass and sipped at his wine absently. "It was the vice president who called," he reminded himself. "He sent the respects of the president. Joey should know. The president of the United States."

"You've done them a great service," Nino said by way of explaining that a call from such a high level was only to be expected.

Albert suddenly leaned forward, his manner indicating he was done reminiscing. "Did Sharif get my request?"

Nino nodded. "Frattiani delivered the message personally to Sharif's brother in Alexandria. He was told it would be relayed to Sharif within the hour."

"And this was his response," Don Trotta concluded.

"There may have been a mistake. Maybe he never got your request."

"I thought of that," Trotta said. "But if he never got the message, then my son would still be held in the school. Why would they single out Joey?"

Nino shook his head. "I don't know, Don Trotta."

"What does Frattiani say?"

"He's shocked, and very angry." Nino tried to remember Frattiani's exact words. "He thinks that Sharif is cutting all his ties with the past."

"By killing a boy?" Trotta asked disgustedly. "Perhaps that's the way an Arab sends you a message. Perhaps this is what I deserve for dealing with Arabs."

Nino shut his eyes to the suggestion. "You can't blame yourself, Albert. It makes no sense. Did we ever hurt another man's family? Another man's son? I hear about governments that let children starve. And then these people who think they can settle a dispute by threatening children? I don't understand it. It's not our way."

Trotta nodded. And then his eyes began to fill again. "I couldn't do it," he agreed. "Even now, if Sharif had a son, I couldn't hurt him just to make things even."

They sat in silence while they finished the wine.

"Thank you for staying with me," the don said finally.

Nino shrugged. He stood the instant that Trotta rose from behind his desk.

"Will you be talking with Frattiani?" Trotta asked as Nino was leaving.

"If you want," his friend offered.

"Yes," Don Trotta said. "Tell him to cut all our ties with the past."

April 19

morning

Sharif sensed the warmth and opened his eyes to the slats of sunlight that were streaming into the back of the truck. For an instant he wondered where he was and then a sudden jolt reminded him that he was traveling over an unpaved road. He pushed away the equipment packing he had used as a blanket during the night and sat up quickly.

The sky was white, not yet colored by the sun that had just broken the horizon ahead. To either side were thin fields, planted in cotton that had not yet begun to flower. Behind him was a cloud of dust that had been kicked up by the tires as they bounced over stones and dropped into potholes. The only sounds were the hum of the engine and the gurgle of the exhaust as it passed beneath the truck bed.

He stood unsteadily and pounded with the flat of his hand against the top of the cab. In response, the engine seemed to die and the truck rolled to a stop at the side of the road. Sharif pushed passed the cargo and climbed down from the tailgate. Without a word of explanation, he wandered to the edge of a field and relieved himself. When he turned back, one of his men had already raised the hood and vented steam from the radiator into a coffeepot. When he reached the cab, he was handed a tin cup of coffee still thick with boiled grounds.

"Where are we?" he asked.

The driver held up three fingers. "Three hours to the river," he answered. "Then we turn north to the highway."

"We're early. I don't want to reach the city until noon."

The driver shrugged. "Maybe we shouldn't wait. On the radio, they are already talking about your arrival. They say that the American under secretary has landed and gone to the American embassy. Everyone knows you're coming, so it may be safer to get to the city as quickly as possible."

Sharif weighed his alternatives as he sipped the bitter coffee. If they were expecting him, people would begin watching the roads and highways. The longer he waited, the greater the chance of his being discovered. He had arranged for a safe house where he could bathe and change into a military uniform. Then he would parade publicly to the Swiss embassy. He probably would be safer in the house than out on the open road.

"You're right," he said at last. "Let's get started."

He tossed the remaining coffee onto the road, then climbed up into the back of the truck. The engine started before he could reach his sanctuary in front of the machinery.

It was all working perfectly. The American had arrived with his hat in his hand, not to visit with any of the established governments, but rather to sit at the bargaining table with Sharif. The implications were staggering. The kings and presidents were being pushed back into the crowd, where they would strain their necks for a glimpse at the negotiations. The Arab people would see them as they were— foolish men, small of stature and devoid of insight. Men with questions instead of answers. They would look past them toward a new leader who could command the presence of the Americans, fix the time and place, write the agenda, and dictate the terms.

The agreement itself wasn't that important. Of course he would release the children. There was no question that the Americans would release Arab prisoners. Financial concessions would also be made, even though they would be thinly disguised as a face-saving for the imperialists. To the Americans, the need to save face was as important as the lives of children. But still, it would be apparent to everyone that the Americans were paying an indemnity. Perhaps they would call it humanitarian aid. Or perhaps a loan. But whatever they called it, they would funnel billions through his hands into relief for the Palestinians. As for the movements of their fleet, what did it matter? The power of the fleet could only threaten property. It was no threat to the ideals of Islam or to his revolutionary cause. Perhaps he would concede it freedom of movement as a magnanimous gesture to a vanquished foe. But all these things were just details.

What was important was that by the very act of meeting with him the Americans were conceding his legitimacy. And if he was legitimate, then his followers were legitimate, anointed to roles of leadership throughout the Arab world. The phantom governments, created by the British as their final curse on the Middle East, would no longer be able to hold power. The religious fanatics, who sold faith in poverty and ignorance, would be driven from their minarets. And the Jews, who had avoided their responsibility to the Arabs they had dispossessed by playing one self-seeking government against another? Now they would face one voice, representating all Arabs from the Atlantic to the Indian Ocean.

As the sun colored the earth and heated the air, Sharif orchestrated the event in his mind. He would leave the safe house in military fatigues, with epaulets on the shoulders of his belted tunic and a white burnoose tied with a red cord, symbolic of his imagined nationless tribe. As he was driven through the streets, crowds would begin to form, pressing against the police that the Egyptian government would station everywhere to prevent an incident. But the police, too, would turn to face his motorcade and join in the warbling chorus of adulation. He would lead his entourage through the courtyard of the embassy, pausing to wave at the television cameras, walk to the assigned conference room, and take his seat at the head of the table without even acknowledging the defeated American.

The American would open with a statement prepared for Western consumption in which he would condemn Sharif's indifference to the safety of children. But he would counter with a statement of his own, recalling the atrocities against Arab children that were a feature of Western occupation of Arab lands. "Why," he would demand, "are American children privileged when Arab boys and girls are sold in the French brothels of Lebanon and made servants in the British garrisons of Palestine?" Then he would dictate his terms, make the inconsequential concessions, and step onto a balcony to wave the surrender document before the throng. He was entering Cairo as a peasant. He would leave as a king.

In his mind he was hearing the crowd thundering his name when he suddenly became aware of the sound of the truck engine. It was slowing, then racing as the driver shifted to a lower gear. Sharif climbed up along the fencing and peered out over the top of the cab. Ahead, he could see a jeep parked across the road, with men standing beside it. He slumped down and sat leaning against the sideboards, his knees drawn up to his chest as the truck rolled to a stop.

There should be no problem, he told himself. Police roadblocks were common, and they had all the necessary papers—passports, work cards, manifests for the cargo. The routine check should take only a few seconds, and in his work clothes there would be no chance of his being recognized. He listened to the official's request for papers and heard his men comply cheerfully. He reached into his own pocket and took out his forged documents, ready to present them when the police climbed into the truck to examine the cargo.

A uniformed figure appeared at the tailgate and ordered him to step down. Sharif pretended for a moment not to understand the dialect clearly, then nodded profusely and crawled past the machinery. He climbed down and offered his papers. It was then that he saw the drawn pistol pointed at his chest.

The official gestured with the gun, guiding Sharif around to the front of the truck. His peasant charade stopped abruptly when he saw his two companions leaning against the hood, their legs spread behind them. Another uniformed figure was covering them with a machine gun. Sharif watched in horror as his men were ordered to lie face down on the ground, their heads under the running board. The police officer opened the hood, reached in, and pulled out the distributor cap. He walked to the side of the road and flung the cap into the grass. Then they walked Sharif to the jeep and pushed him into the passenger seat. One of the officers climbed in behind him, keeping the machine gun trained on the back of his head. The other officer jumped in behind the wheel, started the engine, and aimed the jeep down the road.

Sharif understood what was happening. He was being kidnapped. His companions were being spared so that they could retrieve the distributor cap, repair the truck, and carry the news into Cairo.

He glanced at the driver, who was certainly an Egyptian and perhaps even a legitimate police officer. But undoubtedly he was of higher rank than that indicated by the simple uniform he wore. Lieutenants weren't entrusted the task of capturing the Flaming Sword from the Desert. Who could they be? American CIA perhaps. Were the Americans so foolish as to think they could capture an Arab leader and engineer a trade? There wasn't a single Middle East country that would stand by idly while he was loaded aboard an airplane. And even if he were, no European country would have the courage to grant landing rights or even overflight permission to a plane that was carrying him to captivity.

Maybe the Israelis? Certainly their security forces had the skill and the contacts to locate him and arrange for his kidnapping. But why? They would never hold him away from the bargaining table while American children were being systematically executed. They existed only as a result of the goodwill of the Americans, and they would never risk American approval for the simple pleasure of holding Sharif in one of their prisons.

They drove for only a few miles, but well out of sight of the crippled truck, before the jeep turned onto a side road, scarcely a dirt track that led between two planted fields. His apprehension grew as they drove further away from the main road.

Could it be one of the Arab governments? Were the Egyptians playing lackey to the Americans? Or were the Syrians planning to eliminate a hero of the people before he arrived at his moment of power? He felt the coffee in his stomach go sour. Suddenly, it made sense.

The rise of Sharif was a danger to every one of the Middle East governments. He was a greater danger to them than he was to the Americans. So they would kill him. Kill him at a time when his murder could easily be blamed on the Americans. Or better, on the Jews! With one bullet, they could eliminate a rival who threatened their thrones and at the same time create new reasons for their subjects to hate the Zionist entity.

Sharif shouted over the engine noise at the driver. "You're making a mistake." The driver's eyes never moved from the road. Sharif turned slowly in his seat to face the machine gun. "If you kill me, then they will have to kill you. Whoever sent you to do this will have to eliminate every witness. You will be dead before nightfall."

The eyes that were training the machine gun toward him never flickered. The expression on the man's face remained cold and businesslike.

Sharif tried to think through his growing panic. They had left his men alive. They had let the men see them in their Egyptian uniforms and then left them alive to tell what they had seen. Whoever had taken him prisoner wanted blame to be on the Egyptians. It couldn't be the Israelis. They were friendly with the Egyptians, the only Arab nation that recognized them as a country. Nor the Americans. The Egyptians were their allies. He thought of the Syrians, who feared him and hated the Egyptians. And of the Iranians. Their fundamentalist madmen hated everyone.

"Don't you understand?" he said to the driver. "We're on the verge of a great victory. Talk to your leaders. This can be a great victory for all of us." The driver made no response.

Sharif looked ahead and saw the dusty sedan pulled off into the edge of the field. They were bringing him to meet with someone who was waiting in the car. His terror lessened. At least his fate wouldn't be left in the hands of obedient underlings. No matter who they were, at least he would have a chance to plead his case with someone in authority. Perhaps it was the Americans or the Israelis. At least they would understand reason. He realized then that he felt safer with them than with his own Arab brothers.

The jeep braked to a stop fifty yards short of the sedan. The gun barrel pressed into the center of his back told him to climb out and start toward the parked car. As soon as he was standing on the dirt road, he heard the jeep shift gears. He watched as it backed into a turn, then shifted gears again and drove away.

Sharif started toward the sedan, aware that there was only one person seated behind the dusty windshield. His confusion was total. If it was an American who wanted to negotiate with him, then the Egyptians should have waited to take him back to the truck. If it was a kidnapper or an assassin, then why would he be alone?

For an instant, he thought of diving off the road into the sparse grass. His only chance might be to run, hoping to lose the single figure that waited in the sedan. But then the door pushed open. A short well-built man climbed out of the car and began walking toward him. Sharif raised his hand to block the glare of the sun, but the man approaching him was still distorted by the waves of heat rising from the ground. Before he could recognize the face, he was aware of the pistol that hung from the man's right hand. Sharif stopped, but the man kept walking toward him.

"Wait," he called out. "Who are you?" Before the words had passed his lips, he recognized the face. It was Paul Frattiani, Don Trotta's agent. "Paul, my friend," he babbled in his confusion. "What are you doing here? What do you want?"

Frattiani kept walking until he was only ten yards from Sharif. Then his right arm rose, bringing the gun to bear on Sharif's head. His left hand came up to steady his right hand.

"Paul, what are you doing? Why?" Sharif begged. He couldn't even guess at a reason.

"Don Trotta sends his respects," Frattiani said.

Sharif had no idea what the answer meant. He thought he heard a pistol shot. Then his confusion vanished.

At the sound of the shot, birds screeched and rushed out of the grass and into the air. They darted in one direction, assembled into a ragged formation, then flew back over the body that was lying still in the dust.

Frattiani pulled the sedan up next to Sharif's corpse,

opened the trunk, and lifted the body in next to the spare tire. He drove back to the main road, stopped, and tossed Sharif out onto the packed dirt. Then he drove away.

Moments later, the truck reached the intersection and braked abruptly. Sharif's companions rushed out and turned the body over on its back. The Flaming Sword from the Desert had been extinguished by a small hole in the center of his forehead.

Billy was up before the sun, working on the last piece of his plan. He had blinded the television security cameras, organized the boys for their escape into the wine cellar, and found a way to disarm the radio-controlled explosives. But without the ordinary alarm clock that he was in the process of adjusting, nothing else would work. The clock would initiate the massive distraction that was needed before the plan could be put into motion.

It was a simple matter of converting the hour hand into a mechanical switch. He split the two wires of an extension cord, then cut one of the wires and pared back the insulation. One end was connected to the base of the hour hand, the other secured to the face of the clock at the seven-thirty position. The hand would wind its way around during the day. At seven-thirty it would touch the wire fixed to the face plate and reconnect the lamp cord he had cut.

Next Billy reached behind the books on his bookshelf and found the smoke bomb he had been building for the past three months. He had intended it to be the soul of his next cosmic prank. Now, it had a more practical purpose.

The bomb was its own disguise, designed to escape undetected even if Ferrand or any of the other teachers had pulled a surprise search of his room. "That?" he could have said with typical innocence. "Oh, just some photographs. I'm going to make some prints when I get a chance." He had packed photographic negatives into a milk container on top of a heating coil and a few layers of cellophane. Heat up the coil and the cellophane would catch fire. That would start the film negatives burning, giving off clouds of acrid black smoke. Eventually the milk container would melt and break apart, letting more air reach the negatives and causing still more smoke.

He had planned to sneak down during the night and connect the device into one of the lamp outlets in the faculty lounge, maybe during exam week when the teachers typically retired to the lounge after dinner to correct their test papers. They would sit down with their coffee cups, turn on the lights as darkness fell, and begin their idiotic chuckling over the answers that their students had provided. Two minutes later, they'd be tossing chairs through the windows in their panic to escape the stinking black cloud.

Now he connected the lamp wires to the heating coil and wrapped the wire around his body, holding the alarm clock and the bomb against his chest. Then he covered the whole assembly with his bathrobe, tightened the belt to hold the pieces in position, and opened his door. The guard near the stairwell reacted as soon as he stepped into the corridor. But Billy tried to look unconcerned as he padded down the hall and turned into the bathroom.

Once inside, he pressed against the door and listened to make certain that the guard wasn't coming down the hall to check on him. The only sound, though, was the rhythmic creaking of the old building. Then he crossed the tile floor to the ventilation shaft that rose through the center of the building, connecting the bathrooms on each floor to the roof. It took him only seconds to remove the grating.

Billy lowered the bomb down the shaft, using the extension cord as a drop line, and felt the cord slacken as the container reached the bottom of the blackness below. Then he set the clock hands, wound the spring, and stood the clock on the ledge of the opening. Next he went into one of the booths and removed a roll of toilet paper. He wadded the paper and stuffed it into the pipe that connected the top of the shaft to the roof. Then he replaced the grating. Finally, he stretched the end of the extension cord behind the wash-basins and plugged it into an electrical outlet.

At seven-thirty, the hands of the clock would close the circuit, connecting the outlet to the heat coil two stories be-low. Within seconds, smoke would begin to rise in the shaft, only to be blocked by the paper he had stuffed into the roof outlet. Instead, it would pour through the vents, filling the bathrooms on all three floors and reaching the smoke detec-tors. The detectors would trip the fire alarms throughout the old building and turn on the sprinkler systems. And that, Billy reasoned, would send most of the guards rushing out of the dining hall to fight the fire that was engulfing the man-sion.

He splashed water on his face, readjusted his robe and walked back into the corridor. The guard, who had slumped against the wall, was immediately alert. Billy tossed him a casual wave. "Asshole," he mumbled through a friendly smile. Then he turned into his room and collapsed onto his bed.

One more go go, he thought to himself. Sometime after breakfast he would make his trek from the dining hall to the lavatory and then lift himself into the new building's air ducts. He would wait there until Miss Manetti found an ex-cuse to lure the commander out of the headmaster's office and into the dining hall. Then he would drop down into the administration office and fix the bastard's remote-controlled bombs. After that, it was all up to Ferrand and the Scream-ing Eagles.

His face broke into a grin. Probably, when this was all over, they'd give him a medal. He wondered whether any kid had ever been given the Congressional Medal of Honor. Heck, they might even bring him to Washington so that the president could give it to him personally. Maybe his father would even come, although that was kind of pushing things. His father had already promised that he would try to make it to his graduation, after first explaining to him that he couldn't just drop whatever it was he actually did.

He bounded out of bed as soon as the morning bell sounded. Boy, but this was going to be one exciting day.

Otis Brown found Edward Ferrand on the wooden bench that had been built under the grape arbor behind the farmhouse. Silently, he sat down next to the teacher and joined him in gazing up the hill to where the sun had broken over the trees that surrounded Saint Anselm's.

"The kids are just getting up," Ferrand said as if he were able to see through the walls of the buildings. "They're probably scared out of their wits."

"It won't be long now," Brown said in response. "We've got an under secretary of state waiting in Cairo. Sharif is supposed to be on his way into the city. They should be talking by lunchtime."

Ferrand's eyes never left the hilltop. "I hope so. Five o'clock comes early. It isn't a lot of time."

Brown nodded in agreement. Then he started in on the subject that had brought him out of the house after Ferrand. "We never should have had that discussion last night. Colonel Smiles, of course, has to be ready for anything. He's not anxious to give up the advantage that someone inside the school could give to his troops. But we're not even thinking about attacking Saint Anselm's. We don't make those kinds of decisions."

"Who does?" Ferrand asked sarcastically.

"Washington makes decisions," Brown answered. "We carry them out."

He looked as if he wanted to explain, but Ferrand cut him short. "They didn't make any decisions yesterday."

Brown got up off the bench and walked a bit, examining the construction of the arbor. "No," he finally agreed. "Yesterday wasn't a very good day. We assumed that if we simply indicated a willingness to talk, even through third parties, they would let their deadlines slip. I guess we assumed wrong."

Ferrand remained silent.

"We think we know how these people think," Brown continued. "Our experience tells us that they don't really want to hurt the hostages. They try to sound cold-blooded, but they're as frightened as their prisoners, particularly when they're isolated in a foreign country. Publicly, we talk a tough line to make them think they're not going to get anything. But privately, we start talking to them and offer them something. It's a kind of equation—give them just enough to get the hostages, but not so much that they seem to have won."

"The equation didn't balance," Ferrand reminded him.

Brown shook his head. "No, this time it didn't balance, and I'm not sure I understand why."

Ferrand looked at him for the first time. "I'm sorry. I shouldn't have said that. It's not your fault. You don't make the rules."

Brown accepted the apology with a shrug. "I think I know how you feel. But the danger is over now. We're meeting with them publicly. We're committed to negotiating. So our job here is to make sure that there isn't another tragedy while we're waiting for the negotiations to be wrapped up. That's why I've decided that we have to get Billy Tepper out of there."

Ferrand's gaze had drifted back up toward Saint Anselm's. Now he turned and looked at Brown.

"I think the one thing we were all agreed on last night," Brown continued, "is that Tepper isn't easy to control. You could send him another message telling him that there won't be an attack, but he might not respond to it. He might go ahead with his plans, isn't that right?"

Ferrand nodded.

"That's a very dangerous state of affairs. We want the boys to sit quietly for as long as it takes to negotiate them out of there. Billy might not sit quietly. In fact, from what you've told us, there's a very good chance he won't."

"How are you going to get him out?" Ferrand asked suspiciously.

Brown returned to the bench and sat on the edge. "I think we have to ask Gamel to turn him over to us." He turned and saw the bewilderment in Ferrand's eyes. "Once Gamel knows that we've given in to Sharif," Brown continued, "then he'll want to keep everything quiet at the school. The last thing he'll want is an incident. So, we'll tell him we're afraid one of the boys might cause an incident and ask to take the boy off his hands."

Ferrand's eyes narrowed.

"Put yourself in his place," Brown said. "We're asking for one boy in order to keep something from happening that could jeopardize Sharif's victory. He still has his hostages. What does he have to lose? If you were in his shoes, wouldn't you go for it?"

"I'm not Gamel. My kid wasn't killed by a shell from an American battleship. You just said it was a mistake to think we understand these people. Now you're acting as if you understand just how he's going to react."

"How else can he react?"

Ferrand's expression showed his anger. "Lots of ways. Maybe when you give him the name of the troublemaker, you make it easy for him to pick the next one he leaves at the gate."

"But there won't be a next one," Brown insisted. "Before we'd tell him about Billy, we'd get a firm commitment that there would be no more killing. We'd make him understand that if another boy was hurt then the negotiations would be as good as finished."

"He's crazy," Ferrand said, reminding Brown of his own words. "He's cold-blooded crazy, and you want to tell him which one of the boys is plotting against him?"

"It's the only sure way," Brown argued, but Ferrand had already bolted from the bench and was stalking across the garden.

"There's nothing 'sure' about it," he fired back. "You could get Billy killed."

Brown's anger was rising as well. "And if we leave him in

there, and he tries one of his schemes, he could get a lot of kids killed. You have to look at the percentages."

"Screw the percentages," Ferrand shouted. "We're talking about lives. Kids' lives. You can't play God, deciding whose life should or shouldn't be risked."

Brown pushed his glasses up on his forehead and pressed his fingers against his eyes. "I don't think I'm playing God," he said quietly. "I'm just trying to keep a bad situation from turning into a tragedy. All these kids are at risk. I'm trying to give them a better chance to survive."

"Let's try one more message," Ferrand offered. "We'll do it Smiles' way and tell him to send back a confirmation."

"Now you're playing the odds," Brown reminded him. "The message could be intercepted. He could get caught responding to us."

Ferrand knew that Brown was right. There was danger in anything they did, and even greater danger in doing nothing.

Brown stood up and started toward the house. "It's your school," he told Ferrand kindly. "They're your kids. So you make the call. I'll handle it any way you want. I'd like to tell you to take your time, but I think we should decide quickly. I hate to think of that boy tampering with all those explosives."

Ferrand wanted to scream after him. It wasn't his decision. He knew nothing about dealing with terrorists. Brown was the expert. But he was beginning to understand what the other man had been telling him. There were no experts because there were no answers. All they could do was play the odds. His roll of the dice was as good as anyone else's.

He looked up the hill toward the school and caught a glimpse of the rooftops through the trees. The boys were held hostage to a frail balance of choices. One miscalculation by any of the fallible players could light the fuse to the explosives that surrounded them.

Ferrand cursed their luck. Of all the children in the world, why were his boys the ones locked in captivity? But that wasn't true. They weren't alone. All the world's children were prisoners at Saint Anselm's. There were American children who lived around the targets of Russian rockets, which could make their lethal journies across the pole in a matter of minutes. Russian children played in parks that were a few hundred feet from the Kremlin, which was centered in the crosshairs of American missiles. Jewish children slept in kibbutzim that were targeted by Syrian howitzers. Lebanese boys and girls played under the muzzles of Israeli tanks. Irish children walked to school past British machine guns.

All were held hostage by fanatical leaders. The children were kept alive not by their right to live but rather by a delicate balance of death. Madness was matched by madness until everyone seemed to be sane. The American president seemed rational when he promised to launch a nuclear holocaust to stop the Red Army. Jews seemed courageous when they sent jet fighters to settle the score for an Arab hand grenade. Soviet generals boasted about the number of warheads that could dance on the head of one of their missiles. IRA soldiers explained the logic of gunning down the queen's cousin, and Palestinians fought to take credit for the car bombs they left in front of hotels.

And the children waited. Waited for the mistake in judgment that would set the tanks in motion. For the computer error that would launch the missiles. For the blasphemy that would start a holy war. Like the boys in Saint Anselm's, all the world's children were surrounded by explosives wired to a single fuse. One mistake would touch it off.

"You make the call," Otis Brown had told him. If he made the right decision, then Billy would live through the night. If he made the wrong decision, then Billy would be dumped at the front gate. But don't take it too seriously! All he could do was buy them a little time. Sooner or later someone would make the wrong call and then the missiles and the shells would come crashing through the roof. They were doomed anyway, so what difference did it make who flipped the coin today? Tomorrow, the insane lottery would be played all over again.

Ferrand crossed the garden and walked into the kitchen. Otis Brown was waiting at the table. "I'm afraid to be wrong," he confessed.

"So am I," Brown answered. "What's your best guess?"

"I'd like to try one more message. I'm not sure it will work, but even if it doesn't, it will give us a little more time to figure out what we should do."

Brown nodded. "That's about the best we can do. Buy a little more time."

In Billy Tepper's closet, a message traced neat lines across the display screen of the computer.

> They will release all of you in the next few hours.
> There will be no attack on the school. Do not move
> the boys into the wine cellar. Do not touch the ex-
> plosives. Just wait until you are all released. Send a
> return message telling me that you understand and
> that you will do nothing. Mr. Ferrand.

But Billy Tepper didn't see it. He had already left his room for the dining hall, the component from Jimmy Bradberry's airplane in his pocket.

Billy Tepper was loose in the ventilation shafts.

He had restaged his washroom charade, sending boys in and out until the guards had completely lost count along with any interest in counting. Then he had gone into the washroom, waited until all the other boys had left, and pulled himself up through the grating. He had dropped into the vault to check his connections to the security cable, then pulled himself back into the metal duct. But instead of returning to the washroom, Billy had set out in the opposite direction, along the wall between the new building and the old mansion and then, after a right-angle turn, behind the far wall separating the dining hall from the classrooms and faculty offices.

It was slow going. Every few feet there were branches off

to the right and left, carrying air the short distances to class-room and dining hall vents. He had to stop at each opening, moving close enough to the vent to reestablish his bearings and confirm that all the activity in the building was normal. In the dining hall, he could see the boys leaning painfully on their elbows as they listened to the teachers and scribbled their mandatory notes. Miss Manetti, he noted, was still at the table with her brats. He couldn't go into the adminstration office until she had made her move. To the left he could see the classroom that the guards were using as a dormitory. Two of the terrorists were asleep on the floor, their weapons resting by their sides.

The duct jogged to the left, indicating that he had reached the end of the dining hall. He was now moving along the corridor toward the headmaster's office and, at the end of the line, the administration office. Billy made his final right turn. There were two openings off to the right. He stopped at the first, pushed his head slowly forward, and peered through the vertical louvers into the headmaster's office. Ahead of him was the closed door. Directly below him was the top of Gamel's head. He would go no further until Miss Manetti had lured the terrorist commander away from this wing of the building.

Maria stole a glance from the reader and checked the time on the clock. Nine twenty-five. She swallowed hard and was suddenly aware of the quickened beating of her heart. Gamel was already suspicious of her, ready to push his pistol against her face and pull the trigger if he caught her in a lie. Now she was about to offer him the lie of a ten-year-old boy.

She looked down at the straw-colored hair of Timmy McFarland, a quiet young man whose father had redefined the concept of money-center banking. He was the brightest of the brats and easily the most mature. Timmy had listened unblinkingly as she'd told him exactly what she wanted him to do. "Just say it hurts, and make it look like it hurts. Keep your legs pulled up against your chest and scream every time someone touches you."

"Even a teacher?" he had asked.

"Anyone," she had said. "They'll pick you up and carry you back to your room. I'll stay with you and then I'll tell you what to do next."

Maria reached out and touched Timmy gently on the shoulder. Blue eyes looked up at her. She nodded. It was time.

Timmy pushed his chair back slowly from the table. He stood quietly, walked to the aisle, and turned toward the washroom. Suddenly he stopped, doubled over, and dropped to his knees.

"Timmy," Maria yelled, causing every head in the dining room to turn. Timmy responded with a long groan. Maria rushed to the stricken child and Harold Hutchings arrived at the same time.

"What is it?" Hutchings demanded.

"What's the matter?" Maria asked.

"It hurts," Timmy groaned.

"What hurts?" Hutchings snapped.

"It hurts," Timmy repeated, toppling over on his side.

The guard who was posted by the washroom came over and joined the guard who had left his station at the kitchen door.

"Where does it hurt?" Maria begged.

Timmy pressed both hands low against his right side, under the leg that was drawn up to his chin. "Here," he groaned. "It hurts."

"It's his appendix," Hutchings said. He reached out and probed the area with his fingertips. Timmy shouted and twisted his body away. "He should go to the hospital," he whispered to Maria.

She looked from Harold to the nearest of the guards, and then back to Timmy. His knees were on his chest, just as she had shown him. "Get your commander," she ordered the guard. His face remained blank. "Do you speak English?" she said to the other guard.

He shrugged his shoulders, then said something in his own language to a guard on the other side of the room, who rushed over to the crowd that had surrounded Tim McFarland.

"Please get your commander. We have to get this boy to a hospital."

The guard looked suspiciously at Maria and she felt her cheeks flush. If she couldn't convince a teenaged soldier, how could she ever hope to deceive Gamel.

"Please," she repeated. "Tell him one of the boys is sick."

He spoke a few crisp words to the other two guards, then turned and hurried across the dining hall. Maria noticed that her hands were trembling. She took Timmy's hand and squeezed it in her own, hoping the pressure would stop her shaking.

Billy heard the knock on the door and saw the guard enter. He spoke in Arabic, but there was no mistaking the excitement in his voice. Whatever Maria had done, it had certainly unnerved the bastard. Gamel appeared from behind his desk, asking a question as he strode past the guard. The soldier was in the middle of his answer when the door closed behind them.

He moved quickly, nearly scampering the last twenty feet to the administration office vent. Once there, he pressed his face against the grating and saw that the room was empty. Below him were the filing cabinets that contained the boys' records and in front of them was the countertop over which all their school affairs were conducted. The wires, which were pinched over the top of the locked door, were taped to the ceiling with broad irregular strips of electrical tape. Then they dropped in a bundle to the top of the detonator, which was sitting in the center of the counter.

Billy uncoiled a string from his pocket and tied it to the

center of the grating. Next he pushed the metal grate out of its clamps until it snapped free, catching its fall with the cord. Slowly, he lowered it to the floor, holding it steady so that it didn't bang against the front of the filing cabinets. Then he thrust his legs out through the opening, rolled onto his stomach, and dropped noiselessly to the floor.

Maria's mouth went dry as soon as Gamel appeared in the doorway. Everything was going wrong. She doubted whether she could form the words to explain that Timmy needed medical attention. If she could, it seemed impossible that they would be believed. Timmy was moaning, as she had instructed, and his knees were pulled up against his contorted body. But his eyes were clear and his cheeks were rosy, hardly the picture of a dying child. And her damn hands wouldn't stop shaking! She had lost confidence in her own ability, and with it confidence in Billy's whole scheme. "Piece of cake," he had said with his usual cockiness. How could Ferrand have made a fifteen-year-old boy part of a military action? How could he have trusted him to disable the explosives? She should have stood by her first reaction and refused to help. If she had, she wouldn't be about to confront an insane killer. And Billy wouldn't be fumbling with an electronic device that could bring the whole building down on top of them.

The crowd parted for Gamel without his even having to gesture. The terrorist looked down at Timmy, then from Maria to Hutchings. Harold spoke the words that were still caught in Maria's throat.

"We need to get help for this boy. I think it's his appendix."

Gamel crouched down, turned Timmy's face toward his own, and stared at the blue half-closed eyes. Then he looked up to Maria. "When did this start?" he demanded.

The words came, and she was surprised at how confident they sounded. "Just a few minutes ago. He said he was feeling sick. Then he asked to go to the lavatory. As soon as he started to walk, he doubled over and fell. He seems to be in terrible pain."

Gamel looked back to the boy, then reached with his fingers just as Hutchings had done. Timmy winced the instant he was touched. "It hurts," he yelled, and rolled away from Gamal's hand.

"Take him to his room," Gamel ordered Maria. He turned to one of the guards and spoke in their native tongue. Then he looked back at Maria. "The soldier will help you carry him." He stood quickly and headed back toward the headmaster's office.

Billy Tepper was confused. He had expected to find a battery wired to one side of a control box, with the wires from the explosive charges connected to the other. But there was only one unit—a military-green metal container that received the bundle of wires through a drilled hole. There had been a snap-off cover on the top of Jimmy Bradberry's radio control unit that gave immediate access to the circuits. But there was no opening anywhere on the container. The entire mechanism—batteries, connectors, and radio receiver—was locked inside. He lifted the container and was surprised at its weight, until he realized that it would have to hold a large and powerful battery. Then he turned it carefully in his hands, looking for a seam that could be opened. There were none. The damn thing was a sealed unit, probably designed for military use under the worst of conditions. The frequency component he needed to change was buried somewhere inside.

He tipped it over slowly, listening intently for a click or the swish of liquid. He knew that these things could be made tamper-proof, so that even a slight movement could start the detonation process. His eyes were squeezed shut as he turned the unit onto its side.

There was no sound.

Billy opened his eyes slowly. The base of the canister was made of a different material and slotted into it were four small screws. Now he understood. The entire case was a single casting. The components were mounted on the base, which was then slid up inside the case. If he opened the fastening screws he should be able to slide the top of the detonator up and away from the electronic assembly. He rummaged through the shelves under the counter until he found a letter opener. Carefully, he began to turn the screws.

Maria knew she hadn't given Billy enough time. He was in the administration office, sure that she had drawn Gamel off to another part of the building. Instead, Gamel was headed back to the headmaster's office, only a few feet from where Billy was working.

"What good will that do?" Maria screamed after him. The terrorist leader stopped abruptly, then turned slowly. "He needs a doctor," she said, her voice remaining strong. "We have to get him out of here and to a hospital."

Timmy's rolling eyes suddenly darted toward Maria. A hospital wasn't part of the bargain. She had told him that he would be taken to his room. Now she was talking about a hospital.

"I'm feeling a little better," he said to her in a whisper. "Honest."

Gamel started slowly back toward the stricken boy, his eyes remaining fixed on Maria. He stopped at the edge of the crowd and gave a brief command to the guards. Immediately, one of the soldiers reached down and scooped Timmy up in his arms. Then he followed Gamel toward the faculty lounge that was now empty.

"Where are you taking him?" Maria demanded as Timmy was carried away from her.

Another guard grabbed her by the arm. "You too," he said, and he pushed her through the crowd of boys toward the lounge that Gamel was just entering.

Billy turned the first screw slowly, again listening for the sound of any mechanism inside being disturbed. He knew he was pushing his luck to the limit. You could build detonation devices so that they would explode if anyone attempted to disconnect them. But common sense told him it was safe. This thing was some country's standard military issue, designed to be used by ordinary conscripts. It wouldn't make sense to get too sophisticated with soldiers who had been given only a few hours of training. They would kill themselves more often than they would damage the enemy. Logic told him it was a straightforward, idiot-proof design. But still, the bundle of wires kept reminding him of the consequences should his logic prove faulty.

He slid out the first screw. It was as long as the case, which told him that the base bolted into screw sockets in the top of the housing. "Just like a vacuum cleaner motor." He smiled, and pounced on the rest of the screws.

One by one he turned them free. Then he held the base in one hand and lifted the casting with the other. The top slid off, gliding up along the wires until the entire mechanism was exposed. Billy could see the battery, an assembly of standard dry cells. Attached to its top was a single circuit card. A wire from the circuit card connected to a sealed switch. The switch interrupted the cable that linked the battery to the terminals where the wires were attached.

"Piece of cake," he told himself. His fingers started into the mechanism, but stopped abruptly. There was another wire connected to the switch that came from a small mechanical switch at the base of the connector board. Billy swallowed hard. "Holy shit," he whispered as he recognized the purpose of the design. Had he tried to rip out the wires, the movement of the connectors would have tripped the switch, sending battery current down the lines to the explosives. The damn thing was more sophisticated than he had guessed. His hands drew back away from the mechanism. He had to be sure before he went any further.

The guard dropped Timmy into a soft chair directly in front of Gamel. But the leader wasn't looking at Timmy. Instead, the black lenses were fixed on Maria.

"You're playing a very dangerous game," he told her.

She tried to look calm even though she was holding her hands behind her back to hide their shaking. "What game?" she challenged. "The boy needs help."

"Do you go rushing off to a hospital every time a child has a stomachache?"

She didn't answer.

"You told me that they always have stomachaches. That was why they needed medicine. Now you insist on a hospital the minute the boy complains."

"He's in great pain," Maria said. She saw Timmy react to her words and pull his knees up tighter to his chest.

"Why do you want to get this boy out of the school?" Gamel wondered, ignoring both her response and Timmy's contortions. He didn't seem to expect an answer. Instead he was exploring possibilities. "Is he bringing a message to someone outside? Or perhaps you expect a rescue force to arrive in an ambulance?"

"What rescue force? What message?" she challenged.

Gamel smiled cynically. "That's exactly what we are going to find out." He nodded toward his guard. The guard stepped outside the room and closed the door behind him.

He was taking much too long. When he had examined the radio control for the airplane, he had figured it would take him only a few seconds to change the component in the detonator. But he had already been in this room for nearly ten minutes. Miss Manetti couldn't keep them busy forever!

He was staring at the components on top of the circuit card and beginning to realize how little he knew about electronics. Stringing a camera into a bathroom or connecting a tape player to a cable was easy. But now he was looking at a platform of identical black semiconductor packages arranged in neat rows with no idea of what their functions were. His only clues were Mr. Prinz's explanation that the frequency chips were identical pairs in both the radio and receiver, and his own conclusion that they would probably be easy to insert and remove. He slipped the component from Jimmy's Spitfire out of his pocket and held it close to the circuit card. There were two components it seemed to match.

With the tip of the letter opener, he pushed against the sides of the suspect components. One seemed to be fixed solidly to the board. The other moved. He slipped the blade under the edge of the component and pried it up gently. The metal legs pulled up from their mounting.

He would exchange the components. Christ, it was the only thing he could do. Even if it wasn't the frequency chip, it had to do something. Replacing it with Jimmy's chip had to screw up the circuit somehow!

But it was a gamble. Maybe screwing up the circuit would set the damn thing off. And even if it didn't, he couldn't be sure that the detonator was disabled. He had told Ferrand that he could fix the explosive charges. Ferrand and the Screaming Eagles would be counting on that. If he couldn't be sure—absolutely positive that the explosives were disabled—did it make sense even to touch the damn components?

And yet it seemed right. It was the easiest component to remove, which was exactly what he had figured it would be. And it looked just like the replacement part he held in his hand.

He decided to go ahead and probed into the electronics with the letter opener. At the last second, he hesitated again.

"You have just thirty seconds to tell me exactly what you are up to," Gamel said to Maria. He casually glanced at his wristwatch. "Thirty seconds," he repeated. Then he lifted the pistol from his holster and cocked the hammer with his thumb.

Maria's hands stopped shaking. There was nothing she could tell him. Nothing that wouldn't make Timmy a co-conspirator and bring the madman's cold rage down on the boy. Nothing that wouldn't get Billy Tepper killed.

"Twenty seconds," Gamel said.

She looked at Timmy. He was still curled up in his fetal position, but he had stopped acting. His eyes, open wide, were fixed on the pistol.

"Please," she said. "Not in front of the boy. Have him taken out of here. Please."

Gamel shook his head. "It *is* the boy." He smiled. He raised the cocked pistol and pointed it at Timmy McFarland's head. "Fifteen seconds," he said.

Billy pressed the Spitfire component into the slot, his eyes again squeezing shut as he felt the contacts snap into place. There was no sound. Nothing seemed to move. He opened his eyes slowly. He had changed the components, but he had no idea whether the substitution had had any effect on the detonator. He hoped he had guessed right. But could he let Ferrand lead an attack into the building based on a guess?

There was no cocky smile as he fitted the casting back over the base and began reinserting the long anchor bolts. He was confused. Maybe even frightened. In the past, his pranks had been little more than a game. If his computer control had failed, then the lights wouldn't have come on. No one would have known. If the wrong phone rang, it was no big deal! What did it matter how many phones rang? They would still drive everyone crazy. And if he got caught? So what! They'd yell and they'd threaten and maybe he would even get kicked out of school. But there were always other schools. What was his father going to do? Bring him home?

But this wasn't a game. He was playing with lives. If he made a mistake, people were going to get hurt. Everyone he knew was going to get buried under a burning building. Was he sure that the bombs wouldn't go off? Sure enough to let Ferrand go ahead with the invasion? Jesus, how could you be that sure of anything? And yet, if he stopped the attack . . .

if he sent a message to Ferrand saying that he wasn't sure? Sooner or later the bastard was going to pull out his pistol and fire into another kid. And if he *could* have saved him? If the detonator was *really* dead?

He set the case back on the counter. He had to think. He had to decide what was the best thing to do. But first, he had to get out of there.

"Ten seconds," Gamel said.

Maria tried to scream, but no sound would come out of her mouth. She could only shake her head, lying by her gestures that there was no scheme.

"You were planning something," Gamel taunted, the pistol still aimed at Timmy. "Your last chance. What was it?

She lunged toward Timmy, throwing herself between the boy and the gun barrel. As she threw herself over the boy she began to cry hysterically. "He's done nothing," she managed to say between sobs.

Gamel grabbed her hair and turned her to face the weapon. "You," he hissed into her eyes. "What have *you* done? Your last chance."

Timmy began wretching. His stomach knotted in his terror, and he vomited violently. Then he began to cry.

Gamel's grip on Maria's hair relaxed. He took a step back and lowered the revolver.

"He *was* sick," he said, almost as if embarrassed by his own admission. Maria didn't hear him. She was hugging the boy and crying softly to herself.

Gamel slipped the weapon back into the holster and walked to the door. Then he stopped and turned back to Maria. "Take him to his room. Stay with him."

He opened the door, spoke to the guard, then walked across the dining hall toward the headmaster's office.

Otis Brown rehearsed his words—actually the president's words, which had been relayed from Washington just moments before. He stared at the telephone the Italian police had installed in the bedroom he was using as his private office. It was connected through the telephone switch directly to the Saint Anselm's school. All he had to do was dial three digits and Gamel would pick up at the other end.

They knew that Gamel was aware of the meeting about to take place between Sharif and the high-level American representative. All of the terrorist's information was reaching him over ordinary telephone lines, sometimes in coded digits, sometimes in plain language. Brown's men listened in on the calls, much to Gamel's amusement. He and his conspirators punctuated every conversation with comments that mocked the helplessness of the "arrogant Americans."

"We are completely victorious," the morning's message to Gamel had begun. "The Americans are coming on their hands and knees to plead with our leader."

"Good." Gamel had laughed. "That's where dogs belong. Sniffing at our boots."

Impassively, Brown's men had checked their meters to be sure their recorders were collecting every word.

"You'll be home soon," the voice relaying the message from Cairo had said. "You should have the honor of leading the victory parade."

"I'm in no hurry," Gamel had answered casually. "I may stay another day just to watch the bastards grovel. Or maybe I'll take all the boys with me just to make sure the lying Americans keep their pledges."

Laughter came from the other end of the line and then the connection had been broken.

Now Brown looked at the transcript. Why shouldn't Gamel enjoy his arrogance? He was holding the most powerful nation in the world by its short hairs. He lifted the receiver, took a few deep breaths, and dialed the number. The phone was picked up on the first ring.

"This is Otis Brown," he began. "I am the senior American representative here at Saint Anselm's. I would like to speak to your commanding officer."

"I'm the commanding officer," the voice replied in perfect English.

"I'm ordered to inform you," said Brown, "that American representatives are meeting with your leader within a few hours. We hope to have an agreement before the end of the day."

There was no response, so Brown continued with his message. "Furthermore, all arrangements for the departure of you and your men have been completed. The plane you demanded is already in position, and the helicopters can be on the school grounds within ten minutes of your order."

"Good," Gamel said.

"How will you be informed that your leader is satisfied with an agreement?" Brown asked. He heard laughter at the other end of the line.

"By one of the telephone calls that you will undoubtedly monitor," Gamel replied.

"Fine," Brown said with absolutely no embarrassment. "Then when I know you have received the call, I will contact you over this line for instructions on the arrival of the helicopters."

"I'll expect your call," Gamel said cheerfully.

"I'm further ordered to inform you of two conditions that we regard as vital," Brown hastened to add before Gamel could break off the call.

There was no response at the other end of the line.

"Our representative," Brown continued, "has been instructed to withdraw all concessions and leave the conference table if another of the children is killed. I need your assurance that there will be no reprisals if the negotiations in Cairo are not concluded by your five o'clock deadline."

"I do not give assurances," Gamel answered, the mocking laughter gone from his voice.

It was the answer that Brown had expected. "I understand," he said, forcing himself to sound detached from the implication of the words. "I will inform my superiors that you will not assure the safety of the boys." He changed the tone of his voice. "Personally, I think you're jeopardizing a victory you've already won."

Neither man spoke. Then Gamel broke the silence. "And the second condition?"

"I am instructed to inform you that our unalterable position at the bargaining table is that none of the children or teachers you now hold at Saint Anselm's will be required to leave with you on the helicopters. We will provide alternative hostages—civilian representatives of the United States government—to accompany you as a guarantee of safety to you and your men."

"Members of your Delta Force, no doubt," Gamel said mockingly.

"No," Brown responded immediately. "Civilian volunteers who are now in transit from the United States to Italy."

"Unacceptable," Gamel snapped. "I will select the hostages."

"I am simply informing you," Brown said in a monotone, "that the agreement we reach with your leader will contain that provision. I will contact you when the volunteer hostages arrive. I assume you will want them to enter Saint Anselm's in a controlled fashion so that you can verify their identity."

He could feel the confidence drain from his adversary on the other end of the phone line. If Sharif told him to accept the substitute hostages, he would have little choice but to comply.

"I give no assurances," Gamel repeated. "I will make my decision when the time comes."

Then the connection was broken.

Brown balanced the phone receiver on his fingers, wondering if he had accomplished anything. He would call Washington and tell the director that the message had been delivered. He would repeat verbatim Gamel's reply. But then the director would ask for his evaluation.

Would Gamel let the five o'clock deadline slip by, or would there be another victim to the delay in reaching an agreement in Cairo?

He didn't know. Since Gamel knew the United States was

in the process of making concessions, there was absolutely nothing to gain by executing another boy. That was the logical answer. But, on the other hand, Gamel had nothing to lose by another killing. The United States wouldn't retaliate as long as all the other boys could be killed in an attack. His best guess? Gamel would slip the deadline as long as he thought everything was going his way. But don't give him any reason to doubt his victory. If he thought he was being taken lightly, there would be another victim at the gate.

Would he accept substitute hostages? Why should he? The United States had a poor record of making concessions in order to free adults. But it was jumping through hoops to assure the safety of its children. Its actions were telling him that the boys were the most valuable hostages he could hold. Why should he trade them for anything else?

Still, Brown had to admire Washington's ploy. If it made all its concessions contingent on Gamel's leaving all the children and teachers behind, then it tossed Sharif onto the horns of a dilemma. Should he risk his triumph just to assure Gamel an added measure of safety? Or should he order Gamel to accept substitutes? Brown guessed that Sharif would agree to leave the children behind. But he couldn't be sure. If Gamel sensed a trap, he would load the copters with children no matter what Sharif ordered.

Nothing computed. He couldn't even guess at the odds. It was as Edward Ferrand had told him. The experts had no answers.

Even before Director Clemmons had closed the door to the Oval Office behind him, the president knew he was bringing bad news. The CIA director's face was ashen and his eyes flickered from side to side, refusing to lock onto any of the men who were seated in conversation. Reynolds raised his hand, interrupting the Secretary of state in mid-sentence. "What is it, Bill?" the president asked, not sure he was ready for the answer.

"Mr. President," the director finally managed after taking

a deep breath. "We have just received a very reliable report from Cairo that Sharif has been . . . killed . . . assassinated."

Reynolds jaw dropped.

"It's not confirmed yet," Clemmons hastened to add, but then he confessed, "yet I would regard it as accurate."

"Sweet Jesus," Senator Bradberry said for the entire room, fear darkening his face.

They had met to advise the president on the public relations assault they would launch as soon as the children were released. They expected confirmation from Cairo before the day was out that an agreement had been reached with Sharif, and they expected the children to be free before morning. They would hold the press at arm's length until the few hostages they planned to provide were released wherever Gamel's attack force set down. Then, the president was going on television to begin the process of repairing the enormous damage that they all knew United States' prestige was about to suffer.

Senator Bradberry had struck a bargain with Reynolds about the reaction of the congressional hawks, of which he was the leader. They wouldn't mount the expected campaign of criticism against the president for negotiating with terrorists, he'd said. Instead, they would simply agree that saving the lives of the boys had been everyone's paramount concern, and they would minimize the concessions that the president had been forced to make. They would call, however, for stepped up vigilence around the world to make sure that no more Americans became targets for international extortionists.

Reynolds understood the irony of Bradberry's position. His whole political career, which was firmly on track toward a presidential nomination, had been based on his unshakable faith in America's military might. Were it known that he had agreed to concessions for the sake of his son, after he had repeatedly mocked the notion of concessions for other terrorist victims, his ambitions would suddenly turn hollow. Reynolds had made it clear that he had no intention of embarrassing his rival over a personal issue. And Bradberry had responded with genuine efforts to keep the hawks away from Reynold's naked political carcass.

At the meeting, they had choreographed the public presentation. The boys would be flown north to an Army base in Germany for the ritual physical examinations and psychological evaluations. Simultaneously, the president would announce their freedom, express his regrets that world tensions had turned children into the targets of fanatics, and drum up sentiment for a yellow-ribbon return. The government would remain silent as to the concessions that had been made, admitting only that Arab prisoners had been freed and expressing the hope that the prisoner exchange would open a new era of understanding between the United States and Middle Eastern nations. They were counting on the public celebration to drown out the demands for more information. Then the children would be flown to Washington to be greeted by their president and their parents, who would be the personal guests of the president. Television news, the political leaders had realized, would present an orgy of hair tousling and parental embraces, with little time for facts. The hard questions would probably be asked in the inside pages of *The New York Times* and *Washington Post*, where they could be safely ignored for a few days.

Sometime between the end of the euphoria and the onset of reality, the president would address the nation. He would admit the obvious: that the United States had bargained with the kidnappers for the safety of its children and paid a ransom of terrorist prisoners, made available by friendly and cooperative governments. He would deny that there were any indemnity payments (regardless of what was promised to Sharif) or that the United States offered any substantive concessions. Then he would announce a policy of safeguards to protect Americans from future terrorist attacks and reaffirm a policy of not negotiating with the perpetrators of lawless acts.

The holes in his statement would be obvious. But

Bradberry's hawks would simply pretend they weren't there, letting their silence be mistaken for the kind of restraint Americans expected in a time of national crisis.

The secretary of state had been indicating the type of comments that would be appropriate for friendly governments when the director of the Central Intelligence Agency had been summoned from the room. Director Clemmons' return had caught him at the end of his remarks.

"Do we have any idea who killed Sharif?" the president asked the director.

Clemmons shook his head. "Not yet. All we know is that the Egyptians have been informed that he was killed on his way to the meeting. They're anticipating riots as soon as the word spreads among Sharif's followers. I've suggested to our people that they get out of the country immediately."

"Won't that make us look guilty?" Bradberry suggested.

Clemmons sighed. "They're going to blame us anyway. The Egyptians are doubling their protection at our embassy."

"What will Gamel do?" Reynolds asked.

"We're talking to Otis Brown right now," the director answered. "He's the best man we have. Personally, I don't like it at all. Gamel is unstable. He's sure to think we sprung a trap on his leader. He may conclude that we're ready to spring a trap at the school."

Bradberry was on his feet. "We have to make it plain to continue the negotiations that we had nothing to do with this. We have to continue the negotiations."

"Negotiate with whom?" Reynolds asked. "No one in the Middle East will take over for Sharif. Every leader in the area will be thrilled to be rid of the bastard. The ones who hate us will blame us for killing a popular hero. The ones who like us will blame Israel."

"There must be someone we can talk to," Bradberry said. When he saw no encouragement in the president's face, he looked toward the CIA director. Clemmons threw his hands up in a helpless gesture.

"How long before we have Brown's evaluation?" Reynolds asked Clemmons.

"Any moment," the director responded.

"We'll wait," Reynolds decided for them all.

When it came, the evaluation was concise. Brown reported that "the assassination of Sharif puts the boys in Saint Anselm's at an unacceptable level of risk. Unless there is an immediately available substitute to conduct negotiations, I recommend an attack to free the hostages. I would expect the attack to cause a high level of casualties among the hostages and attacking force." Then Brown asked for immediate instructions. He also asked permission to cut the phone lines into the school and to jam radio transmissions in order to delay Gamel's receipt of information about the death of Sharif. "The boys would probably be killed shortly after Gamel learned of the assassination of his leader," he concluded.

The president frowned at the report. Then he looked at the confused faces of his advisers. "Not much of a choice," he finally said.

"There has to be someone we can talk to," Bradberry repeated. "Maybe Gamel himself. We can treat him as Sharif's successor."

Reynolds shook his head slowly. "Not if he thinks we killed Sharif. Once he gets that information, there's no way he'll trust anything we say. I think we have to decide what's best for the boys. The 'unacceptable risk' of leaving them with Gamel when he learns that Sharif is dead. Or the high level of casualties in an attack." He turned to the director. "Is that about it?"

Director Clemmons nodded. "That's how I see it."

"So if we contact Gamel, or wait until he gets the information, we risk the methodical murder of the boys. But if we're not going to wait, then we ought to cut the lines and attack as soon as possible."

"Those are the choices," the director agreed.

"Give me a minute," the president asked his advisors. They rose immediately and filed silently out of the office. Reynolds fumbled in his jacket pocket and found the crumpled package of cigarettes. He lit one absentmindedly.

The boys, he knew, didn't have much of a chance. Sure, they might get lucky. When Gamel heard that Sharif was dead, he might simply take his soldiers and leave, holding just a few of the boys to ensure his escape. Or, if they attacked, the Delta Force troops might be able to take control without catching the children in the cross fire and before the terrorists could detonate their explosives. But neither of those outcomes was likely. Those who specialized in terrorism were unanimous in their opinion that Gamel would kill before he would retreat. And the military experts had advised him that Saint Anselm's was a difficult target to capture. He had to accept as fact that many of the boys would die.

He weighed the roles he could play in their deaths. If he ordered the attack, then history would see the carnage to be the result of his action. If he continued his efforts to negotiate, then his hands would be left clean. The deaths would be murders committed by an insane terrorist.

Reynolds wondered how he had ever arrived at the edge of such a decision. He had no illusions about himself going down in history as a great American president. He was simply a politician who had danced around the difficult issues and ridden his longevity to ever higher offices. Yet with the highest office came the power of life and death. The 'black box' that could incinerate the planet was constantly by his side. He might, at some point, have to decide whether there would be any children at all left on the face of the Earth. But that decision was still theoretical. The decision confronting him now was frighteningly real.

All he was certain of was that the office was his. There was no one he could turn to for help. He had received the advice of his aides and experts. He had the most relevant information at hand. One way or the other, he was the one who would have to answer for the children. Reynolds decided to disregard the judgements that history would assign to his decision. He decided to give the boys the best chance he could.

He crushed the cigarette out and pushed one of the buttons on the edge of his desk. The door opened and the learned leaders of the free world filed back in, avoiding his gaze as they took their seats.

"Anyone have anything to add?" the president asked forcefully.

There were no takers.

Then he looked at the director. "Cut the lines," he ordered.

afternoon

Colonel William Smiles didn't need to ask Otis Brown what the decision from Washington was. He had watched Brown's jaw tighten as he listened on the telephone, then seen him slump as if he'd been kicked in the stomach. So he gave Brown a moment to compose himself after he had set the telephone back in its cradle.

"When?" he finally asked.

"At our discretion," Brown said. He walked to the window and looked up at the school. "This morning I patiently explained to Ferrand why we wouldn't attack. He told me in no uncertain terms that he didn't think any of us knew what he was talking about. It appears he was right."

"You didn't know Sharif had been killed," Smiles reminded him.

"No, I didn't," Brown agreed. But he wasn't interested in the excuse Smiles was providing. He was thinking of the boys in the school. They were almost out. It would have been just a few hours more. Except the odds had gone off the board. He knew he was no longer calculating but rather simply guessing. The situation was out of control. The accident that had been looming over the children's heads was about to happen.

"We need to get a message to that boy. It has to tell him to disregard this morning's instructions, that we're coming in at seven-thirty, just as he planned."

Smiles agreed.

"I'll get Ferrand to work on it right away. As soon as it's sent, I want the school's telephones disconnected."

"Without waiting for a confirmation?" Smiles asked.

Brown nodded his head. "Billy didn't respond this morning, so maybe he's not getting his mail. I don't want to leave the line open waiting for him to get back to us. The last thing he told us was that he was expecting us at seven-thirty, so we'll go on the assumption that he's still expecting us. Besides, we're going in whether he's ready or not."

Smiles walked to the door and relayed Brown's order to his adjutant. Then he asked a guard to find Edward Ferrand. He turned back to Brown, who was still staring out the window toward the school.

"I have to plan as though the kid isn't going to be any help to us," he told Brown. "If he can get the other boys into the cellar, great. And I'd let the devil take me straight to hell if Billy could disable the explosives. But I can't count on that, either."

"I don't think so," Brown agreed.

"That being the case," the colonel continued, "I want to put my best explosives man over the wall before the attack. I want him standing outside the window of the room where the detonator is before Gamel knows he's under attack."

"Can he get in there?"

"If Ferrand takes him there," Smiles answered. He saw the surprise in Brown's eyes, but didn't wait for him to start asking questions. "I've given this a lot of thought," he continued. "The simple fact is that no matter how quickly we get into the building, we don't stand a chance unless we get to the detonator before Gamel decides that he's beaten. Even if Billy Tepper gets all the boys into the cellar, their chances aren't good if the building comes down on top of them. But if we can get to the detonator, we've got a pretty good shot, even if the kids can't get to safety. We may be able to keep the guards too busy for them to start shooting at the boys."

"Ferrand has no training. He could be more of a problem than a help," Brown said.

"All I need is for him to get my people to the window. Two riflemen and an explosives guy. Then he can go hide in the bushes. Ferrand's an athlete. He won't slow anyone down."

Brown thought for a moment. "You know your people won't have much of a chance. They'll be under fire five seconds after they break into the room. And if they get your people, they'll get Ferrand a few seconds later."

The colonel nodded. "Maybe. But without them, I don't think the kids have any chance at all."

The guard knocked, then pushed open the door so that Ferrand could enter. Brown gestured toward a chair, but Ferrand remained standing, his expression becoming suspicious.

"Edward," Brown began, "we've had a turn for the worse. Some fool has assassinated Sharif. There can't be any negotiations—any settlement for your boys. We think an attack on the school is their best chance."

"Jesus," Ferrand whispered. Then he dropped into one of the chairs.

Brown began filling him in on the conversation with Washington and the factors that had made an attack inevitable. "My advice to the president was that the prospects for an attack were poor, but that the results of doing nothing might be even worse. I don't feel that Gamel will negotiate with us. I think he'll start shooting the second he learns that Sharif has been killed."

Ferrand looked up from the table. "There must be something we can offer him. To attack . . . all those guns . . . the explosives. They don't stand a chance."

Brown slid into the chair across the table from Ferrand.

"Before we could offer him anything, we'd have to tell him why we were talking to him and not Sharif. I'm afraid he would end the conversation right then and there."

"But maybe he wouldn't," Ferrand persisted. "If there's even a chance he would bargain with us . . . Isn't that a better chance than what the boys will have if we attack?"

Colonel Smiles leaned in over the table. "If we can get to the explosives, I think we have an excellent chance. Disable the bombs and hit the place fast and hard, and I think we can save most of them."

Brown continued. "We need to get a message to Tepper immediately. We want him to know we're coming, and we want him to do everything he can."

Ferrand looked from one to the other. "'We don't want a fifteen-year-old boy making national policy.' That's what you said. But we do want him to lead a raid on armed terrorists."

The two men looked away.

"For God's sake," Ferrand said in slow, measured words. "This morning we told him not to do anything. Now we're telling him to do everything. He's fifteen. Fifteen! We're supposed to be protecting him and now we're asking him to protect everyone else. He'll think he's dealing with fools."

"He probably is," Otis Brown whispered. Then he turned aggressively to face Ferrand. "But we still have to send the message."

"You said each message put him in danger."

"They're all in danger," Brown countered. "All the boys. All the soldiers attempting the rescue."

It was Ferrand's turn to look away. Finally, he picked up the pencil and began writing.

When he was done, Brown took the paper to the door and handed it to a soldier who was waiting.

Smiles pushed the pads of note paper to one side and unfolded the plans of the school that Ferrand had corrected at the beginning of the crisis. "Just before we go over the wall," he started to explain, "I want to put three men outside this window." He pointed to the window of the administration office. "Two riflemen and an explosives expert. We're going to try to disarm the explosives before Gamel has a chance to set them off."

Ferrand nodded absently, unconcerned with the details of the attack. Instead, he was remembering Joey Trotta, who had been unaware that the blanket had been pulled down and unconcerned when it was drawn back up over his head. Joey didn't know he was dead. In the same way, none of the boys knew that their lives were about to be snuffed out by the foolish blunders of experts.

"What's the best way to get them there?" the colonel was asking.

Ferrand straightened in his chair and focused on the outlines of the wall and the buildings. "Here," he said, pointing to a section of the wall that was hidden by the trees surrounding the athletic fields. "There's a small break in the wall right about here. It's wired over. If you cut the wire, I think the men can squeeze through. Then they'll have tree coverage all the way to here. That will put them maybe fifty feet from the corner of the building. They'll have to cross fifty feet of open space, but when they reach the building, they'll be right at the window."

"How thick is the coverage?" Smiles asked.

"Overgrown," Ferrand answered. "Trees. Thick bushes. No one goes there. One of the boys got caught trying to squeeze through the break in the wall. We could hear him yelling, but we had the damndest time trying to find him. That's why the opening was wired over. We didn't want the boys trying to get through."

"Could you lead the men through?" Brown asked.

Ferrand nodded. "Yes. I think so."

"Just to the edge of the open area," Smiles added quickly. "We want you to stay under cover. Just get the men to where they can see the building and the window. Can you do that?"

"I've got to do something," Ferrand answered. "I can't just sit here waiting to see how the odds pan out."

A half hour later, he was sitting on the sideline while

Smiles briefed the officers of his attack team. He was startled by how young they were, all younger than himself and perhaps only a half dozen years older than Billy Tepper. Yet they were calm and completely confident about the mission they were about to undertake. He remembered the terrorists who had escorted him into the building for his meeting with Gamel, a meeting that seemed to have occurred years ago. They too were merely boys, like the American soldiers, resigned to the possibility of dying.

But more than anything, he thought of Maria—not of her being killed but being forced to watch the mad slaughter that was likely to take place around her. He imagined her fear when she realized that the danger to her babies was being escalated. And he wondered if she could possibly emerge from her ordeal unscathed. Slaughter had turned Gamel from a teacher into an insensitive robot. What awful transformation might it work on her?

"You have a lot of confidence in Billy Tepper," he heard Colonel Smiles say. He realized that the military briefing was over and that the two of them were alone in the room.

"Nothing could have prepared him for this," he answered. "Until now, everything has been a game. Now . . . he watches his friend get murdered. He sees how confused and helpless we are. And tonight he's going to see some of the wonders we've created for him. It will be a miracle if he just manages to keep his sanity."

"I hope he does," Smiles said. "He can save more lives than we can."

Suppose nothing worked! Suppose the smoke bomb just flared up for a couple of seconds and then went out. He never had a chance to test it, so what made him think all the film was going to burn? One lousy puff of smoke going up the air shaft wouldn't set off the fire alarms and sprinklers. Hell, nobody would even notice it. With all the stinking disinfectant they used in the washrooms, who would smell a puff of smoke? Then there would be nothing to distract the guards, and everybody would be sitting in the dining room with all those machine guns pointing at them. Nobody could escape.

What if the video recorder wasn't connected properly? Terrific! The Screaming Eagles would get more television coverage than the Super Bowl. The terrorists would know they were coming before their feet even hit the ground. They'd be like ducks in a shooting gallery. It should work. Heck, it was the same kind of connection you used with video games. But he hadn't been able to run the tape to be sure he had recorded the wall. So maybe when the recorder cut in, the monitors would just go blank. That would put the bastards on the alert.

"Mr. Tepper, I asked you a question."

Billy looked up into Harold Hutchings' pained eyes. "I don't think I know the answer," he said, trying to look as if he were ashamed of himself.

"And I don't think you even know the question," Hutchings said suspiciously.

Billy looked even more ashamed.

"Who were the participants at the Congress of Vienna?"

Billy pretended to be grasping for the answer. Christ, he was saying to himself, I'm about to get a whole army slaughtered and half of these kids killed, and this idiot wants to talk about the government of Vienna. "You mean what were their names?" he finally said.

"What countries?" Hutchings snapped.

"Besides the United States?"

The teacher buried his face in his hand. From the other end of the table, Billy could hear Jimmy Bradberry snickering.

It was the detonator that had destroyed Billy's confidence. He wasn't sure whether he had disabled it, and he wasn't used to being unsure. If he hadn't been able to figure out the circuits in the detonator, then maybe he hadn't been able to figure anything out.

Or worse. Suppose half the things worked and the other

half didn't? Suppose the smoke bomb got the guards out of the way and the video recorder did its job? That would get Ferrand and the soldiers into the building. But then suppose he had screwed up on the detonator? That would bring the building down on top of the Screaming Eagles. Boy, was he in over his head!

"I'm waiting," Hutchings said. "What was the Congress of Vienna?"

Billy seemed bewildered. Hutchings closed his book and examined its cover. Slowly he raised his eyes. "Have you heard anything I've said today?" he asked softly.

Billy shook his head.

"Anyone?" Hutchings said, glancing around at the other puzzled faces. The boys were waiting for him to explode. Instead, he smiled kindly. "No, I suppose not. Here and now—in our present situation—I guess the Congress of Vienna doesn't seem too important. But it is. It's very important. You see, all these events fit together. . . ." He interlocked his fingers. "What happened long ago helps us understand what is happening now. If we can understand why things happened then, perhaps we won't keep making the same stupid mistakes today. . . ."

He knew they had no idea what he was talking about.

"We'll start over. As soon as these people have left. Let's go back to our rooms. I'll see you again at dinner."

The boys jumped up, stacked their books under their arms, and filed past the guards toward the back door of the dining hall.

Billy dumped his books on the desk and began pacing frantically. He had to do something. But what? He couldn't risk going back into the bathroom and pulling the smoke bomb up to check it. And even if he could, what good would it do? He knew how it was made. What he was no longer sure of was whether it would work. The only way to find out would be to try it, and if he tested it he would destroy it. Just like he couldn't get back into the vault to check his connections to the coaxial cable. Or like he couldn't run the tape through a television receiver to make sure it had recorded the wall.

And the detonator. Even if he was able to get back into the administration office, even if he had the time to open the case, so what? The densely packed circuits and the convoluted wires would still be an unfathomable puzzle. Without a wiring diagram, he would still be guessing. He had lifted the top off the Spitfire and opened the radio control unit. Why had he assumed that the detonator would be just as simple? He had taken the component from the detonator and snapped it into the vacant socket in the airplane. It had fit perfectly. So maybe he had exchanged the right chips. Maybe the damn thing wouldn't go off no matter what Gamel did with the radio transmitter he carried in his pocket. But he couldn't be sure.

Had he ever been sure? Or was it just that when he was pulling pranks it didn't really matter? Now it mattered. Now Mr. Ferrand and the kids and the teachers and the soldiers were all depending on him. Jesus, you couldn't take chances when so many people were involved. You had to be sure.

Billy thought of the messages he had sent to Ferrand. Now they sounded boastful. "No problems," he had said. "Piece of cake." Why did he talk that way? Why did he have to be such a smartass?

There was only one thing to do. He had to call the whole attack off. There was still time. He could send Ferrand a message saying that he hadn't been able to get to the detonator and that the explosives were live. He could tell him that there were problems with the security cameras. "Put it off for another day," he could say. Then maybe something would happen tomorrow so that they wouldn't have to count on him.

He jumped into his chair, picked up a pencil, and began composing his message:

Mr. Ferrand. The bombs are live. Don't attack tonight. I'll fix everything tomorrow. Billy.

He read it back to himself. His panic disappeared. It didn't say he was scared. It didn't admit that he was uncertain. All it did was say that something wasn't ready. Something mechanical or electrical. Something beyond his control. Maybe beyond anyone's control. There was nothing that would get Mr. Ferrand mad at him. All it did was tell him that it was too dangerous to attack. And that was the truth. Once Mr. Ferrand read it, he would call off the attack. And then he wouldn't have to worry about anyone getting killed. It wouldn't be his fault!

He went to the closet and opened the door. Deep in the corner, he could see the soft green glow of the display screen, which told him there was a message waiting. He tore the clothes back and dropped to his knees.

Billy giggled when he read the first message. Mr. Ferrand had called it off. Great. All he had to do was unplug the wire that led to the smoke bomb and stuff it in behind the grate where no one could find it. It wouldn't matter whether the recorder worked because no one would be coming over the wall. And there would be no reason for the son of a bitch of a leader to push his transmitter button, so it wouldn't make any difference whether the detonator was working or not.

Then he read the second message.

"Holy shit," he said to himself. They were coming. At seven-thirty. Less than three hours from now.

Billy sat with his legs crossed in front of him and rushed through the commands that set up his computer. Then he typed in the message he had written, watching it appear across the screen of the display. Next he typed in the access commands that set his modem to transmit the message over the telephone line. He typed in the phone number and listened while the modem dialed a computer somewhere outside the wall—the computer that Mr. Ferrand would be watching.

He was suddenly aware that he hadn't heard the connection signal played back through his modem. Then a message wrote itself at the top corner of the screen.

Unable to access telephone circuit.

"Shit," he said as he rushed through the procedure once more. Again, he heard the modem dialing the number, and again there was no connection signal. The printed message repeated itself at the top of the screen.

Unable to access telephone circuit.

What the hell was wrong? He shut off his computer, then restarted it and moved carefully through the setup procedures. Once again, he typed in his message, correcting the mistakes he seemed to make with every word. He put in the modem access commands and made certain that the interface was connected to the computer. Then he typed in the telephone number.

It dialed. But there was no acknowledgment signal. Again, the message appeared at the top of the screen.

The line was dead, he realized. He wasn't getting a busy signal. It wasn't that the computer at the other end wasn't turned on. There was no telephone line. His modem was dialing into limbo. Somebody had cut the damn telephone line.

"The bastards," he almost screamed. "The rotten bastards." He pounded his anger on the top of the computer. The terrorists had cut the lines. But why? Oh my God, did they know he had been sending messages out? Had they recognized the short burst of computer jabber and figured out that someone in the school had a computer? Did they know who it was?

He turned the machine off and pushed it into the farthest corner. Then he pulled the clothes carefully together and shut the closet door.

They were coming over the wall in just a few hours. Maybe the terrorists had been reading the messages and were going to be waiting for them. Jesus, he had set up Mr. Ferrand and the Screaming Eagles to be slaughtered. And there was no way he could warn them.

*　　*　　*

Despite the student folders lying open on the desk in front of him, Gamel's attention was fixed on the telephone. He needed information, instructions that were supposed to be called in from one of the anonymous and ever-changing numbers Sharif's men were using. But the telephone remained silent.

Their plan seemed to be faltering. Not that there was any danger. He was still firmly in control at the school, with the hostages docile. The explosives planted throughout the buildings and the guns poised over the boys' heads still guaranteed his immunity from attack. The Americans had announced their intention to negotiate both publicly and directly to him. Even now, the negotiations were in progress, leading toward a total victory for Sharif and his followers. Everything was following the script and even more quickly than they had ever expected. But still, he was aware of his own uncertainty. His gut told him something was wrong.

It had begun with the American official's message that there would be substitute hostages to guarantee his escape. That had never been part of the plan. The boys were the most valuable hostages he could hold. Even now, he was in the process of reviewing their files to select the ones he would bring on board the helicopters with him. He had already chosen a congressman's son and the son of an electronics czar who was a close friend of the vice president. With boys like that with him, there was no possibility of the Americans attempting to intercept his plane. The substitutes, on the other hand, would be government employees, perhaps even military men in civilian costume. The Americans wouldn't give them the same consideration they would lavish on the children.

There were also dangers in the very process of exchange. The boys would have to be marched out to the front gate. The substitutes would have to be received, searched, and secured. He would be vulnerable while all this was happening, deprived of the security of having all the hostages locked in one place. If the Americans were planning an attack, that would be the ideal moment. He knew that with his small force he couldn't afford to give the Americans even a momentary advantage.

Yet it would be difficult for Sharif to give up his incredible victory over a small point of procedure. If the United States negotiators were willing to free his brothers from a dozen jails and were about to pay a huge ransom in the form of war reparations, if Sharif were about to be crowned the legitimate leader of the Arab world, should he throw all that away rather than accept other hostages to cover the retreat? If the imperialists yielded on every substantive point, but held fast on this one issue, how could Sharif refuse? In fact, releasing the boys would be exactly the kind of humanitarian gesture he would want for his first act as a world leader.

Gamel needed to get a message to Sharif. He needed to warn him that conceding this point could jeopardize the safety of the troops who held the school. It might encourage an attempt to free the children, which could bring down all that had been gained at the bargaining table. But he couldn't call out. The call would certainly be traced, and that would pinpoint the location of Sharif's agents. No, he had to wait for the call to come in. But the phone wasn't ringing.

He was also uneasy about the woman teacher. She had solved one of his most difficult problems, but she was creating others. From the moment they had conceived the raid on Saint Anselm's, they had been worried about controlling the hostages. The youngest boys were very likely to panic and become unmanageable except by brute force. They had needed the threat of slaughtering the hostages, not the slaughter itself. The woman was minding the youngest boys for them, keeping them calm and out of trouble.

But she had also become a symbol of defiance. She was the leader around whom the prisoners could rally and from whom they could gather courage. It had happened in other raids he'd commanded. One passenger on an airplane would refuse to cower. Or someone would have sense enough to calculate the odds and realize that if they all fought back the terrorists wouldn't be able kill them all before they were overwhelmed. In the past, he had moved quickly to separate the leader from the pack by making him the first victim of the methodical murders that proved his cold-blooded intentions. He knew he should deal the same way with the teacher, leaving the hostages without a unifying and defiant will. He needed her to control the boys, but in the process he had allowed her free run of the building.

The morning's episode still tormented him. He had suspected that the young boy's sudden sickness was feigned, part of some sort of diversion she was planning. But why? She was obviously an intelligent woman and she was honestly concerned for each of the children. What could she hope to achieve that wouldn't put at least some of the boys in mortal danger?

Now he knew that she'd been lying to him. The proof was in the boys' records he had been studying. He had recognized Timothy McFarland immediately from the photograph that was stapled inside his file folder. She had said it was an appendix attack. But his records said the boy had had an appendectomy two years earlier. He also recognized William Tepper from the file photograph and remembered the boy whose room she had visited with medication. But Tepper, according to his file, required no medication. Gamel had gone to the nurse's office and checked the medicine vials. There was none with Tepper's name on it. Was she visiting as many of the boys as possible simply to keep them calm and offer encouragement? Or was she organizing them for something?

Gamel checked his stainless steel wristwatch. The negotiations should already be in their fifth hour. He had to assume that they were still in progress. If they had been concluded, either for good or bad, he would have been called immediately. He looked back to the telephone, which seemed ominously silent. Something was wrong. He couldn't explain why he felt that way, but he had learned to trust his instincts and that was the unmistakable message they were delivering.

He closed the folders on his desk, and put Timmy McFarland and Billy Tepper's files on top of those of the two boys he had already selected to bring with him on his escape. Four boys and one of the teachers wouldn't be freed when his raiding party left the school in helicopters. The teacher would be the woman and as repayment for her defiance, she wouldn't be released even when he was safely home.

Gamel left the headmaster's office and walked to the security office, where one of his soldiers was staring vacantly at the monitors. He studied each of the screens. The Italian police car was still parked outside the front gate, the two officers leaning against one of the fenders and enjoying the sun. Clearly, they weren't poised for any kind of action. He watched four of the screens as their cameras panned the high stone walls, which were monotonously serene. Three screens gave him views over the shoulders of his guards and down the corridors of the old building, where the boys were safely in their rooms awaiting dinner.

"Anything?" he asked.

The soldier shook his head.

"Stay alert," Gamel ordered. "I think something may be happening."

The guard's shoulders straightened.

Gamel opened the door of the empty dining hall, which was brightened by the afternoon sun streaming in dusty beams through the windows. A guard was sitting in a chair by the door of the kitchen, watching the three teachers who were preparing the evening meal. The guard jumped to his feet as Gamel entered the room and walked across to the teachers' lounge. Once there, he pushed open the door and saw the faculty gathered inside. There were papers and books on the tables and he could hear a smattering of quiet conversation. They were relaxed, grown used to their purposeless routine and indifferent to the weapons that their guards carried. Gamel pulled the door closed.

Perhaps he was wrong in his apprehension. Everything seemed to be in order. There was no activity on the grounds outside and not the slightest hint of rebellion inside. Probably, he thought, it was just the isolation that was getting to him. In the past when he had held hostages, he had always been at the center of the negotiations. This time, he had no idea how the negotiations were progressing and was a thousand miles from the scene of the decisions.

It was absurd, he reasoned as he walked back across the dining hall, to worry about whatever ridiculous plots the girl might be organizing among the students. They were in a helpless position and she was certainly smart enough to realize that. He turned his thoughts to the substitute hostages. What could it possibly matter? he asked himself as he walked back into the headmaster's office. All he had to do was demand that the boys remain inside the school until his helicopter had taken off. He would have the substitutes searched and handcuffed as he loaded them into the helicopters. And he would take the teacher as a further guarantee. It wasn't perfect, but it was workable.

He looked down at the telephone and then checked his watch. Something had to be happening. There had to be some news from Cairo.

He walked across the room to the ancient radio, turned on the power, and waited impatiently for the tubes to warm up. After a few seconds, there was a rising crescendo of static. He turned the tuning dial, but the static persisted without any change in its pitch as he moved through the frequency band. Suddenly, he realized what it was he was hearing. The broadcast band was being jammed.

Gamel dropped to one knee so that he was level with the tuning dial and turned the arrow to specific station signals. Static. They were jamming him. But why? They knew his information came over the telephone. Why bother to jam the radio frequencies?

But even as he was asking himself the question, he knew the answer. He sprang across the room to the desk and snatched up the telephone. There was no dial tone. The bastards had cut the line.

Gamel set the phone down gently. Why? Why deny him the information that would cause him to set the boys free? It had to be because there was no such information. The negotiations must have failed. The Americans must have gone back on their word. Or maybe Sharif had seen the danger and refused to allow substitute hostages. Obviously the news from Cairo was bad and the Americans didn't want him to hear it. Or maybe Sharif had promised them another body to make them concede his demands, and this was their desperate attempt to keep the order from being delivered.

Without information he was helpless. True, they couldn't get at him as long as he held the boys. But he couldn't decide what to do with his prisoners unless he knew the situation on the outside. He had to have the telephone fixed. And he had to get them to stop the jamming.

He would send them a message. A message they would have to take seriously. A message so forceful that they wouldn't wait to have it repeated.

He took a piece of paper and printed a note in large block letters.

Restore all telephone lines and cease all radio interference. If you have not complied in two hours, you will get another one of these, and then one every hour until you do comply.

Gamel attached a pin to the note. Then he drew his pistol from the holster, opened the cylinder, and checked the cartridges in each of the chambers. He closed the cylinder, replaced the weapon in its holster, and started out of the office toward the lounge where the captive teachers were waiting.

Ferrand slipped the black flak jacket over the olive-drab fatigues that Colonel Smiles had sent up to his room. He looked at the black crash helmet with the transparent face shield and the heavy boots that were waiting on the bed.

"Do I need all this?" he asked the sergeant who had brought the equipment.

"You'll want it," the sergeant answered.

Ferrand sat and tried on the boots. They seemed grossly oversized. He lifted the helmet over his head and pushed the face guard down over his nose. Then he decided.

"I think I'll stick with my running shoes," he said. "Running is probably all I'm good for. And I won't need this." He removed the helmet and tossed it on the bed.

Smiles was waiting for him in the kitchen along with a young man who was fully outfitted, his face smeared with dark grease. "This is Sergeant Casper," he said. "He's the explosives expert that you're bringing in."

Ferrand nodded at the introduction. It didn't seem like the time for handshaking. Then Smiles gathered them around the table and set out the details of the attack.

Ferrand was to bring Casper and two other soldiers through the break in the wall and under the cover of the trees to the corner of the building. There they were to wait.

"We're holding five minutes, until nineteen thirty-five," Smiles said, "just in case the kid is able to get the boys into the cellar. But whether he does or not, that's when Casper and one of the riflemen go through the window. At the same time, a sharpshooter is going to take out the television camera that's scanning the north wall."

He looked at Ferrand. "As soon as Casper goes in, your job is finished. You work your way back through the trees and get out through the break in the wall. Just keep running. Get away from the place as fast as you can."

"I can help," Ferrand offered.

"No you can't," Smiles said conclusively. He turned to Casper. "We'll have the school under attack about three minutes after you get into the building. Once Gamel knows he's under attack, he could push the button at any time. So you've got three, maybe four minutes to disable the detonator. We'll be on radio silence right up to the time when we go over the wall," Smiles continued. "But then we'll switch from telephones to radio. So take a walkie-talkie in with you. Let me know the second that you've fixed the bombs."

Casper nodded.

Ferrand tried to figure their chances as he listened. It was a daring plan, with no turning back. Casper was going to go after the bomb whether the kids were in the dining hall or not. And Smiles' troops were attacking regardless of whether he succeeded in deactivating the detonator. If the explosives were rendered useless, and if the attackers hit quickly from all sides, most of the boys would survive. But if the attack was poorly coordinated, the terrorists would have time to begin firing at the boys and their teachers. Or if the buildings could be blown, most of the children would die in the rubble.

"Does it have to be this way?" he asked the colonel. "Does it have to be now? Couldn't we give it just a few more hours?"

"We're losing time waiting on the kid," Smiles said. "As soon as Gamel finds out we've cut the phone lines he's going to start killing people. And if he learns about Sharif, he'll kill them all."

Ferrand answered without enthusiasm. "The attack doesn't sound like a great alternative."

Smiles thought for a moment. Then he said, "If your friend Billy Tepper is for real, we'll save them all. If not, our chances are probably about one in three. You're right. It's not a great alternative. But it's the only one we've got."

The two Italian policemen were playing cards on the hood of their car when they noticed movement inside the gate. Two of the terrorists, each carrying a machine gun, were coming toward them, struggling with something they were dragging behind them. One handed his cards over to his partner and took a few steps toward the gate. He stopped abruptly when one of the invaders raised his weapon.

They watched as the terrorists came closer. "It's a body!" one of the policemen said. The other nodded. The terrorists stopped in front of the guard house and dropped the hands of the corpse they were dragging. Then they stepped around the body and backed slowly toward the school, keeping their guns aimed at the policemen.

The Italians watched them until they disappeared into the building, then turned their attention to the rumpled form with its arms stretched out as if begging for help. A piece of paper attached to the body was rustling in the light breeze. One of the officers inched forward, reached down, and tore the note free. Then he ran back to the car, backed up in a small circle, and drove quickly down the hill, leaving his partner to stand vigil over the remains.

Billy could hear the boys filing down the corridor as he opened his closet door and squeezed past the hanging clothes to the computer. He had only a few seconds. Once the boys were on their way to the dining hall, the guard would check each of the rooms. But he wanted to make one last try to get his message to Ferrand.

He turned on the computer and typed in the setup commands, then connected the computer to the modem. Carefully, he keyed in the message telling Ferrand he wasn't ready for the attack. Then he typed in the telephone number. Once again, he listened as the modem dialed and then waited for the connection signal. There was no response, and then the message appeared telling him the phone line was out.

He was nearly crying with frustration. Why hadn't the line been down when he was sending his smartass assurances that everything was under control? Everything had worked fine when he was goading Ferrand into mounting an attack. Now, when he had to warn Ferrand that the attack was suicide, nothing was working.

He heard doors opening and closing in the corridor. The guard was on his way down the hall checking the rooms. He had to try again. He retyped the phone number and waited anxiously. Once more the message appeared telling him that the line was dead.

Billy snapped off the machine just as the guard opened the door to his room. He grabbed a jacket from one of the hangers and stepped quickly out of the closet while slipping his arms into the sleeves. The guard's dark eyes narrowed suspiciously. "I was asleep," Billy lied, and hurried past the guard into the hall. He glanced back when he reached the stairs. The guard was still standing by his open door, watching his every move.

He reached the dining hall just as the lines were forming outside the kitchen door, and looked for Professor Prinz. There were answers he needed. The component he had taken from the airplane fit perfectly into the panel of the detonator. And the detonator component was the right size for the receiver on the Spitfire. Did that mean that they were both frequency components? Could he be certain that the bombs would no longer respond to the frequency of the terrorist's radio controller? If Prinz didn't know, or if the beady-eyed science teacher described a frequency component that was different from the one he had replaced, then he would have to find a way to stop Ferrand and the Screaming Eagles. Maybe he could follow the ventilation duct to the roof, climb down, and then run for the front gate. Or maybe fix his smoke bomb so that it started a real fire and then escape in the confusion. Whatever he did though, he had to do something!

Prinz wasn't with the other teachers, so he pushed into the line directly opposite Harold Hutchings. "Professor Hutchings," he hissed from the corner of his mouth.

The history teacher turned in his direction, but his eyes didn't seem to focus.

"Professor Hutchings," Billy tried again.

Hutchings glanced about absently. His eyes were red and his face was tired. He finally located the voice addressing him and stepped wearily into the line behind Billy.

"Where's Professor Prinz? I need to talk with him."

Hutchings seemed stunned by the request. Instead of answering, he placed a comforting hand on Billy's shoulder.

"I have to ask him a question," Billy explained. What the hell was the matter with Professor Hutchings? he wondered. The guy looked like he had been punched in the stomach.

"Professor Prinz won't be joining us tonight," Hutchings managed. "Maybe I can answer your question."

They shuffled ahead a few paces as the line began to move.

"I don't think so. It's about electronics. Radio controllers and stuff."

Hutchings shook his head slowly. "No, I don't think I can help."

"Listen," Billy said impatiently, "I really need to see Professor Prinz. Where can I find him?"

Hutchings hand squeezed into Billy's shoulder. "Later," he said. "We'll talk about it later."

Jesus, Billy thought, there isn't going to be any later. If I don't get to Prinz right now, it's going to be too late.

"Where's Miss Manetti?" he tried. If Hutchings wouldn't help, then maybe Manetti could get Prinz for him. She knew about the attack. She would understand why it was urgent he talk to Prinz right now.

"Miss Manetti won't be joining us either," Hutchings answered.

Billy looked startled.

Hutchings smiled sympathetically. "It's all right, Mr. Tepper. We'll talk about it later."

Billy glanced quickly at the other teachers. Something was wrong. They all looked like they had been crying. All of them were going through the motions, but none of them seemed to know what was happening.

"Are they all right?" he suddenly demanded. "Did something happen to Professor Prinz and Miss Manetti?"

"We'll talk about it later," Harold Hutchings answered, this time more firmly than before.

*   *   *

The jeep bounced off the edge of the road and glided to a stop in the middle of a stand of trees. The two riflemen, each carrying a stubby assault gun, were out of the car instantly. Ferrand jumped down and waited while Casper slung a canvas equipment bag over his shoulder. He carried the walkie-talkie in his hand.

"Go ahead," Casper ordered.

Without responding, Ferrand turned away from the road and led the procession into the forest.

They walked easily through thin plantings, at first on level ground and then up a gently rising hill. The sun was low in the west, but there was still plenty of light and they were able to move quickly through the undergrowth. Although the south wall of Saint Anselm's was only a half mile away, it was still hidden from view by a curtain of pines.

They had driven from the command post along the road that skirted the hill on which the school stood, starting opposite the front gate and circling south around the southern wall. Now they were climbing in a northerly direction, their route keeping them below the sightlines afforded by the school buildings.

Ferrand walked quickly and, whenever the terrain permitted, broke into a jog. Gradually, the weaving line began struggling to keep up.

"Slow it down," Casper finally ordered from the back of the detail. "We've got plenty of time. No point killing ourselves before we even get there."

The trees began to thicken, and soon their attention was concentrated on moving the branches noiselessly. Suddenly, the stone wall, twelve feet high, blocked their advance.

"Which way?" Casper asked.

Ferrand looked in both directions. "This way, I think," he answered, and started moving toward the east, squeezing himself into the space between the giant stones and the tips of the tree branches. He had traveled less than a hundred yards when he raised his hand and stopped.

The break was minute. A ground cave-in had undermined a small section of the wall. A foundation stone had dropped down and two or three of the stones above it had fallen back onto the school grounds. The hole was about a foot wide and less than three feet high, and was blocked by a heavy wire mesh that was fastened to two posts staked against the inside of the wall.

"Christ," Casper said. "How did anyone ever find this?"

Ferrand smiled. "It drew the boys like a magnet. One kid was actually smuggling girls in through here."

Casper had already taken a heavy pair of wire cutters out of his bag. He cut through the mesh as easily as if it were made of string.

"You could sell a lot of those to the kids," Ferrand told him.

Within a few seconds, Casper was able to lift the mesh out through the hole. One of the riflemen squeezed through first, mumbling a curse as a jagged wire edge cut into the back of his hand. "They must have been flat-chested girls," he said as he crouched inside the wall. Ferrand went through next, then reached back and took the equipment bag from Casper. The sergeant got caught in the wire and had to back out to let Ferrand widen the opening.

Once inside, they began to move westward along the wall, staying low and taking care not to move any branches. Ferrand signaled them to stop when he recognized a clearing at the corner of the athletic fields. He took a folded diagram of the property out of his pocket, showed Casper their approximate location, and then related it to the corner of the school building. Silently, he traced the direction they would follow.

They left the wall and moved through the thick foliage, passing the bent branches from one person to the next. Ferrand remembered the helmet with the face protector he had left on the bed and wished he hadn't been so quick to discard it. His face was already scratched and he was losing precious seconds as he moved each branch away from his eyes. "They brought women through this?" one of the riflemen whispered at one point, and Ferrand knew the stab at humor was masking the apprehension they were all feeling.

He led them along the edge of the athletic field and then turned to the north. The foliage thinned out immediately. After a short distance, he signaled a halt and waited for Casper to catch up with him. "The building is dead ahead, less than a hundred yards. How close do you want to go?"

"Close enough to see the window that I'm going through," the sergeant answered.

Ferrand started forward again, but before he had taken a dozen steps, the back of the new building appeared through the branches. Then he felt Casper's hand on his shoulder.

"Let me lead," the sergeant said.

Casper dropped down on his belly and began to slide along the ground. The two soldiers dropped down next and followed behind him, and then Ferrand tried to imitate their movements. In a few seconds they were lying together under the final row of trees, staring directly at the windows at the near corner of the structure.

"The closest one," Ferrand whispered.

Casper nodded. He checked his watch. "Twenty minutes to go," he said. He looked at one of the soldiers and pointed further up along the line of trees. "Get out there until you can see through the window. That's where you'll cover from." The rifleman rolled away from the clearing and then began to crawl toward the back of the building. "You better go with him," Casper told Ferrand. "As soon as you see me inside, get your ass out of here."

Ferrand pulled back and then moved off in the direction of the first rifleman.

When he reached his new position, he was looking directly through the two back windows. To the left, he could see the edge of the countertop in the administration office. The bundle of wires came in over the opposite door but disappeared before he could see where it ran into the detonator. To the right, he could see the headmaster's desk and most of the office. Both rooms seemed to be empty. He looked down the line of trees and could barely make out the forms of Sergeant Casper and the other rifleman pressed close to the ground.

"I'm going to move up a little further," he said to the soldier he had followed. "Another twenty or thirty yards and I should be able to see into the faculty lounge and dining hall.

The soldier nodded. "Be careful," he said as Ferrand slid away.

The sun had dropped behind the roofline of the building and the shadow of the structure reached all the way to the woods where he was hiding. The darkness made his cover even more secure, and he moved quickly until he was directly behind the back of the building. He could see into the classrooms and through the open doors directly into the dining hall. The children were still at their tables. He saw a guard walk past the doorway and then he noticed another guard standing vigil at the far side of the hall. Ferrand tipped his watch toward the light still left in the sky. Seven-twenty. Only fifteen minutes to go and the boys were still out in the open, defenseless against the impending attack. "Come on Billy," he whispered to himself, "make your move." But there was no response. The meal continued in its familiar routine.

Otis Brown picked up the ringing telephone. Director Clemmons' voice, carried from Washington by military command circuits, was as clear as if the call were coming from the next room.

"Everything is ready," Brown assured the director. "Smiles is in position and the relief forces are organized." Then he recounted the list of preparations. Navy doctors had been flown up from the NATO base near Naples and issued battle gear. They were ready to be rushed into the school as soon as it was secured by the Delta Force. There were two truckloads of medical supplies waiting at the command post that would be rushed up the road to the front gate. Patients had been moved out of two hospitals in Rome and the parking lots had been cleared to serve as helicopter landing zones. Crews were already aboard six helicopter ambulances, waiting the order to take off and fly to Saint Anselm's.

"We've got four Italian construction teams with some heavy equipment waiting just down the road," Brown told the director. "It will take us less than five minutes to start clearing the building if it comes down."

"Sounds as if everything is covered," Clemmons said.

"Everything," Brown said grimly. "We even have a hangar set up as a morgue."

The director didn't respond.

"What's happening in Cairo?" Brown asked.

"Confusion," Clemmons answered. "Government radio keeps saying that Sharif is alive, but some of the Palestinians are claiming to have seen his body. Apparently Sharif's people don't know what to do. They don't want to confirm his death until they decide who's going to take his place. Our State Department people have been told to wait, so it looks as if the Egyptians aren't even sure."

"Any doubts?" Brown asked.

"None," Clemmons said. "We've talked to the man who killed him."

"I'll keep the line open."

"Please," the director said. "And Otis . . . there are a lot of concerned people waiting here. Parents—some of them are part of the government—all close to the president . . ."

"I know that," Brown answered, his voice suddenly becoming sharp. "We'll start reporting as soon as things begin to develop."

"Thank you," the director said. "Naturally, the president wants to tell them—we don't want them hearing from reporters—"

"There is one name," Brown snapped. "Nobody important enough for the president to make a personal call. Just a schoolteacher named Prinz. Gamel just delivered him with a bullet through his head to thank us for turning off his telephones."

There was a pause. "I'm sorry, Otis," Clemmons finally said. "I'll make sure the president makes a personal call."

Ferrand checked his watch. If Billy was going to make something happen, he had just five minutes to do it. And the damn kids were still shuffling through their dinner. What had he told Brown and Smiles? "If Billy Tepper says he can do it, then it will happen." But nothing was happening.

He was suddenly distracted by a flash of light in the faculty lounge. The door had been thrown open and light streamed in from the dining hall. There were two figures silhouetted in the doorway who seemed to be struggling. Then one of the shapes went tumbling out of the light and into the darkness. The door closed and the entire room darkened. Ferrand stared at the opaque window hoping something would happen to set Billy's plan into motion.

After a moment, the lights flashed on. He immediately recognized Gamel, who was standing with his back to the door looking down at the floor. The terrorist suddenly bolted forward, reached down, and pulled the fallen form up from behind the leather sofa.

It was Maria.

night

Colonel Smiles moved along the row of men that had taken position against the base of the north wall, poking shoulders, patting heads, and giving unnecessary assistance with final equipment adjustments as he went. His upbeat comments and relaxed gestures spread a spirit of confidence among the men. Most important, however, they masked his own sense of forboding for the mission that was only a few minutes away.

First, they had to scale a wall, a wall that had been built

precisely to discourage attack. Then they had to push through heavy undergrowth that could break up their attack formations and slow down the progress of the assault. Next, they had to cross open ground in plain sight of rows of windows that could serve as gun ports for the terrorists. Smiles had calculated that if Gamel's troops knew they were coming and manned the windows at the corners of the north side of the old mansion, then his men would be under a murderous cross fire for perhaps twenty seconds. A third of them would never make it to the building.

Once they reached the school, he would have to split his force. It would be safer to keep his men together, so they could provide supporting fire every step of their advance, and it made more sense to work their way carefully through the rooms, being sure to secure the spaces behind them before they moved forward. But that would defeat the prime purpose of the mission. They were attacking to keep the children alive. If they moved slowly and carefully, they would be giving the terrorists time and opportunity for the methodical murder of their hostages. Instead, he'd have to divide his force into small parties that could break in simultaneously from different sides of the building. He was trading safety for speed, and he understood that many of his men would pay with their lives for the trade.

And then there were the explosives. At some point—perhaps minutes, but perhaps only seconds—after they entered the building, Gamel would realize he was beaten. He would have a choice—either surrender or destroy himself, his hostages, and his tormentors in one instant of glorious immolation. There was little in the dossier they had on Gamel to suggest he would surrender.

Smiles' hopes were pinned on the fifteen-year-old boy inside the school, and he clung to the confidence in Billy Tepper that Edward Ferrand had expressed. But he wondered how much of that confidence had survived the contradictory instructions that had been sent over the computer links, instructions that reflected perfectly the confusion of the government that had issued them.

The colonel checked his watch. Nineteen thirty-two. It was past the time when Billy had told them it would be safe to attack. Yet the field telephone that kept in touch with the observation points high up in the hills above the school was telling him that the boys were still in the dining room and his explosives expert still waiting in the underbrush a good fifty yards from the window he was supposed to penetrate.

He turned to his sharpshooter, a tall, thin lad from Idaho, who had learned his trade hunting the lightning-fast wildcats that attacked cattle on his family ranch. "All set?"

The sharpshooter patted his bolt-action rifle.

Smiles looked up at the observer, who was on a ladder near the top of the wall using a periscope to peer over the edge. "Where's the camera?"

"Swinging toward us," the soldier said.

"Better get up," he said to the sharpshooter, pointing to a platform that had been raised almost to the height of the wall. "You'll take it out the next time it swings away from us."

His shot would be the signal for the other members of the Delta Force to start up the ladders and over the top. When they reached the top, they would use nylon climbing ropes to lower themselves quickly to the ground inside the school.

The observer watched the camera. "Right at us and going past," he reported. "It'll be back in thirty seconds."

The sharpshooter slung his rifle over his shoulder and started up to the platform. All along the wall, troops bunched at the base of the ladders that were already fixed in position for the assault.

They must have found out. It was the only explanation Billy could think of. The bastards must have found out about the planned attack and they were taking it apart piece by piece.

First they had locked Prinz up somewhere for helping him

to screw up their explosives. That must be why the science teacher was nowhere to be seen and why nobody would even talk about him. The poor old guy. He didn't even know what he was up to when he'd explained the workings of the radio transmitter and receiver chips. He probably didn't have any idea why they had him locked in a closet or something!

Then they must have gotten to his smoke bomb. They'd probably laughed themselves sick at his stupid alarm-clock fuse. That was probably why the damn thing hadn't gone off. By now, the mansion should be full of smoke and the fire alarm should be rattling the windows. Instead, dinner was over. They were already lining up with their trays and nothing had happened.

And now Miss Manetti. Billy had seen the guard bring her from someplace in the old building into the dining hall, and then watched the leader take her by the arm and toss her into the faculty lounge. He probably knew that she had been organizing the kids for the escape and now he was going to find out just who had been helping her. Which meant they would be coming for him any second.

But that wasn't the real problem. What had him biting his fingernails was the rest of the plan. If they knew about Prinz and Miss Manetti and had found out about the smoke bomb, then it figured they also knew about the television cameras. And that meant they would see Ferrand and the Screaming Eagles the second they stuck their noses over the wall. It also followed that they knew about the detonator and had certainly been able to fix any damage he might have caused. So the bombs were live, just waiting for the Screaming Eagles to get inside the building.

Jesus, how could he have screwed up so badly? Everything he had done had turned into a disaster. But there was still time to fix it. If only he could get outside to warn Ferrand. If the soldiers never came in, at least no one could get hurt. They wouldn't be any worse off than they were before he had started working on his whole crazy scheme.

But he had to move now, before they found out he was the

one who had been working with Prinz and Miss Manetti and locked him up in a closet, or handcuffed him to a radiator, or whatever the heck they had done with Prinz. Once they took him prisoner, he wouldn't have a chance. And then there'd be nobody to warn Mr. Ferrand.

Billy pushed his way to the head of the line that was in the process of forming. As soon as he turned in his dinner tray, he was heading for the washroom. And then he was going into the ventilation shaft and up onto the roof. He didn't know how he was going to get down, and he wasn't sure whether he could make it to the gate without getting caught. But hell, he had to do something.

In the security office, the guard's boring vigil was suddenly interrupted. One of his screens, the one searching the north wall, went blank.

He leaned forward and ran a quick check of the monitors. They were all working perfectly, showing uneventful pictures of the other walls, the entrances to the buildings, and the Italian police car waiting outside the front gate. But there was no picture of the north wall.

He had started up out of his chair when the offending monitor suddenly came back to life. Sections of the picture flickered on and off, interrupted by broad noise traces that ran horizontally across the screen. Then the north wall snapped into focus.

The guard examined the picture carefully. His eyes locked on every tree near the wall as the camera panned across the area, searching for anything that might be suspicious. Then he studied every foot of the top edge of the wall, looking for ropes or grappling hooks or any of the hardware that would give away an attacking force. There was nothing. Just the contrasting shadows of the trees stretched out across the stones by the slanted light of the setting sun.

He eased back into his chair. Whatever had caused the screen to flicker wasn't anything more than the normal static and line noise that were always present. There was nothing to worry about.

Mr. Ferrand. The bombs are live. Don't attack tonight. I'll fix everything tomorrow. Billy.

Maria's trembling fingers held the crumpled paper that Gamel had thrown into her lap and she reread the pencil-written words.

"I don't understand," she decided to say. "I don't know where this came from or what it means."

Gamel was breathing heavily as he stood over her. He had lifted her from the floor and tossed her onto the sofa. Now he was waiting with scarcely controlled rage for her answer.

"It was on the floor of one of the boy's rooms," he told her. "The boy you were visiting last night."

"I was bringing medication—" she started, but Gamel's open hand smashed across her cheek and silenced her.

"Liar," he hissed. "That boy needs no medication. I checked his records and I checked the medicine locker. You're lying."

The back of his hand struck her other cheek.

"And you were lying this morning when you said the other boy needed to go to a hospital. That boy has no appendix. I checked his record."

Maria looked up helplessly. "He was in pain. We thought—"

He silenced her with another blow to her reddened face.

"No more lies," he whispered. "I want the truth. What does that message mean? What attack? How was he going to get the note outside to his teacher?"

"I don't know," she said, her voice cracking. "I don't know."

Gamel loomed over her menacingly, his hands balling into fists. He could beat her senseless, he knew, but she wouldn't tell him anything. She wouldn't save herself if it meant endangering one of the children.

"I will have the boy brought here," he told her, his voice now sounding calm and controlled. "The boy you were talking with. If you haven't told me by the time he gets here, I'm going to shoot him. Then I'll send for another one. You can either tell me what this note means or you can watch the boys die one at a time. Do you understand?"

She tried to protest, but he turned away from her and screamed for the guard who was waiting just outside the door.

"Shoot the son of a bitch," Ferrand nearly screamed to the rifleman who was hidden in the bushes a hundred feet to his left. "He has the detonator in his pocket. Shoot him."

He had watched helplessly while Gamel scooped Maria up from the floor where he had thrown her and pushed her onto the sofa. He had seen his furious blows to her face and watched Maria's head snap as each blow had landed. He had nearly jumped out of his cover and rushed through the window just to get his hands on the killer's throat. But then he had realized Gamel carried the radio transmitter that held the power of life and death over the hostages and Smiles' troops. If the rifleman could put a bullet through his head, everyone would be safe.

"Shoot him," he shouted, suddenly not caring if his voice gave away their positions.

The soldier remained motionless.

Ferrand pulled back from his position and began scampering through the underbrush toward the soldier. Suddenly, the clattering of an alarm bell stopped him in his tracks.

Inside the building, the fire alarm had gone off.

Gamel stopped with his hand resting on the doorknob of the faculty lounge and felt the unfamiliar grip of fear. He knew instantly that the shrill clattering was a fire alarm, but he wasn't thinking of fire. He was thinking of the panic and confusion that would certainly follow. He was thinking of the control of the situation that was quickly slipping through his fingers, of the downed phone lines that deprived him of information, of the plots that seemed to be hatching all around him, and finally of the alarm bell that would command more attention than his own orders. He had to act quickly.

He wheeled around on Maria, who had jumped up from the couch. "Where is it coming from?" he shouted over the near deafening clatter.

"The old building," she screamed back frantically. "It's on fire."

Gamel pulled open the door. The boys and their teachers were frozen near the kitchen door, standing in line with their trays. His guards were looking about the room uneasily, almost as if they expected to see the sound. He grabbed the guard who was outside the door and pulled him into the lounge. Then he shouted his order into the young man's ear as he pointed toward Maria.

"Keep her in here. If she tries to get out, stop her."

The guard nodded and acknowledged the order by pulling back the bolt on his machine gun. Gamel hurried past him and out into the dining hall.

"Stay right where you are," he shouted at the boys, and then, looking into the faces of the teachers, "keep them in line right where they are standing. Nobody is to move."

He rushed across the dining hall and into the security office. His guard was standing over the monitor panel, his eyes flashing from screen to screen.

"What's happening?" Gamel demanded.

The guard threw up his hands. "Nothing! Nothing is happening!"

Gamel pushed him aside. "This would be the perfect cover for an attack," he said as he began to study the screens. But there was no sign of an attack. There was nothing moving along the top of the walls. No one was near the buildings and the police car was still sitting idly at the front gate. He stared at the monitors that were displaying the hallways of the old building. Nothing was happening that would explain the fire alarm.

And then he saw the smoke, a gray haze that seemed to be sliding under the door of the first-floor washroom and climbing up the walls toward the ceiling.

"There," he said to the guard, jabbing his finger at one of the screens. "There *is* a fire." There was relief in his voice. Perhaps the alarm didn't signal anything more ominous than its intended purpose. Perhaps it wasn't cover for an attack or scheme that the teachers had planned with their students. He could handle a small fire that was restricted to one of the washrooms.

"Here too," the guard said excitedly, pointing at another one of the monitors. Smoke was beginning to blur the image of the second-floor corridor.

"Forget the fire," Gamel snapped at the guard. "Watch the walls and the gate. I'm not concerned about a fire. Watch for an attack!"

He was out of the office before he had finished and ran back into the dining hall, where the boys were still frozen in place by the alarm. Immediately, he began screaming orders in his native tongue, his words jolting his troops into action. The guard nearest the kitchen door took a few steps backward to give him full view of the entire room. Then he pulled back the bolt on his weapon. The other guards joined up quickly behind Gamel and followed him as he hurried out of the dining hall and down the corridor leading to the old mansion.

"What the hell is happening?" Smiles screamed into the field telephone. "Where are the boys? Where's Casper? Has he gone in yet?"

He needed answers. The alarm bell had gone off with his sharpshooter atop the tower, crouching just below the rim of the wall. He was seconds from beginning his assault and was desperate for information.

"Nothing at all, sir," a frantic voice came back from one of the observation posts. "The boys are still in the dining hall. They're just standing there. Nobody seems to be moving."

"What about Casper?" Smiles demanded. "Where is he?"

"We can't see him," an observer responded. "He must still be in the bushes. He hasn't made his move into the building."

Smiles had to make a decision immediately. If the fire alarm was Billy Tepper's first ploy, then he wanted to allow time for the plan to unfold. Billy had said he was going to take care of the television cameras. Had he been able to blind them? If so, then he didn't want to announce their arrival by having the sharpshooter fire a shot at the camera that was scanning the wall. Billy had said he was going to disable the explosives. Had he? Then why risk having Casper break in and tip off the attack? If the alarm meant the boy's plan had been set in motion, then he should delay his troops. But if the alarm were legitimate, then he should move now, during the first moments of confusion.

The boys were the answer to his dilemma. If Billy Tepper was in charge, then they should be disappearing from the dining hall into the safety of the wine cellar. The fact that they were still standing in the food line argued that the bell he could hear in the distance wasn't part of Billy's plan.

And what did Casper know? The sergeant was fifty feet from the building, looking directly into the windows. He could hear the alarm and he could see the reaction of the boys and their teachers. For some reason he was staying put, delaying his assault on the detonator. If Casper moved, then he would launch the attack immediately. But as long as Casper waited, he should wait. He needed to talk to Casper, but they were still separated by the radio silence.

"Still nothing," he heard his observer report.

"Damn it, something has to be happening," he shouted back.

There was a moment of silence on the line. "Wait a minute," the observer suddenly shouted. "The guards. I can see them through the windows of the old building. They're all running into the old building. It looks like they've left the kids unprotected."

Billy watched Gamel and most of his men disappear from the dining hall. There were only two guards left. One was in the faculty lounge guarding Miss Manetti. The other was standing just a few feet to his left, swinging the muzzle of his Kalashnikov back and forth in rhythm with his eyes, which were sweeping the line of hostages. The guard was the only thing separating the prisoners from the safety of the wine cellar.

Billy looked back down the line and found Henry Giles, his head towering above the other boys. They made eye contact, and then Billy nodded slightly.

"Hey, can we get rid of these trays?" Billy called to the guard.

The eyes and the muzzle of the gun snapped in his direction.

"The trays," Billy repeated, gesturing with the metal tray that still held his uneaten dinner. "Why don't we put these things in a dishwasher rack?" He stepped out of line and started moving toward the kitchen door, holding his tray out in front of his face so that the guard would understand exactly what he was doing.

"Stop," the guard shouted.

Billy kept moving, again waving the tray as his excuse. "We ought to get rid of these things," he said.

"Stop," the guard ordered ominously. He took three steps forward to keep Billy clearly in his sights.

Billy halted. "Okay . . . okay . . . I just thought . . ." He had the guard turned with his back toward Henry Giles. He could see that Henry had already handed his tray to the boy in front of him. "Can't we put these trays away?" he asked reasonably.

The guard was suddenly aware of Henry's movements behind him. He started to step back, turning his head in Henry's direction while keeping the gun trained on Billy. By the time he saw the massive fist, it was already arcing toward his face. Giles put all his weight into the shattering blow to the terrorist's jaw. At the same time, his left hand clamped on the barrel of the gun. The guard staggered back a few steps, the sling of the weapon slipping from his shoulder. Then he collapsed into dizzy unconsciousness.

Instantly, the younger boys scampered into groups, surrounding the older boys who had been appointed their guardians.

"The kitchen," Billy called as he began to lead the escape. "Come on," he ordered Harold Hutchings, grabbing his sleeve and pulling him into the procession. Hutchings was still staring in shock toward the fallen soldier.

"Come *on*," Billy repeated.

The boys and their teachers moved quickly, tossing their trays on the dishwasher racks as they passed through the kitchen and into the pantry. Henry Giles and Tad Bliss grabbed the guard's hands and began dragging his limp body behind them.

"Give me a hand," Billy told Hutchings as he began pushing one of the pantry shelf sections away from the wall. Hutchings was busy with the shelf when he saw the door and watched Billy pull it open.

The boys began filing down the steps as soon as Billy had switched on the light. He touched each boy as he passed, counting out loud to make sure that all of them were entering the cellar.

"Where are we going?" Hutchings asked, looking down the steps leading to the cellar.

"Just go!" Billy yelled, pushing the teacher through the doorway.

"The wine cellar," the headmaster commented, remembering the room that he hadn't entered in years. He looked at Billy as he passed, smiled, and nodded his approval. "The wine cellar," he said again, this time sounding almost cheerful.

It seemed to be taking forever, but the line was actually

shortening very rapidly. Half the students had already passed through the door and the older boys were herding their charges quickly toward the steps. The younger boys, for the most part, were completely silent and in perfect order, the babies holding the hands and shirttails of the upperclassmen. They were doing exactly what Maria had doubted they would be able to do, but she had trained them well.

The last of the boys went through as Billy finished his count. Then came Henry and Tad, dragging the limp form of the guard. Henry was carrying the machine gun in his free hand. Billy took the gun.

"Just sit on the son of a bitch, Henry," he said. "Don't let him get up."

"He ain't going anywhere." Henry Giles smiled.

He was already three steps into the cellar, with the guard's body bouncing behind him, when he realized that Billy was closing the door.

"Hey, ain't you coming with us?" he called in a stage whisper.

But Billy didn't answer. Instead, he slammed the door shut and threw the bolt, locking the boys into the improvised bunker.

"They're out," the observer confirmed over the field telephone. "All the kids seem to have disappeared from the dining hall."

Smiles felt the corners of his mouth turning up. "Son of a bitch," he said aloud. He looked to the adjutant who was crouched at his side. "The kid did it. He's gotten them all into the wine cellar."

"What about the camera?" the adjutant asked, pointing to the sharpshooter on top of the platform.

Smiles felt as if he were suddenly riding a winning streak. First, the fire alarm indicating that Tepper's scheme was starting just a minute or so behind schedule. Then the boys moved into the cellar exactly as the kid had promised. The dice were hot. He decided to let the money ride.

"No," he answered. "Get him down from there. I'm betting that the camera is already out."

The adjutant looked surprised.

"I think they're watching something else on their goddamn monitors. I think the kid has put them all to sleep. Let's not fire a shot and risk waking them." He turned back to the field telephone. "What about Casper?"

"He still hasn't made his move," came the answer.

"Damn it!" Smiles barked. What in God's name was delaying the sergeant. He must have seen the boys leave the dining hall. He had to know that all the guards were in the old building. He had to get to that fucking bomb now. Right now!

Gamel clamped a wet towel over his nose and squinted into the thick smoke that filled the air shaft. He could see the charred container that one of his troops had doused with a fire extinguisher a few feet below. And he could follow the thick lamp cord as it rose past the second-floor grating and disappeared into the haze near the top floor. He pulled his head back out of the opening and shouted an order that was immediately relayed up the stairs to the top floor. An instant later, one of his men charged into the ground-floor washroom holding an alarm clock.

Gamel pushed the hands of the clock with his finger, recreating the movement that had closed the circuit and charged the lamp cord. Simple, but effective, he thought. And a definitive answer to all his uncertainties. It proved the fire was no accident. It was a diversion, carefully set to go off at a predetermined time.

He was under attack, but certainly not from a trained military force. No army would ever use an old alarm clock to set off its grenades. It was the teachers and students who were striking back—certainly the woman who had defied him and probably the boy whose room she had visited. He tossed the clock idly to one side, ordered one of the troops to stand guard over the now extinguished fire, and took the rest with him as he rushed back toward the new building.

But why? What could they possibly hope to achieve? They couldn't be so stupid as to think that his troops would panic at the sound of a fire alarm, that they would flee the building, leaving their prisoners behind. Could they possibly be hoping for help from the outside? Was their pathetic little act of defiance somehow coordinated with assault forces? Impossible! How could they coordinate an attack? They had no radios, and he had controlled all telephone calls coming in or going out. Besides, the Americans on the outside knew the building was wired and that he held the detonator in his pocket. They would certainly realize that even the most determined attack could only end with the building becoming a mass grave for the hostages. That was why they had agreed to negotiate with Sharif.

Yet they were certainly up to something. There was some reason why they had planted the smoke grenade, why they wanted to get him out of the new building, even if only for a few minutes. He was certain that they were planning some sort of counterattack, the attack described in the note that had been found in the boy's room. And he was equally certain that the teacher was part of the plan and knew what the note meant and who was involved.

So, she would tell him. He would take the boy from his place in the dining hall and bring him into the lounge. Then he would press the barrel of his pistol against the boy's face and cock the hammer. And she would tell him everything he wanted to know. If she hesitated, the boy would become the next victim to be dragged to the gate, and another boy would be brought into the lounge. She would tell him. Of that, Gamel was absolutely certain.

He stopped abruptly when he walked through the door and into the dining hall. The room was empty. The boys had vanished into thin air, and his guard had vanished with them.

Gamel swallowed hard as his eyes searched the corners of the hall. He listened to the silence, grasping for some clue as to what was happening. Involuntarily, his hand shot to his trouser leg and felt the radio transmitter that waited in his pocket. Then he walked slowly toward the center of the empty room, leading a parade of bewildered terrorists whose heads turned uneasily from side to side. Now he understood the reason for the smoke grenade. They had lured him out of the building to give themselves time to hide. But hide where? There was no place they could go.

"Search," he ordered his men without turning to face them. Then he quickened his pace and moved purposefully toward the security office.

His guard was still squinting into the monitors. There was no point in asking him. It was obvious the man had seen nothing out of the ordinary. Gamel stood by his side and scanned the screens, examining the untroubled walls and empty grounds surrounding the buildings. The boys still had to be somewhere inside the new building. They couldn't have gotten to the old building without passing him in the hallway. And they couldn't have escaped to the outside without coming under the eyes of sweeping security cameras.

"Watch carefully," he repeated to his soldier as he left the office and started back toward the teachers' lounge. He was already drawing his pistol. The bitch would shorten his search by telling him where the boys were hiding or he would shoot her fingers off one at a time. Her smug defiance had lasted long enough.

"Now," Casper called to the rifleman who was crouched beside him. He sprang to his feet and started sprinting across the clearing directly toward the window of the administration office. The soldier rose up immediately and followed in his tracks.

Ferrand was startled by the movement. He had been staring into the lounge, watching Maria, who was standing in the center of the room, and the armed guard who waited menacingly by the door. With the door closed, he couldn't see into the dining hall, and he had no idea what was going on with the boys. For the moment, however, his concern was with Maria. One shot could easily bring down the guard, giving him the opening he needed to go through the window and bring her out. But Casper wasn't heading toward Maria. Instead, he was charging toward the other window.

"Get the guard," Ferrand yelled to the second rifleman, who was still crouched in the bushes off to his left. But the soldier wasn't concerned with the guard who watched Maria. His attention was on Casper instead, ready at an instant to open up with supporting fire.

Ferrand jumped up and began running across the clearing toward the window of the lounge. He ignored the shout of the soldier ordering him back and rushed on toward the building. He had no idea of how he could free Maria, but he had to get close enough to act on any opportunity.

Casper never broke stride. He ran directly to the building and, throwing his arms across his face, crashed through the window, shattering the glass and the latticed wooden framing. The impact sent him tumbling across the floor inside the administration office. He managed to hold on to the equipment bag but lost the walkie-talkie, which slid into the center of the room. Ignoring the radio, he pulled himself up at the edge of the counter and reached out and touched the green metal casing of the detonator. He recognized it instantly as a Russian device, rugged and effective, but straightforward. He snatched a screwdriver from his equipment bag and spun the bolts out of the casing as his rifleman took up position at the window, his assault gun aimed at the closed door of the office.

"Casper's in the building," Smiles heard over his telephone.

"Switch to the walkie-talkies," he ordered. "We're breaking radio silence." He threw the telephone handset aside and slung the small radio over his shoulder. Then he raised his hand over his head and swept it down quickly. Instantly, his troops started up the ladders and over the top of the north wall. They formed up into their assault groups as soon as they landed on the schoolgrounds. Then they moved out, trotting through the dense cover without regard for the movement of the branches they were causing. If the cameras were operating, then they had already been seen and had to get across the clearing and into the buildings before Gamel could organize a defense. If the cameras had been disabled, on the other hand, then there was no way the terrorists could see the paths they were beating through the thickets.

Colonel Smiles was oblivious to the slashing branches and streaks of blood that were forming across the backs of his hands. Instead, he was counting seconds, mentally ticking off the moments that were left to Casper. By now the sergeant knew whether he could take the detonator apart. If he could, then he was holding the device in his fingers at this very instant. But just as certainly, Gamel knew that Casper was inside. Within seconds, he would be storming the room to preserve the only advantage he held over his attackers. Smiles had to get to the building immediately; he had to bring the terrorists under fire and relieve the furious assault that would be aimed at his explosives expert from every angle.

And then he had to pray. Pray that Gamel held out enough hope of withstanding the assault that his finger would hesitate on the terrible trigger he carried in his pocket. Pray that he hesitated long enough for Casper to find and disconnect the critical component and report over his radio that the building was safe. Or, in the last resort, pray that Billy Tepper had somehow covered all the bases.

Billy was trapped. He had clumsily pushed the shelves over the wine cellar door and started back out of the kitchen. But then he hesitated, uncertain as to which way to turn. Miss Manetti was the one hostage that was still exposed, held in the teachers' lounge by a single guard. He had to help her escape or else she would pay the price for his stupid scheme. The terrorist leader would slaughter her once he found the boys missing. And even if she somehow survived, she would be caught upstairs when the guy triggered his detonator, the innocent victim of the building's collapse. He had the machine gun, which he didn't know how to use. But maybe if he just pulled the trigger and sprayed some shots, the guard would come flying out of the lounge. And that would give Miss Manetti a chance to get out through the window.

But it would also finish his chances of making it to the front gate. And he had to get outside to warn Mr. Ferrand that the place was still wired. Otherwise the whole army of Screaming Eagles would come charging inside and be blown to bits. That was his most important job. But he couldn't just leave Miss Manetti. Christ, it wasn't her fault he had made a mess of things.

He had been frozen by his own confusion when he heard the terrorist leader march back into the dining hall. Holy shit! Now he couldn't even get out of the kitchen. His head had whipped around. It was too late to get into the wine cellar. They'd catch him with the shelves pulled back and that would give everyone else away. He had taken three quick steps and leaped head first into the tiny space behind the two massive iron stoves. And that was where he was trapped.

Jesus, he thought, it will take them about ten seconds to find me. First creep that pokes around in the kitchen will sure as hell stick his nose behind the stoves. And there I'll be. Holding a machine gun.

He tried to push the gun under the back of the stove. Maybe they wouldn't open fire if he was just kneeling there looking hopeless. But the gun didn't fit.

He heard the leader yell something he didn't understand. Seconds later, he could hear the doors to the classrooms opening and then banging shut. They were searching. Well, what the hell did you expect them to do, stupid. They're tearing the place apart, and here you are hunched up like a frog behind the damn stove. With a fucking machine gun that you don't know how to fire!

He heard footsteps outside the kitchen door and then a *click-click* as heavy boots stepped onto the hard kitchen tiles. The clicking sound meandered along the dish racks and stopped for a moment. Then it started across the floor toward the stove. Billy realized he was about to wet his pants.

Suddenly, the cold silence was shattered. From across the dining hall came an explosion of glass. And then the terrorist leader was shouting orders. He had been crossing the dining hall toward the teachers' lounge when the window of the administration office had been smashed out of its frame. He was under attack and was screaming his orders for a counterattack.

The boots rushed across the kitchen tiles and out into the dining hall. And then there seemed to be a confusion of shouting. Billy scampered on his hands and knees to the edge of the stove and peeked carefully around the corner. The terrorists were rushing out of the dining hall and into the hallway that connected the headmaster's and administration office.

The instant that Gamel heard the crash he knew they had broken into the administration office. And he knew why. They had to get to the detonator before they could launch an attack. If he could keep them away from the device, then he would still be in command. But if he couldn't, then the end was only seconds away. He had no intention of fighting to the last man. If they had reached the detonator, he would push the button he was already holding in his hand.

Two of his guards rushed ahead of him into the corridor. He screamed his orders, calling to two more men to follow him to the office door and directing the others to go out through the classroom windows and attack the administration office from the outside. If it was an advance party, he would have them under fire in seconds. But if it was a full attack force, then there was the button.

The first guard smashed open the administration door with one kick, caught a glimpse of an American soldier at the counter with the detonator, and fired wildly with the gun hanging at his hip. The American dropped behind the counter. In the next instant, the terrorist was jerking in mid-air like a puppet whose strings were being yanked. Automatic fire from the window chopped splinters from the door and door frame and dropped the guard across the threshold.

The American reached up over the edge of the counter and tried to retrieve the detonator, but Gamel's second guard, crouched behind the body of his fallen comrade, fired a short burst into the front of the counter. The rounds punched neat holes in the wooden paneling, and the American's hands dropped from sight, leaving the disassembled detonator behind.

A third guard began firing over Gamel's crouched form, directing a hail of bullets toward the shattered window. The rifleman who had been firing from the outside quickly dropped from sight.

One of the terrorists rushed through the doorway into the administration office, firing through the vacant window to cover his advance. He reached the counter and tried to scoop the detonator up with his free arm but was suddenly spun around by the impact of a bullet fired from outside the building. He staggered back through the doorway, a patch of red spreading rapidly across his shoulder.

The administration office had become a no-man's-land, with the terrorists controlling the door at one end and the attackers controlling the window at the other. There was an American soldier slumped behind the counter and a terrorist soldier crumpled in the doorway. The prize, the dark green canister that connected the wires to the explosive charges, stood on the countertop in plain view.

Gamel's evaluation was instantaneous. If the troops he had sent out through the classrooms could subdue the attackers then he still held the school. The boys were locked somewhere inside the building and he had the live transmitter safely in his pocket. He rushed away from the bloody doorway toward the security office.

The monitors scanning the outside of the building had picked up one of the attackers, a single rifleman in the bushes opposite the shattered window. But there was still no activity over the top of any of the walls.

"You're positive?" Gamel demanded.

"Positive," the guard answered. "Nothing has changed."

"Where's the soldier who was at the window?"

The guard shook his head. "He must be right up against the building, inside the camera's field of vision. But there is only one in the bushes."

It didn't make sense. Why send a small party after the explosives if they weren't following it up with a full-scale attack? But where were the attackers? Certainly they must know that their small advance force wouldn't have a chance on its own. Something was wrong. There was something happening that he didn't understand. There was information he was missing.

Ferrand reached the window of the teachers' lounge just as the firing began in the administration office. He saw the Delta Force soldier crouched outside the window, firing over the sill. Then he saw the sill splinter under a barrage of bullets and watched as the man dropped to the ground. There was another burst of gunfire from inside, which probably meant that they were firing at Casper.

It had happened too quickly. The sergeant was inside the room for only a minute when the shooting had started. Certainly, there hadn't been enough time for him to do anything with the detonator, which meant that the critical phase of Smiles' attack plan had failed. The explosives were still live, ready to do Gamel's bidding.

He could see Maria clearly and the horror on her face told him she knew the school was about to explode. But the guard was still waiting patiently, his machine gun at the ready. If only he had taken a weapon! Even a single shot could have gotten the guard and given him a chance to get Maria out of the building. Instead, all he could do was curse at his own helplessness.

Suddenly, the air exploded with rifle fire that seemed to be coming from his right. He looked around and saw some of Smiles' troops breaking out of the bushes behind the old mansion in a headlong charge toward the buildings. Instantly, they were under fire from Gamel's troops, who were using one of the classroom windows as a gun port. Ferrand dropped to the ground and began crawling away from the battle toward the soldier who was crouched below the administration office window.

"Get Casper," the soldier told him. "He's been hit." Then the rifleman sprang up and aimed a line of fire through the window.

Ferrand could see the sergeant slumped against the wall behind the counter. As he moved into the window frame he could see the detonator. And then the office door came into view. There were two bodies slumped in the opening, and no one seemed to be firing back toward the window. Ferrand took a quick step and leaped through the opening, landing on his face and sliding up against Casper.

"Get it down here," the sergeant gurgled. He raised a bloody hand and pointed to the canister. "Get it down here."

Ferrand reached up and slid the detonator off the counter.

"It's open. Lift the case. The top comes up," Casper instructed him.

Ferrand looked incredulously at the sergeant's clouded eyes and pale skin. "I can't," he answered.

"Lift the case," Casper whispered.

He pulled at the top of the canister and watched it slide up along the wires. A convoluted mass of electronic components appeared. Then he saw where the wires terminated in the connector board. He grabbed for them so that he could pull them free.

"No," Casper's voice hissed.

Ferrand's hand stopped.

Gamel knew it was over. The hail of gunfire had to come from the attack force that had somehow escaped detection by the cameras. There was only one guard left in the doorway of the administration office to keep the attackers out. And he seemed to be pinned down by the automatic-weapons fire that was coming through the window. He had only seconds left to make his move.

He pushed the guard away from the monitor screens and ordered him toward the administration office. "Keep them out as long as you can," he screamed above the gunfire that was now almost deafening. Then he drew his pistol and rushed across the dining hall toward the faculty lounge.

Three of his men were at the dining hall windows, firing at the attackers who seemed to have appeared out of nowhere and were suddenly everywhere. Return fire from outside was methodically tearing out the window frames and ripping holes in the ceiling and walls of the room. He could also hear gunfire echoing in the corridor that led to the old mansion. The attackers were already inside the building. He pushed open the door to the lounge and dropped to the floor inside.

Maria was lying on her face behind the tenuous protection of the leather sofa. The guard was hunched over her, his machine gun aimed at the window, which was not yet under attack.

"Cover me," Gamel ordered. He pushed the revolver back into its holster, then grabbed Maria by the arm and dragged her to her feet.

"As soon as I reach the trees, get our people out of here," Gamel told the guard. "The building goes in one minute."

The young soldier nodded obediently.

Billy crept out from behind the stove just as the world seemed to explode in gunfire. His first instinct was to duck, and he clapped his hands over his ears and buried his face against his knees. One moment, it had been so quiet that he could hear the sound of hard-soled boots on the floor. In the next, the explosive chattering seemed about to crack his head open.

As soon as he had absorbed the shock, he thought of escape. The wine cellar was out. Now it was more dangerous than ever to risk giving away the hiding place. He began crawling toward the kitchen door, dragging the captured machine gun by its buckled sling. When he reached the edge of the door he saw Gamel. Billy watched as the terrorist leader dodged across the battered dining hall and threw himself into the faculty lounge. He remembered Miss Manetti, and knew what the bastard was going to do to her. Somehow, he had to get to her and help her escape.

He slipped through the doorway and looked around quickly. The rats firing out through the windows had their backs to him. There were two more of them in the corridor outside the dining hall, but they were firing toward the administration office. He began to crawl under the tables, making his way carefully across the hall toward the door of the lounge.

Once there, he crept inside, and the noise of the machine guns seemed more distant. Then he slowly raised his head above the back of the sofa. One of the windows was open. A guard was kneeling by the sill, his gun pointed through the opening and his attention riveted on the grounds outside. Miss Manetti and leader of the invaders were gone.

He crouched down again and moved quickly around the edge of the sofa, then behind one of the oversized leather chairs. As he eased himself to his feet, he saw that he was standing directly behind the guard. He lifted the machine gun by its barrel and swung it like a baseball bat. The metal breech twanged like a tuning fork when it struck the side of the soldier's head. Noiselessly, the man slumped forward, his head and arms disappearing outside the window.

Billy stuck his head out the opening. To his right, two American soldiers were hunched beneath the window of the administration office, pinned down by the cross fire that was coming from inside the office and from the terrorist he had just bashed. One of the troops saw him and waved frantically for him to get back inside. Far to his left, two of the terrorists were lying on the ground just outside one of the classrooms. Their fire was holding a group of the Screaming Eagles pinned to the ground at the corner of the old mansion.

Directly ahead, the terrorist commander was staggering toward the edge of the woods, half dragging Miss Manetti, who was serving as a shield. Billy slipped through the window and, still holding the gun by the barrel, began to run after him.

Ferrand was holding the detonator. "Which wire?" he begged. But there was no answer. Sergeant Casper's eyes were opening and closing slowly, seemingly unable to focus.

He looked at the maze of wires and components. Casper had nearly fainted when he'd started to pull the connecting wires free, so some of them had to be dangerous. But which ones? There were connections from the battery to the circuit card and from the card to the connector board. And there were wires that ran from the battery directly to the connector board. Ferrand looked toward the window, hoping there was someone outside who might understand the deadly puzzle. But no one could get through to help him. Each time one of the riflemen raised himself into the vacant window, he was driven back by fire from the doorway on the other side of the counter. He noticed the walkie-talkie that was lying in the center of the floor where it had fallen from Casper's grasp. At least he should warn Smiles that the charges were still live. But he couldn't crawl out to retrieve it without putting himself directly into the cross fire from the window and door. And even if he reached it, he wasn't sure he could operate it.

He took Casper's face in his hand and turned it toward the detonator. "Which wire?" he repeated. The sergeant seemed to bite through his lip in his effort to focus on the device.

"The blue one," he whispered, and then his head rolled toward the wall.

Jesus! There were two blue wires. No, three. And they were in different places. He snapped Casper's head back toward the problem. "Which wire? This one?" He touched one of the blue wires that ran between the circuit card and the battery. But there was no response. The sergeant's eyelids slid shut.

They were failing. The assault was taking too long, and time meant failure. Nearly three minutes had passed since they'd breached the north wall and they still hadn't secured the school.

Smiles and half of his assault team were only thirty feet from the front door of the new building. But they were stopped. Terrorists firing from the dining hall windows had them pinned down behind the low stone walls and hedges that edged the path up from the gate. The other half of his attack force, which had circled around to the back of the building, had fared no better. Some of them had broken quickly into the old mansion, only to be stopped by two terrorists who controlled the main hallway between the buildings. The rest were flattened behind the mansion, exchanging fire with a small patrol of terrorists who had taken a position outside the classrooms.

Smiles needed to know about Casper. If the sergeant had succeeded in disarming the explosives, then he should fire his tear-gas grenades into the school and follow them with a furious assault. That was his best chance of preventing the terrorists from finding the boys and turning their guns on them. But if Casper had failed, then the assault would play right into Gamel's hands. The bastard would want the assault force inside the school before he set off the charges.

He pressed the walkie-talkie to his mouth, but his observer could give him no help. Casper was inside, but there was still a battle raging for control of the administration office. The lack of a report from the advance team wasn't encouraging. It probably meant they were too busy fighting for their lives to get to the detonator. Or worse, that those inside the administration office had already been killed.

There were no answers—only the realization that every moment he hesitated reduced the odds of the boys leaving the school alive.

"Fire the gas," he told his adjutant at last.

The officer unclipped a grenade from his belt and showed it to the line of soldiers who were crouching behind the hedges. Instantly, several of the men set down their guns and pulled grenades from their belts. The remaining troops rose up and fired steadily into the shattered windows of the dining hall. Under the covering fire, the others took aim and hurled the grenades toward the open window casements.

Two of the grenades missed their targets, hitting the face of the building and dropping harmlessly to the ground instead. But four found their mark and disappeared through the openings.

At first, nothing happened. The troops used the moment to pull grotesque gas masks over their faces. Then, without warning, the inside of the dining hall filled with smoke. The firing from the windows stopped abruptly.

Smiles leaped over the driveway wall and raced directly toward the closest window. Half a second later, the rest of his force jumped into the open space and charged the school.

They were the longest minutes of Otis Brown's life. He had listened on the field telephone as Colonel Smiles talked with the observers on the hillside, so he knew about the fire alarm, knew that the boys had disappeared from the dining hall, and knew that Sergeant Casper had rushed the detonator. He heard Smiles order the switch from the telephone lines to the radios, so he knew that the Delta Force had launched its attack. And from that moment on, he knew absolutely nothing.

The radio he was monitoring was no help. All he could hear were Smiles' occasional pleas for information and the confused, uninformed responses that came from the observation post. He was uncertain as to whether the assault force was moving forward, or whether it was being decimated by the terrorists. He didn't know whether the explosives had been deactivated. He wasn't sure what had happened to the boys.

All he knew was that three endless minutes had elapsed and that Smiles still wasn't in control of the school. Three fatal minutes. The assault by Dutch troops on a trainload of hostages had taken less than three minutes. Half the hostages had been found dead. It had taken less than two minutes for Egyptian commandos to take control of a captured airliner. They'd found forty passengers dead in their seats. And what had Smiles told him about his most recent exercise in the Moroccan desert? They had lost about fifteen seconds forcing the airliner door. Half the passengers were machinegunned during the short delay.

Three minutes was an eternity. Long enough for Gamel and his men to find the entrance to the hidden wine cellar. Long enough for the terrorist to pick the perfect moment to detonate his bombs.

In the farmhouse, Brown could hear the distant sound of gunfire, so much like strings of tiny firecrackers at a Chinese New Year's celebration. His imagination began to play games. Half the terrorist force was holding Smiles and his raiders in the narrow hallways of the school. The other half was methodically slaughtering the boys as they were flushed out of the wine cellar. Or maybe Smiles' troops were fighting their way from room to room, backing the terrorists into some final corner of the school. But he had no idea which scenario was accurate. Like Smiles, he had heard nothing from Sergeant Casper. He had to assume that the bombs tucked into the walls of the two buildings were live. As each second ticked away, he waited to feel the ground tremble under the impact of a distant blast. And then would come the deafening roar as the entire school collapsed into its own burning ashes.

*   *   *

Billy raced across the open ground, the machine gun banging at his heels. His goal was the row of trees dead ahead and the still-moving underbrush that marked the spot where the terrorist leader had dragged Miss Manetti. He had to catch up with them. He had to rescue her. It was his fault that she was in trouble.

But how? The bastard was twice his size. And the guy had a pistol that he could hold to Miss Manetti's head. He had the stolen machine gun. But he had never fired a machine gun. He had no idea how the damn thing worked. Oh sure, you pointed it and pulled the trigger. But was there a safety catch? How many bullets did it hold? And what did you do when the bullets ran out?

For an instant, he broke stride. Maybe he should go back. He could tell a couple of the soldiers where the terrorist was and warn them that he was holding a hostage. They'd know what to do. And he could warn them about the explosives. Christ, they were trying to fight their way into a building that was still mined. He had to tell them to stay outside.

Except there wasn't any time. The leader had already disappeared into the woods. By the time he went and got help and then came back, they'd never find the bastard. And what would he do to Miss Manetti? He had used her as a shield while he crossed the open ground. Once he was in the cover of the bushes, he wouldn't need a shield. She'd just be in his way.

Billy picked up his pace and ducked down as he reached the edge of the bushes. They had been only fifty yards ahead of him. But the sun was already down and daylight was fading quickly. Under the trees it was already dark, and he couldn't see anything. He looked down at the gun, then turned it around so that the grips fitted into his hands and the barrel was pointing forward. He raised it slowly and looked down the sights. "Okay," he told himself. "Just aim it. And pull the trigger. And hope." Then he pushed into the underbrush, the weapon raised just under his chin.

He stopped abruptly when he heard the branches crunching under his feet, a sound that seemed louder than the now distant gunfire. He knew the noise he was making would give him away. And then, ahead and a little to his right, he heard Miss Manetti's voice.

She was trying to say something. Maybe trying to scream. But she was gagged, or maybe being choked. And there was another noise, the sound of branches snapping, that told him they were moving. The bastard was still dragging her with him.

Billy moved carefully in the direction of the sounds, the gun still raised to his shoulder. Just ahead he heard her voice, but it was silenced before he could make out even a word. Then he heard the leader's voice seeming to curse at the thrashing of a branch. He kept moving forward, weaving carefully through the bushes and branches, which became visible only when they were inches from his face. And then he saw them.

The terrorist was turned away from him, his right arm wrapped tightly around Miss Manetti's neck. His left hand held one of her arms bent up behind her back. He was forcing her ahead of him, using her as a shield against the branches. He was trying to run, but she was dragging her feet and struggling to break away. Billy started to aim the gun. But they seemed to disappear into the darkness right before his eyes.

He realized then that he couldn't fire. Sure, if the gun worked, he could probably shoot the leader and half the trees in the forest. But Miss Manetti would be hit also. As he threaded his way through the underbrush, he released the grips and slid his hands up onto the barrel. Once again, he was holding the machine gun like a baseball bat.

Ferrand pinched one of the blue wires. Then he held the exposed electronics directly in front of Casper's face. "This one?" he begged. "Is this the right one?" Casper's eyes rolled. Ferrand watched for a reaction. He thought he saw the sergeant begin to nod. But then the man's face contorted in pain and his eyes squeezed shut again. "Is this the right one?" Ferrand yelled. But Casper showed no sign of life.

Ferrand decided. He hooked his finger under the wire. Then he closed his eyes and pulled, feeling it tear free from its pinpoint of solder.

Miss Manetti's scream exploded out of the darkness, but was cut off suddenly by a breathless gasp. Billy jumped forward, and the two of them reappeared in front of him, Miss Manetti on the ground and the terrorist trying to drag her back to her feet. He raised the machine gun and began to swing it in a wide, descending arc.

At the top of the swing, the gun chipped through the tree branches. Gamel began to turn, saw the form behind him, and instinctively dodged to one side. He caught a glimpse of the flashing weapon just in time to drop his head. The metal breech crashed across his back.

Billy felt the gun hit and watched the terrorist drop to his hands and knees. There was an instant in which another swing could have finished off his enemy. But he stood paralyzed by the enormity of what he had just done. "Leave her alone," he screamed, as if the sound of his voice alone would frighten the killer. Then he lifted the gun in a menacing gesture. "Just leave her alone," he repeated, his voice trailing off as he suddenly realized he was in over his head.

Gamel sprang forward, his full weight smashing into Billy. The boy bounced backward and ended up sprawled out on the ground. The automatic weapon dropped beside him. Gamel scampered forward and reached for the gun, but suddenly collapsed as Maria pounced on his back like an enraged lioness protecting her cub. Her hands reached around and her nails dug into his face. He ripped her hands away and spun her off his back. But when he turned back for the machine gun, the boy was pulling it toward himself.

Gamel dove for the gun, but Billy threw it to one side, sending it skidding into the underbrush. The terrorist began to crawl after it, only to have Maria land once again on his back. He struggled to his feet as he tore at her arms and finally was able to throw her to one side. Then he reached for the revolver in his holster. He grasped the butt and was pulling the weapon clear when Billy clamped onto his wrist. Then the boy snapped forward like a cobra and sank his teeth into Gamel's arm. The pistol flew to one side as the terrorist leader jerked his arm free and whipped a backhand blow across the boy's face. Billy dropped in a heap, falling against Maria, who had been struggling to her feet.

Gamel looked around quickly. In the darkness, he couldn't locate either of the guns. Next to him, the woman and boy were trying to pick themselves up from the ground. He took two quick steps backward until he was stopped by the branches of a tree. Then he reached a bloody hand into his pocket and pulled out the small transmitter.

There was no time left. No time to wait for his young soldiers to make their escape from the building. No time to wait for the Americans to fight their way into their own tomb. He was beaten. The occupation of Saint Anselm's had been broken. But he still controlled the lives of the prisoners. The boys were still trapped somewhere inside the building that he had the power to destroy. He held the detonator out at arm's length as if he were aiming its electronic signal.

Maria recognized the weapon and started to scream. Billy ducked his head and buried his face in his arms.

Gamel pressed the button.

The small engine on Jimmy Bradberry's Spitfire snapped to life and then coughed explosively. The propeller cranked for two or three turns, then raced until it became a blur. A cloud of blue smoke pumped from the model's exhaust pipe and disappeared as the buzzing engine reached speed. The plane inched forward, its propeller tugging on a column of air. Then it jumped ahead, rolled quickly to the edge of Billy's desk, and took off across the room. It was moving in a falling arc, clearly destined to crash, when it reached the open lower section of Billy's window and flashed through the outside.

It gained speed as it dove, and then its perfectly proportioned wings began to lift. The nose pulled up and the propeller's pull maintained its speed. The Spitfire leveled off just a few feet from the ground, flying in a straight line away from the building. Then it began to climb until it broke out of the shadow of the school and into the darkening sky.

Smiles' soldiers snapped their attention toward the new threat, then looked curiously at the toy airplane that was climbing into a victory roll just above their heads. They had no idea what they were watching.

The only person who could have told them was Billy Tepper. He could have explained that the buzzing sound of the Spitfire's engine meant they were going to live. But Billy was crouched in the woods watching a madman crush the button of a radio transmitter under his finger.

Gamel squeezed the button again and again, until he was certain that his explosives had been disarmed. In a rage, he flung the device into the forest. Then he looked down at Maria and Billy, who were staring wide-eyed, unable to believe what they had just seen. For an instant, Gamel thought of choking both of them to death with his bare hands, and he balanced indecisively on the balls of his feet. Then he turned abruptly, pushed back the branches, and fled into the woods.

Smiles' men charged into the cloud of tear gas, rolled to the floor, and aimed their automatic weapons. But they found no targets. All around them were disabled terrorists who had discarded their weapons and were staggering blindly in the darkness, desperate for air. The Americans simply dragged them to the windows and threw them to the ground outside.

The two terrorists who were positioned in the hallway and firing through the open door of the administration office suddenly realized there were American soldiers behind them, threw down their machine guns, and locked their hands behind their heads. Three of Smiles' men rushed into the classroom and took up positions in the window behind the terrorists who had pinned down part of the attacking force. The terrorists surrendered immediately. Three more Americans moved cautiously down the corridor toward the old building, surprising the last two members of the terrorist force who had checked the Delta Force advance through the hallways of the mansion. Within two minutes of their charge through the dining hall windows, all the guns were quiet.

Smiles was on the radio immediately, calling in the medical teams that were waiting at the foot of the hill. He heard the sirens begin to wail before he had even completed his message. Then he sent an order to the airport for the medical evacuation helicopters. Finally, he rushed into the administration office, where he found one of the riflemen pressing gauze pads against Sergeant Casper's chest.

"The ambulance is coming," he tried to tell Casper, but the sergeant didn't respond. He grabbed the man's wrist and tried to feel a pulse. "Where the hell is that ambulance?" he shouted back toward the doorway. "I want the doctors in here now!"

He waited on his knees, pressing one of the pads against his explosives expert's chest until a Navy doctor in khaki fatigues pushed him aside. The doctor lifted Casper's eyelids, then laid his fingers along the side of the sergeant's neck. Without a word, he dug into his medical bag and pulled out a hypodermic needle.

"Is he going to make it?" Smiles asked.

"Where's the helicopter?" the doctor responded.

Ferrand heard the choppers pounding overhead but didn't turn to watch them. He rushed immediately into the faculty lounge where he had last seen Maria. All he found was a shabbily dressed terrorist, his legs in the room, his arms and head hanging out the window. He ran into a classroom and found American soldiers covering terrorist troops who were lying flat on the floor.

"There's a woman," he said. "One of the teachers. She was a prisoner in one of these rooms."

The soldiers looked back blankly.

He slipped through the window into the failing light outside and ran along the edge of the building, looking frantically into the shrubs. Then he stopped and screamed her name out, but his voice was lost in the roar of the helicopters' turbines. He raced back into the school.

As he came barreling into the hallway, two soldiers rushed a stretcher out of the administration office. Casper's limp body went by followed by a doctor who was holding an intravenous bottle high over his head. Ferrand spotted Colonel Smiles and clearly saw the anguish in the officer's face.

"Is he . . . ?" Ferrand started to ask.

"He's alive," Smiles answered, but his expression didn't seem convincing. "Get to the wine cellar," he then ordered Ferrand. "See about the boys."

But Ferrand didn't move. He was terrified for Maria's safety and suddenly concerned about Casper's survival. And now he was reminded about the boys. He didn't know which way to turn.

"You can't help him," Smiles said. "Take care of the boys. We have to be sure they're all right."

"One of the teachers is missing," Ferrand answered. "A woman. Gamel was holding her prisoner."

The colonel nodded. "Gamel is missing, too. We're searching. We'll find her. You get to the boys."

Ferrand left in a daze. Smiles was right, of course. The one thing he could do was look after the kids. But his mind was torn, fixed on Maria and the terrible things that might have happened to her, while he prayed that he would find the boys alive.

He crossed the dining hall, choking on the last traces of the tear gas that were drifting through the room, and stumbled into the kitchen. He pulled away the shelves that covered the wine cellar entrance, then pulled the bolt and threw the door open.

No one was on the stairwell. The lights were turned off and the space below was in total darkness.

"Hello," he called into the cellar.

There was no reply. Suddenly, he had the frightening feeling he was calling into a tomb.

"Hello. This is Ferrand. It's over. You're all free."

Still there was no answer.

He was about to scream again when he heard a noise, a shuffling, and then the sound of a footstep on the stairs. A form appeared in the darkness, and then the headmaster stepped up into the light.

"Good evening, Mr. Ferrand," the headmaster said.

The boys followed cautiously, blinking at first, then smiling when they saw Ferrand and the headmaster waiting.

"Are they gone?" one of Maria's brats asked as he stuck his head into the kitchen.

"They're gone," the headmaster answered simply.

Ferrand leaned forward and looked down the line of faces. Maybe Maria had gotten free and made it to the safety of the cellar. But he knew it was a long shot and wasn't surprised when he didn't see her with the others.

"Where's Billy?" he suddenly asked. "Billy Tepper?"

"Ain't he with you?" Henry Giles answered.

Ferrand looked to Hutchings.

"He didn't come down with us," the history teacher said.

Ferrand bolted past the boys and back out through the dining hall until he found Colonel Smiles. "Two of them are missing," he said breathlessly. "The teacher and one of the boys. Billy Tepper."

Smiles started to answer but was interrupted by the noise of one of the medical helicopters pounding the air as it lifted off the ground. They had no choice but to watch until the chopper disappeared over the roof, and then Smiles said,

"One of our men thinks he saw Gamel escape into the woods. He had a woman with him."

Ferrand's eyes closed.

"He thinks that one of the boys followed them. It was probably Tepper. We've got a patrol out looking for them, but they're moving very slowly. If Gamel has the teacher or the boy, we don't want to rush in and shoot the place up."

Ferrand understood.

"Everyone else is okay?" the colonel asked.

"Fine. They're all safe."

Smiles nodded. "All but two," he said. He turned and walked to the front door, where his adjutant was waiting with the field radio.

Otis Brown could hardly believe the report. He had expected to hear the grim tally of a body count. Instead, it was news of nearly total victory. The boys had been rescued unharmed. Only one was unaccounted for, William Tepper, the only one he knew by name. One of the teachers was missing as well. The rest had been rescued unharmed.

The attack force had suffered only one serious casualty, the explosives expert who was now being airlifted to the hospital, where doctors were waiting. The prognosis was uncertain. There were numerous minor injuries, the kinds that were suffered in training exercises. Only two of the soldiers had been wounded by gunfire, and both were in good condition.

Three of the terrorists had been killed, and three wounded. They were being taken to an Italian hospital under a military guard. The rest were being held as prisoners. There would probably be a diplomatic flap with the Italians over whose prisoners they were, but Otis Brown didn't give a damn.

There was only one cause for alarm. Gamel had escaped onto the grounds. American troops were searching inside the walls, and the Italian military was sealing off the entire area.

Brown wanted Gamel either dead or in prison. If he escaped, it increased the odds of there being another Saint Anselm's, probably in another country, sometime in the future.

He heard his call being connected and found himself speaking directly to the president.

"All the boys?" President Reynolds asked incredulously.

"They're all fine," Brown repeated buoyantly. "The Tepper boy is the only one unaccounted for, and we expect to know about him very shortly. I would advise against saying anything to his family until we're certain."

"Then the rescue was a success?" the president asked.

"The best we've had yet," Otis Brown was able to report.

The boys were gathered in the dining hall while the military doctors went through the mandatory routine of cursory physicals. It was a needless exercise. They had revived the moment they understood they were free, and the laughter and storytelling was better evidence of their health than anything the doctors could possibly discover.

"You were scared shitless," Henry Giles was telling Snuffy Bradberry.

"I was not," Snuffy said defensively. "I didn't see you throwing a coughing fit in front of those guys."

"Yeah, well how many of them did you punch out?" Giles asked.

"Hey, Mr. Hutchings," an upperclassman wondered, "we're not going to have a test on that thing in Austria, are we?"

"Happily not," Hutchings said. "And it wasn't a 'thing in Austria.' It was the Congress of Vienna."

His answer was drowned out by hearty cheering.

Ferrand stood to one side, unable to join the horseplay. His mind was fixed on Maria and the search parties that hadn't yet reported back. He almost resented the sound of the boys' laughter, which somehow seemed obscene while one of their classmates—the one who had probably saved their lives—was missing.

"She'll be all right," he heard the headmaster whisper to him.

Ferrand looked startled.

"A very lovely woman. And an excellent teacher," the Old Mouse added. "You'll be very good for each other."

"You knew about us?" Ferrand nearly smiled.

The pince-nez and the mustache bobbed up and down. "And the Tepper boy—the one who sent me to Russia—he'll be fine. He has such courage. . . ."

Ferrand had never suspected that the headmaster knew who any of the boys were.

"Every Friday he brought me cheese," the headmaster said wistfully. "A very fine boy."

"Hey, Billy!" The whoop came from Snuffy Bradberry, who bolted out from under a doctor's stethoscope and charged across the dining hall.

Ferrand looked up to see Billy Tepper in the doorway. And over his shoulder was Maria.

The boys rushed toward Billy as one, leaving the doctors shaking their heads.

"Where the hell were you?" a voice demanded.

"Outside where the shooting was," Billy answered casually.

"Bullshit!" It was Henry Giles' baritone above the higher-pitched screams of the brats. "You were probably hiding in the can." And then everyone was talking at once, exaggerating experiences that needed no adornment.

Ferrand and Maria looked at each other over the bobbing heads of the boys. Then he walked toward her, weaving through the jostling bodies without even noticing them.

"We'll live here," he told her. "Wherever you want." Then he eased his arms around her and kissed her battered lips.

"Get the wine cellar ready," Billy Tepper said to the boys. They had heard the sensational stories about Maria and Ferrand, and now they screamed their approval.

Ferrand reached out and mussed Billy's hair. "Your best prank yet," he said.

"Piece of cake," Billy told him.

April 21

afternoon

The boys were organized onto buses and driven to an Italian air base where United States aircraft were waiting for them. From there, they were flown immediately to an American hospital in Germany.

"These children have been through a profound trauma," an expert on terrorism said, justifying the detour. "We need to evaluate them individually so that we can recommend proper counseling procedures." It was simply an excuse to give the president and his aides a chance to organize a triumphant return that could be thoroughly mined for political gold. The boys would spend their day of evaluation cleaning out the military hospital's ice cream supply.

Maria had been taken to a civilian hospital in Rome, where a plastic surgeon sutured the gash on her face that she had suffered in the first moments of captivity. They also taped up a rib that had been broken in her struggle with Gamel, sedated her, and put her to bed.

Ferrand shuttled between the hospital and the school, where the teachers were helping with the cleanup and assuring the headmaster that Saint Anselm's would be ready to open in just a few weeks. But the Old Mouse knew better. Certainly the buildings could be repaired quickly. There was some smoke damage in the mansion, and a film on the walls and ceiling of the dining hall, the residue of the tear gas. All the windows needed to be replaced, but that could be done in a few days.

But the headmaster knew that the facilities had little to do with the school. A school was a sanctuary, set apart from the daily badgering of commerce. It was a community of young minds and learned heads where all that was decent in civilization was passed on carefully to the next generation in the hopes that they would value it and therefore preserve it. Their sanctuary, however, had been defiled by a bloodletting that was more than anything a monument to stupidity. By a senseless power struggle in which there could be no winner, but in which humanity was the certain loser.

There could be no school without seclusion. But Saint Anselm's would forever be the target of curious publicity. There could be no school without young minds, but even before the occupation had been lifted, parents had been rescuing their children from schools all over the continent. The boys probably wouldn't be coming back for some time. And there could be no school without teachers. Yet the very honors that Professor Prinz's body deserved would discourage teachers from ever coming to the historic mansion on a hilltop north of Rome.

So he watched the repairs and thanked his teachers for their efforts. But he spent most of his time on the telephone calling schools in England and Ireland to see if there might be openings for his faculty. And he gathered his texts and his papers and toyed with the idea of a more contemporary translation of Virgil. The boys were bored with the existing texts, and certainly someone had to rekindle their interest in the Latin poets!

Ferrand was on a ladder, knocking the splintered framing out of a window well, when he looked down and saw Otis Brown. He climbed down and offered Brown a cup of coffee, then led him into the kitchen, where he lifted a large pot from the giant steel stove and filled two mugs. They walked back to one of the tables that had served as a classroom during the crisis.

"We never thanked you properly," Brown began, and he raised his mug in a toast. "Everyone in Washington is taking credit for the victory. The president. The chairman of the Joint Chiefs. They've even tossed some of the accolades my way. But so far, your name hasn't come up."

"I don't think I was very helpful," Ferrand answered. "As I recall, I didn't agree with you most of the time."

"No, you didn't," Brown admitted. "But you were invaluable in planning the attack. And then in leading in the advanced party.

"In the debriefing, one of the soldiers mentioned you had jumped through the window to defuse the detonator. I don't think I would have been that courageous. You were supposed to get out of there as soon as you showed Casper the window."

"I got distracted." Ferrand laughed. Then his face grew serious. "I heard Sergeant Casper is in a bad way."

Brown nodded. "But he's going to make it. He won't make the reception in Washington. But he should be able to travel in a month or so. The Army is pushing to get him the Congressional Medal of Honor."

Then Ferrand asked, "Did I really get the bomb? I pulled the wire that I thought Casper was after, but I never knew. . . ."

"You did indeed." Brown laughed. "The thing was examined by the experts and they concluded that you had disabled it."

Ferrand grinned.

"Of course, it didn't make a damn bit of difference," Brown added mischievously. "In the course of examining it they discovered that the frequency filter on the device had been changed. It couldn't have responded to Gamel's radio transmitter."

Ferrand looked confused.

"It really had them baffled. Why would anyone use a transmitter and a receiver that were set for two different frequencies. And then they found a toy airplane that had crashed near the front gate. A Spitfire, I think it was."

"Jimmy Bradberry's?"

Brown nodded. "It had a frequency filter that matched the one on the transmitter Gamel threw away in the woods. And then, of course, they found out that the filter in the detonator matched the transmitter in the Bradberry boy's radio controller. Your friend Billy Tepper must have switched them."

"Jesus . . ."

"So when Gamel tried to blow the building, his signal started the engine on the Spitfire."

Ferrand was laughing.

Brown smiled, then said, "It's a good story, but we've decided not to tell Sergeant Casper. And with a medal pending, we don't want to make too much of it in Washington."

"You ought to figure out a way to give Billy a medal," Ferrand suggested.

Otis Brown sighed. "It's a shame, but Billy won't even be coming to Washington. His father didn't want him included in the ceremony."

Ferrand was startled.

"His company does a lot of business in the Middle East. The directors didn't want to aggravate a few million customers."

"Bullshit," Ferrand said. "So what are they going to do? Hide him in the boardroom closet?"

"In Germany, actually," Brown answered. "A school near Mannheim called Schiller."

Ferrand had to laugh. "It's called 'Shriller,'" he corrected. "It's a prison camp with barbed wire and light towers and guard dogs." Brown didn't understand, but Ferrand decided not to enlighten him. "Billy told me about it," was all he said.

They finished their coffee, and Brown followed Ferrand back into the kitchen to rinse the cups. "I understand you're planning to stay in Italy," he said, easing into the real reason for his visit.

Ferrand nodded. "Maria is going to find us an Italian school," he explained. "We'll be here for quite a while."

Brown turned his cup over on the drainboard. "Why don't

you and Maria come back to the States for a while. Show her our country. I'm sure I can arrange some way to get you the funds—a 'thank you,' you might call it."

"No." Ferrand smiled. "When she gets out of the hospital, she'll want to get back to work."

Brown dropped his conversational tone. "I think you should come back. For your own safety. Just for a year. Maybe only six months."

Ferrand's eyes narrowed.

"We never did get Gamel," he explained. "He got out of the school grounds before our boys could find him, and he somehow managed to slip past the Italians. That means he got to Rome, where he can hide out forever."

Ferrand didn't seem to be following him.

"He's a very dangerous man. He knows you and he knows Maria. With all the publicity, he probably knows her room number. You and Maria made him a laughingstock. He might want to settle the score."

Ferrand shook his head in disbelief.

"The fact is, the Italian police think he'll try to get to you. They have guards on Maria's room, and they've asked us to get you out of the country. Naturally, I thought it would be more appealing if I suggested you take her with you."

Ferrand looked directly at Brown. "What do you think? Is there any real danger?"

Brown shrugged. "Well, he is armed. One of the plastic explosive charges was missing when our people made their sweep. We have to assume Gamel took it with him. He certainly has enough of the stuff to blow up a small building— or a hospital room. And there's a very large Moslem fundamentalist community in Rome. So there's no doubt he could get his hands on weapons. I guess if I were him, I wouldn't hang around looking for revenge. I'd be trying to get out of the country. But he hasn't left yet, as far as we've been able to tell. So I begin to wonder why he's sticking around. Maybe to settle a score?"

Ferrand nodded. "I'll talk to her."

"Be persuasive. The Italians have already talked to her. They don't like the idea of providing a guard for the rest of her life. But she told them 'no' in rather direct terms."

"I'll talk to her," Ferrand repeated.

April 25

morning

Washington had given in to its worst instincts. There were television cameras everywhere, and lines of elected officials and political appointees jostled one another for even a few seconds of air time. The Saint Anselm's boys and their rescuers had become national heroes, and everyone who was serious about a government career wanted to get in on the action.

The president's role had been carefully orchestrated. It had begun with a national hookup over all three networks on which he announced the safe rescue of the boys without a single fatality to the rescue force. He expressed his prayerful gratitude, but sprinkled in several phrases about the determination of the United States to protect its citizens and the swift and decisive response of his administration to terrorists. The facts that he had been fumbling to bring about negotiations and that his government had no hand in quenching the Flaming Sword from the Desert were carefully omitted.

Next came his appearance on the podium as the bodies of Professor Prinz and Joey Trotta were landed at Andrews. It was a simple ceremony with no speeches and no relatives in attendance. The intention was to make Reynolds look sympathetic without forcing him to pay public respects to the head of organized crime in New Jersey. Don Trotta understood. He was planning to bury his son privately and then take his wife home to Italy.

Then there'd been a reception for Colonel Smiles, who was decorated with a Silver Star. The exchange of salutes was intended to reinforce the image of Reynolds as the commander-in-chief, implying that he had somehow directed the rescue. But the president was embarrassed by the charade; he threw away his prepared remarks and simply said, "Thank you for a brilliant and brave operation." Smiles' only comment was that "We were lucky. Damn lucky." Presidential aides chose to characterize the rescue as meticulously planned and dismissed Smiles' comment as "refreshing modesty."

Now Reynolds was to greet the boys of Saint Anselm's. They and their families, who had quickly forgotten their attempts to bargain directly for the release of their sons, were to assemble at the White House for a luncheon with the president and then parade in open cars to the steps of the Lincoln Memorial. There, Reynolds was to address the gathering.

He read the speech that had been prepared for him and then tossed it aside. "Who wrote this?" he demanded of his special assistant.

John Powers smiled. "Flanders," he answered, naming a former political columnist who had become the administration's chief speechwriter.

"He's getting senile," Reynolds said. "I can't say this."

"It is a bit heavy-handed." Powers laughed.

"It isn't true," the president said peevishly. "It's all lies." He reached into his desk for his cigarettes, and Powers stood with a lighter. "Why don't we just tell the truth?"

Powers teased him with a look of disbelief.

"Well then, let's just have some minister offer a prayer of thanks. That's what I really want to say. 'Thank God these boys have survived our stupidity.'"

"You'd need to have a priest and a rabbi, too," Powers said. "You don't want to offend any voters."

They sat in silence, and then the president started through the speech again. "'These boys have sent a clear and courageous message to our enemies all over the world,'" he quoted sarcastically. He turned a page and read, "'The United States will risk all in the defense of freedom. We have risked our sons in world wars and in the defense of freedom in all quarters of the globe. And now we have risked them in a small school in the hills of Rome.'" He fired the script at his wastebasket. Powers was surprised by his anger.

"You know what the truth is?" Reynolds demanded. "The truth is that we haven't sent a clear and courageous message to anyone! What we've sent is clear evidence that we're completely out of touch with the hopes and needs of people all over the world. They hate us, and we don't have the slightest idea why they hate us. Risk our sons? For what? To try to keep a lid on millions of angry people? To preserve a status quo that's left over from colonialism? Exactly what is it that we're risking them for?"

Powers endured his boss's tirade, waiting patiently until Reynolds was calm enough to smile at his own frustration. "We have to say these things," he advised gently. "It's what Bradberry and his hawks are saying. He'll keep saying it all the way to the White House, and he'll make it here if you decide to spill out your conscience."

The president pointed across his desk to the chair next to the one in which Powers was sitting. "He sat right there. Right in that chair. And he thanked me for risking the whole damn country to save his son. I ought to go on television and tell the country exactly how much faith Warhawk Bradberry had in American principles and in American military might when his kid was under the gun."

"Why don't you?"

"Oh, hell," the president sneered. "He's a politician on the make. He's entitled to forget his moments of weakness."

"Then you be a politician," Powers advised. "Read the speech. You made the call for the attack, not Bradberry. You're more entitled to take credit for its success than he is."

"I'd be too damn embarrassed," Reynolds muttered.

He knew that the victory of Saint Anselm's hadn't solved anything. There were still hundreds of millions of people around the world who hadn't been allowed a shred of human dignity, and who would fight for it with any weapon they could command—even the lives of innocent people. And he knew it hadn't stopped anything. Somewhere, in some stinking hut or bombed-out building, there was another Sharif planning his next assault on the power brokers. An attack on an airplane, or a bus, or an embassy, or perhaps even another schoolhouse. Of course the terrorists were crazy. But to stop them, he had to understand what had made them crazy. He couldn't save future victims with a policy fashioned out of clichés.

That was precisely what Senator Bradberry was doing. In his comments on the Saint Anselm's kidnapping, which seemed to be turning up everywhere, he was crediting American military might backed by American values for the safe release of the children. "Sharif," he had bellowed to an audience of financiers, "has been reduced to food for the vultures, bleached bones lying in the desert sun. His henchmen are in prison, awaiting the verdict of an outraged world. America's policy of standing firm on the side of justice has been vindicated. And American children, protected by the might we have marshaled in the cause of justice, are free." Then he'd reminded his audience of his constant determination to resist terrorists, and his equally ardent support for the military budget needed to resist terrorists. And he had basked in the long, loud applause, which seemed fervent enough to carry him to the presidency.

"I'll write my own speech," Reynolds decided finally.

"I wouldn't," Powers advised. "Maybe Flanders is laying it on a bit thick. But I think he knows what the people want to hear."

"Maybe. But he doesn't know what I want to say. He doesn't even have a clue."

*   *   *

Powers watched the motorcade roll through the White House gates, carrying the bewildered boys past teary-eyed throngs. In the last car, the president conversed quietly with Colonel Smiles, both of them feeling guilty for accepting praise for an outcome they both knew was due to blind luck. "By all rights, half of these boys should be dead," Smiles had admitted to Reynolds.

"When I gave the order, I would have been grateful for half," the president had answered.

At the Lincoln Memorial, instead of a speech, Reynolds led the huge crowd in a brief prayer of thanks. Then he reminded his audience that there was no victory in killing other men, no triumph in freeing children so they could anxiously await the next threat on their lives. "Victory will come when justice isn't equated with military might," he said. "The final triumph will be when children are freed from the fear that a leader's mistake or a technician's miscalculation will obliterate their world, whether that world is a home, a camp, a kibbutz, or a school."

The polite applause convinced Senator Bradberry's followers that Reynolds could be beaten. It convinced John Powers that Edward Reynolds had no intention of seeking a second term.

April 26

morning

"Up yours, Freddie," Billy Tepper said by way of greeting, as he gazed for the first time at the marble figure of Friedrich Schiller.

The statue was in the center of the circular driveway, closer to the front gate than it was to the steps of the school. Its base was a miniature turret, perhaps twelve feet high, with two small windows and a diminutive door. Schiller stood atop the rampart in frock coat and knee breeches, a book of poetry clasped to his breast, his free hand extended as if he were conducting an orchestra. He was leaning forward precariously, his jaw thrust out defiantly.

"Your luggage, young man," the rotund porter said as he lifted Billy's suitcase from the top of the van. He noticed that that boy seemed to be in awe of the figure towering over their heads. "That is our inspiration, Friedrich von Schiller," the porter whispered.

"I figured it wasn't Joe DiMaggio."

"You notice that he is standing on the top of a fortress," the porter continued. "That was very important when the school was opened. Do you know what it means?"

Billy looked suspicious. "That he was the warden of a prison," he tried.

"No, no." The big man laughed. "Of course not. Schiller is a poet—a philosopher—not a jailer. No. What it symbolizes is the triumph of learning and wisdom over brute force. Schiller"—he gestured to the school—"was founded in the first days of the German Republic. In 1920, at the end of the Great War, and it was hoped that generals and soldiers would never again rule the country. So Schiller, a poet, was placed on the ramparts of the nation, the position that had always been occupied by soldiers."

"What happened?" Billy asked.

The porter picked up his suitcases and began laboring toward the arched doorway of the school. "It didn't work very well," he answered.

Billy turned and walked backward, his eyes fixed on the figure of Schiller. "The way he's leaning, it looks like he's getting ready to jump over the wall," Billy said.

The porter laughed heartily.

The room was like the one he had left in Saint Anselm's—

a closet to the right as he entered, a desk and bookcase on one wall, and a bed on the other. But it didn't look as comfortable. Instead of the light-wood desk with rounded corners, his new room featured a dark wooden cube. Instead of the bright bedspread, there was a deep purple cover. The bedframe was iron, right out of a hospital, and the pillow was as hard as a rock.

Billy lifted his suitcases onto the bed, which squeaked under the weight, and began unpacking slowly. He was in no hurry. There was no place to go. It was late in the term, probably too late to make any friends. Besides, there were no American kids. They had all been pulled out in the panic caused by the Saint Anselm's kidnapping. Chances were they wouldn't be coming back for the summer session. So all he had to look forward to were dreary classes with guys who probably wouldn't even talk to him, and then a summer session with different guys who wouldn't even talk to him. No wonder the place was called Shriller!

"Lunch will be in twenty minutes," the porter had said. Screw it. The last thing he wanted to do was walk into a dining room filled with sour-faced strangers and carry his lunch around in circles while he looked for an empty seat. If he found one, it would probably belong to a two-hundred-pound class bully who carried a riding crop and wore an armband!

He lifted his dress slacks and blazers out of a suitcase and carried them to the closet, where he found a row of wire hangers, all fastened to the bar. "Nice touch," he said to himself. "Makes you feel right at home." He dumped his underwear into the vaultlike drawer of the dresser that sat next to the small window and fired his socks into the top drawer. His shoes and three pairs of sneakers were dumped onto the closet floor and his sweaters onto the shelf.

He opened the second suitcase, took out his dress shirts, and hung them next to his jackets in the closet. He left his jeans and sport shirts rolled up and simply stuffed them in the dresser next to his underwear. The computer had been wedged between his sport shirts for protection, and Billy lifted it carefully onto the desk. Next to it, he set the box of floppy disks that held his programs and computer games.

The last thing he unpacked was a small paper bag, which he opened carefully. Inside was a tinfoil package, its folds crimped to form a seal. He worked the wrapping slowly until he was able to lay back the tinfoil.

Inside was a white lump of putty—the plastic explosive he had detatched from two of the wires in the old building seconds before the Army explosives squad had made its sweep. He repacked the plastic in the tinfoil and slipped it into one of the discolored sneakers at the back of the closet.

When he had taken the plastic explosive, he had had no idea what he was going to do with it. But it was too good an opportunity to pass up. The stuff had power. You could really shake things up with a cherry bomb or an M-80, and they were just toys. This was the real stuff! But after just a few seconds at Schiller, he had decided on the superprank to end all pranks.

He was going to help Friedrich make it over the wall.

April 30

afternoon

Maria balanced the ice cream as she rushed down the ramp toward the vaporetti landing, then jumped over the widening rush of water and into Ferrand's arms. He pulled her over the chain and onto the open deck of the water taxi, laughing as the ice cream smeared against his face. Then they turned, smiling to the two policemen in black suits who had tumbled down the ramp and stopped at the water's edge. "Wave goodbye," Ferrand said, and Maria blew a kiss back toward the dock.

It had become a game. They knew that their freedom would be short-lived and that when the boat reached its final landing or when they returned to their hotel, the two policemen would be waiting. They followed them everywhere—dining at nearby tables in restaurants, window-shopping outside the stores they entered, lounging in the powered taxis that followed their gondolas. Maria and Ferrand had accepted the intrusion that the police insisted was a necessary precaution. "Just until we find Gamel, or are assured he is out of the country," the Italian official had explained when Maria was leaving the hospital in Rome. Their protests had been ignored with a solicitous smile.

A policeman had slept uncomfortably on a lobby sofa on their first night at a hotel in Rome. Two policemen had been in the next compartment when they took the train to Venice. And ever since their arrival, two policemen had been close behind as they toured the city, plainly visible in dark jackets and light ties that stood out in any crowd of tourists.

They had begged for privacy. Their first evening in Venice, they had dined well over their budget on a rooftop that looked out across the San Marco at the basilica of San Giorgio. When they had looked up from their blackened pasta, they had seen the policemen playing with the bread sticks at a table near the door.

"Christ," Ferrand had said, tossing his napkin on the table. Then he had walked through the restaurant and slipped into a chair between the two men. "We'd like to be alone," he'd explained.

One of the officers had smiled appreciatively. The other had shrugged sadly. "That's not possible," he apologized.

"Look," Ferrand had continued. "You know our hotel. Our clothes are there, so we're not going to change hotels. And we can't get off the island without going through the railroad station. We can't get away from you. So why don't you give us an evening to ourselves. Wait at the hotel. We'll be back."

"We have orders," one of the policemen had explained.

"We won't tell a soul," Ferrand had promised, making a cross over his heart with his fingertip. "If anyone asks, we'll say you ate at the next table and slept in our bed. Anything you want. We would just like a few hours alone."

Both men had looked down sadly at the bread sticks.

So they'd taken up the challenge of losing them. On their second day in the city, they had jumped out of a gondola just after it made a sharp turn in a narrow canal and dashed into a street that was squeezed between two decaying buildings. The launch had rumbled by, following the empty gondola, its two passengers with their heads tipped back to take the sun. Then they'd joined a tour of the Doge's Palace and suddenly broken from the group into a labyrinth of rooms in the armory. They'd walked out with a different group of tourists while the policemen were searching the building and entered a small church, famous for the hundreds of oil paintings covering its walls. They'd sprung into a confessional and stifled their laughter, watching through the latticework as their protectors had rushed up and down the aisles and into the street.

That night, they'd entered their room and left one of the policemen at each end of the corridor. They knew they were being protected, not spied upon, but still the presence of the two men outside their door had intruded on their lovemaking. Maria had tiptoed out of the bathroom wearing her robe and slipped it off at the edge of the bed, leaving a full-length nightgown on as she slid beneath the sheets.

"You're not going to wear that all night?" Ferrand had begged.

"I'm not going to undress in front of the Italian army," she had answered.

On their third night, they had entered the room, gone straight to the louvered doors that served as their window, and stepped out onto the railed balcony. The iron grating over the ground-floor windows served as a perfect ladder for their escape. They'd spent an hour alone, sipping wine at a sidewalk table outside a café. Then they'd returned to the hotel, walking past the policeman who was slumped against the wall at the end of the corridor. "Good evening," Maria had said politely as they passed, and then they'd laughed all the way to their room.

They had lost the two men early the next morning by jumping off a vaporetto just as it pulled away from the landing, leaving their protectors on board. The day, they'd thought, was theirs, and they'd wandered through the shops along the Grand Canal enjoying a freedom that had not been theirs since the night three weeks earlier when Ferrand had left Maria at the gate of Saint Anselm's and driven down the hill to return the rented car. But as they had browsed through a glass shop, looking at decorative pieces that cost as much as their combined savings, they'd seen the policemen looking in through the window.

It had been Maria's idea to use the water buses for another escape. They'd walked to the Rialto landing, their guards following a hundred feet behind. Ferrand had walked down the ramp and sat easily on one of the benches at the dock. Maria had gone into an ice cream shop, one of the policemen following her as the other waited at the top of the ramp. She'd bought an ice cream and stood with it until the boat slid up to the dock. Then she'd sauntered back toward the ramp. As the boat began to pull away, Ferrand had jumped aboard and reached out for Maria as she raced ahead of the policemen. Now they were alone again, gliding down the Grand Canal toward the railroad station bridge.

"Free again." He laughed, luxuriating in the warm spring sun. But her gaiety was suddenly gone.

"For how long?" she challenged. "When we get off, they'll be waiting at the dock. We shouldn't have come here. There's no place to hide."

"We're not in hiding," Ferrand said.

Maria's voice dropped to a whisper. "In the school, when I was prisoner, I kept thinking that soon it would all be over. I didn't know how it would end, but I knew it couldn't go on very long. But it hasn't ended. I'm still a prisoner."

He took her hand and held it tightly, but her morbid mood wouldn't be appeased.

"How long are they going to be with us? Will we ever be free of them?"

"Of course we will," Ferrand promised. "They can't keep police on us forever. They'll find Gamel, or they'll learn that he's back in Beirut, or Tripoli, or wherever he lives. Or else they'll just lose interest."

"When?" she demanded. But he didn't have an answer.

They rode the vaporetto to the end of the route, past the railroad station, then boarded another boat headed back up the canal. The policemen hadn't caught up with them yet, so they had at least another few minutes to themselves.

"Maybe we ought to go away for a while," Ferrand said as they moved past the ornate palaces rising up out of the water. "I'd like to give you the chance to see the United States."

"You mean run away," Maria snapped.

He shook his head. "I mean travel. One of the American government men offered us a chance to spend a few months touring the States at their expense. It would fill the summer. And we wouldn't have to escape from the police twice a day."

"I'm not going to flee my own country," she said defiantly. And then she fell deeper into her brooding silence.

When they got off the boat at the Piazza landing, the policemen were waiting for them. Maria fixed them with her eyes, one at a time. Then she turned to Ferrand and said, "Take me back to the hotel."

He nodded, but then added, "They'll be right behind us."

"I want to go to bed with you," she answered. "Without a nightgown. They can come in and sit on the foot of the bed if they want to. And if Gamel shows up, he can sit with them and watch!"

May 1

morning

Gamel watched from the window while the girl struggled across the sidewalk with the last of the heavy bags. She lifted the hatchback of the beat-up black Volkswagon and pushed the bag into the luggage compartment. Then she slammed the hatchback shut, walked to the driver's door, and paused to look up at the window.

Gamel nodded toward her. Then he glanced carefully up and down the street, searching the tangle of parked cars and scooters. There were no unfamiliar vehicles, nor was there anyone waiting in a car. He scanned the blank windows of the rundown apartment houses. Everything seemed normal.

He turned to the mirror and made a final evaluation of his appearance. His head had been shaved, leaving just a fringe, which was colored with gray. He had used the same gray coloring to lighten the beard that he had allowed to grow in. The combination had added thirty years to his age, and when he slipped on the wire-framed glasses, he looked like an old man. No one searching for a fit, vigorous man in his mid-thirties would give him even a second glance.

He reached into the inside pocket of his oversized suit jacket, pulled out the passport, and glanced from the small, poorly focused photograph to the image in the mirror. The match was perfect. Even if they should be stopped at a routine checkpoint, the document would arouse no suspicion.

Gamel went to the closet and retrieved the final piece of luggage, a small leather two-suiter, tied with an old belt. He opened it, lifted out the tangle of laundry, and then pulled up the false bottom. The pieces of the rifle were packed in graphite-impregnated rubber, the long barrel separated from the firing chamber, the stock and telescopic sight detatched. There were also three gracefully curved ammunition clips. He repacked the suitcase, took one more look out into the street, and then down at the waiting Volkswagan with the woman already in the driver's seat.

He crossed the sidewalk leisurely but unsteadily, as if even this simple activity were a great effort. The woman helped him pull the case into the back seat, and then she covered it with other packages while he climbed into the passenger seat.

"You could be my father," she said, smiling, as they pulled away from the curb and began navigating the narrow streets of the neighborhood.

"Good," he answered, but his expression was distracted. Then he asked, "Are we leaving too early?"

She shook her head. "We'll be catching the morning rush. There will be plenty of traffic before we reach the highway."

"Good," he said, and he slumped down in the seat, leaning his head against the door as if he were asleep.

"You don't have to do this," she said after a few minutes. "In that disguise you'd have no trouble going home. You could probably even get into Israel and become a citizen."

Gamel smiled at the idea without opening his eyes.

"There are plenty of people who could do this for you," she continued. "There's just no reason for you to risk your life."

"We discussed this," he reminded her. "For me, there's every reason. And it's something I have to do myself."

The traffic she had promised was waiting—long rows of angry cars jostling for position at noisy intersections. Soon, they were nearly at a standstill.

"There's too much traffic," she said finally.

Gamel shook his head. "It's perfect. The police would never set up a roadblock during the morning rush hour. The people would get out of their cars and beat them to death."

They began to move when they made a turn away from Rome, toward the major highway that led north. The cars were still closely packed in parallel lines, but they were moving quickly, buiding up to highway speed as they got further from the city.

"When we get there—right at the last moment—I want to dress in my fatigues."

She looked at him with an expression of disbelief.

"When I begin firing, I want them to know exactly who I am. I want the whole world to know that Gamel paid his debts."

"It's suicide," she said. "They'll kill you on sight."

He opened his eyes and looked at her. "I'll do my killing first."

afternoon

"You were a rocket scientist," Billy Tepper had said during his second day at Schiller. His face had been shining in admiration.

Professor Emil Werner had nodded, his white goatee bobbing with the movement of his head. "Of course," he'd answered, surprised at the curiosity of the new American student. It was his experience that American boys weren't interested in mathematics, or any other subject for that matter. They knew that their futures were assured by the same trust funds that were paying their tuition. All they needed was a bit of social polishing in traditional European manners and a touch of the arrogant indifference that would befit their station in American society.

"I mean a real rocket expert," Billy had continued in awe. "You really know how to make those things take off . . . and to fly exactly where you want them. . ."

"Naturally," the professor had said. "It's really quite simple."

"I'll bet I could never learn it," Billy had said, setting up his mark.

"Of course you could," Werner had answered, suddenly flooded with enthusiasm for his profession. He snatched a razor-sharp pencil from the leather holder on his desk. "Come around here where you can see."

Billy had bounded out of the chair and run around the desk so that he could look over the professor's shoulder. The old man's hand had flown as it sketched in the basic vectoral diagrams.

"You begin with the center of gravity of the rocket, a force pushing straight down through the center of the cylinder. What we need is an opposite force—a thrust—positioned directly below the center of gravity. As long as we can keep the thrust directly below the center of gravity, the entire apparatus will move upward in a straight line."

"How much thrust?" Billy had interrupted.

The man's eyes had filled with tears of joy. A question! An intelligent question! He'd torn off the first sheet of paper and begun writing math equations across the next sheet.

"You understand the calculus?" he'd asked.

"I don't think so."

"No matter. I can show you what is involved."

He had ripped through page after page, relating the weight of the rocket to the thrust and then the whole thing to the forces of inertia that had to be overcome.

"So the thrust force has to be at least half again the force of gravity," Billy had concluded.

"At least," the professor had agreed.

"Now suppose you don't want it to go straight up?" Billy had asked. "Suppose you want it to take off on an angle?"

"Then you change the balance." Werner had been inwardly rejoicing. "Here, let me show you." He had gone back to his vectors, with the thrust slightly offset from its position directly beneath the center of gravity.

Billy had gathered up the scraps of paper, thanked Werner profusely, and promised to return for another session. Then he had gone off to the library, searching through the dusty tombs that held the chronicles of the school's illustrious history. "They put the statue up when the school first opened," the porter had told him. So he had begun turning through the pages of the first volumes. And there it had been. A photograph of the statue being lifted on top of the rampart by a small crane, while frail men in dress suits looked on in admiration. He'd struggled through the text until he'd found the detailed specifications of the statue. Thank God for the Germans! They recorded the specifications of everything.

Professor Emil Werner had happened into the library that night and seen Billy's head over a pile of reference books. He had never seen a student in the library before and he rushed off to find the headmaster. The two men had crept back to the library door and stood watching in amazement while Billy dashed up and down the ladder, replacing the volumes of Schiller history with reference works on chemistry. The teachers had hugged each other in their joy.

Now Billy was back in Werner's office with a new problem. It was easy to find the center of gravity in a regularly shaped object. But what did you do with an irregularly shaped object? You might know how much the material weighs, and you could probably figure out how much an object weighed that was made of the material. But how could you find the center of gravity under which to position the center of thrust?

Werner took a new pencil and a fresh pad. He was close to ecstasy. He drew a number of irregular shapes, then shaded some sections as he fit them into spaces to create a more uniform configuration. "The shape doesn't really matter," he explained.

But, of course, it mattered very much. For each shape the mathematician created, Billy's mind substituted the shape of Schiller, clearly visible through the window in his position at the center of the circular driveway. He looked up from Werner's drawings that positioned the exact point at which the thrust should be located and mentally moved the center of thrust forward toward the poet's toes.

You're a lucky man, Freddy, he thought to himself. Tomorrow you're going to be the first poet into orbit.

night

"Maybe the other guy can't stand Vivaldi," Ferrand speculated.

"No," Maria answered, her head turning as she scanned the audience. "All Italians love Vivaldi. Especially in Venice."

They were in the courtyard of Vivaldi's church, seated with two hundred other spectators who had gathered for the first concert of the season. The orchestra had just entered and the musicians were in the process of tuning their instruments while they waited for the conductor to make his dramatic entrance. Ferrand had spotted one of the policemen seated near the entrance to the courtyard. The other was nowhere to be seen.

"He's probably outside in the street," he said. "Or maybe they're losing interest in us already. Maybe we're only worth one guard."

The conductor entered in white tie, the tails of his coat shiny from years of wear. The first of the Four Seasons began. It was the perfect spring evening to be under the stars and enveloped by the historic music of the city—the perfect ending to their brief vacation. The next morning they would head back to Rome and begin tracking down the many rumors of summer employment. One of the airlines, they had heard, was looking for guides to accompany bus tours of Americans that were shuttling through Rome, Florence, and Venice. Teachers who were fluent in both Italian and English were excellent prospects. But tour bookings were down; the trauma of Saint Anselm's had caused hundreds of cancellations. There might not be any tours, or any job openings.

Another possibility was a meeting of auto industrialists in Milan. The organizers needed simultaneous translators in several languages. Maria could handle the Italian-English work easily. Ferrand wasn't so sure of his own ability. But again, there was the possibility that the whole conference would be cancelled. The chance of a terrorist attack was making all meetings in Europe dangerous.

They left the concert in a somber mood. It wasn't just the end of the vacation, but also the uncertainty of the future. Their world was fracturing, and the pieces were beginning to separate. The fear that terrorists used as a weapon was proving surprisingly effective. Even when they failed, as they had at Saint Anselm's, they still succeeded. People worried about the next attack and locked themselves in their houses with the shutters pulled tight.

Logic told Ferrand that he should pack his things and return to America as he had always intended. Both Maria and he knew that was the sensible course. And they knew it would become harder to avoid talking about it if there were no summer jobs, or teaching positions in the fall. If they were going to stay together, Maria should think seriously about leaving Italy and traveling to the States with him. While it might have been a choice she would have made freely not too long ago, she was now determined that she wouldn't allow herself to be exiled from her own country. She had to prove her right to live in Italy before she could even consider leaving it.

They took a last ride in a gondola, moving silently through the lightless canals beneath flat stone walls with shuttered windows. Occasionally, they could hear the wash of the gondola that followed them with the remaining policeman as its only passenger, but the intrusion on their privacy was no longer a great concern.

The officer followed them back to their hotel, but settled into a stuffed chair in the small lobby instead of taking his normal post at the end of the corridor. It wasn't that he had abandoned his charges. Instead, he seemed to sense that on this one night it was more important that they be left alone. They made love on top of the sheets, with the shuttered door open so that the moonlight could find its way into their room. And then they lay awake until the first hint of dawn sent the birds into a musical frenzy.

"I wonder what it would take to re-open Saint Anselm's?" Ferrand asked suddenly.

Maria smiled in response. "I've been wondering the same thing. But it seems impossible. The headmaster certainly thought it was impossible."

Ferrand rolled over on his side, raising his head on his arm. "It wouldn't be easy. You would have to start very small and build it back up over time. It might take several years."

"But it would be worth it," she answered with the first trace of enthusiasm she had shown in days. "Saint Anselm's is too important to just abandon. If we close down schools like Saint Anselm's, then everyone loses. If there is ever going to be an end to all these murders, it's got to come from the schools."

"Probably," he said. "But my reasons were simpler. I was thinking that I really don't want to be a tour guide, or a translator. I want to be a schoolteacher."

"So do I," she said. "And I want to be with you."

They talked about the difficulties as they dressed and packed their small suitcases. Just maintaining the buildings and grounds would cost a staggering sum, a fixed amount that they couldn't really cut back on no matter how many students they had. And then the teachers. They had to get good people and they had to cover at least the major subjects. They were plunged into despair when they added up the costs and realized how many students they would have to attract.

But then they thought of other ways of funding the operation. It didn't just have to be rich families who could pay a fortune. There were foundations all over the world that might see the school as an important institution that had to be preserved. Their spirits soared at the possibilities.

May 2

morning

They were still assembling the pieces over their breakfast coffee when the policeman came to their table and slipped into an empty chair.

"Good morning," he began cheerily. He turned his cup over and poured coffee without waiting to be invited. "A beautiful day. And I'm happy to begin it with very good news." He waited until he had their undivided attention. "We won't be joining you for your trip back to Rome. You won't be needing our protection any longer."

"You've caught him?" Maria nearly shouted.

The policeman shook his head. "I wish we had. No, he seems to have slipped through our fingers. But we're certain that he is out of the country."

Maria and Ferrand seemed disappointed.

"We learned through informants that he had been living in Rome, and that he left the city yesterday morning. In an automobile in the company of a woman. We know the woman well. She is Italian, a leader of one of our radical communist groups. They were heading north, so we were concerned that he knew you were in Venice and was heading here."

"He came here?" Ferrand whispered.

"No . . . no . . . not here. Not at all. But we thought that he might, so we called in reinforcements. We had people in the room right across the hall from you, and others in the building across the street."

He sipped his coffee while Ferrand and Maria thought of the window they had left wide open. At least the police hadn't lacked for entertainment.

"We also checked the trains coming across the lagoon, and the automobiles going onto the parking dock. That was fairly simple. The difficult part was intercepting all the speedboats that were coming over from the mainland. You really had us all very busy. It took a dozen men to make sure that your last night in Venice was an enjoyable one." He smiled knowingly. Ferrand guessed that he had probably spent the night in the apartment across the street.

"Well if he didn't come here, where did he go?" he finally asked.

"Germany," the Italian police officer answered. "Interpol picked up the woman in the car early this morning. Gamel, unfortunately, wasn't with her. But he can't have gone far. Apparently, she was caught just moments after she had dropped him off. We would have had him if the car had been identified just a few minutes earlier."

"Germany?" Maria asked. "Are you sure? He'd be much safer staying in Italy. It doesn't make any sense."

The policeman nodded as he blotted his mustache with a napkin. "Sensible or not, that's where he is. Which means that you don't need to be protected any longer. I was enjoying Venice, but keeping up with you two was exhausting. I need to go back to my office so that I can get some rest."

He stood up and extended his hand to Maria. "You're very beautiful," he told her sincerely. Then he turned to Ferrand. "And you're a very fortunate man."

"Where in Germany?" Ferrand asked as they were shaking hands.

"Mannheim," the policeman answered. "It's near—"

"I know where it's near," he said, interrupting. "It's near a school called Schiller." He turned to Maria. "The school where they sent Billy Tepper."

"Billy!" she gasped.

He grabbed the policeman by the sleeve and began dragging him toward the door. "You're working night and day protecting us, and we're not the ones Gamel is after. He's after Billy. The son of a bitch has gone to Schiller to kill Billy Tepper."

afternoon

"Piece of cake." Billy smiled to himself. He leaned back in the chair and admired the rocket engine he had just assembled on his desk. Well, not really a rocket engine, of course. Rocket engines poured out a steady stream of energy over a long time. It was really just a bomb, ready to release all of its awesome energy in one blinding flash. But if Herr Professor Werner's calculations were on target, it would have the same effect as a rocket. It would lift Freddy Schiller about fifteen feet in the air and toss him in a graceful trajectory right over the wall. Wouldn't it be a gas if he landed on his feet! They'd all be standing there looking up at their rampart, wondering where in hell the great poet had gone. And he'd be standing outside, up to his ass in the bushes, reading his verse to the outside of the wall.

Billy's launcher was simplicity itself. The plastic explosive, with its tiny detonator, was wrapped in a transparent sandwich bag that he had taken out of the dining hall. The battery had come right out of his penlight. And the control mechanism was lifted from a radio-controlled model Porsche he had picked up in a Mannheim toy store. Press the "forward" button on the toy's control unit, and the receiver clicked, connecting the battery to the plastic. Half a second later Freddy would be on his way!

The problem had been keeping the whole package very thin. The space between the stone turf that Schiller's figure stood on and the top of the turret was less than an inch at the point where the charge had to be placed. To get it right under Werner's calculated center of gravity, it had to be pushed in from the outside edge of the statue. So the thickness of the penlight battery was the maximum dimension he could allow. Flattening the plastic was no problem. But the controller he had taken out of the toy Porsche was nearly an inch high. He had to remove the protective case and reposition one of the components to the side of the miniature circuit card. But when he was finished, it tested out perfectly. He had connected the battery and the controller to a flashlight bulb, then stood across the room and touched the button on his controller. The light bulb had winked back at him.

Now he had to put the device into position. Billy disconnected the battery and slipped it into his pocket along with the radio controller. He pushed the sandwich bag into his belt and zippered his windbreaker over it. Then he strolled out of his room and into the empty corridor.

The building was silent. Final examinations were in progress, which had all the boys trapped in classrooms, sweating their way through long lists of impossibly obscure questions. The teachers were pacing around the perimeters of the classrooms, their attention riveted on their students lest a confused eye should wander to another boy's paper. Billy had been excused from the tests. He hadn't been at Schiller long enough to master any of the courses, and the German faculty knew better than to expect correct answers from a boy who had studied at an Italian school.

He wandered down the stairs and out the front door, nodding politely at the Wagnerian secretary who peered out through the sliding glass window of the reception office. There was a gardener on his hands and knees in the flowerbed that surrounded the front steps. The man never even looked up.

He started around the circular driveway, making it a point to ignore Schiller's statue, and continued halfway around the circle until the turret was directly between him and the building. Then he left the path and cut across the grass to the base of the structure. In an instant, he was down on his hands and knees, scampering through the turret's miniature doorway. When he stood up, he was inside the cylinder, with Friedrich Schiller standing directly overhead. The darkness inside was broken by shafts of light that streamed in through the miniature gunports and illuminated the spiderwebs on the walls. "Jesus," Billy said as he realized his shoes were sinking into a carpet of animal droppings. He stepped up into one of the gunports and reached up high to get a handhold on another. Then he climbed up the inside of the tower. At the top, he pulled himself through the gunport that faced away from the school and sat outside the opening with the feet of Friedrich Schiller only inches from his nose.

Billy slipped the sandwich bag out of his belt and placed it on the pedestal. Then he found the battery in his pocket and carefully clipped the terminals to the connectors that protruded from the bag. "All systems go," he said with a smile. He slid the assembly carefully under the pedestal and pushed it into position with fingertips. "Begin countdown," he said, and then pulled himself back through the port and climbed down the inside of the turret.

"Piece of cake," he said again as he crouched in front of the door ready to make his escape. But he was brought up short by the screech of automobile tires, and he looked out through the doorway toward the front gate. Two Mercedes sedans with flashing lights mounted on their tops turned quickly into the driveway and swung around the circle as they sped to the front door of the school. Then policemen jumped out and slammed the doors behind them as they rushed up the steps.

"Holy shit," Billy whispered. "These Germans just can't take a joke!"

Gamel sat in the waiting room of the train station, the belted suitcase resting on his knees. Travelers rushed back and forth around him, followed by dark-coated porters who struggled with armloads of luggage. In the busy and confused setting, he was completely invisible, exactly as he had planned to be.

He had told the woman that he was staying at a small

hotel and had given substance to the lie by having her circle the block around the hotel before dropping him at the corner. After she had driven away, he had lifted his suitcase and walked nearly a mile to the train station. In the men's room, he had altered his disguise, changing into a short jacket, discarding the wire-framed glasses, and trimming the unkempt ends of his beard. He had changed his brimmed hat for a cap and, in his new identity, strolled out into the waiting room. Now there was no one in the world who knew how he was dressed or where he could be found. No one would disturb him while he waited for darkness to close in around the Friedrich Schiller School for Boys.

He would have no trouble recognizing William Tepper. He could still see the boy, his expression calm and untroubled, casually discussing the model airplane that had sat on his desk. He remembered the face that had assaulted him in the woods, swinging the machine gun like an ax. It wasn't the American troops who had defeated him at Saint Anselm's. It was the boy. The schoolboy and the two teachers—the woman inside the school and the man called Ferrand. They would all pay for their momentary victory!

It had come together for him while he was hiding in the basement of the safe house in Rome. First, the woman and boy in the room with the model airplane, the plane he had held in his own hands. Had they already used the controls from the toy airplane to disable the bombs that were scattered throughout the school? Or were they just in the process of formulating their plans? It didn't matter. Either way, they were laughing at him, confident they were playing him for the fool. And he had been a fool. He should have shot them the moment he had become suspicious of them.

And then the message. The note that had been found in Tepper's room addressed to Ferrand and talking about an attack. He had wasted precious minutes questioning the teacher when the answer was so obvious. They had to be the inside contacts for a raid that was coming from the outside. If he had simply killed the pair of them and dragged them out through the gates, the attackers would have known that their scheme had been compromised. Or at least they would have been thrown off balance. But he had waited, losing the precious minutes that had cost him control of the situation.

The details of his defeat had been trumpeted in the newspapers and on television. He read how the children had vanished into a wine cellar right under his feet. A television commentator demonstrated how a simple video recorder had been used to show him tranquil scenes of the grounds while an entire attack force was making its way over the walls. "Students and teachers inside the school rendered the terrorists helpless seconds before the American commandos attacked," the media had reported. And Gamel realized that he had watched their schemes unfolding around him and done nothing about them.

He had watched the Americans boasting about their victory. "We have stood up to terrorism," an American senator gloated to an Italian interviewer. "We have shown them exactly how we deal with international outlaws. Their leaders are dead and their troops are in prison. They'll think twice before they make Americans a target for their criminal activities. Now they know what the consequences will be."

The fools thought it was over. They thought that Saint Anselm's was the war and they had won. But Gamel knew better. The war was still on. And it wouldn't end until the last Westerner had packed his bags and left the Middle East to the people of the Middle East. Until the Zionist entity was destroyed and not a stone was left standing upon a stone. Until the Moslem nation was given its rightful place of honor at the table with other world governments.

He would show them that they had won nothing. First the boy and then the two teachers would die, each body announcing that the struggle was still being fought. That Americans would remain targets until they abandoned their economic colonialism and gave the deserts back to the Arabs.

Gamel stood and stretched, then joined the crowds milling through the station. He sauntered past two policemen who looked right through him as they searched faces in the disorderly parade of humanity. Who were they looking for? A lean young man with Semitic features? Or, if their informers had seen him leaving Rome, an old Italian with a scraggly beard and ridiculous hat? He turned into the street and began walking past the rows of parked cars, glancing through their windows. It wouldn't take long to find one with the doors unlocked and the keys hanging from the ignition. And then he would be on his way to the Schiller school, where he would begin his counterattack.

Maria and Ferrand sat silently in the back of the speedboat as it skipped across the surface of the lagoon toward the Venice airport. The two Italian policemen sat opposite them, looking curiously at the wake of white foam that spread out behind the craft and at the ancient buildings that were growing smaller in the distance.

"How much longer?" Ferrand suddenly demanded.

One of the policemen shrugged. "A few minutes," he answered, "but there's no reason to hurry. The plane won't get here for another hour."

They had wasted the morning arguing with officials in Rome during a dozen separate telephone calls. The Italian national police, then the military, and finally high-ranking government figures had been skeptical about any link between Gamel's appearance in Mannheim and the fact that the Tepper boy was at the Schiller school. The official position was that Italian responsibility had ended the moment Gamel was known to be out of the country. It was now a problem for the Germans to deal with. Of course they would notify German officials about Ferrand's fears. Yes, they would call back to inform Ferrand about the German response. No, they saw no reason why they should send the two teachers to Mannheim, unless the Germans wanted them there. And then they would have to discuss the arrangements with the Germans.

Maria and Ferrand had listened carefully to their end of

the conversations between their police guards and various authorities in Rome, their fears growing with each minute that passed. Each time the policemen had ended a conversation an argument had ensued, the police assuring the two teachers that everything was under control and the two of them screaming that the boy was in terrible danger. Finally, their guards had relayed the best thinking of their superiors. The Germans were questioning the woman who had driven Gamel to Mannheim. Nothing could be done until the woman gave them sufficient information to act on.

Ferrand had found his own telephone and called the American embassy in Rome. Again he'd endured the calming assurances that the Germans were on top of the situation and screamed back that an American citizen, William Tepper, would be dead before the end of the day if he wasn't put into protective custody immediately. The embassy officials hadn't been impressed. Then he had thought of Otis Brown and urged the embassy to contact Brown in Washington. Nearly an hour passed before his phone had rung. It had been Brown's voice on the other end with the first intelligent response he'd heard all day.

"I've talked to the Germans," Brown had said immediately. "They sent the local police to get Billy out of the school."

"Thank God," Ferrand had answered, giving Maria a thumbs-up signal

"I've warned them that it's dangerous to wait for information from the woman," Brown had continued. "She may never cooperate, and even if she does, Gamel probably didn't tell her anything about his true plans. They're starting an intensive manhunt in the Mannheim area. They probably won't find him. Hell, we couldn't find him on the school grounds. But they should be able to keep him away from Billy."

"Great," Ferrand had answered.

"And I agree that we ought to get you and Maria to Schiller," Brown had concluded. "You're the only people that Billy knows well enough to trust. The Air Force is sending a plane down from Germany to pick you up at the Venice airport."

"Seems as if you have quite a bit of clout in Washington," Ferrand had teased.

"Not me. The order came from the White House. Billy's father is a close friend of the president."

Now, the speedboat slowed as it turned into the channel alongside the airport, and they could see a police car waiting at the dock. Maria, Ferrand, and the two Italian policemen were driven to the security office at the airport.

"Your plane is in the air," they were told by an Italian army colonel who was waiting for them. Then he handed them an overseas telephone number and led them to his desk with instructions that they were to return the call immediately. It was Otis Brown who answered.

"We seem to have a problem in Mannheim," Brown said without any preliminaries. Ferrand felt his heart stop. "The police are at the school, but they can't find Billy. Do you know of any reason why he might have run away?"

"No," Ferrand answered. "Unless he knows that Gamel is looking for him."

"There's no way he could know. Is there any other reason why he would just disappear?"

Ferrand could think of only one. Gamel could have gotten there before the police.

Billy crouched inside the turret, looking out at the police officers who were gathered on the steps of the school. He had seen them rush into the building, then emerge a few minutes later and begin searching the grounds. A half hour after that a third police car had swung into the driveway and four more uniforms had joined in the search. Now they were all assembled by the cars, taking instructions from the officer who seemed to be in charge. The headmaster was standing in the doorway behind them, and students were watching from the windows above.

How the hell had they found out? he kept asking himself. No one knew he had taken the plastic explosive from Saint Anselm's. If they did, they never would have let him out of Italy. And what was suspicious about buying a radio-controlled toy car? How had they figured out that he didn't want the car but rather the cheap electronic controls that came with it? Maybe it was Werner. Maybe the math professor had realized he had been lecturing a kid in the art of demolition. But he obviously hadn't figured out that he was going to launch Schiller's statue, because the police had walked all around it without searching inside the turret. But Werner might have looked at the books that he had borrowed in the library, recalled their conversations, and finally put all the information together. Maybe he'd suddenly slapped himself on the forehead, yelled "dumbkopf," and rushed off to tell the headmaster that there was a mad bomber loose inside the school.

And that's just what the police must be searching for—a mad bomber. A kid with plastic explosive in a sandwich bag and a radio detonator stuck in his pocket. So what was he supposed to do when they found him? Just chuckle and say that it was all a joke? Bet they wouldn't lose any time laughing! They'd have him in handcuffs before you could say "Friedrich Schiller." Bet they didn't do much laughing in German prisons, either!

He couldn't just come strolling out of the turret while they were holding the policemen's ball on the front steps! Jesus, they'd trample one another in their rush to make the arrest— if they didn't all just draw their pistols and get in some target practice. No, he had to stay right where he was with the spiders making webs between his legs and his feet sinking in rat shit. No matter how loud they called his name, he wasn't going to answer. They'd get tired of looking, and sooner or later they'd climb back into their cars and head out the gate. They'd probably leave a cop or two behind, but he should be able to slip around them once it got dark.

The only problem was where would he sneak to. Maybe

he could slip into town, throw the detonator into the river where they could never find it, and then telephone the school. He could tell them that he had gone in to watch a movie and had missed the bus back. The worst they could do would be to kick him out of Schiller, which would make his father mad. But not as mad as if he telephoned home from a German jail. Or maybe he should just sneak into the library and pretend that he had fallen asleep behind the stacks. Of course they wouldn't believe him, but if he could get rid of the detonator, what the hell could they prove?

Jesus, it was such a great idea. I mean, getting Schiller to jump over the damn wall was better than anything he had done at Saint Anselm's. How in God's name had they ever found out? Billy leaned wearily against the inside wall of the turret. It was going to be a long wait.

night

The police cars had left by the time Gamel drove past the gates of Schiller. He could see the statue in the center of the circular drive and behind it the facade of the ivy-covered building. But because of the position of the statue, he couldn't see the front door, or the lone policeman who had been left to stand guard. It seemed quiet, with no hint of the futile search of the grounds that had just been concluded. There was no reason for him to believe the Germans knew even that he was in the country, much less that his target was inside the school.

He continued along the road, the land to his right sloping down to a river and to his left swelling into gentle hills. It grew suddenly dark as he drove into their shadow, and he reached down and switched on the headlights. A few more minutes, he thought. In the rolling countryside, night would come quickly. He wanted to plan his attack while there was still enough light to see. The attack itself would occur under the cover of darkness.

Gamel used the entrance to a side road to make a u-turn and then retraced his route back toward Schiller. He was looking for a path that led into the forest, some place where he could leave the car without its being quickly discovered. He would approach the school on foot, scale the wall, and find a vantage point from which he could see into the common rooms. Sooner or later he would spot William Tepper— at dinner, in a study hall, or perhaps even in the chapel. Wherever it was, he would attack immediately. There would be no time to stalk his prey and wait for a better shot. He had to seize the opportunity the moment it appeared.

He had thought long about that moment and knew exactly how he would handle it. In his military uniform, he would break through a doorway or smash through a window. For an instant every head would swing toward him. Then he would scream the boy's name. There would be a second— probably only a fraction of a second—when Tepper's and his eyes would meet. But in that moment, he would see understanding flash across the boy's face. William Tepper would know that Gamel had not been defeated. He would know that he had been found and was about to answer for his arrogance. Then Gamel would pull the trigger.

The shots would be followed by panic. Everyone—teachers, boys, even the geriatric security guards that the school probably employed—would dive for cover. And when they looked up, he would be gone.

There would be no pursuit. They would waste seconds hovering over the bleeding body of the dead student, then minutes calling for an ambulance and the police. By the time help came, he would be across the grounds and back over the wall, on his way to his car. In all likelihood, the police cruisers and ambulance with their frantically wailing sirens would rocket past him as he leisurely drove away in the opposite direction.

He saw a path. It was just a small break in the bushes that lined the road, but beyond it was a dirt path pitted with stones. Gamel stopped the car, slipped the transmission into reverse, and backed through the bushes. The car lurched on the uneven surface as it rolled between the trees, tall grass and branches scraping at its sides. Gamel turned the wheel sharply, swinging the car behind the foliage, where it would be invisible from the road. He stopped the engine, forced the door open, and climbed out slowly.

In the top of the suitcase, he found his uniform—drab khaki fatigues with the leather belt that held the pistol holster. He stripped out of his disguise and dressed for combat. Then he lifted the false bottom of the case, removed the oiled components of the weapon, and placed them carefully on the roof of the car. Gamel smiled at the precise machining of the metal as he screwed the barrel into the breech and slipped the slot of the wooden stock into position. He pushed two of the curved magazines into the belt, then snapped the third into the chamber opening at the bottom of the weapon. He took a moment to examine the precise workmanship of the rifle. Then he pulled the bolt back and let it fly forward, stripping a round from the top of the magazine and sliding it into the chamber.

He looked up. The treetops were barely visible against the blackening sky. He made a quick check of his position. On his return, all he had to do was move through the woods in this general direction until he reached the road. The road would lead him back to the automobile. Then he pushed aside a branch and started deeper into the woods, toward the walls of the Schiller school.

Maria and Ferrand listened patiently while the German police captain tried to calm their fears.

"He is probably in a movie house or an ice cream parlor. Somewhere in the city where he is perfectly safe. He left the school of his own accord, by himself. The secretary at the front door saw him leave. She remembered his polite smile."

"But you haven't located him," Maria interrupted.

The captain dismissed her concern with a wave of his hand. "It's a large city. There are many places that a boy could go. But we are searching. It's only a matter of time before we find him."

"Or before Gamel finds him," Ferrand said softly.

The German folded his hands on the edge of his desk and sighed his impatience. "We're taking every precaution," he repeated, "but there is no reason for panic. First, we can't be positive that your terrorist is even in the city. The woman has told us nothing, and she could have dropped him anywhere between Rome and here. Second, even if he is in the city, he would have no way of knowing where your young man might be. His target might be the Schiller school, but we have searched the school and the grounds and we are certain that he is not there. If this man goes to the school, he will find a police officer waiting for him."

"One man?" Maria challenged.

"One man who can summon a hundred men in an instant," the captain responded. "It seems to me that the best use of our police force is searching for the boy, as well as the terrorist."

"You don't have to search for them," Ferrand nearly shouted. "Wherever Billy is, he has to go back to the school. That's where he lives. And Gamel will head directly for the school. That's where he expects to find his victim."

The police captain smiled at the rebuke. "So you want us to abandon our search and barricade the school? Turn Schiller into a fortress?"

"Can't you do both?" Maria begged.

The man shook his head. "I have all the men assigned that I can possibly spare. More than I should assign to a crime that hasn't taken place, that is really only a rumor. I don't even know for certain that your man is in my city."

They were getting nowhere. The police captain's assessment was logical and correct. But it didn't take into account Gamel. Maria and Ferrand knew he was in the area. And they knew that a perfunctory guard, posted at the door of the school, wouldn't keep him from getting at Billy.

"Will you take us to Schiller?" Ferrand asked.

"Of course," the German answered, delighted that the interview which had been forced on him by his government was finally coming to a close. "And I hope I will be delivering your boy there within the next few hours. I'm sure we'll pick him up before long."

They were halfway to the school before Maria broke the silence. "Where do you think he would have gone?" she asked.

"That's what I've been asking myself," Ferrand said. "He's only been here for a week. He can't have made any friends. He wouldn't know where to go. But I was thinking of all the hidden places that he found at Saint Anselm's. The old wine cellar and the vault between the two buildings. If he found out that Gamel was coming for him, he might have gone into hiding." Then he laughed. "Or maybe he's down in a deserted basement of Schiller cutting through the telephone wires. Hell, there's no telling where Billy Tepper might be."

It was time. The only thing Billy could see were the lights of the school, so he was sure no one would be able to see him. And he certainly couldn't stay in the turret forever.

But he couldn't just walk back through the front door. The damn cop had been standing there for the last two hours, with occasional trips inside to freshen his cup of coffee. If he was going to let himself be found inside Schiller, he would have to work his way around the building and come in through the back door. And if he waited any longer, the back door would be locked for the night. He had to move now!

Billy got down on his hands and knees and crept out through the doorway. With his body pressed against the curved wall of the turret, he inched along until he could see the front door. The damn stormtrooper was still at his post, pacing back and forth, raising his head to look out over the grounds each time he turned and started in the other direction. Billy waited until he began walking away from his side of the tower. Then he bolted across the circular lawn and dove behind the hedges that framed the driveway.

He scrambled to his knees and slowly peered over the top
of the hedge. The cop had reached the far end of his beat and
was looking across the front of the building, his head tipped
back so that he could see under the bill of his cap. Then he
turned and headed back in Billy's direction.

Billy held his breath, lying perfectly still until the uniformed figure had once again turned away from him. Then
he jumped up, hurdled the hedge, and scampered across the
driveway, falling flat to the ground on the other side.

Billy turned his head. The cop had stopped dead in his
tracks right at the center of the doorway. His head was
swinging like an antenna, panning in his direction. "Holy
shit," Billy whispered. His hand shot into his pocket and he
fumbled for the transmitter. If he was going to be caught, at
least he didn't want them to find the damn thing on him.

And then the moon came out. It broke through the clouds
just above the trees, bathing the school grounds in a soft but
pervasive light. "Fucking wonderful," Billy cursed. "Here I
am lying out on the lawn and the goddamn moon comes
out." He was as good as in prison.

At the same instant, the policeman's head snapped around
toward the sound of a car engine at the gate. Headlights appeared through the opening and swept over the grounds as
the automobile turned into the driveway and curved its way
around the statue. The wheels spun by not twenty feet from
where Billy was lying, and then the car braked at the front
steps. A police officer climbed out and there were a few comical seconds of heel clicking and saluting. Then the patrolling
officer reached down and opened the back door of the car.

Reinforcements, Billy thought. But the two people who
got out and stood beside the car were civilians. "Jesus
Christ," he said when he recognized them. It was Miss Manetti and Mr. Ferrand.

They started up the steps behind the two officers. But
Billy wasn't about to let them get out of sight. He jumped to
his feet. "Hey, Miss Manetti," he screamed joyfully. "Mr.
Ferrand." He was already running toward them waving a

cheery greeting, thinking to himself that a good offense was the best defense. "Hey, great to see you. What brings you to Schiller?"

Maria stood paralyzed for an instant, then ran down the stairs to meet Billy. At the bottom step, she caught him in her arms as if he were a long-lost child. A second later, Ferrand was standing beside them, his arms wrapped around both Maria and Billy as if it were a family reunion.

"Where in God's name have you been?" Ferrand finally scolded the boy.

"Around," Billy said casually.

"Is that the boy?" one of the police officers asked, interrupting the reunion.

"You bet it is," Ferrand fired back.

The policeman began to laugh.

"What the hell is going on?" Billy demanded. He had been counting on the two teachers to rescue him from the stormtroopers. Instead, everyone was laughing as if finding him was some sort of joke. Just what the hell was going on?

"Please call your headquarters and tell them we've found him," Maria told the officer. At the same time Ferrand was turning Billy back toward the parked car.

"Come on," the teacher said. "You're coming with us."

Billy stopped dead. "Where?" he demanded. "Where are you taking me?"

"To police headquarters." Ferrand smiled.

Billy backed away. "What for?"

Ferrand laughed again. "Don't worry. Everything is okay. I'll explain everything in the car."

Billy looked at Miss Manetti, who was smiling at him fondly. "Why is everyone so damn happy if I'm going to prison?"

Ferrand was about to tell him when the crack of a gunshot fractured the quiet of the night.

*   *   *

Gamel had made it over the wall easily, simply climbing a tree and sliding out on a branch that reached over the school grounds. He had moved quickly through the scattered shrubbery, circling around toward the front of the school. The windows were ablaze, with activity behind every panel of glass. He had decided to cross the open ground to the edge of the building, then move silently from window to window until he spotted William Tepper. He was about to dart out of the trees when he saw the policeman pacing nervously across the front door.

Gamel settled back into the bushes, setting the butt of the rifle on the ground next to his foot. Why a police guard? He had expected that there would be security people attached to the school. But not this. The man was a police officer, wearing the identical uniform he had seen in the train station and on the streets of Mannheim. What could have brought him to the door of a private school?

He thought of the woman who had driven him from Rome. What did he know of her? That she was a political radical who would join the most violent opposition to any government that could possibly be formed in any country. A slogan-spouting crusader who would fall into line with any opposition parade no matter where the parade was heading. She had joined with the Palestinians simply because they were the only armed opposition that was left. She had served him simply because he was introduced as a terrorist.

Could she possibly have gone to the police? Unlikely, because she hated anyone who wore the uniform of order. But how would she act if she was captured by the police? Would she crack under their threats? Would she trade his mission for the promise of freedom? Perhaps it had been a mistake to allow her to drive him into the city. He had considered killing her on the roadside and taking the car for himself just to assure the absolute security of his plan. But why would the police have picked her up? And if they had, did it make sense that she would have talked so quickly? It didn't seem possible. Yet the police were guarding Schiller. Someone must have told them that he was headed there.

Or perhaps it was the car. Certainly, by now, it had been reported stolen. But the police weren't likely to react so quickly to a stolen-car report. And how could they have found it buried in the trees miles from where he had taken it?

There must be another reason why the police were at the school. They couldn't be waiting for him. "It has to be a coincidence," he assured himself. "Just bad luck."

But still, he would have to be very cautious. He couldn't just dash across the grounds, particularly now that the moon had slipped through the clouds. His movement would certainly attract attention, and he hadn't come all this way just to kill a policeman. He had come for William Tepper.

He began backtracking, keeping his eye fixed on the front door while moving further away from it. He would work his way around to the side of the building, where he couldn't be seen by the officer posted at the front door. Then he would cross to the buildings and begin searching through the windows. But he had to remember the policeman. When he killed Tepper, it wouldn't be just amateurs who would be rushing to the scene. There would be at least one professional who would move very quickly.

And then his thoughts were interrupted by the lights of the car that turned onto the grounds. Gamel watched it suspiciously until it stopped at the front gate, and bit down hard in anger when he saw another policeman climb out. Something was happening! Something had gone wrong! It had to be the girl.

He was truly startled when he saw the woman and the one called Ferrand stand up beside the car. "They must know," he told himself. "They must know I've come for the boy." He began backing away toward the wall, trying to organize his options.

But then he saw the form moving in the moonlight. He leaned forward, heard a boyish voice and, at the same time, recognized Tepper walking into the light that came through the windows of the building. They were together. All three of them standing together less than fifty yards from where he was crouching.

Gamel calculated quickly. Two officers up on the steps and one still seated inside the car. If he fired at the boy, he would only get one of them. The police would return his fire before he could aim a second shot. But if he could hit the police officers who were standing at the top of the steps, then he would have all three of them trapped. Whether they tried to run up the steps and into the school or darted out to either side of the parked car, they would be running across his sights, backlighted by the glowing windows of Schiller. He could have them all, and perhaps leave a policeman as a witness to tell the world who had finally triumphed at the battle of Saint Anselm's.

He rushed forward to the edge of the bushes and dropped to one knee. Ahead of him, the teachers and the boy were locked in an embrace. Two of the policeman were standing side by side in the glaring lights at the front door. He raised the rifle and fixed the cross hairs on one of the officers.

They were still frozen by the sound of the shot when they heard the glass doors shatter behind them. Ferrand wheeled just in time to see one of the police officers fall backward through the door. The other had his hand on his holster, his head whipping around as he looked for shelter. He had started to move toward one of the stone pillars that flanked the entrance when a second shot cracked through the air. The officer twisted and collapsed onto the ground.

Still, Ferrand remained motionless, his mind struggling to sort out the last two seconds. They had found Billy. They were safe. They were laughing away their anxieties. And now there was shooting. Someone was firing at them. Why?

"Get down," he heard Maria scream, and at the same time he felt her pulling his arm. She had already pushed Billy across the sidewalk and up against the parked police car. Now she was trying to drag him down on top of the boy.

A third shot exploded, and with its sound the driver's window and passenger window of the car shattered. Powdery fragments of glass sprayed out on top of Billy and across Ferrand's legs. He threw his arm over Maria and pulled her behind the car, falling down beside her.

"What's going on?" Billy started to scream, but he was struck by the passenger door as it suddenly swung open. The policeman tried to scramble out of the car, his drawn pistol already in his hand.

There was another explosion, and simultaneously the sound of the bullet smashing against the side of the car like a hammer. The German officer tumbled out of the seat head-first. His hand shot out to break his fall, and the pistol clattered to the ground, bouncing off the edge of the curbstone and skittering into the glare of the headlights.

"That dumb son of a bitch is going to kill somebody," Billy said.

"It's Gamel," Maria said. "We have to run for it."

She started to pull Billy away from the car, but Ferrand held her back. "We can't," he hissed at her. "We'd never make the door. Stay behind the car."

But even as he said it, he knew it was no answer. Gamel was out there in the shrubbery at the other side of the circular driveway. It would take him perhaps fifteen seconds to cross the circle and walk up next to the car. If they ran, they would only be giving him target practice. And if they stayed hidden behind the car, they would only be delaying the inevitable.

"Wait," the policeman ordered. He began crawling toward the front of the automobile. His pistol—their only hope for survival—was no more than three feet beyond the front bumper. If he could reach it, they had at least a small chance of holding off Gamel. He crawled as far as the headlight, his face appearing ghostly white in its glow. Then he flattened his chest against the pavement and slowly stretched his arm out toward the weapon. His fingers inched forward through the darkness until they were less than a foot from the butt of the gun. Then they slipped into the illumination of the head-light, now just inches from their goal.

Another shot sounded and immediately the officer's body snapped like a whip. He screamed in pain as he recoiled out of the light and crumpled onto the sidewalk, clutching his arm, which was bent at a sickening angle. Ferrand lifted him until his back was leaning against the front wheel of the car. "You have to run for it," he said through teeth clenched in pain.

Ferrand looked back up the steps at the brightly lit door-way. One officer was lying in front of it. The other's legs hung limply through the doorframe. Gamel had proven he could hit anything on the steps. The seconds it would take to free the door from the fallen policeman's legs and push it open would give Gamel ample time for a shot.

"Why is he shooting at us?" Billy asked, but Ferrand ig-nored the question. Instead, he began to rattle off the details of the only escape route that seemed open to them.

"I'll run for the doorway," he told them. "As soon as he fires, you both run in different directions. You go that way," he ordered Billy, pointing past the rear of the car. "Run as fast as you can and then dive into the bushes next to the building."

He turned to Maria and pointed past the front of the car. "You go that way. Don't stop."

"You'll be killed," Maria protested.

"Not if we confuse him. Even for a second," Ferrand in-sisted. But even as he gave the order, he knew the plan was bound to fail. Gamel would get him as soon as his head came into view above the roof of the car. Then he would get one of the others fleeing in the opposite direction, and simply spend a few seconds to hunt down the third. But what choice did they have? If they stayed where they were, they would hear Gamel's footsteps approaching and then watch as he came around one end of the car or the other. They would have a few moments to look at the satisfied smile on his face and the metallic glimmer of his eyes. Then they would be slaughtered methodically.

"I'm coming for you." The words came in a sing-song cadence from somewhere out in the darkness.

The three of them froze in fright, listening intently to the silence.

"Did you think I wouldn't come back?" The question was mocking. "Did you think I would run away?"

The voice seemed to be coming from across the driveway, from the foliage behind the statue. But it was growing louder as their attacker moved in for the kill.

"Where are your soldiers?" it asked. "Did they run away and leave you to die by yourselves?"

Billy suddenly changed his position, stretching out on the ground so that he could look out under the police car.

"Why don't you reach for the pistol," the voice taunted. "It's your only chance." It was much louder, much closer.

Billy saw him, a shadow in the moonlight. He had emerged from the cover of the trees and was crossing the circle, carrying a rifle at the ready.

"I have to get that gun," Ferrand said as he slipped past the wounded policeman toward the front of the car.

"He'll see you," Maria protested, but Ferrand didn't hesitate. He inched up next to the headlight, then suddenly dove forward and reached for the gun. Instantly, Gamel snapped the rifle to his shoulder and the muzzle flashed. There was a shower of sparks as the bullet skipped off the pavement an inch from Ferrand's fingers. By the time the next shot rang out, the teacher was holding the weapon clutched to his chest.

He rolled back along the side of the car until he reached the front window. Then he jumped up, firing two shots through the splintered window openings without even aiming. He had barely dropped down again when the return fire shattered the remaining window fragments, showering them all with pieces of glass.

"Good," came the mocking voice from out of the darkness. "You have a gun. Now we will see if you have the courage to use it."

Ferrand inched back up toward the window, trying to gauge the direction the voice was coming from. But as the hand with the pistol reached the edge of the window another shot cracked through the night and glass slivers drove like knives into his skin. He pulled the gun back, and then watched it slip through his blood-soaked fingers and land at his feet.

Billy had seen Gamel suddenly stop and fire when his teacher had reached for the pistol. Then he had darted a few steps to his left, disappearing into the shadow of the turret that acted as the base for Schiller's statue. Now the form reappeared in the moonlight, pressed against the turret for protection as it aimed the rifle toward the windows of the car.

"Try again," the taunting voice challenged.

Billy's hand slipped into his pocket and touched the radio controller. He fingered the switch.

"Give me your best shot." Gamel laughed.

Billy pushed the switch to "forward."

They were blinded by the flash of light. Then they felt the car lurch against them as if a giant hand had slapped the other side. And finally they heard the explosion—a thunderclap that was echoed by the rattling of windows across the face of the school.

Friedrich Schiller bounded from the top of his turret, his arm still extended and the book of verse pressed to his breast. He turned an acrobatic somersault at the top of his trajectory and then disappeared over the wall.

Gamel was thrown away from the side of the turret like a rag doll tossed at a toy chest. His rifle flew aimlessly into the air. He landed on his feet and seemed to stagger for a few steps. Then he collapsed onto the ground.

"Holy shit," Billy Tepper whispered from beneath the car.

Gravel and dirt were falling like rain all around them as

Ferrand raised himself back up into the opening of the car window. He could see the turret, its top still glowing with the heat of the dying explosion. He could see the form crumpled on the ground. He lifted the pistol in his left hand and steadied it with the bloody fingers of his right hand. Slowly, he stepped around the back of the car and moved toward the fallen body, the gun trained ahead of him. He heard Gamel moaning as he drew close and circled cautiously around the writhing shape. Then he stepped forward and aimed the tiny sights at the back of Gamel's head.

"Don't move," he ordered. But even as he said it, he knew the command was unnecessary. The back of Gamel's shirt was torn open as if he had been hit by a shotgun blast. There were a hundred wounds, each beginning to bleed. He was lucky to be alive.

"Call an ambulance," Ferrand screamed back toward the building. Maria, who had been rushing toward him, stopped and ran back up the steps of Schiller, now crowded with students who had pushed out to investigate the uproar.

"What happened?" the wounded police officer asked Ferrand as he came close, still clutching his battered arm.

The teacher looked bewildered. "He was firing at us . . . and then he just . . . exploded." He saw Billy standing by his side, looking down sympathetically at the shattered body. "What happened?" he asked suspiciously.

Innocent eyes turned up toward him. "Amazing," Billy Tepper answered. And then, when he noticed Ferrand's eyes narrowing, "Hey, Mr. Ferrand. You don't think I had anything to do with this. I mean, how am I supposed to know what he does with his old hand grenades?"

May 3

morning

They had gone to the hospital in Mannheim to say a word of thanks to the German policemen who had been wounded at Schiller. Two had superficial wounds and were already walking the corridors, one with an arm set in plaster, the other with bandages across his back to protect the repairs on the hole that had been blown through the top of his shoulder. The first officer who had been hit, the one who had fallen backward through the glass door, was the only one still in guarded condition. He had undergone surgery to remove a bullet that had lodged against the ribs in his back. There would be another operation to repair the damage that the round had caused while passing through his chest.

The police captain had given them the official version of the events. Gamel had apparently been carrying explosives— a plastic charge according to their expert investigators. For some reason, he had decided to dispose of the explosive. Given the situation, he had probably thought he had his victims cornered and that the rifle would be all that he'd need. But no matter. He had obviously thrown the plastic through one of the gunports of the turret, and it had gone off accidentally.

"Could he have been trying to throw it at us?" Ferrand had asked.

"No," the captain had replied. They were absolutely certain that the explosion had occurred inside the turret. "The whole top of the structure was lifted up into the air," he'd explained, shaping one hand into a cylinder and poking a finger of the other hand up through the bottom. "The energy was directed upward, like this. It actually threw the statue of Schiller right over the wall."

Ferrand had noticed the grin that was trying to force itself onto Billy Tepper's face. "Imagine that," he'd said, his eyes fixed on Billy.

"Of course, we'll get a better explanation from Gamel as soon as he is well enough to be questioned," the captain had concluded.

Now, Ferrand and Maria were getting into the front seat of the car. Billy stretched out in the back. They pulled away from the hospital and drove out of the city toward the Schiller school.

"Are you going to be able to visit me?" Billy suddenly asked from the back seat.

"Of course," Maria assured him.

"Thanks," Billy said. But his voice was filled with despair. He didn't sound convinced.

Maria turned around in her seat. "I mean it," she said.

Billy looked idly out the window. "I know," he answered without looking at Maria. "But you'll probably both be going to America. That's a long way to come for a visit."

"We're not going to America," Ferrand said firmly, his eyes fixed on the road ahead. "Miss Manetti and I are going back to Saint Anselm's. We're going to try to reopen the school." His glance drifted hesitantly toward Maria, seeking confirmation. He found her looking back suspiciously. "Aren't we?" he asked.

She smiled and then looked back at Billy. "That's right. So you see, we'll only be a few hours away. It will be easy to visit you."

He seemed pleased.

They were well out of the city, driving along the river toward the school, when Billy spoke again.

"Can I come with you? To Saint Anselm's?"

Maria and Ferrand exchanged awkward glances. It was Ferrand who answered.

"There isn't much there. We won't be able to open until the fall term. And even then it might not be much of an opening. We might not have any students."

"There isn't much here, either," Billy said.

Maria tried to present a more optimistic picture. "You have your summer classes, Billy. And then graduation at the end of the summer. There will be nothing at Saint Anselm's except a lot of work to get the place ready. Maybe not even that if we can't raise enough money."

"You'll be there," Billy answered, and neither of them could think of a response.

They drove in silence until they reached the road that led to the school.

"Do I have to go back?" Billy tried again. "I just don't think I'm what they're looking for at Schiller."

"Of course you are," Maria said. But there was no conviction in her voice.

As they rounded a turn, Ferrand suddenly slammed on the brakes, bringing the car to a skidding halt. Friedrich Schiller was standing in the middle of the road, blocking the way to the front gate, his hand raised like a traffic officer signaling for them to stop.

"Will you look at this," Ferrand marveled. The workmen had levered the statue out of the bushes by the roadside. They were in the process of rolling it up onto a dolly so that it could be hauled back to its place of honor atop the turret. "How do we get around this?"

Maria rolled down the window and called to one of the workmen. "We have to get to the Schiller school," she tried to explain. But the workman shook his head, then untied the handkerchief he was wearing on top of his head and used it to mop his brow.

"You can't get past," he said, gesturing with both of his hands back toward the statue. "You'll have to wait."

"Like hell we will," Ferrand said. He slammed the car into reverse and began backing up to the road's edge. Then he shifted it into gear, swinging the front of the car away from the school. "If Friedrich Schiller doesn't want Billy Tepper to go back to his school, then we'll take him with us. I'll bet you we won't find Saint Anselm standing in the road trying to keep us out of his school!"

Billy's eyes went from one teacher to the other. Both were smiling. He folded his hands behind his head and leaned back into the seat.

Ferrand took one last glance in the sideview mirror at the statue that now seemed to be pointing away from the Schiller school. It almost looked as if the great poet were ordering them off his property. "Screw you," he said to the image in his mirror. He pushed down on the accelerator until the tires squealed. "We're going home to Saint Anselm's," he shouted. "All of us."